MW00852166

the *Hollywood* horse

Ocala Horse Girls

Book 4

Natalie Keller Reinert

This book is a work of fiction. Names, characters, businesses, places, events, locales, and incidents are either the products of the author's imagination or used in a fictitious manner. Any resemblance to actual persons, living or dead, or actual events is purely coincidental.

Copyright © 2023 Natalie Keller Reinert

All rights reserved.

"The Hollywood Horse"

ISBN: 978-1-956575-37-8

Cover Photos: Callipso_Art/depositphotos

Cover Design & Interior Design: Natalie Keller Reinert

No portion of this book may be reproduced in any form without written permission from the publisher or author, except as permitted by U.S. copyright law.

Also by Natalie Keller Reinert

Briar Hill Farm
Foaling Season
Friends With Horses
Outside Rein

The Ocala Equestrians Collection
Alex & Alexander: A Horse Racing Saga
The Eventing Series: A Three-Day Eventing Saga
Sea Horse Ranch: A Beach Read Series
Ocala Horse Girls: A Romantic Comedy Series
The Hidden Horses of New York: A Novel
Grabbing Mane: A Duet Series
Show Barn Blues: A Duet Series

Romantic Comedy
The Settle Down Society: A New York City Rom-Com Series
Sorry I Kissed You: A Rock Star Romance

Catoctin Creek: Sweet Romance
Sunset at Catoctin Creek
Snowfall at Catoctin Creek
Springtime at Catoctin Creek
Christmas at Catoctin Creek

Learn more and find bonus stories at nataliekreinert.com

Chapter One

HOW DO YOU know when something's not going to work out?

"Up—down. Up...and down. Up and *down*, Sarah!"

My student flushes and kicks out her feet in the stirrups, but her attempts at rising trot do not demonstrably change.

How do you know when to throw in the towel?

"Up, down. And *up*—Sarah, what now?"

This child is exhausting. If she weren't a child, I'd take her off the lunge line, let her finish out her riding lesson on a loose rein, and then kindly suggest she come up with a new hobby or fitness plan, because horseback riding ain't it for her. At least, not English riding.

But Sarah's only ten and she isn't even the one choosing riding lessons for herself. That's her mother, who is on her phone with her back to the riding arena, blissfully unaware that Sarah is crying in the saddle again.

How do you know when a plan is just not going to pan out?

Asking for a friend.

"Okay, Sarah, break time."

I reel in the lunge line attached to Nando's halter. The tall chestnut horse walks towards me with a look of relief on his long face. When he reaches me, he shoves his head against my shoulder, his meaning clear: *Save me from this life.*

Blessed are the school horses, they say, and they're not wrong. I don't know how Nando does it. I don't know how *I* do it, and I'm the one on the ground, yelling instructions.

Atop his back, Sarah's face is crumpled and red.

I'd feel bad, but I know it's all for show. Sarah is a chronic sobber, with crocodile tears that could put most Hollywood stars to shame. She inherited that talent from her mother, I assume: Kat Castellano-Marquis, retired soap opera star and the author of *Sunshine and Rainbows: Positive Living for the Win.* Unfortunately, Sarah is immune to her mother's positive living mantras.

"Sarah, honey," I say, struggling to keep my tone soft—hey, I can act, too—"can you tell me what's the matter?"

In reply, Sarah bawls with the clear satisfaction of a film star nailing the big scene. It's good crying, lusty and filled with tragedy. I'd be more impressed, though, if she didn't pull this nonsense with me every single riding lesson.

"Sarah," I hiss, giving up on the sweet act. There's a time and a place for everything in the horse business. Now it's time to be strict. "Pull yourself together, girl, or get off this horse!"

Unimpressed, Sarah opens her mouth wide for a particularly despondent howl of grief. Nando shifts nervously beneath her and she clutches at the saddle pommel as if he has threatened to run away. And that's something Nando would *never* do, thank you very much.

"You're scaring my horse," I scold her, "and you're *annoying* me."

That, at least, earns me a beady-eyed glare. This girl has the diva act down pat. She needs to get out of the saddle and into the studio.

"Alison?"

I turn. Sarah's mother is off the phone. She calls, "Alison, is everything okay?"

"It's fine, Mrs. C," I reply. "Sarah thought she saw a bee about to sting Nando."

A total fabrication, but the kid's mother buys it. Looks like I can act, too. "Oh, sweetie," she coos, "a little bee won't hurt you or the pony! It'll just fly by looking for some flowers." She glances around as if to point out a flower-bed. Unfortunately, there's a total lack of flora around my dusty little barn. Mrs. C lifts an eyebrow and looks back at me questioningly, as if she has just noticed how plain this place is.

Fair. It's not exactly the prettiest farm in Ocala. But it's only me running this show, and do I have time to be a landscaper *and* a horse trainer *and* a riding instructor *and* a barn manager? I think we all know the answer to that.

Still, I feel my face flush. The sultry heat of this late summer day has already made my cheeks pink, and yet somehow, they are turning a brighter shade of maroon now. Yes, I am self-conscious about my farm.

I know the place needs prettied up, but right now, gardening is pretty far down my to-do list. It's actually about fifty spots below 'Don't lose this place,' and 'Remember, your life savings went into starting this business.' I love a good list, because organization is everything, but this one is just depressing.

"I want off now," Sarah pouts, having abruptly turned off the waterworks. "Mom! I want down!"

"But you're just learning to post the trot," Mrs. C says encouragingly. "You're doing so well!"

This is a lie, and Mrs. C knows it. Sarah has been 'just' learning to post the trot for the past six lessons, and I am not confident this is a hurdle she'll ever clear. To master rising with the horse's trot, a person must be motivated. They either have a strong desire to do it well or they learn out of necessity.

Sarah's not being kidnapped on horseback, so she has to care enough to learn.

And Sarah just does not care.

"You're getting so close, darling," Mrs C calls, ever the cheerleader, even in the face of insurmountable adversity. "I'm sure you've almost got it!"

Before she was a soap star, Mrs. C was an equitation star. I figure she became an actress because she was searching for that blue-ribbon rush in her adult life. Meanwhile, Sarah is her mother's daughter, but without the horse bug; I can tell she would be much happier as a Disney Channel star, which is something else a child never recovers from.

But maybe she'll be luckier than others and get the chance to chase her dreams. I'm grateful to my parents for letting me chase mine. And look what I've got now. Ten acres of gritty sand and scruffy pasture and a barn that never seems clean enough.

Stop that, Alison.

It's not like me to be negative. Things are just...well, they're tough right now. The beginner riding lessons, the messy farm, the daily struggle to get everything done all alone...I admit, this isn't the part I would have written for myself. It's definitely not the role I auditioned for.

But this is what I have.

Teaching up-down lessons wasn't part of the business plan. I was supposed to move straight into selling horses and taking on prospects for training, the same way my former boss, Malcolm, started his business. I neglected to note how much financial backing Malcolm had at the beginning, though. I oversaw his barn and ensured that every horse paid its own way through the program, but I hadn't experienced the difficulties of starting from scratch myself.

I guess I only saw the good parts. The top horses, the adoring fans, the owners frantic to get their ponies into his program. Malcolm hired me to run a mature business, which couldn't be more different from the baby business I've poured my life savings into.

I blink and realize Mrs. C is looking at me anxiously, wondering how I will rescue her daughter's riding lesson. As if this kid's non-existent equestrian career could possibly be saved.

But I have to try. That's the job. And if there's one thing I *always* do to the best of my abilities, it's my job.

"We have five more minutes," I say to Sarah, who is wiping her face with the tail of her shirt. "Tell you what. Can you walk Nando around off the lunge line and hold yourself up nice and pretty in the position we talked about? Or do I have to keep you on this boring old circle? Be honest."

Sarah sniffles and considers for a moment. "Off the lunge line," she finally says. "I can sit up straight."

Thank goodness. I'm dizzy from turning in circles for nearly an hour.

"Okay, go sit up there nice and pretty like a princess," I say, sending Nando away with a gentle shove.

The chestnut horse sighs and flicks his long ears as he heads for the rail.

Thank god for Nando. If I didn't have him, I'd lose half my income. Such as it is.

You just have to survive the summer, I remind myself. *Winter will be better.*

"You look great," Mrs. C trills. "Remember to keep your eyes up!"

Sarah tilts her chin skyward, as if she is looking for enemy aircraft.

"How is she doing?" Mrs. C asks as I join her at the rail. "She seems to be getting it!"

"Closer," I hedge, leaning against the top rail. The rough wood cuts into my bare arms, but it's worth it to have something besides my own two legs holding me up. "I think once she just relaxes into the rising trot, she'll be ready for anything."

"She's very tense," Mrs. C agrees. "That's her biggest problem. Her therapist says she carries her tension in her shoulders, like a little businessman."

I'd scoff at the idea of a ten-year-old from an unbroken household needing a therapist, but I've met Sarah, so I approve of the judgment. I say, "Maybe she could try some other sports, too. Like gymnastics. It would tighten up her core, help her balance."

"I can look into it," Mrs. C assures me. "I'm sure there's something —oh, excuse me. My phone."

I take a few steps away to give her privacy as she answers, "Kat Castellano-Marquis speaking."

I always feel a moment of shock when Mrs. C answers the phone with her full, famous name. What is she doing here? Why is her daughter riding with me? All I can think is that all the nice equestrian centers in town already kicked Sarah out.

Then again, Ocala's not a big beginner-lesson kind of town, anyway. Trainers in the Horse Capital of the World take pride in producing new Olympic mounts, and their riding students are often skilled amateurs who moved here to devote more of their income to their hobby. Being a beginner in Ocala is a bit like being a pedi-cab driver at the Indy 500—you're going to get shoved out of the way a lot.

So, I never meant to teach little kids to get by, but the summer has been slower than I'd hoped. This rented barn sits more than half-empty. Nando is bringing in the bulk of my income right now. Three sales horses eat their heads off while I prep them for the winter show season; two horses are in training for clients, with drastically discounted introductory rates. Those two are basically paying for their own upkeep and not much else.

It's going to be okay, though. I'm pushing through. We're already almost through August. The winter season is coming and it will bring boarders, horses in training, and hopefully, a few more advanced and interesting riding students. Opening up my schedule to teaching beginners was just a survival tactic, and one I hope I won't need much longer.

In the arena, Nando ambles along, his long ears flicking as he takes in the scenery. I seriously love that horse. He's a Thoroughbred and Dutch cross with a heart of gold, retired off the jumper circuit when he decided he was ready for the minor leagues. When I get on him, he still burns jet fuel, but with kids, he's a big old sofa. Exactly what I need for up-down lessons—you know, the kind of riding lesson where you just call, "up, down, up, down," for half an hour while they slowly, slowly learn rising trot?

Still on the phone, Mrs. C suddenly waves her free hand, startling me. I jump and Nando glances my way with his ears pricked. *Something scary?*

Mrs. C raises her voice. "No, no, no, I am telling you, Cary Davies, or no one. Yes, his screen test was perfect! Why are you asking me that? Why—*oh*."

The change in her voice is abrupt enough to pull my attention from Sarah and Nando. Mrs. C pushes her luxurious dark curls behind her ears and nods, listening to whoever's on the other end with a serious expression on her face.

"Fine," she says at last. "That's fixable. It's *fixable,* Janine! Send him out here. Yes, to *Ocala.* There's no reason to say it like that. This is exactly where he needs to be. We'll fix the problem here and have him ready for preliminary shooting in late October."

Oh, this sounds really interesting. Sarah and Nando walk past and I give her a thumbs-up, not wanting to speak and miss the end of Mrs. C's conversation.

"Perfect. Yes, I'll have the guest-house made up for him. No, he doesn't need to bring boots. We'll get him fitted here. Trust me, Janine. We have everything we need out here. Perfect."

Mrs. C slips the phone back into her purse and sighs. She fluffs her hair with manicured fingers and gives me an apologetic smile. "Sorry about that. Work crisis."

"I thought you were retired from acting," I say.

"Producing now," she says with satisfaction. "We're working on a feature for Arrowhead Pictures. A Western."

"A Western? Like cowboys and gunfights? I didn't know they still made those."

"No, heavens," she laughs. "Maybe *Western* is too grand a title. Let's say it's a 'cowboy-themed romance picture'. You know, Wyoming mountains and a big city girl and a big rodeo prize to save the ranch. That kind of thing. Only, hopefully we transcend a few cliches." She sounds a little doubtful they can pull it off, but her smile is still bright. She likes the idea, I can tell.

"Ah," I say.

"You don't sound impressed."

"I'm not into 'western' anything," I explain. "I know it makes me sound like a snob, but it's just how I was raised. I like English riding, English countryside, English romances. Now, if you ever do a Jane Austen, you call me, because I will be an extra for free."

Mrs. C laughs. "Don't ever work for free, darling! Speaking of which, I might have a new job for you." She looks at Nando, who is idly walking across the diagonal of the arena—something I suspect was not Sarah's idea at all. He knows how to cut corners, my clever school-horse. "That horse there...will he go in western tack?"

"If I had any, yeah." His former owner, an old friend from my Virginia days, would ride him western for fun. "He's actually been in parades and stuff in western gear, with the American flag dangling and everything."

"What if I said I could finance the tack...would you consider taking on an adult beginner? It's no good trying to teach him in English tack. We don't have that kind of time. I just need him to be capable and balanced in a western saddle for a few scenes." She laughs. "We can edit out any disasters. And he doesn't need to learn rising trot."

I want to tell her that not every kid takes three months to learn to rise the trot and I don't know what's wrong with Sarah, but tamp down the urge. Diplomacy is one of my skills. I needed it working for Malcolm, since that notorious grump was forever on the urge of offending someone with his unfiltered personality. I think I taught him a few things about how to deal with clients, and his girlfriend Evie picks up the slack for me now.

I'm grateful to that girl; I never could have left Malcolm without knowing he was in good hands. But then again, maybe I should have stayed.

I wonder about the life I gave up to try for independence at least a dozen times a day. It didn't use to come up so often. But nowadays, specifically anytime I'm providing my credit card number to pay for something Malcolm's tack room already has in drawers, or while avoiding my creepy landlord, I can't help but think of my simpler life running Fine Day Farm.

I know, I know. I wanted my own place so badly, and now I have it, and of course it's not what I expected...and I can't very well turn down Mrs. C if she's providing me with a new student.

Even if it's yet another beginner.

Maybe an adult will be easier?

Not likely, but a girl can dream.

She pulls her phone out again, misreading my hesitation. "This is him," she says, scrolling through her photos. "Could this face tempt you?"

I take the phone and screen it against the sunlight. A real Hollywood leading man grins back at me—he has the lazy smile, secretive dark eyes, and broad shoulders that make the killer movie combination. Dark brown hair floats back from a high forehead and curls gently just above his shoulders. He's handsome. Too handsome, actually.

Tempting, alright. Imagine having this guy around the barn! I should take his picture, put it on a sign, and stick it out front. I'd have all the boarders I could want in no time at all.

"Well?" Mrs. C takes her phone back. She doesn't exactly have to pry it out of my fingers, but I'm not proud of how long it takes me to give the thing up, either. Her smile is knowing as she says, "A hunk of a man like Cary could be good for business. I'll give you full credit for teaching him to ride. Maybe you could move into the Hollywood business, too!"

Clever of her. If she gives me all the credit, I have to do an *amazing* job. A lot better than I've done with her daughter.

It's like she hears me thinking, because next she says, "I know Sarah's no rider. I just want her to stick something out. Cary will try for you because he wants this role. Are you up for a challenge?"

Her words are casual, but calculated. Mrs. C is shrewd, alright. She can see I'm struggling here. Physically, it's obvious: the barn needs painted, the arena has grass poking through the footing, and I've been replacing broken wooden fence-boards with cheap electric braid while my landlord delays fixing it properly.

But, teaching some actor to ride western? Is this the way forward?

My aunt would be shaking her head right now. *The art of English equitation is a privilege to learn,* she told me, more times than I could count. *Don't muddy the waters with fads and trends. Stay focused on your discipline.*

Western riding is hardly a fad or a trend, but her meaning still applies. Do one thing with everything you've got. I've lived by that rule for my entire life. Certainly, as a teenager I had no choice, but it's served me well as an adult, too.

At least, I think it has.

"I don't teach western riding," I explain to Mrs. C, feeling like Aunt Kate is standing behind me, nodding her head with that precise way of hers. "This is an eventing barn. We focus on dressage and proper equitation over fences as we prepare riders for three-phase competition."

I think I've stated things pretty well, so I'm shocked when Mrs. C just rolls her eyes at me. She says, "Don't be stubborn, Alison. This is a good thing for you. He'll be here on Monday. Pick out the tack you want and send me the invoices. And triple your lesson price on every bill you send me, too. Arrowhead's paying for this."

I try to protest, but stutter into silence. She's not even looking at me. Her will is law, apparently.

I'm not used to someone else taking control so easily. Maybe I'm not the tough girl I was a few months ago. Maybe the struggle of keeping this farm together has finally broken me down.

Or maybe Mrs. C is simply too powerful.

She takes my silence for acquiescence. "Good girl. Now get my daughter off that horse. Her therapy session is in half an hour and the office is all the way across town."

Chapter Two

LATE AUGUST TWILIGHT has settled over the farm like a blue velvet blanket by the time I have a single second to myself. The lesson after Sarah's is another up-down rider, with slightly more talent than Sarah, thank goodness. She finally leaves, excitedly chattering to her mother about the moment Nando spooked at a shadow—his one true pleasure in the afternoon, my sweet school-horse. With the place deserted at last, I look up and down my barn aisle in glorious solitude, mentally calculating how long it would take to clean all the stalls now, versus leaving them for the morning.

I know I won't leave them for the morning; I'm incapable of going upstairs for the night while dirty stalls sit untouched. It's just a game I play with myself, pretending that for once I might give in to my exhaustion and put my feet up for the evening. Instead of working until eight or nine o'clock, then trundling upstairs so tired I can hardly heat up a cup of ramen, which is my usual routine.

Nando pushes against his stall door and grumbles, setting off the other horses in the barn. Everyone is nickering and rumbling, kicking at the doors, making nuisances of themselves as if I habitually forget they exist.

"Fine!" I tell them. "Dinner is coming. Everyone sit tight."

Feeding the horses is a routine I have down like clockwork: setting up buckets in order, scooping grain, doling out supplements, mixing them all with warm water, and leaving them to soak for a few minutes. It still surprises me how quickly the job goes by. Some aspects of a six-horse stable whip past in record time. At Fine Day Farm, I took care of two dozen event horses throughout the year. Not alone, of course. I had plenty of people to clean stalls, groom horses, and dump grain. But still, occasionally having only half-a-dozen horses in my care makes me feel like I've spent my life savings on a hobby, not a training stable.

Don't worry, though, I manage to fill my days and work from dawn to dusk, because I'm a perfectionist and the barn is never quite spotless enough to please me. Still, I have to admit that Highbury Sport Horses isn't taking off quite as quickly as I'd hoped.

Nando bangs on his stall door, and I hoist the feed buckets in both hands, the metal handles pulling at my fingers. "Coming, bossy!" I call. "Keep your big old chestnut knickers on..."

I trail off when I realize there's someone else in the barn. My landlord is standing in the doorway, blocking my path to the barn aisle. Ugh, not now, Nathan! This guy is such a creep. And he's lazy, besides. I think being lazy might be worse than being a creep.

"Hi, Nathan," I say, trying to put some strength back into my tired voice. "What's up?"

Sensing a delay in the feeding process, Nando trumpets his hunger again. Five other horses raise a chorus behind him. Man, my school-horse has these horses trained. He's a master teacher.

"Well, shoot, can I help you feed?" Nathan is all big eyes and comforting tone. That means he is up to something. I watch him push back his white cowboy hat—Floridian cowboys all wear white hats, and please don't ask me why, because I don't know—in order to better give me the kindly neighbor act.

Well, it won't work on me. I already know why he's here, and it's not to be my groom.

"I got it under control," I assure him, pushing past him with my elbows out. "Excuse me! Horses wait for no man."

I emphasize *man* just a little.

He's waiting for me in the office once I have finished dumping grain and returned my empty buckets to the feed room. I lean against the doorframe and look at him, sitting in my creaking old desk-chair like he owns the place.

Because he does.

"Rent's late," Nathan says, holding out his hands in faux apology. "Had to come by and check on ya."

"My last lesson tonight just hit my Venmo," I say, folding my arms. "Let me transfer the funds and you'll get paid tomorrow."

"You were waiting for fifty dollars in order to pay me the rent?" Nathan asks incredulously.

Actually, I was waiting for five *hundred*, but I moved some money around when no surprise check arrived in my mailbox. Eh, who needs an emergency savings account, anyway? I shrug instead of answering. It's none of his business how I pay my rent.

As long as I actually pay it.

"If you're having trouble running the farm at a profit," he says, "I can find renters for the remaining stalls. You all can share the arena and the facilities. How does that sound?"

It sounds like exactly what he wants, to charge per stall instead of for the entire facility. Nathan knows the winter show season is coming. He knows what an empty stall is worth in this town once the horse show people descend. And he'd rather that check goes directly to him, instead of letting me get my share.

"I need the entire farm," I tell him. "We're absolutely not sharing the ring."

This is non-negotiable. If I get winter boarders, they will not want to feel like they're training their horses at some kind of equestrian community pool. People who can afford to winter in Florida for the show season are not used to sharing with any old riff-raff who wants to gallop around the arena.

"Why not just let me rent the stalls?" Nathan demands, giving up the aw-shucks routine. "You've been here four months and you're using half the stalls you're paying for. It's a waste for both of us."

"I have some prospects," I lie. "Some folks are thinking about boarding with me for the winter. It's only August. Give me time."

"Most of the barns in Ocala are already booked for winter."

"That's good. I like my odds in getting some boarders if everyone else is booked. Why don't you let me run my business my way and not worry about where my money comes from?"

"I just want to be sure this arrangement works out," Nathan says, affecting a sympathetic expression. I guess he's playing good cop/ dumb cop or something. He's not a good enough actor to play one role, let alone two. For a moment, my mind wanders back to the actor Mrs. C showed me on her phone. Cary Davis? Something like that.

"You're a good prospect," Nathan continues. "I want to say I knew you back when."

He's such a liar. He just wants to be sure he doesn't have to evict me *halfway* through the lucrative winter season, when it would be so much more effective to do it now. He probably already has someone lined up to rent the entire property at twice what I'm paying per month. I wonder if he even thought I'd make it through a year lease when I signed with him back in spring. Or if someone told him after the fact he should have been doing six-month leases instead. Starting a short contract in October, and charging double during the show season, is pretty common practice here.

October is when the winter show season officially starts to heat up in Ocala. And even though it's only the end of August, a few big rigs from up north are already beginning to pull into town. They're towing show, sport, and breeding horses to Florida from the northern states. Traffic is already snarling around the town's various show-grounds, and our local Publix is slammed every time I walk in. Want a Pub Sub from the deli but you didn't call ahead? Hope you have an hour and a good game on your phone.

Oh, in winter-time, there's *plenty* of business to go around in this town. I'll get some boarders, just to spite Nathan if nothing else. My Aunt Kate didn't raise a quitter. Neither did my parents, even if they weren't as involved as she was.

"I have a rental contract for a year," I remind him, slumping against the door-frame to show just how casual and confident I am. "It's going to work out just fine, down to the letter. And if you're *very* lucky, I'll renew the lease next year and you won't have to find a new tenant."

Nathan nods slowly, his eyes drooping with hound-dog sadness, like he'd love to believe me, but he just can't.

I sigh. I don't have to prove anything to this man. Yes, the rent is a day or two late. That's what grace periods are for, and I have a three-day one spelled out in my lease. And anyway, I'm still finding my footing in this business. I need some more money? Okay, I'll add some lessons, put out a few more feelers about getting winter boarders, and everything will be fine. During the season, I'll be able to sell a few of my sales horses as amateur horses. Then, I'll get some fresh retired racehorses in spring to work on all summer, and start the cycle all over again, a little stronger than I did this year.

This is how it works. It's a proven formula. This is how Malcolm built up his business in the beginning, and it's how I'm going to build mine.

Yes, Malcolm had more financial backing to begin, but it's *fine.* Splitting hairs, really, to even think about that. I'm doing fine.

Fine.

Nathan laboriously stands up and comes around the desk. I watch my chair swing behind him and feel my lip curling. He has no business sitting in my desk chair like that—or standing so close to me. I try to back away from him and find the wall behind me. My fingers spread out across it.

He tips back his hat again. "I am *sure* we can make it work," he drawls.

For a moment, I think he's going to kiss me, and if he does, that's going to make things horribly awkward in our landlord/tenant relationship, what with the restraining order I'll have to take out on him. And will his wife still love him when he's missing a few front teeth? It will be a true test of their union. Mentally, I begin to review everything I know about making a fist.

But luckily, it doesn't come to violence. Nathan steps to the side and leaves me in the office, my fingers still pressed against the wood paneling at my back, a whiff of cigarette smoke hanging in the air.

Did he just light up in my aisle?

Only a real ass would smoke in a barn.

I listen to his truck start up and leave, then count to ten, before heading back into the aisle. The horses have finished eating their dinner and now they watch me eagerly, ready for turnout.

"Come on, Nando," I say to my tall chestnut, who presses his nose against the stall bars in anticipation. "Let's get you outside and raising hell for the night."

A little over an hour later, the stalls are clean and the aisle is swept. My barn is pristine, as all barns should be. I give it a satisfied three-sixty, turning in place to take in the pleasing sight of all my hard work.

It's a hell of a job keeping this barn dust and cobweb-free; this place was built on the cheap, with wooden walls that don't reach the eaves and an aisle paved in blacktop that rolls a little with the settling ground underneath. But the stalls are roomy and the electricity works—mostly—and there's a full-size arena outside along with six grassy paddocks and one large pasture in the back. As a starter farm, it definitely works. Daily, my perfectionist self struggles with its general untidiness compared to the pure ritz of Fine Day Farm, and my aunt's farm back in Virginia, where I learned to keep horses properly. But I comfort myself with the hope of a brighter, cleaner, and fancier future.

My day will come. And I know exactly what it will look like.

A concrete-block barn, brass nameplates on every stall, ceiling fans turning overhead, an air-conditioned tack room with a washer and dryer, lockers for my boarders, a full jump course in the manicured arena...oh yeah, I can see it all.

Someday.

In the meantime, though, I do the best I can.

Back in the office, I flip open my laptop and look at my schedule, double-checking tomorrow and making sure the weekend is mapped out in neat, hour-by-hour rows. Some people might call my scheduling obsessive, but what do they know? Life is full and chaotic; spreadsheets and PDFs make it manageable.

Friday looks normal, just riding in the morning and lessons in the evening. On Saturday, though, I'm hauling my two youngsters to a nearby jumper show in the morning, then getting back in time for afternoon lessons. It's going to be a long day; thank goodness I don't have to braid or do anything special for the show. We're just running through a few schooling rounds to prep them for the first event I've entered them into, coming up in mid-October. Both horses are young off-track Thoroughbreds, about to get their feet wet in the world of eventing for the first time.

"Literally wet, if I can get Plato to put his hooves in water," I mutter, thinking of the last time I took him cross-country schooling. The tall bay Thoroughbred, veteran of twenty-two races and winner of a princely fifteen thousand dollars, thought trotting through water was absolutely out of the question. We eventually got through the water complex, but it wasn't pretty.

His stablemate Sebastian is an easier ride; with a coat of patchy rose-gray that is fading to flea-bitten, he'll be some adult amateur rider's silvery unicorn, once I have some show miles on him. Or a pro could take him on, too. I'm not picky as long as I make some money on him. And I think I will. Sebastian is talented, gentle, and gray. He'll sell before Plato unless I'm very much mistaken.

"And you both have to sell," I say softly, "to pay off my bills. So I can rack up some more with new horses."

I click to my monthly lay-out and ahead to October. Events and jumper shows line themselves up on the boxes. The winter rush is so very, very close.

A text pops up on the screen and I lean forward, clicking it open.

Malcolm. I smile. I miss my old boss sometimes. Just a few miles away, but he's so busy, and I'm working so hard trying to be busy, that we never get together unless I'm bringing horses over to school fences in his arena or fields. "What's up, Malcolm?" I mutter, reading the text.

Have I got a horse for you.

I sigh and shake my head. I don't need a horse. I need to *sell* horses. I need—

A picture pops up on the screen.

"Whoa," I say, enlarging the picture.

Goosebumps raise on my arms.

The horse is jumping a cross-country fence in one of Malcolm's fields, just Novice height, but a formidable-looking log for all that. The horse is dark bay, without even a tiny star to relieve the darkness of his intense face, and his knees are nearly up to his chin as he clears the fence with miles to spare. Tiny Evie, Malcolm's girlfriend, is perched on his back and folded up like a jockey. The horse's back-cracking jump seems to be shoving her out of the saddle.

The horse is really something. I let my eyes rove over his lines, the curves of his muscles, the determined look in his dark eye.

Malcolm thinks this is a good horse for me? He's delusional. I couldn't possibly afford a horse like this. I have a horse fund in my annual budget, and it's tapped out for the year. But even if I hadn't bought Sebastian and Plato from a racehorse trainer looking to retire them into sport, or Nando for a great price from my friend, I wouldn't have the cash for a horse like this, already schooling cross-country and clearly showing aptitude to go far. This is an expensive prospect.

But damn, a girl can dream. There really is something about this horse that gives me chills.

Like I know him already.

Like I've been waiting for him my entire life.

Nice, I tap back, shaking my head again. No chance. And no use being sentimental and dreamy about him.

Malcolm replies: *He has Alison written all over him. Too tough for an amateur. Owner looking to sell fast. Are you interested?*

I nearly laugh. Of course I'm interested. But there's no way.

Malcolm keeps going.

I know you're just starting, but we could go in on him together. You take the ride.

The laughter fades. Could I make that work? Halfsies on a horse who will probably sell for the cost of a down-payment on a small farm?

Of course I can't.

I can barely make my rent.

The silence stretches out, then Malcolm types. *Or you could do payments. We can work something out. Just come ride him. I know you two are perfect for each other.*

It's insane. Terrible idea. But the thing is—I trust Malcolm. If he thinks he's found my horse—the Big Horse we are all waiting for—I believe him. Everyone's looking for the horse that's going to take them to the moon and back. Everyone wants that funny feeling in their chest, that flutter of premonition, that I'm feeling right now. I run my fingers over my heart now, telling it to settle, but that stupid old organ doesn't listen. It just imagines riding that horse, galloping cross-country, leaping every obstacle, and it thumps in a rapid, dangerous tattoo against my ribs.

Well, you can't fight love at first sight, I think. Some people feel this way about other people; apparently, I feel this way about good horses.

I'll come ride him tomorrow, I text back, figuring I can fit the horse in before my first lesson. *Two okay?*

See you then.

I take a breath and look at the show calendar again, willing it to fast-forward to April, when I will hopefully have a nice fat wallet from selling Sebastian and Plato, plus a full barn of boarders all winter. *Then* I could possibly pay Malcolm a few hundred a month for my share of a horse like this.

But now?

Where will I find any extra money?

I sigh. Charge triple, Mrs. C said. Is she really my only hope?

Chapter Three

"HE'S NOT GOING to suck," Evie says with certainty, punching a hole in a stirrup leather with one mighty squeeze of her tiny hands. Evie is short and the stirrup leathers we use for cross-country riding (doubled leather with a reinforced nylon belt in the center) do not come in a child-size length. So when she gets in a new set, they all receive the special Evie holes, several inches above the top hole the leathers came with.

I throw myself down on a monogrammed tack trunk belonging to one of Malcolm Horsham's well-heeled students. Chin in my hand, I remind her, "He's a Hollywood actor. They all suck."

I've decided I'm not excited about Mrs. C's proposition to train her movie star for the saddle. This decision came after a wakeful night criss-crossed with way too many short, suggestive dreams about what it might be like to train a man with those particular cheekbones and dark, flashing eyes. He's a distraction, and he hasn't even arrived in Ocala yet. Hell, I never even told Mrs. C for sure that I'd take him on. Although, knowing her, that's not up for discussion. I'd still like to pretend I have a choice.

Evie pushes back her short, dark hair and kneels next to a sleek cross-country saddle resting on a wooden rack, calmly awaiting its new stirrup leathers. As she wriggles the leather into place, she says, "Alison, I love and respect you very much, but you are a hater."

"Excuse me?" I snort, amused. "I am not a hater. I just know how things work in this world. And people who work in movies all suck. Have you ever worked with a Hollywood type? No? Because I have. Mrs. C puts on a good show, but she's not really as nice as she acts."

I feel guilty as soon as I say this because the truth is, I don't really know Mrs. C that well, and I am making assumptions about her because I'm mad at her. She is going to force my hand on this new student, and she'll do it with no effort. She just said I was doing it and left, even after I'd told her no.

How can she have that kind of power? It's infuriating, really. Although I don't actually feel furious.

Just annoyed.

And certain that this actor is going to be a lot of trouble. Did I really dream that I caught him as he was sliding out of the saddle? The memory of his eyes on mine is enough to make my stomach flutter, and it was a dream. A very stupid dream.

Trouble, I'm sure of it.

"Mrs. C is probably not the only example of Hollywood types," Evie says patiently, wiggling the stirrup leather back and forth as it resists sliding beneath the metal stirrup bar. "I am sure they have all kinds out there. And anyway, she's giving you a lot of money! So you can take that giant horse off my hands!" She gestures to the barn aisle, as if the promised perfect horse is waiting for us on the soft equine pavers.

"Maybe I'll be taking that horse," I hazard. "If I like him."

Even though deep down I'm anxious to see him, I haven't laid eyes on this promised perfect horse yet. Sydney, the farm's working student, has been sent out to retrieve him from his paddock. He'll be here in a few minutes. I can only hope he's not as good in person as he is in photos. That way, I won't do something stupid like try to buy him.

"Oh, you'll like him," Evie says. "Malcolm knows what you're looking for. That's what he's good at, remember? Matching up horses and riders is kind of his special talent."

"I used to run his barn for him, so yes. I remember."

Evie sighs, pushing out her lower lip. "You're a handful today, Alison," she says.

Malcolm sticks his head through the doorway. Six feet and change of muscled athlete in tan breeches and a moss-green jersey, Malcolm Horsham is one gorgeous man. *He* ought to be the one in movies, I think ruefully. Although I can't deny that dark-haired, dark-eyed devil of a movie star has definitely stuck with me after Mrs. C showed me his headshot on her phone. He's slighter and lankier than the broad-shouldered Malcolm, but both guys are truly hot stuff.

I don't typically notice people's looks, so that should tell you how impressive both men really are.

"Alison, a handful?" Malcolm demands, sarcastic grin flashing. His short, black beard and perfect dark skin make the perfect contrast to his gleaming white teeth. Women swoon before Malcolm's grins. Well, some women. Not me. But only because I know him so well.

"I don't believe it!" he continues. "Can't be true."

Oh yes, I ran his barn with an iron fist. Has that been mentioned? But he's lucky he had me, and he knows it.

"Malcolm," I say, "Evie has been claiming that this horse will change my life. Wouldn't you say that's a tad bit dramatic?"

I'm not willing to let on how hard I've fallen for this horse already. I've stared at all the pictures and replayed all the videos he's sent me, watching them again and again instead of going to sleep last night and between horses today, trying to find something wrong, something I won't like. I can't even explain why this horse matters so much to me. It's like witchcraft.

It's like the real thing. Like love.

I'm not one for falling in love with horses. The truth is, I haven't had a horse for longer than two years since I was a teenager. Everything I rode belonged to my aunt, and she made sure I understood the purpose of owning and training horses was to make them into easier horses for someone else to ride. Once I sold a horse, that was so that I could buy a better horse with the profit, and sell *it* on for more money. And so on and so on. The great circle of horse sales.

And so even as an adult, I try to sell a horse within six months, having developed a horse that is better and stronger than the one I started with. I find horses that are perfect for someone else, but not for me. I just don't get that close to them. I can like a horse without falling in love with it.

Something about this horse is very different.

But falling in love is a terrible business model. So, I'm going to give this horse a very skeptical test-ride, just like I would any other. I'll look at his radiographs and exam results, since Malcolm very kindly pulled that information for me already. I'll be cold and pragmatic and look at the horse's overall potential as a competitor and as an investment—all the while knowing he couldn't possibly work out as an investment for me in my current business plan.

And that is something I will *not* deviate from. You can't build a business plan and then just go willy-nilly off-book. That's something else Aunt Kate taught me. *There a thousand ways to go broke in the horse world, and about three ways to make money,* she'd told me over and over as a teenager. *Stick to the ways that work at making money.*

So, that's fine. All well and good. But some little voice deep within me says that this horse is different.

A foolish voice, probably.

But Mrs. C's terms for teaching her actor to ride hit my inbox this morning and they're....generous. To say the least.

So I'm allowing myself a possibility. A condition.

If I'm still somehow smitten with this horse after I've checked all the logical boxes, I'm going to call her back and tell her yes, I'll train her Hollywood star for the six weeks she is requesting.

And I'll give myself until the end of September to get in enough winter boarders to cover my bills and leave something leftover at the end of each month to cover this horse's payments. I did the math. I built the payment chart. I was thorough. And I think it will work out perfectly.

As things usually do, right?

I shake my head at myself. I know I'm being silly. I'm putting too much faith in other people, in the season's potential, in my own horse-girl math.

But hey, at this point? Blind faith is just about all I've got left. Faith that I'm right, faith that my methods will work, faith that I didn't make the mistake of a lifetime when I left Malcolm's employment and headed off on my own.

"Well, let's tack up Hansie and see what he's got," Malcolm declares, ending my mental gymnastics. "Sydney got him inside. Evie, which saddle has he been going in?"

"Use the black Stubben dressage," Evie says, not looking up from the cross-country saddle she's still working on. "And the brown bridle with the baucher snaffle. No flash necessary. He doesn't like tight nosebands." She glances at me. "Use the flash on cross-country, naturally."

"Of course," I say.

"Got it, boss." Malcolm looks at me expectantly, and I realize he still thinks I'm supposed to tack the horse up, even though I'm the potential client today.

I sigh and pick up the familiar saddle and bridle. After all, I'm the one who organized this tack room. I know it better than Malcolm does. I slide a girth over the top of the saddle, then pick up a clean, sage-green saddle pad from the pile on a shelf. *Fine Day Farm* is embroidered along the bottom corner. I had that embroidery done. I personalized everything in this tack room. Appearance is half the business when you're selling high-dollar horses.

Sometimes it's more than half.

"Malcolm?" Evie calls.

"Yes, dear," Malcolm sings, swinging back into the door.

"You know that Alison doesn't work for you anymore, right?"

He looks at me, arms draped in his horse's tack, and a rueful grin splits his cheeks. "Well, *damn*, Alison. I think Evie wants me to tack that horse up for you!"

"I'll do it," I tell him, shrugging. "Better for me to get to know the horse this way, anyway."

Malcolm skips ahead of me and slips into a stall, emerging with the tall, dark, and handsome horse of my dreams on the end of a leather lead shank. Hansie, as they call WL Hans Silverskates, comes out of the stall on his toes, ears up and eyes bright. I take a step back and let Malcolm walk the big horse into the grooming bay, where he turns him and clips the cross-ties to either side of the horse's halter.

Hansie stands perfectly still in the cross-ties, but his eyes are drinking me in as his nostrils flutter, showing the pink skin inside.

"Well, hello, Mister," I tell him, trying to ignore that insistent thump of my heart.

This horse has the strangest effect on me!

While I get to work grooming the horse—ticklish and wiggly, which doesn't surprise me given his high head and wide eyes— Malcolm fills me in on his breeding and prior training. The facts he lists are enough to remind me I can't afford this horse: he's by a champion eventing stallion and out of an elite Dutch mare with consistently high scores in the dressage arena; he's seven years old and experienced through Novice eventing along with some outings in the hunter ring (too forward) and the jumper ring (too slow over the big jumps).

"He spends too much time in the air," Malcolm explains. "When you're forward on the cross-country course, it's not a problem, but in the ring, he's very careful."

"And he's a back-breaking jumper," Evie adds. "Never touches a thing. It's just the wrong kind of scope for the big jumper classes."

"I get it," I say, picking up his front left hoof and admiring his angles.

"So," Malcolm continues, "he's an ideal event horse. But he's too spicy for the guy who owns him. This guy is looking for a field hunter type to take care of him. He's in his sixties, so that's fair."

"Totally fair." I put down the hoof and move to the right front. Something catches my eye—a thin hoop of white hair crossing his black pastern, just above the heel. I glance at the other fore-hoof and see a second hoop, nearly identical on the inside, though it fades on the outside. I guess that's why I didn't see it. "Wait a minute," I say, tracing the hoop with my finger.

Malcolm laughs. "You found the skates!"

I'm completely charmed. "These are adorable. Is this why he's called Hans Silverskates?"

"Has to be."

"What would these markings even be called?"

"Just coronets," Malcolm guesses. "Just funny little coronets."

"I love them." I pick some packed shavings from his hooves and admire his soles, the clean triangle of his frog. "I love this entire foot, actually."

"Damn, Alison, at least play it cool, so I don't jack up the price."

"I'm relying on you to get me a friends and family discount," I remind him.

"I'll see what I can do."

Horse tacked and helmet buckled, I lead Hansie towards the covered arena at the end of the barn aisle. Evie emerges from the tack room, ready to watch. "You going to put Malcolm on him first?" she asks, holding up Malcolm's helmet.

"Oh, for sure," I say, giving Malcolm a pointed look.

He sighs and takes his helmet, like he somehow thought he'd get out of showing me the horse under saddle just because we're old friends.

"Not just dressage," I tell him. "Jumps, too."

"It's *hot* outside," Malcolm moans. "And he's in a dressage saddle. Let's jump another day."

"A couple of little fences? Five minutes and some long stirrups won't kill you."

"She's right," Evie says. "Warm up in here and then take him out for a quick jump school."

"You women love bossing me around," Malcolm grumbles, but we all know he's going to do as he's told, so we let him grouse.

While Malcolm mounts Hansie, my phone buzzes and I look at the caller. Mrs. C, of course. She's the only one who calls me when a text would do. I let it go to voicemail, then read the transcript. *Great news, Cary arrives later today and he's excited to start riding. Need you to begin teaching tomorrow, thanks so much, bye-bye.*

What happened to starting him on Monday? I have a horse show tomorrow, for goodness' sake. Not to mention I didn't even tell her I'd take the job. She's just making these huge assumptions about me.

I sigh so heavily Hansie flicks his ears at me from across the arena. Evie glances at me curiously. "Client giving you trouble?"

"Mrs. C, of course." I show her the message.

"Wait," Evie says. "You said a Hollywood guy. But...Cary *who?*"

"Cary Davis—no, that's not right." I look through my email. "Hang on, I'll find it."

"Cary—*Davies?*" Evie gasps.

"Yeah! You've heard of him?"

"He was a Nickelodeon star," Evie says. "And he did a big teen surfing movie. Didn't you watch TV when you were a child?"

"Not really after I moved to my aunt's," I say, shrugging. "We didn't have cable." Windy Hill Farm is too remote for cable, and the house is too shadowed by trees to get decent satellite. Even today, Aunt Kate barely has basic internet.

"Didn't have cable—okay, we are digging into your troubled childhood later," Evie promises. "But first we need to talk about how Cary Davies was the cutest guy on TV in the early 2000s and everyone had a crush on him, me included."

"Crushes? Are we talking about me?" Malcolm calls, passing us on a walking Hansie.

"Oh, you wish," Evie scoffs. "Ride your horse."

"Alison's horse," Malcolm corrects her, walking on.

"Alison, I need to meet him," Evie says.

"Because you thought he was cute when you were fifteen?"

"Yes. Isn't that a good enough reason?"

"I wasn't even going to take him on unless I buy this horse, though." I'm ignoring the fact that Mrs. C is bringing Cary over whether I agree to teach him or not.

"Oh, get over it," Evie scoffs. "You are one hundred percent buying this horse. Just watch him move. Then imagine riding that moment yourself. Then actually get on. The horse is a done deal. Cary Davies, on the other hand..." She actually gives a delighted shiver.

"You're living with the hottest guy in three-day eventing," I remind her. "Possibly all of equestrian sports. I realize he's annoying, but if we're going solely on looks, you are actually all set."

"Just wait until you see Cary Davies," Evie says. "Have you Googled him? Google him."

"I've seen him," I say. But on reflection, I remember I've only seen the picture Mrs C showed me. The one where he looks like a self-satisfied model I'd like to smack. First with my lips and then with the palm of my hand. Then maybe with my lips again. I take my phone back from Evie and do a more thorough search.

"Oh," I realize, astonished. "He was awfully cute as a surfer."

"Mmhmm," Evie agrees, looking over my shoulder. "And that's not even—here—" She scrolls down and a picture of the Teenage American Dream fills the screen. "Sixteen years old there."

"This is illegal," I say. "We can't lust after a teenager like this."

"He's thirty-something now," Evie says. "It's fine."

A shout interrupts us, and we look up to see Hansie spooking hard as Malcolm exits the saddle. He hits the ground with a thud, and Hansie takes off, bucking and snorting.

"Oops," I say, as Evie swears and takes off across the arena to check Malcolm.

What set Hansie off? That's what I get for not watching the horse. Thanks a lot, Cary Davies.

You cute so-and-so.

Chapter Four

HANSIE RUNS RIGHT for me.

Listen, I'm a pragmatic professional; I'm not into touchie-feelie woo-woo *ooooh he loves me* nonsense when it comes to horses. I mean, I know horses and humans are capable of very special relationships, and I fully believe horses love humans who deserve it. Hell, sometimes they even love humans who *don't* deserve it—horses are forgiving and foolish that way. I think I've had a few horses love me in my time, mostly as a tween, before I had to get serious about showing and selling under my aunt's strict tutelage.

As for right now, I think Nando is very fond of me; Sebastian and Plato clearly like me, even if we've only known each other for a few short months.

Hansie doesn't know me at all. So when he comes right for me, ears pricked and eyes wide, arena footing flying from his hooves, I assume he's actually aiming for the doorway to the barn aisle behind me, and I step to one side. There's a pole across the doorway for precisely this situation, to keep horses from running out of the arena. What I'd like to know is if he's going to respect the barrier by turning away, or if he's the renegade type that will just jump it and head back to his stall, anyway.

I would prefer a horse that respects barriers and only jumps when asked to by a human. Have I mentioned my fences are often in need of repair? I don't need any horses deciding a fallen top board is a fine reason to explore the neighborhood.

My impromptu personality test fails, as Hansie doesn't even glance at the doorway. He veers off course immediately and keeps running right at me.

Okay, *weird.*

There's only one thing to do when a horse is running right at you —make yourself big and scary and give the horse no excuse to run you over. I throw up my arms and yell, *"Whoa!"*

The big horse screeches to a halt in front of me, sending clay and sand showering over my paddock boots.

Then he lowers his head and blows, hard, from his red-rimmed nostrils.

Goodness.

Taking his dangling reins in one hand, I run my other hand along his left cheek, feeling the muscles there flex as he works his jaw. A sign of relaxation and trust, the classic lick-and-chew response.

Seriously? For me?

"Dammit, Hansie," I say. "This is all a big scam, isn't it? You're a damn circus horse."

"What are you calling a scam?" Malcolm demands, brushing dirt from his perfect tan breeches as he pounds across the arena. He's pissed that he fell off, which will make him more difficult than usual. "You think I trained him to chase you?"

"I wouldn't put it past you," I drawl, even though I know it's a ridiculous idea. But it leaves behind an even more ridiculous idea.

Did Hansie just...*choose* me?

Do horses actually do that?

"I think he really likes you," Evie says, and I hear the surprise in her voice.

Hansie is drooling on my breeches, his head low and his ears at half-mast, even though his nostrils are still puffing with the effort it took to buck off Malcolm in the first place. "Yeah," I say dubiously. "I guess he does."

"I told you this was the horse for you," Malcolm says triumphantly. "Now, get on him and show us what he looks like when he isn't dumping me in the corner like a school-pony. Clearly, you've got something I haven't."

"Big of you to admit that," I snort. "But you're going to have to check that corner and make sure there's not a ghost over there. *Something* made him dump you. It wasn't just your total incompetence on horseback."

Malcolm snorts and waves a hand at Evie. "Come on, let's make sure Princess Alison isn't going to get any dirt on her britches."

They do a quick inspection of the far corner of the covered arena while I walk Hansie in a circle, letting the horse rub his muzzle against my shoulder and generally act as if he's fallen in love with me. It's bewitching. I'm already feeling half-in-love myself.

"Some mouse turds behind the cones stored over there," Evie reports back. "Looks like Madam Mouser isn't doing her job."

"No cat can get them all," Malcolm says, quickly rising to his cat's defense.

"I'll have to call the Operation Catnip people and get a second one," Evie says, making a note on her phone. "Can't have too many barn cats."

I watch her note-taking with pleasure. Oh, I've trained that girl well; she's almost as ruthlessly organized as I am. Evie won't forget to get a new barn cat. Malcolm would forget in less than five minutes.

"So it could have been mice," Malcolm says, looking over Hansie. "What if it wasn't?"

"Well...anything, really. It's a scary corner, you know that."

He's right, the far corner is classically the scary one. Every arena has a scary corner.

"Get on him again," I say, handing over the reins.

Hansie gives me a hurt look.

I mean, no, he doesn't. He's a horse. He just glances over at me.

I must be crazy to let myself get so emotional and silly over a horse like this.

"Go on," Evie tells Malcolm. "Get on the horse and be a professional."

Malcolm knows he's cornered. So, he mounts back up and shows off Hansie's three smashing gaits, but I can't help noticing the horse avoids bending into the corner where he spooked. There's something over there upsetting him. Mice, or the general scariness of the scary corner.

Or maybe it's something about the way Malcolm is riding him right there that's doing it. Horses can feel *everything*.

Malcolm grunts and gives Hansie a poke in the ribs with his heel as the horse balloons inwards, shoving his shoulder away from the scary corner.

"Whatever it is, he's not fixing it today," Evie says. "But I swear he hasn't been doing it with me."

"Lady's horse?"

"Could be. His owner is an older guy and they *really* don't get along."

That's probably it, then. Some horses just need a woman's touch.

"Let's go outside and see the jumps," I call, partially to put Malcolm out of his misery and partially because I'm eager to try this horse for myself. "Then I'll get on him."

A HALF-HOUR later, I'm done for.

Evie sets the higher jumps back down to Novice height, just under three feet, and then we step back to watch Malcolm take the horse over a few fences individually, stopping and backing him up after each one.

I glance at Evie. "Gets strong after he jumps?"

She grins and nods. "He's a freight train once he gets rolling. You have to keep his head up, and then you won't have any problems. But the good thing is, he doesn't have a stop in him. And that includes on cross-country."

"Have you done a whole course with him?"

"Big chunks, like five or six fences, but not a full course."

"Close enough, I guess."

"He'll do water, he'll do a ditch," Evie says, ticking off the different jumps on her fingers. "He'll do a skinny, but you have to steer. He won't try to run out the side, but he'll get himself too close to the edges and take down the flag-pole with a foreleg."

"Is that a penalty on course? I can never remember."

"Depends on the jump judge, I think?" She shrugs. "We can check. But you know what you're doing. It won't be a problem."

When Malcolm brings Hansie over, the horse immediately shoves his nose against my shoulder. Like he's been missing me and can't believe we're reunited at last.

This is crazy, I think.

Malcolm and Evie exchange glances, then Evie bursts into laughter. "I *swear* I didn't teach him that!"

"Sure," I scoff, as Hansie gives my wrist a long, wet lap with his tongue. "Like you aren't trying every trick in the book to get this old plow-horse off your hands."

Malcolm dismounts and hands me the reins. "Take this plow-horse for a spin, then you can apologize."

Hansie feels electric underneath of me; before I even have my feet in the stirrups or contact with the bit, I can sense the connection between us. Sometimes, you sit on a horse and you just know.

Hansie and I both know.

Delicately, he mouths the bit and takes me around the arena with a big, but polite, step. I'm dying to jump him, so I barely notice the blazing-hot summer sun or the awkwardness of the deep-seated dressage saddle as his sure strides eat up the ground between fences.

As advertised, Hansie's signature leap is the high, flat-in-the-middle jump of an upper-level event horse. And he has a way of flicking back his ears to listen to me, even when I'm only thinking, that touches my heart.

No, it doesn't touch it. It reaches out and *squeezes* it. I feel wrung out, emotionally and physically, after we finish jumping. To distance myself from the jumping emotions, I slide him into a dressage frame and we do a few transitions, dance through a few leg yields. It all feels so good, so right.

Evie grins as I walk the horse back over to the in-gate, where she's standing alongside Malcolm. "Well?"

"Let's figure out the payment plan," I say, shaking my head at myself.

Malcolm nods. "I knew it."

WITH THE PAYMENT-plan contract on the way over to Hansie's current owner, I know I have no choice but to take on Mrs. C's

Hollywood boy. I call her while I'm still in the Fine Day Farm parking lot, putting her on speaker as I turn up the air conditioning to full blast. Cold air on this hot day will make my decision a lot easier to swallow.

She offers me the first week's payment right away and I blink at the amount about to bolster my tanking checking account in exchange for five measly riding lessons, but recover myself in time to remind her that I also need to expense her for the western tack I currently don't own.

"Just take pictures of the receipts and send them to me," she trills. "I have to go, movie business on the other line!"

Movie business. I bet she loves saying that.

I tap my finger against the steering wheel, trying to decide if I have time to get the tack before my afternoon lessons. I figure I better do it now; there won't be any time tomorrow, with the jumper show taking up my morning and the usual Saturday students in the afternoon. So I turn right instead of left after the farm gate, and head towards Ocala—where the only question is which of the many tack shops in town I should visit first. I don't usually have a blank check to play with.

This could be fun.

My phone buzzes as I drive through the rolling horse country north of town, black-board fences and broad green pastures stretching away from the narrow road on either side. The roadsides are thick with late-summer grass and soggy with late-summer monsoons, and there's no shoulder for a buffer zone if a tire should slip off the road, so I quickly stab the answer button before locking both hands tightly around the wheel again.

I know good days can go bad quickly. I don't trust them. Never have.

"Hello, this is Alison," I say into the air. It must be Mrs. C again. I wonder what she wants this time.

If she changed her mind about all this, right after I signed that payment plan with Malcolm and he emailed the document to the horse's owner for approval, I'm going to die. That's all. I'll just die. Because being dead will be preferable to the professional embarrassment of not being able to live up to the contract. Word will get around—word *always* gets around in the horse business.

I can't afford to have people thinking my business is running on fumes. No one will board or train with me if they expect me to close up shop within six months.

"Hi there," a man says. Even in those two syllables, I can hear something smooth and silky about his voice. Something that makes me shift a little in my seat. "I'm Cary."

"Oh!" I stop looking at the narrow road ahead of me and stare at my phone instead, as if I expect Cary Davies' dark-haired head to pop up and start talking to me. But it's just my phone, resting on the center console, screen blazing with a phone number I don't recognize.

"Um, hi," I say. "I'm Alison."

"Yes, you said that," he says, a smile in that smooth voice. I shift again. What a weird effect his voice is having on me! "It's so nice to talk to you at last. Kat has told me the nicest things about you."

"Oh, she has?" I wish I didn't sound so surprised. "I mean, that's great."

"Absolutely," Cary assures me. This guy's *voice,* my god—

I realize I'm still looking at the phone. I flick my gaze up to the road, just in time to see that I'm over the center line and there's another truck approaching fast. I swing hard to the right, over-correcting, and the truck careens towards the edge of the road.

I grip the wheel tightly, trying to fix things, my breath catching a little in my chest.

It's fine, it's fine—

"Oh, *shit!*" I shriek, forgetting all about the new student still on speaker-phone.

The truck hits a pothole along the crumbling edge of the road, and the tires swerve to the right, spinning the wheel through my frantically clutching fingers.

With a lurch and a crunch, the front right tire drops off the road. It hits the deep, wet sand lurking beneath the over-ripe grass and immediately starts to swing around as I frantically slam my booted foot down on the brakes.

Worst-case scenario, I'll *only* end up in the ditch and not slam all the way through Starry Sky Equine's gorgeous four-board fence on the other side.

The truck grinds to a halt and I take a deep, shuddering breath.

I have managed to avoid the fence.

But only because the ditch stopped my momentum. The truck is tipped nose-first into the muddy swale. Still running, thank goodness. No warning lights on the dashboard, air conditioning roaring strong.

Hmm.

Maybe this could still be a good day?

I hear a squeal as the other truck hits its brakes a few dozen feet up the road. I should probably get out, let the other driver know I'm okay. But ugh—how embarrassing! I drove off the road because I was looking at my phone, like a teenager or something.

I stare at the fence rising just beyond the swale and try to mentally prepare myself for a ticking-off from some old Ocala guy who has just about had it with the empty-headed horse girls zooming around these narrow country roads looking at their phones instead of paying attention.

On the other side of the fence, fresh company approaches: a herd of well-bred Thoroughbred weanlings, recently introduced to adult life away from their mothers, come trotting up to inspect the new truck which has appeared just outside their fence. No doubt they get fed in the field from a pickup bed and they think I'm a new food truck, come to give them lunch.

They lean over the top rail and look at me with interest, eyes bright and ears pricked.

"I don't have any food," I say aloud, as if they can hear me.

"Um, hello? Is everything okay?" The voice coming through the Bluetooth startles me so hard I jump.

I do a quick double-take at my dashboard, realizing that Cary's number is still on the screen. Did I just assume the call would drop off while I was busy trying not to wreck my truck? He heard *everything*—ugh, he must think I'm a total psycho.

Well, welcome to horse-land, Cary. We're all mad here.

I scoop up the phone from its landing spot on the passenger side floor and deposit it back in the cupholder where it belongs.

"Yeah, I just wrecked my truck a little bit," I say. "Hopefully not too bad, though."

I hear Cary gasp. "Holy shit! That's insane! I should let you go deal with that. I'm so sorry—"

"It's fine," I say dreamily, because I'm clearly going into shock. My hands are shaking, but my thoughts are foggy. I watch the horses—at least six weanlings have lined up along the fence now, and they're staring at me with huge, round eyes. Their pricked ears remind me of Hansie, the way he watched me with laser-focus even after I dismounted and left him with Evie while I went into the office to look over the paperwork with Malcolm. It was like he didn't want to let me out of his sight, and I felt bad when I left him there. I wanted to put him in the back of my truck and drive him straight back to my farm. Maybe bunk down in his stall with him tonight.

"It's fine?" Cary asks, his voice surprised. "Are you sure? Listen, I can postpone the riding lessons a few days if you need me to. We don't have to start tomorrow."

Suddenly, I jolt back to life. It's extremely urgent that he not postpone. Cary can't do *anything* to jeopardize this deal. I just literally signed my life away to buy a horse relying on his lessons to cover the first few payments, and now I might have truck repairs to deal with, too? Everything has to go smoothly from here on out.

"I'll be ready for you tomorrow," I assure him. "Everything is fine. Really. You just caught me at a weird moment."

You made me drive off the road. But he didn't, not really. I did that to myself.

I didn't *have* to stare at the phone like an idiot, after all. That was my own weird, inexplicable choice.

"Well, okay, if you say so." Cary hesitates. "Um, do you want me to stay on the line in case you need help?"

A man in breeches, boot socks, and a pair of clay-stained sneakers is walking up to my window. After a moment's staring, I recognize him as a jumper trainer. What a way to meet a fellow professional. Oh, Ocala.

"Thanks, but I promise I'm safe," I say. "I'll see you tomorrow."

And with Cary Davies disposed with until tomorrow, I pop open the door and step down from the truck, ready to inspect the damage and see just how far down the spectrum my good day has shifted.

Chapter Five

"I'M JIM," THE familiar guy says, extending a hand for me to shake. He looks me up and down, then his gaze flicks to the truck behind me. "Jim Brewer. You okay?"

"I'm Alison, and yes," I reply, taking his steady hand in my shaking one. Callouses brush my palm. He must not ride in gloves. *A man's man*, I think somewhat hysterically, smothering a smile. *Deep breaths. Don't say anything stupid.*

I glance back at my poor truck, which looks forlorn in the deep grass. The weanlings just beyond the fence shove against one another, anxious to get a closer look, maybe lean over the fence far enough to take a bite off the side mirror.

"I'm okay," I repeat. "But my truck..." I trail off, feeling smothered beneath a layer of despondency which isn't my natural state. If my truck is damaged, I am beyond screwed.

"She actually looks fine," Jim says, kneeling to inspect the front tires, which are six inches deep in Florida's signature swamp-muck. He glances back at me. "I think you might get away with this one. Want me to try hauling you out? Then we can see what the axles look like. That's the only thing I'd be worried about."

I take another deep breath, trying not to fixate on the wreckage of my schedule. Instead, I will fixate on keeping his intact. "That would be amazing, thanks, but I can call a tow truck and not make you late for wherever you're heading."

I can't afford a tow truck, obviously, but there's a stupid side of me which can't stand letting other people put themselves out for me. And this wasn't even Jim's fault. It's entirely mine.

Why did I stare at my phone like that? Did I really think I was going to *see* the fabulously gorgeous Cary Davies grinning back at me? Maybe I thought he'd blow me a little kiss? What came over me?

I'm Alison. I'm the *steady* one around here, the woman who takes names and gets things done. I don't get giddy over former teen heartthrobs and swerve off the road like an idiot.

Maybe I need more sleep. They say anything less than eight hours can cause drunken-like behavior. I should try going to bed at eight thirty instead of nine thirty, add in an extra hour and see if that fixes my brain. Of course, I don't usually finish the barn until eight, so that won't give me much time to eat or shower or anything. Maybe that's not the solution—

"No, please let me. I'm happy to help," Jim says, running a hand along his jaw.

It's a very well-cut jaw, I reflect, and with that thought, I realize I've gone around the bend. Yup, I am definitely moving back my bedtime.

"I can't ask that of you," I insist again, but Jim holds up his hand.

"Don't be silly. I've got a chain in the back. Give me a minute and we'll get you fixed up."

And sure enough, within ten minutes, Jim has my truck back on the southbound lane of the road, pointing towards Ocala and none the worse for wear. He rolls up the tow chain with a practiced hand while I try not to look too impressed. It's an uphill battle, though, because I *am* impressed. In my experience, men in breeches are not particularly handy. I don't think Malcolm would know how to check his windshield wiper fluid, let alone figure out where to attach a tow chain. I used to have to schedule his truck's oil changes, for heaven's sake, or the engine would have just fallen out of the thing on the way to an event.

"Thanks," I tell Jim. "I'm lucky you're so handy with a tow chain. I bet you can change your own oil, too."

He barks a surprised laugh, then looks embarrassed at the noise that came out of his mouth. "I can, actually," he says. "And you're welcome. It was no problem, I promise. Anyway, couldn't leave you here on the side of the road when I'm sure you have important places to be."

"I have saddles to buy," I say gravely.

Jim nods, equally serious. "Doesn't get much more pressing than that. I better let you get on with it." He hesitates a moment, then grins and says roguishly, "This is when you say you don't know how to thank me, and I say, 'Let me buy you dinner.' "

I feel a smile tugging at my lips. Oh my, Jim's a player! How about that? An oil-changing, breeches-wearing player.

"I didn't realize we were supposed to learn our lines beforehand," I say.

"I learned both parts for you," he replies pertly. "Just in case you didn't show up prepared. Now you say, 'Oh, Jim, I'd love to!' "

"I'd *definitely* let you buy me dinner," I answer, shrugging. "As long as you don't mind dropping it off around eight? You can leave it in the barn. I'll walk down and pick it up after you're gone."

He laughs, holding up his hands. "Outsmarted already. My mom always told me girls were smarter than boys."

"She was right." I study him for a moment, trying to make up my mind. Jim Brewer is a good-looking guy: laughing green eyes, tousled brown hair, a farmer's tan that shows just below the sleeves of his tech-fabric riding shirt. He seems nice. And he did just haul my truck out of the mud when he had absolutely no hand in getting it stuck there. Maybe I *should* give him a chance. I never give anyone a chance—that's really not my style—but hey, free dinner with a funny, nice horse trainer?

It could be fun, and it will definitely be more nutritious than any of the cheap meals in my pantry. I can't remember the last time my protein source wasn't from a box of Zatarain's red beans and rice.

"Okay," I say, deciding to go for it. "I'll let you eat *with* me, if you want. But you should know I just decided my new bedtime is nine thirty, precisely to prevent situations like this." I nod at my muddy truck. "So I can't be out late."

"Fair enough," Jim says. "My mornings come pretty early, anyway. I'll text you, okay?"

And he takes a picture of the magnet on my driver's side door, the big square one that reads *HIGHBURY SPORT HORSES* and includes my phone number.

Well, fair enough, I think, as I restart my truck and proceed into Ocala—where I proceed to spend so much money it makes me nervous. If Mrs. C changes her mind about this, I'm absolutely out of luck.

It's past time to head home and feed dinner before I'm finished raiding the tack stores. I glance back at the gleaming chestnut-colored western saddle in the backseat of my truck, nestled alongside its woolen saddle pad and cotton cinch, and wonder just what I'm getting myself into.

I'd better look at some western riding videos tonight and make sure I don't try to teach this poor guy how to ride hunt-seat in a cowboy saddle. The last thing I need is to be the reason *another* Hollywood movie gets horses wrong.

SATURDAY MORNING SWEEPS by in a busy haze of hauling horses, jumping courses, and turning them out again so that I can clean the barn before Cary's arrival—all before one o'clock in the afternoon. To be fair, the barn was already pretty clean, but I had to leave in a rush around six thirty this morning to get to the show on time, and anyway, by my standards, a barn can always be cleaner. I certainly don't want to scare Hollywood Boy off with something scary, like a cobweb in a door-frame, or an eight-legged friend the size of a dessert plate where he least expects it.

My white-splashed tabby cat, Lily Marlene, sits in the office doorway and watches me sweep down dusty webs clinging to the tops of stall doors, slowly blinking her large green eyes as if to ask, *Why are humans like this?*

It's a good question, I say to myself, as I realize that now I'm a sweaty and dirty mess—not exactly how I'd like to greet *any* new client, let alone a movie star who has already provided some questionable cameos in my dreams.

So, I run upstairs to my apartment, a tiny living quarters positioned above the tack room and office, and quickly shimmy out of my sweaty, messy breeches and top. I'll just put on something clean and presentable. I try to look the part of an equestrian professional—someone who has people to do the dirty work for her, not someone who has to do everything herself.

I leave the apartment door open behind me, in case Lily Marlene wants to come up and nose around her food dish. The good food only gets served inside, to keep out other critters.

With a cool breeze blowing directly from my A/C unit to the open door, I glance around my little apartment with a critical eye. Just in case Cary were to see it for some strange reason, would it be presentable? Would it seem cozy to him, or embarrassingly small? At twelve feet wide and twenty-four feet long, it's big enough for a tiny bathroom, a bed, a small table with two chairs, an itty-bitty sofa, and a kitchen set-up against one short wall.

As a horse-person would measure it, my apartment is the size of a foaling stall, and if this space is big enough for a mare and her foal, it's certainly big enough for one human and the occasional feline friend.

The only downside to my living space is that the laundry facilities are in the tack room, and when I don't feel like schlepping back downstairs (that last flight of stairs can feel daunting after a full day of barn work and riding) I sometimes just give my riding breeches a good scrubbing in the shower stall rather than throwing them in the washing machine. There's more than laziness at work here. I wear *nice* things—nice being a code word for *very expensive*, because I believe looking successful is halfway there. Malcolm is a fantastic example of this philosophy in action. And nice things benefit from hand-washing.

That's my rationalization, anyway.

A gorgeous pair of moss-green Romfh breeches I scrubbed last night are currently drying over the back of a kitchen chair. They'd be perfect for my needs right now—I put my hand on them and sigh. Not quite dry. That's okay; it's hot out, they'll dry on me. Once I get them on, that is. Damp breeches can take a while to coax into place.

I'm sitting on the edge of my bed, topless and wrestling my way into the breeches, when I hear a sound through the open front door.

Tires, crunching over the gravel in the driveway.

I freeze. He's not—

A car door slams.

I look at the breeches crumpled in my grip, at my white thighs and bare knees, then at my open door. I should really stop leaving that open. It's just that I'm pretty much always the only one here, with the exception of afternoon riding lessons...

Suddenly, I hear the patter of little feet on the stairs, and then Lily Marlene races into the apartment.

That's a bad sign—Lily Marlene is something of a self-appointed watch-cat.

She meows frantically at me, showing her pink mouth and sharp mouse-eating teeth. *Human, dress yourself!* Lily Marlene's warnings say.

In short order, I hear much larger footsteps on the stairs.

He's here.

He must have seen the open door, the light spilling out. With the downstairs clearly deserted, the upstairs is the next logical place to check. I can't fault him for that.

I look down at my sweaty legs, still exposed from the knees up because that's as far as I've gotten these lovely, but damp, breeches, and then my gaze shoots up again as a shadow crosses the doorway.

Instantly, I drop my hands from the waistband of my breeches and put them over the cups of my sports bra.

Pure instinct. Possibly not the best one. The bra has pretty full coverage already. Everything below the waist, on the other hand...

"Hello—?" Cary's voice is even more charming in person. I see a hand pushing back the door to get a good view inside—

"Don't look!" I gasp.

"Oh god—sorry!"

For a split second, time stops and I stare into the dark eyes of the one and only Cary Davies. Not just his eyes—his entire lovely face.

He seems like a fascinating hybrid of the teenaged star I ogled yesterday with Evie and the handsome man I admired on Mrs. C's phone a few days ago when this whole debacle started to shamble into existence. Mahogany-brown hair that curls around his ears and shoulders. A prominent nose offset by two sharp cheekbones. Eyelashes that would make a socialite squeak in envy. Full lips and perfect, perfect Hollywood teeth.

Not my type, but damn, I don't care, I think, and then remember I'm perched on the edge of my bed with my pants around my ankles and my hands cupped over my breasts.

Cary seems to register the inappropriate nature of our first meeting at the same time. He blushes—like a *girl,* I think hysterically —and then ducks out of the doorway, pulling the door closed behind him.

"Sorry!" he calls through the door. "Sorry, sorry, sorry!"

I look down at my gleaming white thighs and wonder if it's too late to call Mrs. C and tell her I'm sorry I can't teach Cary, because I'm dead.

A person can die of embarrassment, can't they?

Chapter Six

EVENTUALLY, I RECOVER myself enough to tug my breeches the rest of the way up and get them zipped and buttoned. I find a decent shirt and tug it over my head. And now that I'm presentable, there's nothing to do but go down and face the music.

It's not *that* big a deal, right?

I mean, yes, I just met my new client for the first time while half-naked. And that is unfortunate.

But Cary needs to understand something: this is the horse business. And nothing is sacred in this world—nothing but taking care of our horses. He'll just have to get used to the weird and unorthodox ways horse-people behave. Occasionally seeing us with our tight pants halfway off. That kind of thing.

I guess.

That's how I'm going to spin it, anyway.

Or...maybe it won't even come up?

Resolved to be a big girl about this, no matter how the conversation to follow turns out, I cautiously open the front door and step onto the creaking landing, looking up and down the barn aisle below.

I don't see anyone.

He's wandered off? He's left? He's been frightened away by my gleaming white thighs?

Cary steps back into the barn aisle from outside, where he must have been taking in the uninspiring vista of my dusty little farm.

Ugh. I'd almost rather he was staring at my bare legs again.

Truthfully, when I look at my farm, I wish *everything* could be the interior of the barn, which I've worked so hard to scrub clean and organize into something at least *resembling* a high-end stable.

Despite the weary look of the unpainted stall fronts and the uneven black-top aisle, this barn still looks a hundred times better than it did the day I rented it—thanks in part to the new halter hooks and blanket bars I installed myself, the sparkling clean wash-stall I scrub every afternoon when the horses are finished for the day, and the spotless rubber mats seen through the open door of every stall, the shavings atop them swept back four feet precisely to keep bedding from spilling into the aisle.

Inside, I have the closest thing to complete control over my domain that I can manage at this unruly rented farm.

Whereas outside, I don't have the same magic touch. I'm struggling to turn straw into compost, let alone gold. It would take a full-time landscaping crew a few weeks to whip this neglected property into something as shapely and dignified as Fine Day Farm. I don't have to step outside to know what Cary is seeing: a sandy driveway lined with overgrown grass; a parking area dotted by potholes where the crushed lime-rock has washed away in heavy summer rains earlier in the season, an apron of scrubby weeds surrounding the barn.

I wish one of those summer storms would materialize now. At least things would look clean. This past week has been dry and so the sand is getting deep, the arena is getting dusty, and everything is tired and brown.

Things get messy so quickly, from one extreme to the other. In a few days, I'll probably be dealing with floods.

I shake my head and remind myself, for the millionth time, that it's unreasonable to expect the perfection that I was accustomed to achieving at Fine Day Farm. How can I compare my one-woman operation to a place where we had professional landscapers come handle the flower-beds, clean the fountain, and mow the grass? The outside of the barn simply doesn't stand a chance without hiring a crew to help me keep the place up.

But a lack of help doesn't change my high standards. It can't. My brain is wired for perfection, and that's not going to change.

With a final sigh, I head down the stairs—followed closely by Lily Marlene, who is still on high alert regarding a stranger in the barn. Her tail twitches against my leg as we reach the barn aisle, then she takes off ahead of me, ready to protect me from the handsome stranger lounging at the end of the aisle.

Cary turns around as the cat reaches him and offers up one tiny, defiant *mew*.

"Well, hello there," he says, bending down to give Lily a pat. She backs up, sitting just out of reach. He raises his hands in surrender, and says, "No petting. Fair enough."

Then he straightens and looks at me.

Silhouetted as he is against the blinding sunlight of late August, I can't see his expression, or even those impressive cheekbones I had time to clock upstairs. But I can still tell he's giving me a tentative smile. His ears seem to lift ever-so-slightly, giving his expression away.

"Hiya," he says in that warm baritone that nearly made me wreck my truck only yesterday. "I hope I didn't catch you at a bad time."

"Just an ordinary everyday game of breeches-wrestling," I joke, strolling up to him. I stoop to give Lily a little pat, then straighten and rest one fist on my hip. A power pose. I say, "Kind of comes with the territory when you ride horses in Florida."

Cary looks down at my breeches, which are moss green, skin-tight, and patterned on the inner legs and seat with a subtle horse-head design in silicone. They're meant to help me stick to the saddle in desperate moments. I let him examine my legs without embarrassment. He's already seen what's under the stretchy fabric. Muscled legs the color of the moon.

"Now, should I be in breeches?" he asks after a moment, his gaze flicking back to mine. "Or are jeans the right thing? I figured I'd be in jeans when we shoot the riding scenes, so that's what I went with today. They're hot as hell, though."

I imagine Cary in one of Malcolm's smart riding outfits, tan breeches and a sage-colored riding jersey. Cary's dark hair would look gorgeous against green. And it would bring out little pinpricks of color in his hazel eyes, too.

But there's no point treating this guy like a male Brenda Breyer— *was* there a male version of Brenda Breyer? I can't remember—when he's here to be a cowboy. I shake my head with some regret and say, "Oh, you're good in those. You'll be riding western. I think jeans are the most appropriate thing for you. As long as they don't rub your legs or your—um—crotch."

Two dimples appear beneath Cary's perfect cheekbones, because of course they do. "I guess, as my riding instructor, it's your business to care about my crotch."

"I'm afraid it is." I let myself grin back. I like his sense of humor. "Let me introduce myself properly, now that I'm fully clothed. I'm Alison, and this is Highbury Sport Horses."

"Cute name." He extends a hand and I take it, feeling strength in his warm fingers. He gives my hand a little squeeze before he lets go.

"My name, or the farm?" I ask coyly.

"Both. You ever go by Ali?"

"Never."

"Fair enough," he says again. "Alison it is."

We look at each other for a moment. I feel a strange urge to take his hand again. "Let me give you a tour of the farm," I suggest, shoving my fingertips into the small pockets of my breeches to keep them from doing anything funny.

The tour is brief. In fact, we can conduct it simply by standing here at the end of the barn aisle.

"I know it's small," I say, pointing out the collection of paddocks which circle around the arena, where the horses have space to graze and nap. Most of them are currently snoozing beneath the shade of a few oak trees, which spread their boughs like protective wings over the shared fence-lines. "And it's a little plain-Jane compared to some of the spreads in Ocala. But I'm just getting started on my own. I think it has a lot of potential."

When I can afford some employees to help me, I might even reach it.

"I think it looks nice," Cary says, shrugging. "You don't need a hundred acres to have a nice farm."

"It could use some sprucing up," I say, unable to stop myself from a little light criticism of all the work I can't fit in. "I never seem to find the time to get the outside worked on."

"Well, I guess it takes a lot of time, taking care of all these horses," he says reasonably.

Does it take a lot of time? Somehow, it takes all of my time, but I don't feel like it should. I look at the six horses in my paddocks. Sebastian, Plato, Nando, and the other horses here on training board —Lucy, Gidget, and Roddy. This little herd is such a far cry from the twenty-plus I was responsible for at Fine Day Farm, along with all the trailer-in lessons, the conditioning rides, the rehabilitation work, and everything else that was part of my job running a top eventing barn. Sometimes I go to bed embarrassed that I'm so worn out handling just six horses and a few riding lessons.

But it's somehow more tiring doing *everything* alone. Something else I didn't know about running my own business.

"Yeah," I say finally. "It does take a lot of time. But all we need to do for you is get you riding, right? Have you ridden before?"

"Pony rides as a kid." Cary gives me that toothy grin again. He's quick with a smile. "And once when I guest-starred on an episode of *Molly H2O,* I rode a horse."

"Wasn't *Molly H2O* about a teenage mermaid?" I recall, perplexed. That show was on network television, not cable, so I occasionally got to watch it. "How...?"

"Yeah, but in this one episode, she rescued a handsome stranger on a deserted island, and he tamed a wild horse while he was there. Well, my stunt double did. But Molly fell for *me.*" Cary's tone is triumphant.

"Oh, so *you* were the handsome stranger?"

"Is that so hard to believe? I admit I was much better-looking when I was a kid." Cary laughs.

I give him a sidelong glance. "I don't know about *much,*" I say. "If anything, you're probably equally good-looking."

"Well, my career ended at eighteen," he says. "I put it down to never growing into my nose."

"It's not a tiny nose, but who wants a tiny nose?" I happen to like Roman noses, in horses and in people, but I don't tell Cary that. He's clearly fishing for compliments. Nice try, buddy. Being cute and self-deprecating can't disguise his movie-star narcissism from me. I knew it would be there.

"So, you admit my nose is big." Cary pats the offending organ mournfully.

I study his nose. It's really only a *little* larger than necessary. "It's fine, like I said. You want to talk about big noses? Let's look at the horse you're going to ride today. I'll let you two compare schnozes, and may the best snoot win."

"Ouch," Cary says, staggering backwards like I've mortally wounded him. "Comparing me to a horse? That was straight to the heart, madam."

"You'll be fine," I say loftily. Am I smiling too much? I feel like I'm smiling too much. He's not *that* funny, is he? I look away from him deliberately and point towards the paddock where Nando is snoozing. "Come on, let's bring in Nando and I'll show you which end bites and which end kicks. You've probably forgotten, if the last time you rode a horse was back in your distant child-star days."

"Distant? Another stab to the chest," Cary groans, clutching his chest, but he falls into step beside me.

Our shoes slip and slide in the dry sugar sand, and I have to watch where I put each foot. My paddock boots rise and fall next to his sensible round-toed western boots.

Okay, first impression? I like him. I'm sure he has that child-star craving for attention that Mrs. C's dreadful daughter exhibits on a weekly basis in her tragic riding lessons, but maybe having a career dry spell between the ages of eighteen and thirty has been good for this man. Maybe he's learned a little humility.

For his sake, I hope so. Because nothing can quite make mincemeat of an overly confident person like learning to ride, *especially* as an adult. Even on my saintly school-horse, dear old Cary Davies is in for a wild ride.

Into his own psyche, more than likely.

"THIS END BITES, right?" Cary pulls a few strands of Nando's tail across his face like he is Cousin It's mustachioed nephew.

"You're lucky this horse is a saint," I tell him. "Try that with my guy Plato out there and you'll end up with a hoof-shaped bruise on your chest."

"Cool, I could use a new tattoo pattern," Cary jokes, dropping Nando's copper-colored tail.

"I didn't peg you for a tattoo guy." I toss him a tail brush and he catches it. Surprisingly dextrous, our movie star. "Nothing's showing. Are your other ones all on your ass, or what?"

"Oh, I'm totally lying to impress you. I'm terrified of needles." He starts at the bottom with Nando's tail, which is the correct form. I guess someone on the set of *Molly H2O* showed him how to groom a horse, once upon a time. "In fact," he continues, "I'm so afraid of needles that I don't have any piercings, not even in my ears, and I have to get my flu vaccine up my nose, like a child."

"Thanks for telling me the truth. I respect you more because of it."

"Really?"

"No," I say blandly. "Horsewomen like me keep needles within easy reach at all times." And I scoop a few disposable needles out of my grooming box just to prove it. They're still locked in their sterile caps, but it gets the point across—too well.

Cary literally takes a few steps backwards.

"You're *that* freaked out?" I snort. "I'm not going to stab you, big baby."

"I'm going to find out what you're afraid of," Cary promises, still keeping his distance, "and I'm going to scare you with it."

I drop the needles and pick up a hoof pick. "The only thing I'm afraid of is mediocrity."

Cary grins. "Well, honey, you're looking at it. Scared yet?"

I shake my head. "I see a guy who hasn't had to work a real job in his life, and I think, how nice for him."

"Being a child star isn't exactly working in the salt mines," Cary says thoughtfully, "but in a lot of ways it's probably comparable."

"Oh, please. Try working your way up in the horse business."

"Maybe we can compare notes. I'll bet we both have mental trauma we aren't dealing with." He grins.

"If I have PTSD from my childhood riding horses," I say, whisking a soft brush along Nando's back, "I am going to bury it under a mountain of blue ribbons and big checks."

"Over-achieving to counteract the scars of adolescence. I like it. I wish I'd done the same." He gets back to work on Nando's tail, teasing out a tangle with gentle fingers.

"You have a movie coming up, so things can't be all bad." I lean against Nando's right fore-leg and he picks it up, letting me scoop his hoof into my hand. "Hey, get over here and learn about hooves. You should be able to clean out your horse's hooves all by yourself."

"I did it once before," he says, but he drops Nando's tail and comes to my side. I gesture for him to stand at my right and he bends over next to me while I point out the basics of equine hoof anatomy. The frog, the sole, the heel. *Tap tap tap* with the hoof pick. Cary is close to me, watching avidly.

"And this is the white line," I say, gently rubbing the brush on the back of the hoof pick, showing him the line marking the division between hoof wall and hoof sole. "Don't stick anything too sharp here. When the ground is wet, the white line can get soft and crumbly, and then bacteria can find its way in between the wall and the bits inside. We don't want that."

"Seems bad," Cary agrees. He cranes his neck past my shoulder to get a closer look, and I'm hit with a scent of his shampoo—something lavish, eucalyptus paired with a fragrant flower too expensive for a lowly horse trainer like me to identify by nose alone. I have to resist the urge to breathe it in with a long, luxurious sniff. "Don't horses wear shoes?" he asks.

"Some horses. Not this one. He has nice feet and doesn't work hard enough to bother with them."

"Oh, lucky horse. In all my days of not working hard, I have still always had to wear shoes."

I glance down at his boots. They are refreshingly low key. Some of the things people wear in the name of western attire make my traditional English eyeballs ache. I probably have Mrs. C to thank for Cary not showing up in a fringed vest and snakeskin, high-heeled boots. She's pretty sensible.

"What have you been doing for the past decade, anyway?" I ask casually, setting Nando's hoof down. The horse sighs and adjusts his position.

"Not a whole lot," Cary confesses, straightening slowly. He puts his hands on the small of his back and stretches. "Sorry, I know I'm not old enough to be this stiff, but the plane ride out here was long and I'm still sore from sitting so long. I mostly work out," he adds, "to answer your question."

"That's not true. What do you *really* do?"

Cary flashes that million-dollar grin, and I feel my heart gallop a few beats before settling down again. "Secret," he says naughtily.

I study him for a moment. He's definitely used to seeking attention, being cute to keep everyone in the room happy. He's a people-pleaser.

Well, I like him anyway.

I hand him the hoof pick. "Okay, mystery man. Let's see you pick up one of Nando's hooves."

"With sheer brute strength?" He stands next to Nando, facing the horse's shoulder, and examines the horse's long foreleg. "Oh, did I let you see me flex, Mr. Horse? That's my bad."

"No, muscle man, don't be ridiculous. We don't do anything with horses using sheer brute strength."

"Thank goodness," Cary says. "Because I lied. I don't work out most of the time."

"Big surprise. Stand here—" I step behind Cary and position him properly with my hands on his shoulders, so that he's facing towards the horse's tail instead of the shoulder. "There you go. Now, pat your horse."

Cary obligingly pats Nando's shoulder.

Nando turns and glances at Cary, then looks back at me. He gives me a friendly nudge with his long head. Nando's version of *friendly* is like being patted on the back by a giant, so before I can stop myself, I'm toppling forward against Cary. My chest smacks into his back and I find myself leaning against him for a moment before I recover myself.

Just a split-second, really, but that can feel like a long time to have your chest pressed against a handsome man you've only just met.

He grins over his shoulder at me. "Wow! Is this part of picking hooves?"

"Nando's an overly friendly horse," I grit out through clenched teeth, wishing Cary didn't get both a visual *and* a tactile on my boobs before lunch. Might as well have him grip my thighs while we're at it. I turn things into a joke before it can get any weirder. "You know, most of my clients don't get this personal with me. I guess you're lucky."

"I guess I am," Cary says, and damn if he doesn't sound like he's joking at all.

"Hoof," I say, before he can act all intimate and caring with me. I don't have time for any funny business. "Bend over, squeeze his lower leg, and say, 'hoof, please.'"

"What if I forget to say 'please'?"

"Then he'll kick you."

Chapter Seven

"SERIOUSLY?" CARY LOOKS back at Nando with new respect in his eyes. "Man, this horse knows how he wants to be treated. He's like a modern woman."

"Always tell my Nando 'please' when you want anything," I laugh. "He has a tough life teaching beginners like you and he deserves all the respect. You should probably also get in the habit of bringing him bags of carrots. He says he prefers the twenty-pound box from the guy with the produce stand down by the airport."

"Duly noted, Nando," Cary says, bending over. He addresses Nando's hoof with courtly charm. "Now, kind sir, will you please lift your beautiful and mighty hoof for me?"

Nothing happens.

"Not even a muscle twitch?" Cary asks despondently. "Do I have to take him to dinner first?"

"You have to squeeze his lower leg, too," I remind him. "Try again."

Cary adds leg-squeezing to his flowery speech, and Nando obliges with a put-upon sigh.

"Good boy," I tell my horse.

"Good boy," Cary echoes. "Oh god, what am I looking at? This is nothing like the last one. Does he have two different types of feet?"

"It's just sand," I say, leaning over to look at the packed hoof. "Go gently with the pick. I promise there's a foot under all that."

It takes some time, but we get Nando's hooves cleaned to a shine. Next, I go over brushing, and then there's a twenty-minute struggle to get the saddle on and cinched properly. It doesn't help that everything I know about cinching a western saddle comes from the videos I watched last night, on my back in bed with my phone held over my face, and this is the first time I've attempted the job. I'm left feeling utterly confused by the process—why are we tying a saddle on instead of just using buckles?

"I think I should have bought a different kind of cinch," I say, plucking at the knot we've finally gotten into place. "I was trying to be authentic, because of the cowboy thing, but of course you'll have someone else tacking up your horse for you, anyway."

Cary is pleased with himself despite how long the whole business took us. "Never thought of myself as a sailor, but now I think I might tie knots well enough to try it."

"I think you have to go a *little* faster to keep a boat from flipping over on you." I hold up a bridle; this should take another twenty minutes, I guess. Bridles are mysterious to beginners.

"Is that what you think knots do in sailing?" Cary asks with great interest. "Keep boats from flipping over on you?"

"How should I know? I've never been on a boat. Here, let's talk about the parts of the bridle." I hold up Nando's bridle, dangling it from one finger.

"Hmm." Cary takes the bridle from me with a studious air. It's a padded eventing bridle with a crystal-bedazzled brow-band. Very clearly not western in nature. He flicks a finger across the shiny crystals. "Doesn't look like something a cowboy would use."

"It's Nando's bridle. I can't change it out just because we changed the saddle. A horse's bridle is a special thing. It's tailored to their likes and dislikes, the shape of their head—"

"Their preference for sparkly things?"

"Don't make fun of his sparkly brow-band," I warn, "or—"

"He'll kick me? I'm starting to think you're just using that as an empty threat, madam riding coach of the year."

"No," I say, holding back a laugh, "or he'll *bite* you."

Cary eyes Nando's mouth. The horse is snoozing and his lower lip is hanging a good half-inch below the upper lip, exposing a row of yellow teeth. "Fair enough," Cary says. "Nando, I love your sparkles."

Bridling is another task that involves a lot of close-up bodies and guiding of hands when it's being taught. Nothing about bridling a horse appears intuitive to beginners; at least, not with an English bridle, which has a few more straps and buckles than a western one. Throughout the process, I'm treated to a few more whiffs of Cary's expensive shampoo, and his back gets a little more boob action, too.

I decide that this contact is just part of teaching beginner adults and I shouldn't be embarrassed about it, while simultaneously feeling pretty grateful all of my child students are so short that there isn't any question of them pressing up against my chest while I'm helping them understand how to slip a head-stall over a horse's ears.

And then, at last, Nando is fully tacked up, Cary is wearing one of my schooling helmets, and the time has come to get him into the saddle. I glance at my watch; nearly an hour gone already. Maybe Mrs. C isn't paying me too much, after all.

"The mounting block is next to the arena," I say, gesturing to the end of the barn aisle. "So if you just take the reins in your right hand, we'll head out there—"

"The what is next to the arena?" Cary asks, like he heard me wrong.

"The mounting block," I enunciate. "Where we step up and mount from?"

"Oh." Cary looks at the stirrup dangling from the saddle. He picks it up and drops it again, watching it fall gently against Nando's gleaming coat. "Uh. Well, I'm pretty sure that as a cowboy, I have to stick my foot in there and swing up. So maybe we should learn that...?"

"Absolutely not," I say, shaking my head. "That's an advanced move. And even then, I *never* mount from the ground unless I absolutely have to. Only show-offs do that."

"But...shouldn't I start that way so I don't learn to lean on the mounting block? I mean, I'm not trying to show off, but as a cowboy, I think they'll laugh at me if I mount using a log or something during a take."

I snort at the image. "That would be hilarious. And I'd let you start out from the ground...if I wanted to ruin my horse's back. But he doesn't deserve all your beginner weight hanging off his spine like that, so forget it. You'll probably learn mounting from the ground *last,* once you're totally balanced."

If he ever learns to be balanced. I hope this guy has a natural affinity for riding. Otherwise, Mrs. C would have been better off casting one of the stunt doubles for the leading man role. Imagine if he's as untalented as her graceless daughter!

No, I can't even let that possibility arise in my mind. Begone, bad vibes. This arrangement has to work. My financial future depends on it, as does my competitive future with one dark bay horse just down the road, who is going to be delivered in a few days.

As soon as that first deposit from Mrs. C is accepted by my bank and is ready to hand over to the owner, that is.

Cary accepts my curt retort with more grace than I probably deserve, and allows me to show him how to lead Nando by the reins and position him alongside the mounting block. Nando could do this part of the lesson in his sleep, and indeed, the horse closes his eyes against the glaring afternoon sunlight as I stand at his head, pretending to hold him still for Cary.

Our future cowboy stands on the top step and looks down at the waiting saddle with a rueful expression. "Haven't done this in a long time," he says. "Not since I was sixteen, actually. And I was really doing it because of the big kissing scene with the teenage mermaid."

"The time for cold feet was before you accepted this role, movie star," I tell him, going fully merciless because he strikes me as the sort who needs tough love at pivotal moments. And also because that is my nature. "Now, hands on the saddle, resting on either side of the seat, then stick your left boot in the stirrup and push off with your right one."

"And then what?" He positions his hands at the horn and cantle, as commanded.

"Swing around and sit down," I say. "*Gently.*"

"Okay." Cary takes a breath, looks at the saddle, then back at me. "There's something you should know in case I die up here."

"Last words? I like it. Go on." I lean my head against Nando's cheek. "I'll put it on your tombstone, cowboy."

He smiles winningly. "Well...okay. Here goes. I, uh—I think you're pretty cute."

HE THINKS I'M cute? I stare at Cary, numbed by his unexpected statement, and then he gives me the most delighted grin I've ever seen on any face, ever, before leaping nimbly into the saddle. Nando flicks back his ears, like he's surprised by the deftness of Cary's moves, too.

Son of a—

"Well, here I am!" Cary announces triumphantly, gazing down at me from Nando's back. "Now what?"

I am tempted to tell him to pick up the reins and go for a gallop. The smart-ass. Why did he think it would be fun to throw me off my game like that? Not that I especially want or need my students to think I'm cute, but I'm only human. Not *completely* made of stone when it comes to getting a compliment from a good-looking fellow human.

A really, really ridiculously good-looking fellow human, at that.

But whatever. Hollywood here is just showing up to learn to ride, and in six weeks he's going to be John-freaking-Wayne in the saddle. That's a promise to me, Mrs. C, and him.

Oh, and Nando, who will be doing the heavy lifting here.

"Feet in stirrups," I say sternly, snapping myself right back into trainer mode. "You can lean down, just bend at the waist—*easy*—!"

I put up a steadying hand as Cary overdoes the bend to reach his stirrup and starts to slip to the left. I grab his arm and heave him back into place, right in the middle of the saddle. "Stay *there*," I tell him.

Cary just laughs, shaking his head.

Nando steps sideways, sighing like this is *exactly* the nonsense he expected.

Eventually, Cary gets his boots into the fat leather-wrapped stirrups, and I help him position his fingers on the reins. "Pinkie underneath," I instruct, pulling the little finger of his left hand from atop the leather and sliding it beneath. Touching his skin gives me a little shiver of—something—but I ignore it. Professional mode only.

"Why is my pinkie underneath?"

"Pinkies are worthless. They're too short to be sensitive. Your ring finger will do the talking—so you grip the rein with it, instead."

"Poor pinky finger," Cary says. "I still love you, tiny fingers."

"They do hold the rein against the ring finger," I say, relenting slightly in my stance against pinkies. "I admit you would miss them if they were gone."

"I remember some of this from the *Molly* set," Cary says, looking thoughtfully at his hands. "I seem to remember one of the rules being, 'Pull back on my horse's mouth and I will kill you,' does that sound familiar to you?"

"That's literally the very next rule," I laugh. "You can pull back about as hard as you'd like someone to pull on a piece of twine in your mouth."

Cary looks suitably horrified.

"Exactly. Okay, I think we're ready to walk."

I'm not sure how much of the horse's motion is translated to the rider in a western saddle. I should probably give this saddle a try when I have time. But for now, I figure it can't hurt to teach Cary the same way I do my English students. Balance and feel come first.

"We're going to start out by feeling the horse's motion," I say, putting a hand on Nando's left rein. "So I'm going to walk Nando, and you're going to let his side-to-side motion move your hips. Don't brace against him."

Cary nods and puts his hand on the horn.

"Nope, take your hand off that. Nothing to steady you. Just think hips. Your core will hold you up."

He nods, tension slowly replacing the constant mirth of his boyish face.

"And breathe," I remind him. "Pretend you're doing yoga. And... drinking green smoothies."

"What?"

"Hollywood stuff," I explain. "That's what you guys all do, right?"

Cary just shakes his head.

"Okay, Nando, buddy, let's walk on."

Cary lurches as Nando steps off with his long-striding walk. "Eek," he exclaims, already breathless. "He really does move side to side!"

"It's his hips moving yours," I say, playing slightly loose with equine anatomy. "Go with it. Sink left, into your left stirrup, then right, into your right stirrup, then back again. You can over-do it while you get used to the movement. Okay?"

"Okay," Cary says tightly.

He's actually kind of scared.

I smile to myself and give Nando a pat on the neck. There's something empowering about knowing horses so well that their movement is engrained on my deepest muscle memories, while a person who is in every way better connected and better compensated by this world is struggling with what I would find the simplest task of all: to walk horseback without falling off. Cary's devilish confidence has already put me on my back foot several times—that *I think you're cute* gag was a prime example—but now that he's in the tack, his fear puts me firmly back in charge.

And that's where I like to be.

The lesson goes smoothly, as a first lesson should, since there isn't much to it but letting the student get in touch with the horse's motion. After twenty minutes, I decide I've had enough of the hot midday sun glaring down on my sandy area and reflecting into my eyes, so I walk slowly to the gate. Nando follows at a snail's pace, while Cary sways on top like a rajah riding an elephant.

"We're done?" Cary asks, and I hear the relief in his voice. He's not used to Florida's muggy heat; sweat runs in rivulets down that lovely face of his and his cheeks have a pink flush.

"All done. Kick your feet out of the stirrups and hop down."

I like this part. You get the strangest looks from beginners when you give the bare minimum instruction on how to get *off* the horse. Like they've been working so hard for so long to stay on, there is simply no instinct left to get them down.

"It can't be that simple," Cary says, looking at the ground dubiously.

"Are you sure? You seemed awfully confident about mounting."

"I gave you my last words, remember?"

I'm surprised to hear him say that so softly, as if those silly words he'd thrown at me before mounting Nando were more than just a brash boy's showing off before he took on a new task with way too much confidence.

Something in my cool heart warms ever so slightly. "Okay," I say, relenting. "Here's what you're going to do..."

When he's safely on the ground, I let him lead Nando to the barn while I check my phone. To my surprise, there's a text from Jim Brewer, jumper trainer and truck tower of my dreams.

About that dinner—next Friday at Legends?

"Fun!" I exclaim.

Cary glances back at me. "Fun?" he echoes.

"A date," I say, replying quickly to tell Jim that I'd love to go to Legends Equestrian Center on Friday. "A date with a nice horse trainer."

"Ah," Cary says, turning around again. "Well, that's nice."

Chapter Eight

"STOP TAPPING YOUR foot," Cary says. "I'm hosing off this giant animal as fast as I can."

"I'm not tapping my foot." I look down at my boot and observe it bopping up and down on the pavement. How is that happening without my permission? I press down my toe and admit, "Okay, so I am. But not at you."

Instead of tapping my foot more, I opt to look at my phone again. I've been glancing at my phone every thirty seconds for the past ten minutes, even as I showed Cary how to unsaddle and unbridle a horse, a task seemingly as difficult to learn in reverse as in forward motion. We settled Nando in the cross-ties of the wash stall and I gave Cary instructions on how to hose him off. I'm not sure he'll need that information for his movie role, but I figure if he's going to be spending time here, he might as well leave with a thorough understanding of horse-keeping.

Which leaves *me* plenty of time to look at my phone, waiting for Jim to reply to my text.

I thought a simple, *Legends sounds great. What time and where should we meet?* would be the perfect response to his invitation, but apparently it flummoxed my would-be beau, because he left my text on read and has gone to ground, sly fox style.

"Who is ignoring you?" Cary asks, noticing my phone obsession. "I'll punch him in the nose for you."

"You can't punch people," I scoff, meaning that assault is frowned upon.

"No, I actually can," he says, purposely misunderstanding me. "I took boxing lessons for an audition a couple of years ago. I didn't get the role, but I can absolutely hit a guy in the nose now. It hasn't come up as often as I hoped, though."

"You go *looking* for fights?"

"I mean, I would like to feel I got my money's worth from those lessons. They weren't cheap." Cary sprays the water a little too close to Nando's head and the horse steps away from him, fixing him with an evil glare from his closest eye. "Whoa, that's *some* side-eye, buddy," he says to Nando. "I absolutely didn't mean to get your little face wet."

"Looks like Nando's jonesing for a fight," I tease.

"I would never punch a horse," Cary says solemnly. "I'd be too afraid he'd bite me."

He throws me a grin to remind me that I assured him Nando would bite him for any insult.

I grin back before I can help myself. This guy keeps my cheeks exercised, that's for sure. And why is he still looking at me? Look back at Nando. Look at the horse. Stop looking at me, before I start blushing and say something stupid—

Luckily, my phone buzzes before I can get deeper into this flirty little tête-à-tête. I mean, it *is* flirty, right? I'm not imagining this? Maybe it's just the Hollywood way. Mrs. C is terribly charming in her own way, too.

Jim's text is a welcome distraction, even if he doesn't bother apologizing for leaving me hanging all this time. He just writes: *7ish by the pizza cart would be great. Send me your order ahead of time and I might even have it waiting for you.*

Oh, the pizza cart at Legends Equestrian Center! My mouth is watering already. Excellent choice, Jimmy-boy. *Margherita,* I reply. *See you there.*

"Who ya textin'?" Cary asks in a mockingly upbeat tone. "Is it your special friend?"

"None of your business," I retort, pocketing the phone. "Is that horse hosed off yet?"

"Yes, boss, he's soaked to the skin, as requested. What's next?"

"Sweat scraper," I say, and I show him how to squeegee the excess water out of Nando's coat.

Cary is seriously impressed by this step. "Ancient horse-people truly thought of everything," he says solemnly. "We owe them so much."

"Well, you laugh, but horses are delicate," I tell him. "If you do one little thing wrong, they up and die on you. Or they get a gross skin fungus."

"Oh, no! Nando, please don't die. Don't get fungus." Flinging the sweat scraper aside, Cary wraps his arms around Nando's damp neck.

The horse gives me a pleading look. I can't blame him. This lesson has gone on for two hours and Cary shows no sign of running out of steam. Must be nice.

"Alright, buddy, that's enough. Give him a carrot and turn him out in his paddock. He gets a break before his next lesson."

"Outside in this *heat?* It's scorching out there." Cary puts his hands to his mouth in mock horror. Or maybe he's serious.

"He has shade, and water. He'd rather be outside than in, anyway." I'm hanging on to my brusque and serious trainer voice, but it's only by a thread at this point. Cary's dramatics are cracking me up—on the inside, where no one can see.

Once we've got Nando outside, I expect Cary to take off for the afternoon—but instead, he just follows me around like a faithful dog while I sweep up the cross-ties and hose out the wash-stall, so the barn will once again be pristine and perfect, even though I have two lessons this evening who will mess it up all over again.

"You're a very tidy person," he says, watching me at work. "Almost frighteningly so."

"It's the way I was raised," I reply, looping the hose on its hanger so that it forms a perfect oval. "A clean barn is a happy barn." I straighten the scrub brushes and sweat scrapers stacked in the mesh baskets hanging in the wash-stall, and squeeze excess water out of a sponge still wet from scrubbing Plato's dirty white socks before the horse show this morning. Wouldn't want to risk mildew. This is a good sponge.

"I don't know," Cary says dubiously as I clip the loose cross-ties back to the hooks they hang from. "Have you considered medication, instead?"

"What are you saying?" I put my hands on my hips and look up and down my barn aisle. It's spotless, but something about it is still bothering me. I can't quite put my finger on it. "You think I should live in filth?"

"I'm not saying anything." Cary spreads his hands in a supplicating gesture. "You do you, by all means."

Oh, *there* is the problem! I need to straighten up the hay bales stored in the stall next to the feed room. The open bale left over from this morning's feeding is spilling onto the stall floor, right where everyone can see it as they walk through the barn.

I'm halfway through picking up the loose flakes of hay when I notice Cary is still watching me closely. "What?" I snap. "Stop trying to make me feel weird for being tidy!"

"Were you raised in a cult?" Cary asks, tilting his head to one side. "I'm just trying to understand."

"I was raised by my aunt, if you must know," I inform him loftily. "She was a British Horse Society-accredited trainer and held herself to a higher standard. And she held me to those standards, too."

Standards, standards, standards. The word simply means that the work never stopped at Windy Hill. My aunt was never satisfied, and she taught me to feel the same way. Morning, noon, and night, we kept our farm, tack, and horses in pristine condition. Sure, it was hard. Yes, I hated getting up at five o'clock to feed and do a dozen other chores before school. But the early hour was worthwhile because it left the afternoons wide open for joining as many riding lessons as I could while Aunt Kate taught from the center of the ring, her critical voice cracking like a whip as she spotted crooked wrists, bouncing hands, slumped shoulders. After riding and feeding, we finished up late in the evening with a spotless stable, swept and scrubbed clean of the workday's debris.

The house was another story, but we didn't spend much time in the house, anyway. It was hard to mess up a place where you really only slept and ate.

My parents were kind to let me stay with Aunt Kate. They lived an hour away, in Washington, D.C., and there wasn't enough time in the day for them to work, get me to school, *and* satisfy my insatiable urge to ride. I begged to be allowed to move to Windy Hill, and I never let them know for a second how hard I worked there. They wouldn't have approved.

But that's only because they aren't horse-people. They don't know, like I do, how important the hard work is. Perfection *is* the standard, not the goal.

I bend back over to grab another handful of hay, imagining what Aunt Kate would say if she saw me leave an open bale falling over like this, instead of immediately tying it back up with the loose ends of hay-string. "My aunt would be appalled I left this hay loose all day long," I say. "She'd say, 'Alison, maybe you've given up all your standards but I haven't, so get in there and tidy that hay-room up!' "

Cary is looking at me very strangely, like I've said something wrong. "Was your aunt...nice to you?" he asks, and I instantly realize what he's getting at. People have been like this before, insinuating that Aunt Kate had a problem.

Which is uncool of them, because they're then implying that I have a problem, too.

"She was amazing," I reply flatly, aware that I didn't really answer the question. But being nice and being amazing aren't necessarily the same things. She was strict, and driven, and determined to make me the best horsewoman I could be. That's pretty amazing, in my book.

Maybe there wasn't always time for her to be nice, but that's just life, isn't it? You can't fit everything you might want into one day. The work comes first. And on most days, second and third and last, as well.

"I learned everything from her," I say at last. I look around my tidied hay stall, then back at Cary. He's still got a concerned look on his face, as if he sees something that I don't.

Suddenly, I wish he'd just go already. "Don't you have anywhere to be?" I ask, more sharply than is strictly professional.

But our conversation has strayed from professional bounds, anyway.

"I don't actually," Cary says, shrugging. "But trust me, I can take a hint."

Chapter Nine

EVIE THINKS THE whole situation is very funny.

Evie thinks everything is funny these days. Now that she's coming to the end of a long, hot summer working endless hours with Malcolm, the girl is completely slap-happy. So when she stops by late in the evening to drop off some paperwork from Hansie's seller, she has a loopy grin on her face which says she's been enjoying her car's air conditioning just a little too much.

I invite her up to the apartment for a cold drink before she succumbs to the sticky heat in my barn aisle. There's a thunderstorm off to the east, rumbling enthusiastically and sparking like a faulty electrical outlet, but the sunset light filtering through the western-facing stall windows is still hot enough to strip paint off a wall. In late summer, six o'clock can be the hottest hour of the day.

My students have all tottered off for the evening, drenched in sweat and looking dazed, which I think means I did a good job. But I'm also glad I wasn't the one riding.

"Drink this Coke and tell me about the doings at Fine Day Farm," I command, sitting Evie on my loveseat with a cold soda can in her hands. "I miss working at a real farm, with big-time horses, and a nice, even aisle that's easy to sweep."

"I'm sure Malcolm would take you back," Evie says. "I know I would."

"No, I'm going to make this place work." I throw myself down on my bed. We're both too sweaty to sit close together on that tiny sofa. "Hansie's going to help me. I need a flashy horse like him to get some attention."

"I hope he does it for you," Evie says sincerely. "But I do mean it when I say we'd love to have you back. This summer was a crash-course in how much work a person can do in tropical weather and somehow not drop dead. It really made me miss galloping racehorses. I was always done work before eleven a.m." Evie's voice turns wistful at the end. "I napped in the afternoon. Life was so good."

"Nuh-uh!" I tell her, sitting up again and wagging a finger at her. "None of that! You were bored and going nowhere. Now you've got a good horse in Bucky and an excellent shot at going places with Malcolm."

"And he's a good boyfriend," Evie admits, taking a sip of Coke. "When he's not making me crazy in the barn."

"You're welcome," I snort, because I taught her everything she needs to know about managing Malcolm. And it really is a full-time job, especially the part where he isn't supposed to know he's being managed. "So, how is my Hansie? Excited to move here tomorrow?" Mrs. C's money hit the account before five, despite it being a weekend, and I immediately forwarded it on to Hansie's seller as the first payment. He's officially almost-mine now, and Malcolm promised to bring him over on Sunday after training was wrapped up for the day.

"Shoot," Evie laughs. "We forgot to tell Hansie!"

"It'll be a fun surprise for him. I bedded my nicest stall for him, too."

"Well, he'll be so happy about that," Evie agrees amiably, well aware that all my stalls are exactly the same. "And I will be happy to have one fewer horses in the barn. For a few weeks, anyway."

"That October rush creeping up on you?"

Evie nods and rubs her forehead wearily. I know she's looking at a tough season ahead. The only difference between us right now is that Evie is dreading a barn full of seasonal boarders, and I'm longing for some.

"You know you can send any overflow my way, right?" I remind her.

"Of course! It's just..."

"What?"

Evie shrugs. "Well, your place...it's just a little...um..."

"Spit it out," I command, flopping backwards again and staring at the ceiling. I know exactly what Evie is trying to say.

"I know it's just you working here," Evie begins.

"But it's a dump," I finish for her.

"No, it's *not* a dump. Don't say that. But it could use some touch-ups if you want to impress the type of clients you're looking for," Evie says diplomatically.

She's so good at that. Perfect for her job, which involves smoothing ruffled feathers when Malcolm's frank words upset students and horse owners.

And Evie's right, too. If I don't spruce this place up, I can't count on getting boarders in who can actually pay me enough to justify the time and cost of keeping their horses. The best I could offer is "dry stall" rental, and I definitely don't want horse owners dropping in at all hours, stalls getting cleaned whenever they feel like it, horses getting fed at all different hours...absolutely not. I don't need that kind of mayhem in my life, and neither do my horses.

"What would you suggest?" I ask, still staring at my ceiling. There's a wiggle of a crack in the plaster. That can't be good.

Evie sips her soda thoughtfully, then says, "You could probably throw together some cheap flower-beds at the ends of the barn aisle. You'd be surprised by the way flowers spruce up a place. Put some by the arena gate, too."

The idea of digging up the hard-packed sand in front of the barn entrance and dragging around bags of potting soil makes me sigh. But I put on the best front I can, replying, "Okay. I can probably do that. What about inside the barn? What would you change? Or is it good enough?"

"You need to slap some stain on those stall fronts," Evie says promptly, like she had that answer locked and loaded. "It makes a barn look totally luxurious. I couldn't believe how shiny everything was when I walked into Malcolm's barn for the first time."

"Ugh, you're right. That's probably what bothers me most about this place, but I thought maybe I was getting away with it." The raw, unfinished look of plain wood is fine for the average horse barn, but not one catering to wealthy competitors in a crowded, upscale market like Ocala. "I guess in an ideal world I'd have rubber pavers instead of that black-top, too, but this place is just a rental, so that's not happening."

Also, it would cost thousands of dollars I don't have, so even if I somehow bought this place, pavers aren't coming anytime soon. They're a lottery-winner type item.

"Try those two things," Evie urges. "Flowers and stain. And then update your website with new pictures. I'll forward it to everyone on our waiting list."

"You already have a waiting list?" I demand, sitting upright again. It"s very early for that.

Evie nods meekly. "So the sooner you get this stuff done, the better, okay? I'm sure I can get you some boarders. It's winter in Ocala. Everyone wants to be here."

EVIE'S REVELATION OF an early wait-list for stalls at Fine Day Farm lights a little fire in my belly to get this place dressed up nice and pretty, but mere inspiration doesn't equal the time or money to get a job done. And before I can even get started, things actually get a worse. A thunderstorm finally breaks over the farm well after nightfall, sending a torrent of water and sand flooding down the barn aisle overnight. When I head downstairs to face Sunday morning head-on, I find half a day's worth of mud-scraping and shoveling waiting for me.

Because the horses' schedules come first, though, I have to grin and bear the mud caking my boots while I groom and saddle Sebastian, then Plato, and then the horses on training board. The work we're doing can't be compromised, certainly not this close to the season.

By the time I've ridden all six horses, the clock above the tack room door tells me it's well after one o'clock, and the sky outside is clouding over, thunder shuddering through the humid air again.

Florida tends to be fire or flood. This week, apparently, will be flood.

"What happened to just one rain storm at three o'clock every day?" I ask my last horse, Gidget, and the lanky mare tosses her head in reply. *Who knows, silly human?*

With Gidget turned out and my stomach rumbling, I tramp upstairs with Lily Marlene at my heels. The plan is to make myself a sandwich and cool off for a brief but necessary half-hour before it's time for Cary's riding lesson. Even though I really want to clean up the aisle.

I'm embarrassed to think of someone like him—or really, any client—seeing the filthy barn aisle. The debris from the flooding looks ten times worse now after having horses traipsing back and forth through it.

But a person has to have some priorities, and those horses aren't going to prep for the show season on their own while I'm scraping the aisle clean.

So, even though I wince every time I think of the mess downstairs, I fill in the training spreadsheet on my laptop as I moodily munch my way through a ham-and-cheese on whole wheat. Training first. Everything else has to come after, no matter how much it hurts.

The schedules for each horse are worked backward from their planned competition calendar. Sebastian and Plato had a good day out in the jumper ring yesterday, and they did a judged dressage test back in early August, so with one more cross-country school over at Malcolm's, we'll still be on track for a three-phase horse trials at Sunshine State Horse Park in October.

Hopefully by then, we'll have somewhat nicer weather, not too scalding, and not too hurricane-y—although in Florida, you never do know for sure. I've definitely done my cross-country round in fifty-mile-per-hour wind gusts before, and I'm sure it will happen again.

Sandwich finished, training sheet filled in, fifteen minutes to go before Cary should get here. Suddenly, I'm filled with conflicting ways about how best to fill the next quarter of an hour.

Do I go downstairs and work on the aisle?

Or do I stay upstairs in the air conditioning, get changed into dry and clean clothes, and appear the perfect professional when my student arrives?

I mean, will it really hurt our business relationship if he sees me drenched in sweat and heaving sand into a wheelbarrow?

What would Aunt Kate say? In times of confusion, I can always count on my aunt's strict rules to help me find the right answer.

"Yes, it would hurt, because that's not the way you present yourself," I murmur, imitating her clipped speech. "You're a *professional trainer*. He doesn't need to know you do all the dirty work yourself."

With that decided, I walk over to the mirror hanging on the bathroom door to assess what can stay and what needs to go. I wipe a smudge from the morning rides off my breeches, then pull off my dirty long-sleeved sun-shirt, and take out a clean one.

This is one of my favorites: emerald green with darker green color blocks up the side, a color combination that works with my pale blonde hair and blue-green eyes. I've been buying up high-end riding clothes in dark greens for a while now, whenever I find a clearance sale, so that I have a good collection for wearing in public and in front of clients. Wearing your own farm colors is just good branding.

After I left Fine Day Farm, I had a boxful of sage and moss-green riding tops and breeches, because we were religious about wearing our farm colors at shows and in front of clients. I decided to represent Highbury Sport Horses with a darker shade of green because I could sneak the older shirts and breeches into the mix and not waste all those expensive clothes.

Waste not, want not.

"And now you're clean, and you wait for your client," I say primly to my reflection, having swept my hair up into a bun and tucked the flyaways behind my ears. I snatch a pair of sunglasses and a straw hat from the little shelf next to the door before opening it, looking out at my barn. Aunt Kate would be proud of my presentation, I think, but this barn...

The dirty aisle looks back at me. It's like staring into the abyss.

Maybe if I just shovel a *little* bit of the sand up, I won't get too sweaty and dirty—

"Control yourself," I murmur.

It's hard work putting aside my need to present a clean, perfect barn at all times. That might be one of the toughest things about this whole exercise in running my own barn, aside from getting used to being alone, all the time, instead of working alongside other people, friends whose company I enjoy.

I miss Malcolm, and Evie, and the nice retired couple who muck the stalls, and even their working student Sydney, as annoying and hard to train as she was in the beginning.

But a dream's a dream, and I couldn't have stayed with Malcolm forever. It was time for me to strike out on my own. I still believe that, even if things are tougher than I expected.

"I will clean up the mud *after* Cary leaves, and *after* Hansie arrives," I announce, and remembering Hansie is coming late this afternoon gives me a delicious shiver of anticipation. I wonder if he'll still watch me with that brown-eyed devotion I'd felt at Malcolm's farm, or if that was just a weird moment in time.

I hope it's not the latter. I've spent a future fortune on this horse, based on a gut feeling that had better not turn out to be a lie.

Chapter Ten

"HELLOOOO," CARY SINGS out, walking into the barn with his arms spread wide.

Someone's in a good mood. I shake my head, but then again, there's something about Cary that cheers me up, even when he's being way over the top.

It's like I'm charmed by his child-star charisma. So weird. Ordinarily, I'd be annoyed at someone this exuberant for no reason. After all, riding is a serious business, and I like my students to approach it that way.

"Hellooooo," he yodels again. "Is anyone out there?"

"Up here," I call, waving back.

"Ah!" Cary looks up and spots me. A smile splits his face from ear to ear. Then he puts a hand to his heart, affecting a romantic pose. He puts on a theatrical accent as he pronounces, "Hark yon lady on the highest perch, with thy complexion of the rosiest sheen!"

He's absolutely crazy. But I can't help smiling. "Is that from Shakespeare?" I ask.

I've never had time to read Shakespeare, but I watched *Shakespeare in Love* quite a lot in my early twenties. Who wouldn't?

"No, I made it up. Because your cheeks are pink." Cary laughs.

"Oh—" I touch my warm cheeks. Now I can feel the blush, and it's deepening by the second. "Must be from the heat," I say, surprised at myself.

Yes, the heat, though I've been inside for the past half-hour with my air conditioning roaring like an arctic blizzard.

"It's very hot," Cary agrees. He puts his hands on his hips and looks up at me.

We stare at each other for a moment. I get the feeling he's holding back laughter.

What is so funny? Surely not *me*. I'm very serious and important.

Cary looks like he thinks otherwise.

I give in first and start down the stairs. "Right, so let's get your horse and get you tacked up. Remember anything from yesterday?"

"Not much," Cary says, smiling sheepishly. "And I have some sore places," he adds in a confiding tone.

"Where at?" I merely ask to be polite; I know exactly where. Cary is feeling like he did the splits all day yesterday. That's totally normal. I even get sore between my hips if I have to take a few days off riding for a bad cold or something.

"I don't want to be untoward," Cary murmurs in a hushed voice, looking from side to side as if to be sure no one can overhear our conversation, "but it's in my—*unmentionable*—region."

I snort. "The part that was split in two over the back of a horse for almost an hour yesterday?"

"Yes, that's the general area," he agrees, his voice going so abruptly back to normal that I burst out laughing.

Cary affects a hurt expression, fixing me with puppy-dog eyes. "You're laughing at my sore nether-regions?" he demands. "How could you?"

"No, I'm laughing at *you*."

"I believe that's the same thing, hurtful woman." His dark eyes are wells of tragedy.

I can't take it.

"I'm laughing at your performance, not your sore parts—oh, forget it." I wave him away, still laughing. "Let's see if you remember how to use a halter."

Once he focuses, Cary does make a credible attempt to get the halter over Nando's long nose. Hell, if he'd had it right-side up, he might have succeeded. Nando takes a step backward and shakes his head.

Cary looks at me beseechingly.

I help him straighten the leather out, our fingers brushing companionably. His skin is so smooth I can't stop myself from commenting on it.

"You must use Hoof-maker every day on these beauties," I say.

He raises his eyebrows at me. "*Hoof*-maker?"

"It's a hoof cream that some people use on their hands and nails. They sell it at Walgreens."

Cary grins. "Will it make my hooves shiny and strong?"

"That's what they say. Going to try it?"

"Why not? You have any?"

"I don't, sadly. I have Keratex, but that's mostly acetone, I think—"

"That's not the same at all." Cary sniffs.

"It's a hoof *hardener*," I say. "Maybe that's really what you need for your baby-fingers, because we're going to be looking at some serious blisters from the reins."

"Ugh." Cary pauses to snap the cross-ties onto Nando's halter. "Can't I ride in gloves?"

"I ride in gloves...but I'm not sure cowboys do. We can check some movies to see."

"Why can't I be civilized and ride like you? I don't want blisters!" Cary cries out. He has a completely neutral face, but his voice sounds like he's a teenage girl being dragged away to boarding school. It's uncanny.

I hand him a curry-comb. "You're really dramatic. Anyone ever tell you that?"

"Yeah," Cary drawls. "My acting coach."

I suppose I walked into that one. But seriously, Cary turns everything into a life or death situation. Funny or die, that kind of thing. It should be exhausting. Dramatic people are not my cup of tea.

But instead, he just makes me want to laugh.

Like, sit down in my muddy barn aisle, lean back against the wall, and laugh until I cry.

"Okay, drama-llama," I say, seeing no other way to get hold of the situation but to be as stern as possible. "Let's focus up. Groom that horse until he sparkles."

Cary's in the saddle and halfway through his riding lesson when I hear the squeaking of brakes on the main road, and the growl of an engine that could only be a truck hauling a trailer. My heart skips a beat.

"My horse is here!" I exclaim.

Cary looks up from the reins in his hands—we haven't worked on *eyes up* yet. "Alison, you have horses all over the place," he says.

"No, my *new* one. Ride Nando over to the gate and hop off a minute. Unless you think you're okay on your own while I unload Hansie." I'm already heading for the arena gate.

"What kind of name is Hansie? You give horses the strangest names," Cary complains, riding Nando alongside me. "What is poor Nando named for? The chicken restaurant?"

"It's short for Fernando Z," I say. "His registered name. What chicken restaurant?"

"It's in the U.K. They have spicy chicken. At first, I just thought it meant Nando was one spicy chicken." He pats the horse. "But so far, no spice."

"You might get some spice if Hansie is a bad boy when he unloads."

The trailer pulls up in front of the barn and arena, and Evie waves from the driver's seat. I guess Malcolm is still busy riding.

I glance up at Cary and say, "Hop off a minute. It's good practice to mount and dismount a few times, anyway."

"You're making that up," Cary grumbles, but he carefully kicks his feet free and slides out of the saddle the way I showed him yesterday.

"That was a really nice job!" I'm momentarily distracted from Hansie's imminent appearance by Cary's smooth dismount. He brushed against the saddle on the way down, and now his shirt is clinging to his sweaty abdomen and chest.

Someone works out, I think. *A lot.*

Maybe he wasn't just teasing when he said his job was working out.

Cary runs a hand over his chest and grins at me. "My eyes are up here," he says.

I shake my head at him. Such a dork. Such a dramatic, funny, cute dork.

Yeah, I can admit he's cute. Especially with those ripped muscles beneath his t-shirt. Oh, Hollywood. Your unrealistic standards of beauty are doing the Lord's work with this man.

The sound of whinnying from inside the trailer gets my attention back on the matter at hand—my new horse! I have the giddiness of a little kid as I leave Nando's reins securely in Cary's soft hands and run across the parking area, bypassing a few cloudy puddles on the way.

Evie hops out of the truck and comes around to meet me, her eyes bright.

"You look *so* excited," she says, grabbing my hands. "I'm so happy this is working out for you guys!"

"Hansie and I are going to be very happy," I assure her. "Thanks to that guy behind us."

Evie's gaze flicks over my shoulder. "Oh, my," she says, eyes going round. "That's our movie star?"

"In the flesh."

"He looks..."

"Hot?"

"Yeah," Evie agrees. "Hot is an understatement. He's got that Hollywood sparkle. Speaking of which...any sparks flying yet?"

I snort. "Not hardly. Also, I have a date on Friday night at Legends."

"Oooh—the horse guy date is happening!"

"Yes!" I'm about to fill her in when Hansie whinnies again. All the horses on the property reply, Nando included. I'll bet *that* echoed in Cary's brain. "Let's get my baby off this truck. Boys can wait."

There's definitely no time to talk about boys when ponies are waiting.

Hansie strolls down the side-ramp of the Fine Day Farm trailer with his head high and his ears swiveling. He's sweaty from the short ride, and fat veins are standing up on his neck and beneath his barrel, making it look like he's just run a hard cross-country course.

"Let's get you a shower, buddy," I tell him, and after giving him a slow circle around the parking area so he can see the paddocks and lay of the land, I walk him into the barn. Evie follows, taking pictures of us along the way.

"This is a historic day," she says as I walk Hansie into the wash-stall. "I think we're going to be looking back at this day and saying, 'Wow, remember when he first came to your barn?' in just a few years."

"That would be nice." Hansie swings his hindquarters back and forth in the wash-stall, too keyed up to be tied, so Evie takes his lead-shank while I hose him off. "I'm thinking we event at Novice level in October with the other guys, and just go right through the winter until he's ready to step up to Training before the end of the season. Assuming everything goes okay."

"Oh, of course," Evie agrees.

We're both so cool, like everything going okay isn't the least likely scenario. We both know a million things can go wrong between now and the end of the Florida winter season in six months' time. Hell, a million things can go wrong between now and the end of this bath. Horses are like time-bombs just waiting to go off. You're cantering along and *boom*, squirrel runs by, catches the horse's eye, you get a spook and a soft-tissue injury that sidelines him for a year. You're hosing your horse off and *boom*, the horse sidesteps to get away from the hose, steps on his own horseshoe and tears up his hoof wall, requiring months off and expensive hoof repair.

You know what? I don't want to make this list anymore. It's too scary.

"Look at that throat-latch," I coo as Hansie arches his neck to look down the aisle. "So curvy! It's killing me! What's he looking at, anyway?"

Evie looks down the aisle too. She laughs in a breathless kind of way. "Your riding lesson."

"Oh my god!" I drop the hose. "I completely forgot about him!"

What kind of riding instructor am I, anyway? Leaving a beginner rider out in the sun while I just casually give my new horse a bath? Unreal. I pick up the hose and hand it to Evie, then haul down the barn aisle to meet Cary and Nando.

He's grinning—Cary, not Nando—and walking the horse along at a careful pace, watching his feet in relation to Nando's hooves to make sure he doesn't get stepped on. "Look, Ma, I walked the horse in!" he calls.

"I'm so sorry," I gasp. "I can't believe—"

"It's fine. Nando wanted to see the new horse, too. He must be pretty special if he drove us right out of your head. That's what Nando thinks, anyway." Cary pats Nando on the neck in a familiar sort of way.

It's nice to see them bonding. "I shouldn't have left you, though," I say. "That was bad. Forgive me and expect more of me."

Cary shakes his head, that charming smile of his in full force. "You're hard on yourself, Alison, you know that?"

I shrug. He already knows I have high standards. That's not going to change. I don't even want it to. "Can you hang out a minute while I get Hansie settled in a stall? And I promise to introduce you after we finish our lesson."

"Nando and I will wait right here," Cary says, patting him again. "We're buds now."

Evie gives me a thumbs-up when I return to the wash-stall. "He really likes you," she confides, voice low.

"Hansie?"

"No, silly...Cary."

I shake my head, amused. Evie just wants to see everyone fall in love, since she's so happy with Malcolm. And I can't blame her for that, but...Cary? Hardly what I'm looking for in a boyfriend. "He's just nice."

"He's watching you."

And I realize I don't have to ask if she means Hansie this time. I can feel Cary's gaze on my back.

Like a physical touch.

I straighten my shoulders as a little shower of sparks seems to cascade down my spine.

Evie gives me a knowing grin. "What were you saying about a date on Friday night?"

"That's still happening," I say, "because Jim is an actual local person who asked me out, not a student who will only be here for a few weeks."

"But you're thinking about it," she says. "You're thinking about *Hollywood.*"

"Nope," I reply. "I mean it, too. Not thinking about him. He's an overgrown kid!"

"If you say so," Evie smirks.

"I do say so."

Chapter Eleven

CARY MAKES PLANS to come back in the morning for another lesson.

But I don't usually ride or teach on Mondays, so I try to get him to take a day off. It's my one day off a week, and I would like to have a single morning where I can feed, turn the horses back out, and go back to bed without thinking about someone coming over that I will have to clean the place up for for, babysit while they're here, and then clean up after.

"Two days in a row is enough for just getting started, hotshot," is how I put it, giving him a sidelong look as I pick up the horse to start power-washing the aisle once he's put Nando away.

It's not the most professional way to suggest a pause in lessons. But somehow I find it really hard to be professional with Cary. He just brings out my looser side. And because it's sarcastic, that side of me is not usually allowed to see the light of day around clients.

But Cary seems to like it when I get snarky with him. He crosses his legs one over the other and leans back in the folding chair next to my office door, where he has settled down to enjoy the air conditioning while I purposely hose right around his feet. Cleaning up after him, like I said. "Well, Ah gotta learn to ride, don't Ah?" he drawls, like he's playing cowboy already and he's got a jaw hanging off its hinge from too many plugs of tobacco wedged into his cheek.

"You're going to be so stiff and sore after the two long riding lessons you've just had, you're not going to want to get out of bed tomorrow," I inform him, picking up the plastic shovel I use for scooping big messes. "Trust me. You want the day off."

I feel his eyes on me as I carefully sweep an ever-dwindling pile of debris into the shovel, and my back stiffens. For some reason, he makes me feel self-conscious when I'm doing the most simple, necessary jobs: like sweeping up or hosing dirt away. Like he thinks I'm an over-the-top clean freak.

Okay, so, he's not *wrong*; I would just rather not be made to feel that way. There's no point in fighting who I am, so why bother bringing it up? Or insinuating it with knowing glances and raised eyebrows, which is what Cary does.

Which is what Cary *is* doing, right now.

"I can push through pain," Cary says, returning his face to neutral as I dump the shovel and hang it up again. "In fact, I want to work with you outside my lesson, too. Work around the barn, get to know horses better. Won't that stretch me out?"

"You've never felt anything quite like this," I say, brushing aside his supposed interest in horse care. He's so full of it. He's probably just looking to avoid Mrs. C or something; I'm sure she's full of extra assignments for her little movie star. "Like I told you before, getting your body used to riding is like you just started doing the splits all day. But you've never actually *practiced* doing a split before. See how that might end up hurting in unmentionable places? It's going to get worse before it gets better. Wait and see."

"Now, we agreed that you put my crotch first," Cary says, nodding as if I've presented some very strong arguments to the committee.

"And I appreciate the consideration. But old Kat isn't going to let me hang around her guest-house doing nothing all day. She'll cook up some job for me. Or make me give acting lessons to that horrible daughter of hers. I'd rather tell the boss I'm here, earning my keep with you."

So I was right! I narrow my eyes at him, pushing back at his argument, which is full of flaws. "You'd rather be out here, on a sweltering-hot horse farm, than back at Kat's—well, I assume *mansion*—in the air conditioning? The kid's in school all day, so don't use that excuse. What kind of work would she make you do?"

He leers and manages to insinuate some very bawdy tasks.

I feel myself blush and look away. "No! That's ridiculous."

"I'm kidding, I'm kidding," Cary laughs. "I don't *think* she's got me doing this movie because she lusts after my body. I could be wrong, though. Do you want me to hang around the house tomorrow and find out? Is that really what you want for me?"

He's so ridiculous. I can't help but grin. "You poor thing. I still find it hard to believe there's nowhere else you'd rather be than here. I'm going to force you to work, you know. You can't just sit in that folding chair all the time. I don't allow loitering."

"I can do work," Cary promises. "You won't even believe how helpful I can be."

I gaze at his smiling face for a moment, weighing the likelihood of his *actually* hanging around the barn all day. The weather has been awful this month, and it promises to be just as bad tomorrow as every other day in the past few weeks, melt-your-skin-off hot with a chance of thunderstorms in the very late afternoon, a chance at a cool-down that comes long after the lion's share of work and riding around the farm has been completed. The last week of August is fading into September with the kind of end-of-summer misery that makes a person rethink living in Florida, until they remember winter exists in other places and that the horses will still need to eat and train in freezing rain and snow.

I remember those days, and I don't want them back.

He'll wuss out and leave by noon, I figure.

"Fine," I say at last. "You can come tomorrow and help around the barn. I don't usually ride on Monday, but I want to get on Hansie first thing, so if you want to be here for that..."

"What time do you feed the horses their brekkies?"

"Seven." I eye him, waiting to see if he'll change his mind, or say he'll be here around ten.

"I'll be here at six-fifty," Cary promises. "And I'll bring coffee, too."

Well, when a guy puts it like that...

"Write down my order," I command, and Cary produces his phone and opens his notes app, waiting.

I'M UP AT six-thirty, with a mug of coffee poured from yesterday's leftovers, and doing some quick laptop work before I head downstairs. Cary has promised me coffee, but I have a routine to stick to. Anyway, it's not like I can drink too much coffee.

I've been going through the Eventing Entries website and double-checking the open and closing date for the various events I want to take horses to in the next few months. My calendar spreadsheet is open on a separate tab, so that I can triple-check my plans. My mind is humming happily. I love scheduling my show season. There's so much promise to it, so much potential. And the organizational aspect hits all my brain's pleasure centers.

Hmm...there's another open jumpers show on Saturday morning that I can take the horses to—not Hansie though, not yet, even though I'd love to get him out and try his paces on a professionally-set course. Sebastian, Plato, and the client horses can go. A couple more rounds in the jumper ring will only help me tighten their coursework before the first event of the season.

Outside, a car door slams. I look up automatically, but the apartment's small windows crammed under the eaves look out over the arena, not the parking area. I have to open the front door to see who is here, and when I do, I'm pleased to see Cary swaggering into the barn, a carry tray from Starbucks in one hand.

He drove into town and got Starbucks? Oh, Hollywood. I would have expected two big Styrofoam cups from the gas station; in this part of the country, that passes for a thoughtful gesture. But not only did he backtrack and deal with morning traffic in Ocala, he got proper iced coffees, in massive cups.

The nectar of summer...and most of winter, around here.

He sees me standing on the landing in my stocking-feet and waves like Forrest Gump on the shrimp boat. "I hope you like giant cold brews, boss!"

"I worship them. Let me get a couple Yetis to keep those things icy," I suggest, and duck back inside.

Stimulated by a rush of warm air from the open door, the air conditioner clicks on and caresses my skin. It feels so good I want to throw myself back on my little sofa. That devilish machine has a way of trying to keep me inside in the morning. But the horses will have seen Cary's car and they'll already be standing at their paddock gates, whinnying and rattling the chains. No rest for the wicked.

I pull a couple of green Yeti mugs from the cabinet over the sink, then slide my feet into my paddock boots. Wearing bike shorts paired with tall socks, I look like an overgrown Boy Scout, but there's a fine line between staying cool and keeping horse-flies off my shins, and I don't want to pull on breeches if I don't have to.

"Whoa," Cary says as I clomp down the steps in my high-fashion scuffed boots and knee socks. "I had no idea we were going on safari today, professor."

"If you want to work here all day, you should probably know about my frequent costume changes," I tell him, taking a frosty coffee cup from him. I throw back a long, grateful gulp before I dump the rest into my Yeti cup. "On training days, I will be making several. This is the early morning outfit—just throwing on clothes to get the horses in and fed. Then I switch to breeches and a sleeveless shirt for a couple of rides. Then, when the sun gets bad, I change into a long-sleeved sun shirt."

I don't mention that I also change my sports bra. In this weather, a girl can only stand being so wet all day. I might go through three sports bras on a day like this, and as many tech-fabric shirts, between morning coffee and the end-of-day shower.

"Of course today," I add, "I'm just riding one horse, so I'll probably only change once or twice."

"Wow," Cary says admiringly. "You must have a huge closet."

He fixates on the weirdest details. It's like his brain operates on some unique frequency which picks up inferences no one else would notice.

"I have a few large piles of clothes that are semi-folded at the end of my bed," I admit. "I'm not quite as tidy in my personal life as in my professional."

Cary strokes his light shorts and flicks at his athletic t-shirt. "As you can see, I also dressed for the weather, not the sport."

"Did you bring jeans?"

"I did, but yesterday, getting out of those sweaty jeans was an exercise in itself."

"Yeah, jeans are kind of a nightmare in Florida." Again, I wonder if I should get him into breeches. The tech fabric makes all the difference in the heat. But he'll be riding in jeans in the movie. Obviously, a cowboy would not be riding the range and picking up defenseless females in a pair of full-seat breeches. Although they'd be a lot more comfortable if they did.

"Well," I say, deciding it can be up to him, "if you end up feeling too gross, I can make some recommendations for riding clothes that won't stick to your skin."

"I'm gonna be dressed up like you before the end of the week," Cary guesses.

I imagine him in clinging stretchy breeches, a riding jersey tucked into his waistband and pressing against those abs of his. "If you are, all of Ocala will thank me," I joke, and then I try to ignore the slow unfurling of pressure in my core as Cary's smile widens and his sparkling eyes laugh back at me.

Time to get horses, I think. *Time to work out all these weird feelings.*

Chapter Twelve

IT TURNS OUT Cary can be fairly helpful at the little stuff, dumping feed where I tell him to and bringing in the horses while keeping his feet well clear of hooves, never running short of inane jokes and chatty conversation with each horse. The horses know where to go anyway, and first thing in the morning they're really not concerned with anything but getting to their stalls and devouring their breakfasts, so he doesn't need much observation outside of getting their halters on and off correctly.

I do notice he has a sway in his walk that wasn't there yesterday, so my prediction about his inner thighs feeling like he just learned to do a split without any warmup was not wrong, but he's pushing through the discomfort pretty impressively.

And I must say, I love a person who can push through physical pain without complaining. Maybe this is not the best trait to admire if you're looking out for someone's well-being, but it makes me feel like he can get through a day on a horse farm without being annoying. I really don't have room in my life for weenies who are going to cry every time they get a blister or have a pulled muscle. There just isn't time in the day...and anyway, my tragic up-down students give me all the grief I can handle in that department. This is Monday. I am free of whining on Mondays.

When everyone's inside and eating, I give Cary permission to enjoy the air conditioning in the office while I go upstairs to change into my breeches. Lily Marlene follows him into the office and curls up on the desk, purring loudly.

"Ah, a mascot," Cary says warmly, rubbing her ears in just the right spots.

"Don't steal my cat," I warn him. "I'll hunt you down."

"I would never. I'm more of a dog person," he says, as Lily presses her head against him and closes her eyes, utterly content.

"Yeah, I can tell," I scoff.

Upstairs, I brush at my bare legs with a damp towel, getting the dust and dirt off them, then scuffle through my stack of breeches, looking for...what? Something flattering, for some reason. I usually just take whatever pair is on top of the pile. But somehow the slightly tatty pair of plum-colored riding tights staring at me from atop the heap just don't convey the look I want with Cary following me around.

"And anyway, I'm going to ride Hansie for the first time and he can take some pictures," I rationalize, as I disturb the pile's order to take out a lovely pair of sage-green breeches. I wore them often at Fine Day Farm, but since they're really in Malcolm's farm colors, they haven't gotten a lot of riding time since I moved here. They're absolutely beautiful, with all the show-ring touches, like belt-loops and false rear pockets.

Plus, I know I look great in them.

Perfect for a few commemorative photos of Hansie's first ride at the farm, right?

I wriggle into them, check my appearance, and straighten my belt. "You look good," I tell my reflection.

You never look at me this much, my reflection snipes back.

Or it would, if it was doing its own thing, Mary Poppins-style.

"Whoa," Cary says when I reappear in the office, dressed like I'm ready to show a horse in the Grand Prix ring at Legends Equestrian Center.

"Whoa?" I echo teasingly, putting a hand on a hip and jutting it saucily. "What's that supposed to mean?"

"You look...uh..."

I wait for him to say *hot* with an expectancy that grosses me out.

"Professional," he says.

"Oh." How deflating.

He smirks, and I realize he knew exactly what I was thinking. This guy loves to get into my head! And it's completely annoying.

But also...kind of nice?

When I was riding and working with Malcolm, I got used to being a crew of one in so many ways. Malcolm is a self-centered human; Evie is the first person who ever turned his interest away from himself and onto another person. It's charming to watch them together, but also a little frustrating at times—I ran his life for years, and I never garnered the kind of attention and interest that he lavished on Evie from the moment she walked into his barn.

(Although "walked" is kind of a misnomer for what happened the day she arrived at Fine Day Farm. That's Evie's story to tell, though.)

When it came to Malcolm and me, our relationship was always about what I could do for him, not what he could do for me. That's not to say I didn't learn from him; riding with Malcolm was invaluable. He changed my life on many levels. I wouldn't be here today, with my own place, without Malcolm.

For whatever that is worth, I think wryly, considering my current position.

Having Cary watch me with such keen interest, having him listen to me, ask for my opinion and look for my attention and actually try to compete with my other responsibilities to get it...

That's refreshing, and fun.

I make up my mind that for now, I like having him around. And until I don't anymore, he can continue to hang out.

But he needs to be useful. No one drapes themselves around my farm to live a life of leisure. I tap the desk with my fist and demand, "Are you ready to play photographer and videographer? I'm going to get on Hansie and I'd love to see it documented."

"Documented!" Cary leaps up, disappointing Lily Marlene, who stretches and leaves the room. "Are we going to produce a special? Do a YouTube series? I'm up for anything. Oh, I have *so* many ideas!"

Outwardly, I scoff at his excitement, but inwardly, I'm intrigued. What if we *did* record Hansie's training progress? What if in three or four years, Hansie and I are upper-level competitors and the equestrian world wants to know everything about us? Having archived footage to produce a YouTube series would actually be pretty valuable for the business. "Let's say we are," I suggest, noncommittally as if I really don't care, "and that way we have the video if we decide to do it."

"You got it, boss," Cary says. "And I like the way you say 'we,' like we are starting a production company together. You're a real girl boss, just like Kat."

"I'm not a girl boss," I demur. "But thanks. Kat's a pretty powerful woman."

"Terrifying, some people say," Cary murmurs, almost to himself.

I wonder how things are going at home.

Hansie seems eager to come out for a ride, nearly plowing me over when I open the stall door. The interest he showed in me at

Malcolm's farm is still gratifyingly present the entire time I'm grooming and tacking up; when he isn't watching a bird hopping in the barn aisle or listening to a horse whinnying from a neighboring farm, he is watching me, his head turning and his body shifting as I move around him in the cross-ties. Cary might as well not exist. I love every second of his attention.

I feel like I have a special place in my heart for Hansie, a spot that has been open and waiting for years, just hoping he'd turn up. This is a special horse; I can feel it, and I've seen him in action—and the enormity of what we could do together is almost frightening. I've never felt this way about a horse before. I've heard about it, I know heart horses exist, but until Hansie arrived in my life, I assumed it was something that happened to other people, with less regimented nervous systems—and hearts—than mine.

And with love, comes fear. What if I mess him up in some way? What if I do something stupid and this partnership never has a chance to get off the ground?

What if I'm not good enough to help him give his best?

I settle the saddle pad over his back with steady hands, putting on a strong, armored expression for the iPhone that Cary is training on me, getting our future documentary footage with dogged determination.

"And what are you going to do with him today?" he asks, a rich and deep tone entering his voice. It suits him. I realize this must be his Hollywood voice in action.

"I'm going to do some basic flatwork to start," I respond, placing my favorite jumping saddle on Hansie's back and sliding my fingers around the panels, checking the fit. "Just stretch him out, let him feel the ground in the arena. And then if he wants to do more, I'll let him pop over a few fences."

Ordinarily I wouldn't start the week of riding with a jumping school, but this is a stretch-out day to feel each other out. Today, we're just going to have fun.

"Well, we're all excited for this first ride," Cary assures me, as if there are a dozen people in the background awaiting my debut on Hansie's back. "Anything you want to say for posterity before this historic moment?"

I have to laugh, covering my mouth with one hand as I do, because I'm afraid that if we actually use this video someday, I'll look toothy and insane and completely overwrought with nerves. "Yes, Cary, I just want to say that I have just met this horse and I love him."

Cary laughs as well, struggling to hold the iPhone steady. Then he clicks the camera off and lowers his arms. "You can't beat a talking dog quote," he says. "Hopefully we don't have to get permission from Pixar to use it."

"I'm pretty sure a paraphrase that broad will get by their lawyers," I laugh. I'm loving this fake documentary game way more than I expected. "Okay, let me put on my hard hat and bridle this big boy, and then we can head out!"

The sun is climbing slowly, but it's already hot in the arena, or maybe it was always hot, all night, and I'm just privileged enough to enjoy the residual effects of yesterday's sunlight. Despite the recent rain, a fine cloud of dust accompanies Hansie's dark hooves as he walks alongside me, head high and ears swiveling to take in the surrounding countryside. There are broodmares out on the pasture neighboring my farm, a few scattered foals still in the mix although most have been weaned and taken elsewhere. They graze slowly across the slope of their field, and Hansie stares at them as if he has come across a herd of deer.

Oh, wait, there *are* a few deer, heads down amongst the mares. Hansie's nostrils flare and he stops, standing with his head high. It's the *Danger! Predator!* position, and the follow-up for this pose is either a fluttering release of breath and relaxation, or a quick turnaround and the horse's intense flight response kicking into high gear.

I'm hoping for the former. "Let's walk on, Hansie," I tell him, jiggling the bit. He ignores me, his breath coming out in one hard puff.

Oh, not the herd stallion routine! "Hansie," I say more forcefully. "Buddy, listen to me. Come on!"

I tap his neck to get his ear to swing down to me, then pull him forward again.

Hansie snorts and bounces forward, then swings his hindquarters around to the right and sidesteps anxiously, his ears still waving back and forth between the deer and me. His legs cross each other and I'm immediately afraid he's going to step on himself. I should have put him in boots. But it's so hot, and leg boots hold in heat...ugh, there is never just a simple, right answer to anything in this world!

"A little high-spirited," I hear Cary intone, still using his announcer voice, as I try to straighten Hansie out. I realize he's filming all this.

Not what I want in the documentary!

"Cary," I hiss, "not now!"

"But this is real and raw," Cary says. "And anyway, you've got him settled down. Nice work, boss. This is real horsemanship in action," he tells our invisible audience. "A woman who can settle a frightened horse with just her words, her hands, and her expression."

That makes me seriously question the look on my face right now. It's probably not pretty. I work to flatten out whatever grimace I'm making as I walk the snorting Hansie to the mounting block. In the distance, the deer move on, leaving the broodmares to their grazing.

He lets out a flutter of air through his nose, the breath he's been holding.

Oh, thank goodness.

Under saddle, Hansie is tense, but no more than I would expect... no less, really. He mouths the bit carefully and over-bends, tucking his chin close to his chest. I give him some room, figuring he'll take a while to chill out and start stretching his spine out. "No need to film this part," I call to Cary. "He's probably going to look kind of hunched up for the next ten minutes."

"What if I miss something good?" Cary replies. He's standing in the center of the arena, next to a jump standard, with the iPhone held up.

There's no way he's going to keep up this kind of enthusiasm, I think. He's just found a shiny object to keep him occupied for a little while during this weird, boring stay in Ocala. I'll let him do whatever he wants until he gets tired of it.

Chapter Thirteen

"WHEN IS HE going to loosen up?" Cary calls half an hour later. "Or is this how he looks? He's pretty," Cary adds hastily, as my silence continues. "Don't get me wrong or anything."

I know we've been riding half an hour because I have a ride tracking app on my phone that's occasionally calling out time markers. And it has been a solid ten minutes since the twenty-minute cue, which is when I first began to lose all hope in this ride. Now, at the thirty-minute marker, I'm running on the fumes of my initial fizzy high. This isn't going the way I'd hoped.

Meanwhile, Hansie is apparently still fully gassed up, and revving at very high RPMs, because his neck is tight, his ears are pricked, and he's trotting with about the right tempo *if* I wanted him to win the final heat of the Hambletonian. I'm mixing my racing metaphors there, but I'm sure the point is clear.

The only thing in this arena that isn't going anywhere fast is Hansie's tension.

That's fine, I remind myself, flexing my inside ring finger on the reins, gently opening and closing my grip as I try to supple the line of communication between my hand and his mouth. It's fine that he's tense on his first ride in a new arena, in a new place. Doesn't mean a thing. We'll just get a little suppling work done, ask him to bring his pace down a touch, lower his poll and drop his neck, and maybe gently mouth the bit instead of clenching his jaw around it—

Hansie responds to my soft, suppling hand by bowing his neck to the inside of the ring and bulging his outside shoulder towards the rail, trotting with his forelegs farther into the arena than his hind legs. It's not a shoulder-in; it's more like a deranged crab-trot.

"Ugh," I sigh, pushing my inside leg against the girth to see if I can salvage the bend and make it something useful, something graceful, something *dressage* instead of just a messy complaint. "Hansie, buddy, relax."

"Wow, that's a nice sideways move!" Cary shouts. "I'm getting all of this!"

"No, it's not—that's not what I'm asking him for," I reply, trying a sitting trot to see if that will help my seat influence his body more effectively. Hansie takes the change as an invitation to canter and bursts forward in an explosive upward transition. "Whoa, buddy— whoa, now *stop* it—" My breath bursts out of me in exasperated huffs.

Hansie is shaking his head as I rein back and I have to sit down on my bum, tilt back my pelvis a little, and drive Hansie down to the trot without using my reins. He responds nicely to my seat, but now walking is out of the question.

Oh no, because we are *prancing*!

"He looks super athletic," Cary enthuses from a few feet away, iPhone trained on us with a steady hand. "Absolutely incredible dance work here!"

Idiot, I think, aware I'm being mean in my head because I'm pissed off about this ride and there's no one around to blame but Cary.

"Isn't that phone battery dead yet?" I snark at him as Hansie jigs past.

Cary tilts his head back to look at the phone's screen without taking the lens off Hansie and me. He shakes his head and says, "No, it's still good. I've got a charger in the car, anyway."

"I think you've got more than enough."

"You can never have too much film to play with. I'm telling you, you're going to want all of this someday."

"What could I *do* with it?" I demand, nodding down at my demonic horse.

Hansie swishes his tail and snorts.

"There are a million things you can do with iPhone footage," Cary says, sounding like he's being patient with the dummy who doesn't understand.

The idea that I'm the thick one here irritates me; I tighten my fingers on the reins for a moment, then have to release the pressure as Hansie's jig becomes a feverishly collected trot. Hansie's intensely sensitive; the horse feeds off everything and amplifies it.

Cary continues blithely in his praise of film footage. "I mean, obviously I haven't had much set work in the past ten years, so I've done a lot of independent stuff. YouTube has been such a gift. How about starting there? You could set up a channel, do training videos. People would like that, right?"

"They're not going to learn anything from this ride," I say grimly. "I'd rather die than let this go public."

"But he looks really pretty," Cary persists gamely. "And if he's not doing what you want today, then that's *good*, because it gives you a story arc. If he were just perfect every day, there wouldn't be any drama and no one would tune in to watch the next episode."

"The next—" I start to splutter that there won't be *any next* episodes, not until Hansie gets his shit together and moves into the bridle the way he did at Fine Day Farm, but I'm interrupted by a clap of thunder that sends my horse jitterbugging sideways. And by the time I've got him back in hand, it's time to go back inside as a storm rapidly arrives from the southwest, the part of the sky that's so conveniently blocked by the barn, I had no idea it was coming.

"HMM," CARY MUSES, watching the rain pour down. "This isn't exactly what I had in mind for the day when I decided to become a horse expert."

"*That* was the plan?" I glance at him, then back at Hansie, who is standing in the wash-stall accepting his shower with remarkable good grace.

In fact, everything about him improved the minute I dismounted. He's watching me carefully again, and a part of me wonders if he's been keeping his eyes fixed firmly on me because he's *wary*, not because we're best friends and destined horse/human partners who have been brought together to wow the world.

I'd still really prefer it's the latter, but unfortunately, I'm a realist and it's getting harder by the minute to hang on to that particular spark of magic.

"I mean, yeah," Cary says. "Being a horse expert would be great for my brand. Not that it's my brand anymore, but I guess I still think that way."

"What exactly is...was...your brand?" I ask, slopping shampoo into a sponge. Thunder echoes through the rafters, but Hansie ignores it, keeping his dark ears trained on me. "Teen star turns into cowboy. I get that's what is happening now, but what happened in the middle?"

"The past ten years where I was messing around on my phone, you mean?" Cary laughs. "I was an expert! I mean, a pseudo-expert. I tried a few different podcasts and vlogs, but the thing that stuck was this YouTube show I produced where I interviewed quirky people and then tried to do their specialties, like surfing or mushroom foraging or, I don't know, building reproduction French furniture. I did that once."

"You're allowed to use power tools?" I gasp. "Surely that was a mistake."

"I do have some neat scars from that one." Cary holds out his left hand for me to inspect. "The crescent-shape one, see? And this one down the middle of my palm? *That* one bled like a mother—"

"I don't want to know." I go back to scrubbing Hansie, who leans into my efforts. I half-expect a groan of satisfaction. "So, you're not planning on doing the same thing with me, are you? I didn't sign off on being a segment on your show."

"No, not at all. I'm on hiatus from it...hopefully forever, because the jobs my viewers were asking me to try were getting more and more dangerous."

"Would you say no to anything?"

"I said no to alligator-trapping in the Everglades."

I glance at him, trying to imagine his smiling good looks wrassling a gator. "Good call."

Cary grins. "Right? But I like this cowboy thing. I like horses. So, I guess it's just my natural reaction now...when I walk into an unfamiliar space I feel like I have to learn it as quickly as possible, because it's about to be my new job and a bunch of people are gonna watch me to see how I screw it up."

Well, that explains the way he showed up this morning asking to do everything. I can't help a feeling of mild disappointment, though I'm not actually sure why. Did I want it to be about spending time with me?

"Pass me the hose, will you?" I say, tossing the sponge into its wire tray. "Let me get this horse rinsed off."

Cary hands me the hose dutifully. "I'm not filming this part," he says, like he's making me a promise. "Working with you...that isn't for my show."

I find myself watching his dark eyes carefully. It's alarming, how easily I am pulled into his magnetic orbit. "Thanks," I say. "I mean— because—"

"It'll be our thing," Cary says.

He smiles at me like we're the best of friends, and his Hollywood sparkle almost tricks me into believing it's all real.

I CALL EVIE while Cary is out finding us some lunch. That's the way he put it, "finding" lunch, as if he's going foraging in the outback. I suggested he just go to Hopper's, an old service station/ lunch counter combo that has been in the neighborhood for something like seventy years, but he has to do things his way, so he says he'll be back in an hour with something exciting.

"In Ocala?" Evie asks when I update her on the goings-on around the barn. "Let me know what he finds that's more exciting than a new taco truck."

"I'd love it if he brought back tacos," I reflect. "I could go for the barbacoa from that truck that sets up at the gas station on 441."

"Oh, big same," Evie sighs. "Sounds amazing. But I don't think we have time for more than a pack of peanut butter crackers over here today. Unless I take matters into my own hands and send out Sydney without permission."

"You have the authority to send her out for lunch, trust me. And how is she doing? Still loving the working student life?"

"She really is! I thought we'd break her immediately, but she's tougher than she looks."

Sydney, still a teenager, had been one of Malcolm's wealthy winter-season students until she rebelled against her mother and insisted she wanted to work with horses full-time. I could use her energy. I sigh and say, "I need a Sydney to help me around here."

"You have a Sydney," Evie says. "His name is Cary."

"Hah! We'll see how long that lasts."

"I've got my money on a long and loving partnership," Evie teases.

"That's *so* not what is going on around here."

"Sure, sure," she scoffs. "Listen, I have to go in a minute. Malcolm is designing a jumper course for the weekday show series, and he's making me come with him to do measurements. Even though I *said* it's my day *off!*"

That last line was not directed at me and I know it means Malcolm is a few feet away, making an impatient face at her.

"Did you call about Hansie?" Evie asks.

"I did," I say. "How did you know?"

Did she expect my first ride to be a disaster?

"Because you've had him twenty-four hours, and I expect by now you've had the first ride and it wasn't what you expected."

"How do you know that?" I demand, trying to ignore a sudden prickle of suspicion. Evie and Malcolm are my closest friends. There's no way they would have purposely sold me a lemon, or not shared the horse's problems beforehand.

"It was the look on your face when you first saw him," Evie says, surprising me. "Like you just met your soul-mate. The first ride on a new farm is always messy, especially for a horse that green, and you were just not thinking clearly. I figure this morning you got on and he gave you a wake-up call. Am I right?"

I sigh. She's got my number, alright. "Evie, that's exactly what happened. He was so tense, it was like riding a volcano ready to blow. And everything I did just seemed to make him worse."

"So, you'll do something a little different tomorrow," Evie says reasonably. "And the next day. And in a couple of days, you'll see what he wants and he'll be used to your property and everything will be fine."

"You think so?" I know she's right, but I am craving reassurance. Because, like she said, my good sense went right out the window the moment I saw Hansie.

"Everything is going to be fine," she says. "And if you have trouble, we'll help you. But you won't run into anything you can't handle. You're Alison. You've got this."

"Yeah," I say, trying to wrap my usual cloak of confidence around me. "I've got this."

But have I, really? I stand in the barn aisle and watch Hansie attacking his alfalfa, rummaging through the bright green hay like he's never eaten anything so delicious in his life before this. It feels like forever stands between this moment and tomorrow morning, when I can get on and try again with him. I just want that feeling back, the feeling of connection we had in the covered arena back at Malcolm and Evie's place, and I'm afraid the craving for it is going to make everything I do in the next twenty-four hours feel boring and flat.

Chapter Fourteen

CARY DOESN'T SHOW up on Tuesday morning. Instead, I get an apologetic message, something about muscles he's never used before, blah-blah-blah. Since he stuck around until evening feeding on Monday, I do something unusual for me when someone cops out of their riding lesson.

I smile and shake my head, and write back, *No problem, you'll be missed!*

If I did that to one of my regular students, they'd think someone stole my phone. Someone really, really nice and forgiving—a welcome change from strict old Alison, who never seems satisfied.

After I put down the phone, I gaze moodily into my fridge. There are a few aluminum foil takeout containers in there, stuffed with leftovers from the massive lunch he brought us yesterday—yes, from the taco truck on 441. Adventure in Ocala, Cary is realizing, doesn't often take the form of culinary masterpieces. He made up for the anti-climatic lunch by bringing home an a*stonishing number of assorted* tacos, a styrofoam container containing a heap of nachos drowning in sour cream and guacamole, and two massive burritos.

"I panicked," he explained. "I don't know what you like, and I had no cell service."

So, my fridge is packed with leftovers.

I usually have a banana or a yogurt for breakfast; this morning, annoyed with life, I devour two cold tacos.

Of course, tacos don't keep well. So, these don't do much for my mood. With acidic tomato salsa running roughshod over my esophagus and stomach lining, I head out to face another lonesome Tuesday.

The day seems to drag, and I feel as if I'm just going through the motions of my first rides of the week. It's flavorless today, doing the stretching and balancing work that will feed our schooling and new skill practice for the following five rides. Boring, even.

Giving Hansie "Big Horse" status, I ride him first. He is marginally better than the day before, but still tense, still holding his breath, still vaguely volcanic, as if he's just looking for an excuse to blow. I force myself to let it go and move on to my other horses without beating myself up about my riding. Even though it's upsetting, underneath my initial bout of hurt feelings, I do know his tension is not about me. And it's not *really* what I can expect from Hansie long-term. We're just dealing with a new situation for a young horse. He has to settle in. And when he does, everything will be fine.

But the loss of our initial connection continues to nag at me as I ride my other horses, and all of our rides are a little stiff and jerky because of it. I try to soothe ruffled feathers when I ask for too much and reward too little, and eventually, the horses accept my belated apologies.

I'm cooling Plato out on a long rein after a ride that was just a little too tough on him, watching the clouds thicken overhead and gauging how long I have before the rain begins. I figure it's about half an hour.

My phone pings with a text message, interrupting my thoughts. I tug the phone out of the side pocket in my riding breeches, marginally disgusted by how sweaty it is, and flick past the lock screen.

For some reason, I expect the text to be some silly message from Cary, so I'm a little disappointed when it isn't his name on the notification. But then I cheer up—it's Jim Brewer. I'm reminded that someone in this town actually wants to spend time with me. We have a date coming up! Can't remember the last time I went on one of those. I wriggle a little in the saddle and Plato shakes his head at my movement, his ears waggling.

"Let's see what Jim has to say," I mutter, opening the text.

Saw this and thought of you, with a wink emoji.

I see "this" and can't help snorting with laughter, startling Plato. He's sent me a picture of a horse in a mud-hole, four legs in the air. I can practically hear that horse groaning with satisfaction as he grinds the muddy water into his back. He's happy as a pig in muck.

I type back, *Where did you get this picture of me?!*

Jim sends back a few more wink emojis.

Okay, a man of few words. But that's okay. I like his sense of humor.

This is good, I think. This could be good.

Then I get another message, from a student's mom, asking if she can come tonight instead of Friday.

Of course, I text back, thinking that this day is just a total wash. Might as well put all my eggs in Friday's basket. I'll have one fewer lesson to deal with before I head out on the town, Ocala-style, with Jim.

"BYE, MARLEE," I call to my departing student. "See you next week! Have fun on your vacation!"

The six-year-old waves as she climbs into a waiting SUV. She's a cute kid, I reflect. She'd look great in jodhpurs and little black jodhpur boots, big blue bows tying up her brown pigtails. If she ever learns to sit back and stop clutching the pommel of her saddle. She's way too small for Nando and the smart thing to do would be to refer her to one of the riding schools around here with a plethora of ponies lined up for young riders, but her mother, flatteringly, likes the way I teach and is willing to stick it out while the kid finds her balance on a full-size horse.

I learned to ride on horses a little too large for me, too, so I know she can do it. These things just take time. Riding's a lifelong lesson, I remind the kids when they think they're not progressing, and then I have their moms show them some bouncy phone video of how awful they looked in their first lesson. At that point, everyone usually laughs and then begs their mom to delete the video.

Mom never does.

As Marlee's mom drives off, I brush loose hair back from my face and turn around, surveying my barn. After a full day's work and an hour spent teaching Marlee, it's in a sad state. We got another rough storm before her lesson, and it has never been more obvious that this place's drainage is shot to hell. There are huge puddles at the barn entrance and the arena gate, and the dirty water, churned-up ground, and muddy slats of the barn walls combine to paint a picture that couldn't be farther from the professional excellence I'd cultivated at Fine Day Farm.

To make matters worse, Evie has actually lined up a potential boarder from her wait-list, but the client wants to see pictures of the farm before she commits. Evie is still adamant that I have to fix the place up a little before she sends anyone photos. And she was talking about a *clean, non-flooded* barn when she set that stipulation.

I heave a deep sigh, shaking my head. I never thought I'd stand at the barn door at the end of the day and shrug off this kind of mess, but right now all I want to do is turn out the horses for the night, go upstairs, and stay in the air conditioning for as long as possible.

This isn't working, a little voice in my head says.

"You're not a failure," I remind myself, silencing this little voice before it can get any louder and do some real damage. Aunt Kate always says the voice in your head is just doubt that needs to be squashed. "You're just understaffed. It won't be like this forever."

And as I start to head into the barn to get chores finished (because how could I ever relax if I went upstairs with the barn in this kind of state?) I hear a car coming up the drive. Oh lord, it must be someone lost, or some tourist who wants to look at pretty horses. I turn around again, ready to send them on their way.

But to my surprise, I see Cary pulling in, driving his black rental SUV.

"What are you doing here?" I ask as he parks by the barn, window down, so I can see his grinning face.

For some reason, that smile of his cheers me up instantly.

"I had a little project in mind," he says mysteriously, "and I was waiting for the weather to cool down a little so I could do it. Pretty nice now, isn't it?"

"Well..." *Nice* isn't exactly what I'd call the evening, but the temperature is below ninety degrees, anyway. "What kind of project are we talking here?"

Cary smiles and pops the back hatch.

Together, we walk around and he gestures triumphantly towards the pots of blooming flowers stuffed in the back of the SUV.

"What's all this?" I ask, confused.

"I'm going to do a little gardening," he declares.

"Gardening!" I exclaim, staring at him. "Gardening where?"

"Right here." He gestures to the muddy mess in front of my barn. "Along either side of the barn door, we'll do a neat little flower-bed. I can knock it out in an hour."

"You...garden?" I ask weakly, feeling like I've been blindsided by a freight train. Cary's energy is a lot at the end of the day. "Or are you just experimenting? Is this another one of your weird fake-job situations?" Maybe he played a landscaper on his web series and that is giving him ideas. My barn area might be ugly, but I don't want him experimenting on it. Suppose he makes it worse!

I gaze at the sad, muddy sand piled up against the front of the barn.

Okay, he probably can't make it worse.

"No, this is something I'm *actually* good at, without having to shadow professionals first," Cary says. He starts hauling plants out, handing them to me, so that I've got armfuls of potted flowers before I know what's happening. I start lining them up alongside the barn wall. "I've always had a green thumb. Learned how to garden from my mom. It's her passion."

I step back as Cary confidently starts spading into the muck with a newly bought shovel. He clears out my drains first, then starts in on the sand along the barn wall. "Grab me those bags of garden soil, will you?"

Obediently, I trot back to the car and return with a few big bags of dirt.

"Good girl," Cary says cheerfully. "Now I'm all set. You can go do your thing. No need to stand here and watch me."

Feeling oddly like I've been dismissed from my own property, I head into the barn. The entire time I'm turning out horses and mucking out stalls, Cary is out there gardening.

It feels good having him nearby. His presence is a comfort, which is strange, because I didn't even realize I needed comforting.

STALLS ARE DONE and I've just finished blowing the mess of the day out of the aisle with a leaf-blower when Cary strolls in the doorway, hands on his hips, and gives me a satisfied look. Against the swirl of a pink-and-purple stormy sunset, he has a heroic air, like a knight who has just won his battle against the dragon.

"Gardening done?" I rasp, trying to swallow the dust in my throat.

"It looks bee-*you*-ti-ful," he enthuses, spreading his arms out. "Come and see!"

A smile tugging at my lips, I follow him out to the parking lot and then turn, dramatically, to observe the change he's made to the front of my barn.

"Whoa!"

"Right?"

I can't believe the difference. Where there was previously a muddy, sad mess of sand and weeds, there are two heaped garden beds on either side of the barn door, with bright red, purple, and yellow blooms nodding above their fresh soil. I can't identify them—not a flower person, I'm afraid—but they look tropical and exciting, and they lend a stylish flair to the entire barn front, as if we've suddenly transformed into a cosmopolitan training stable instead of a sandy rental.

"The yellow and purple ones are butterfly bushes, so they'll attract butterflies," Cary says, pointing out some round clusters of blossoms. "And the big red ones, of course, those are hibiscus, because it's Florida and you need hibiscus. They'll get really tall and spread out along the barn walls, so in three months, it'll look like they've been there for years."

"It looks incredible," I say, feeling completely choked up. "Thank you so much. I can't believe you just showed up and planted a flower garden for me!"

"Well, I felt silly not coming out this morning, but wow, I could barely move." He grins sheepishly. "And then I spent half the day stretching myself out so I could get moving, and I thought, how can I salvage this day and have something to show for it? I remembered this area looking a little weedy, so..."

"Really," I say, "I can't believe it." And I can't. He's made such a difference in an hour, without even being asked. I turn and touch his shoulder, feeling an intense urge to draw closer to him, and then, without warning, going against all my cool, professional instincts, I pull him into a hug.

His arms go around my back and his chin rests just above my head, hovering there for a moment before he settles into the embrace and allows its weight to settle gently atop me. I suppose I'm just very tired and that's why I lean into him so hard, letting my chin press against his shoulder, my face snuggle close to his warm neck. His hands are comforting against my back, and I like the feel of his back beneath mine, so I spread out my fingers and let them sprawl there, pressing against his muscles.

And then, without warning, a flood of warmth spills from my core and soaks all the way from spine to seat, fingers to toes, tingling in my joints and my skin and my muscles. The skin of my chest seems to tighten and my breath comes faster.

I step back quickly, and let my hands fall to my sides, digging my fingertips into the slim pockets of my breeches.

Cary looks at me with an almost wary expression. His pupils are dilated, his lips parted.

Something absolutely terrifying occurs to me as we stare at each other: *I think I almost turned up my head and kissed him. I think if I'd stayed there in his embrace another second, I might have done it.*

The realization does nothing to cool the sizzling heat gathering inside me.

Tired, I tell myself, *I'm just really tired.*

Cary brushes a lock of loose hair back from his face and sighs, and when he does, it feels like he's trying to let go of something taut within.

As if he almost kissed me, too.

Chapter Fifteen

IT TURNS OUT Mrs. C has some kind of press nonsense and wardrobe fittings for Cary to deal with over the next few days, which means he only has time to come out for his lesson. That's good for me, I think, because I need a little distance to think about the weird feelings his hug gave me last night.

And not just his hug, I reflect, as I teach him on a cloudy Friday afternoon, watching him practice swinging his hips along with Nando's walk on the far side of the arena. I'm getting vibes from all angles, from his charm, his charisma, his *thoughtfulness*—which is something I find both alien and impossibly desirable in a man. I'm not saying horsemen are typically cruel and unfeeling—actually, most of the men I know in this business are *so* in touch with their feelings that they can get far too emotionally invested in their horses. But they're self-centered. At least, the competitive ones are. And I can't blame them for that. This isn't a sport with a lot of room for other people; as a rider, you're kept busy trying to take care of your partner, the horse.

I wouldn't have expected a former teen television star from Los Angeles to be the least self-centered person I've talked to in a while, but this career is full of surprises.

"Nando is the best boy," Cary calls, smiling, as they walk past me.

"He's a saint," I reply, thinking of the two lessons Nando will cart around later today. Sarah will be coming with her nanny, since Mrs. C is busy with production company work. "I'm glad you recognize it."

"I wish I could take him out of the arena." Cary opens his left arm to tug gently at the inside of Nando's mouth, and the horse amiably turns to walk a misshapen circle. "Think we could go on a trail ride, boss?"

"Oh my goodness, no," I snort, startled into laughter. "You've ridden, what, five times? You're not taking a horse out of the ring for ages yet."

"But I know Nando would be a good boy," Cary argues. He keeps Nando walking on their lopsided circle while he turns in the saddle to face me, pleading, "Come on, Alison, let's go play. Five rides in the arena is four too many."

He's like a child, face bright and shining with his newest idea. "Absolutely not," I say sternly. "You have a lot to learn in a short amount of time. We're doing arena work. Now get back on the rail and work on your hips; they're locked again."

"My hips are moving just fine," Cary grumbles. "Nando's going slow, that's all."

"Nando's going slowly because your hips are holding still and keeping him from moving his back. Don't you know everything your body does affects his? His back can't swing from side to side if you're pressing him into a straight line! Now, shoulders back, and lift your chest, and feel his movement—why are you stopping?"

Cary looks at me for a moment. A resigned expression comes over his face, and he shakes his head at me.

"Alison," he says, "I really hate to tell you this, but you're a terrible riding instructor."

"Cary!" I'm shocked; I can't believe he'd say that to me. I guess I thought we were friends. "What's the *matter* with you?"

"Maybe not terrible," Cary amends. "Maybe just not great."

"Seriously, dude, why would you say that to me?" Now I'm just exasperated.

"I mean well. It's just that you're trying to teach me way, way more than I need to know about this stuff."

I force myself to look stern, even though deep down, I suspect he's on to something. This guy isn't gunning for his silver medal in dressage. He just wants to look not-scary in a western saddle for a few frames on film. But still!

"I'm making sure you have the fundamentals," I insist. "If you don't even know how your horse *moves*—"

"Imagine I'm five years old," Cary interrupts. "Would you teach me this stuff if I were a little kid? Or would you teach me to steer and stay on and save the tough stuff for when I'm older and more experienced, and can grasp the concepts?"

I stare at him, perplexed. "Yes," I say at last.

"It wasn't a yes or no question." He grins.

"Yes, I'd teach you all of this stuff. It's hard, but it's important!" I do believe that.

Cary shakes his head at me. "I think you're jumping ahead with your lesson plans. So, maybe you're not a great teacher. That's okay. I think you're trying your best."

"Well, *I* think you have no idea what you're talking about!" I feel my face getting hot. "But if you're so good at teaching, what do you think comes next?"

"I think I should work on my jogging," he says amiably. "And I looked it up, and cowboys say *jogging*, and it's slower than your trotting."

Oh, he looked it up, did he? "Fine. Let's *jog.*"

Weird feelings? Yeah, I'll give him weird feelings.

Weird feelings in his crotch.

Wait...that's not what I meant.

I meant because he's going to *bounce* when he—

Forget it.

"Sit on your butt," I holler, as he puts his heels to Nando's sides and slowly trots—I mean, jogs—the horse away.

SARAH PIDDLES THROUGH her lesson with a minimum of drama, and then a pop-up storm cancels the next riding lesson. It's still crashing around outside while I run upstairs after evening feeding to get showered and dressed for my date with Jim. I have to make it a quick shower; if you live in Florida long enough, you will inevitably hear a story about someone being struck by lightning through their plumbing. Are any of these stories true? I don't want to find out.

Dressing for a date in Florida, especially in the give-up days of late summer, is pretty easy. With weather this hot and humid, there's no shame in smoothing wet hair into a bun, glopping some leave-in conditioner on top to (hopefully) smother as much frizz as possible, and slipping on a little tinted sunscreen in lieu of actual makeup. Because we're going to be outside at Legends Equestrian Center, which is like a theme park but for horse showing instead of roller coasters, I pull on a nice riding shirt patterned with stylized horses and pair it with loose linen capris that feel like water against my skin after weeks on end of living in riding tights and breeches. I give myself a quick glance in the mirror and head out the door, confident that I look like a successful and fit horsewoman out for a rare non-riding engagement.

That's all I can really ask of myself.

Legends is across town and the evening traffic is heavy, which gives me plenty of time to get nervous about the evening ahead. I don't date—because I don't have time and rarely meet anyone out of the saddle, not because I'm against the concept. Just like Malcolm met Evie at work, I have just assumed that's how I'll meet someone special...otherwise, the only way I can think of finding Mr. Right would be at a competitor party at a three-day event, or maybe we'd bump into each other at the feed store and have some adorable meet-cute, possibly involving me knocking down a shelving unit of fly spray or a display of horse cookies?

The cookies would definitely be cuter, I think, parking my truck in the crowded lot in front of the equestrian center. Ahead of me, through the criss-crossed paths between huge indoor arenas and the looming white hotel that overlooks the Grand Prix arena, I see the usual blend of local equestrians out for the evening, competitors still in their show attire, and mildly perplexed tourists loudly dressed in cruise wear and Hawaiian shirts. The latter group are the reason why I'm always careful to keep my equestrian identity close when picking out clothes for nice occasions. I'd hate to be mistaken for anything but a local taking a rare evening off from the farm grind.

After all, I've spent my whole life working to achieve this persona.

My phone buzzes as I walk beneath the twinkling lights strung over the main promenade, white indoor arenas rising on either side of me, their metallic panels hiding the vast arenas and hard-working horses inside. The text is from Jim, asking me to meet him at the pastry shop off one side of the Grand Prix arena, instead of the pizza cart.

Dessert first? I text back, smiling to myself. I watch my phone for the reply, hoping it's something moderately spicy.

A senior couple just ahead of me comes to an abrupt halt, in the tourist move that has exhausted Floridians since the first tin-canner drove to the state in search of mermaid shows and fresh oranges, and since I'm looking down, I ram right into the man. He stumbles sideways and I reach out to catch him, dropping my phone in my panic to avoid breaking a senior citizen.

"Whoops!" I exclaim, as his companion yelps in terror and several other people on the walkway come to horrified halts of their own.

"Oh, gosh," he gasps, once he's righted and the blood has stopped rushing in my ears. "You need to be more careful, young woman!"

I blink at him for a moment. "But, you stopped right in front of me," I sputter, but he's already turning away, shaking his head. His companion mutters something about young people today.

"At least you're young," a rich baritone voice, thick with laughter, murmurs in my ear.

"Cary!" I jump sideways in surprise, nearly taking out another oldster bopping along with a cane. "What are you *doing* here?"

Cary gives me a crooked smile and holds out my phone. "You dropped this," he says. "And I'm here to see the competition."

For a moment, I think he means Jim, and my stomach does a weird kind of somersault. But then he nods at the huge LED screens mounted on either side of the Grand Prix arena, and as they flicker to life to prepare for the first ride of the evening, I realize he just means the show jumping competition.

"Oh, of course," I say confusedly.

"Here comes your date, I'd guess," Cary says good-naturedly, nodding to a man heading towards us. It's Jim, looking dapper in his own set of saddle-to-sidewalk togs. He holds up a hand to greet me, his gaze sliding to Cary for a single, suspicious once-over before jerking back to my face. I can see the question in his gaze.

"That's him," I say hastily. "Nice to see you, Cary. I'm sorry about before, about your lesson—"

"No worries," Cary says. "It was hot. Sometimes we argue when it's hot."

I look at him thoughtfully. "That's true."

Cary smiles down at me.

And he makes no move to leave as Jim walks up.

Chapter Sixteen

JIM AND I greet each other as awkwardly as possible, which I kind of like. It's no fun being the only socially inept person in the room—another solid check in the column for only hanging out with other horse-people. We're sort of half-hugging when Cary clears his throat.

Both of us pull back and glare at him.

Cary beams at us, the happiest third wheel you ever did see. And with a startling premonition, I realize that he's not planning on going anywhere.

"Wow, I have no idea what's going on around here," Cary says blithely. "My first time. Seems big!"

He's playing wide-eyed innocent, which I've discovered is his favorite character. I shake my head at him slightly, but he's not looking at me. He's gazing around with the bright, interested eyes of a toddler in a toy store. But why?

Okay, what game are you playing, Cary?

I grit my teeth as Jim holds out a stiff hand to him and says, "Sorry, I don't think we've met."

"Cary Davies," Cary says, leaning in to shake his hand. "I'm from California."

"That name seems familiar..."

"It's Welsh," Cary says. "Are you a Welshman, Jim?"

"I—uh—"

"Just messing with you! My family's mostly from Arizona." Cary grins and looks back at me. "I like your friend here, Alison."

That's nice, because I'm going to kill you. "If you want to see the show jumping from the best spot, go and grab a table over there," I suggest. "You'll be able to follow along in no time."

Clunk. A pole hits the ground in the Grand Prix arena, and a few people around the arena say, *oooooh,* in that bad-luck tone. Jim included.

"Ouch," he says. "Erin's gonna be kicking herself over that rail."

"Why?" Cary asks eagerly. "What happens with the rails?"

"Google 'show jumping,'" I suggest coolly, but Jim actually starts pointing out the different types of fences on the course, giving commentary as his friend Erin jumps around the big arena on a solidly built dark bay warmblood.

"Jim," I say, as soon as Erin is trotting out of the arena, "you'd said something about the pastry shop. I was hoping you meant we were having dessert first..." And I smile to show what a fun-loving freewheeler I can be.

"Oh, right," Jim says, looking back at me like he just remembered I exist. "Yeah, let me just watch the next round, okay? It's a friend, Lauren Albright, she's got a real up-and-coming horse—"

"Wow, you know everyone," Cary interrupts, sounding so eager he can't even let Jim finish a sentence. "I'm impressed. You must be pretty important around here."

I stare at the two men with deep irritation, their heads close as Jim points out the finer points of Lauren's supposed up-and-coming horse. I honestly can't believe what I'm seeing. Cary is playing a ridiculously hick character, straight out of some nineteen-thirties screwball comedy, and Jim is just lapping up the attention.

Meanwhile, I'm left out completely. It makes no sense. Why doesn't Jim want to tell *me* about Lauren Albright's fancy horse? I would actually know what he's talking about!

As Ms Albright jumps a brilliant round, I pull out my phone and text Evie about the situation.

Her reply is quick. *Make sure he introduces you to Lauren later.*

I furrow my brow at the phone. *What? Why?*

It's kind of a giveaway when a guy doesn't introduce a girl he's dating to another woman he knows.

A giveaway...

What? Oh, Evie, come on. *He isn't seeing Lauren Albright! She's a big-time rider.*

Evie replies, *It's Ocala. Half the people here are big-time riders. Someone's gotta date them.*

She has me there.

Well, thanks for reassuring me that the weird date is going to get better, Evie. Before, I was just annoyed that Cary has decided it would be fun to completely monopolize my date. Now, I have to wonder if Jim is talking to Cary about the women riding around the Grand Prix arena because he doesn't want to give away that he's seeing them as well.

See? This is why I don't date. I could be at home on my sofa right now, watching TV on my laptop and patting Lily Marlene.

When Lauren trots out of the arena, looking smug about her clear round, Jim seems all prepared to watch the next rider, and Cary appears happy to continue their private viewing party. But I'm finished with being ignored.

I touch Jim on the shoulder, and he turns quickly, as if I surprised him. "Can we go get something to eat, please?" I ask, trying to keep my tension out of my tone. "It's been a long day, and I haven't had anything since my lunch of one slice of bread with peanut butter."

Jim quirks an eyebrow. "Hearty lunch."

I shrug. "My cabinets are empty. Due for a grocery shop." Monday with Cary around threw off my weekly schedule. Also, I am not spending much on food for myself until my winter income is secured. I should be home cleaning the barn, I think with a sudden pang of regret. Getting it ready for those pictures Evie is waiting for. Not out here goofing around with Jim.

But...free dinner...that counts for something. If I can make it happen.

"I should have brought you lunch earlier!" Cary exclaims. "Why didn't you say anything? I could have picked something up on the way over—"

I shoot him a freezing look that finally seems to get the message through his thick skull: *I am not happy you are here.* Cary subsides, looking a little sheepish as he shuffles his feet next to Jim.

"Cary, if you can excuse Jim and I," I say, "we had plans tonight."

"Okay then," Cary agrees, dropping the hick act at last. Jim glances at him as his accent evens out, but doesn't say anything. Cary says, still in his normal voice, "Have fun, you two. I'm going to just wander over there and try that pizza." And he turns away, heading for the pizza cart on the other side of the arena seating.

Which doesn't help me a lot, since I was planning to eat dinner there, too. I sigh.

"Wow," Jim says, glancing at me with surprise. "You can be pretty tough."

I shake my head at him. "I wasn't being tough," I say. "He was being a pest on purpose, to annoy me."

Jim raises his eyebrows. "Now, I didn't think he was being a pest! Just curious about show jumping."

"Trust me," I say, turning to walk towards the pastry shop. "He was being a pest on purpose."

Jim falls into stride next to me, but it takes a moment.

I don't think this is going well. But maybe I can pull it together. Pastry will help. Chocolate, sugar, butter—surely they're the key to a successful date? We'll eat something and reassess the evening.

OVER COLD BREW coffee and a chocolate-filled eclair, which does a lot for my mood, I give Jim a notecard-version of my riding history with Malcolm and my plans for my new farm. Then, I wait for him to tell me more about himself. But he is constantly distracted, watching various riders in the arena with all of his attention, then texting the ones he considers his friends. At one point he even texts a rider's *groom*, to tell them how nice the horse looks.

"That's very nice of you," I say, wishing I could slap the phone out of his hand. "Grooms don't get enough praise for their hard work."

"I would hate to be a groom," Jim says, eyes on his phone. "Backbreaking, thankless work."

You prefer to spend your time schmoozing, I think. Aloud, I say, "I groomed for my aunt, at Windy Hill Farm in Virginia. I liked it."

Jim finally glances up. "Windy Hill? Katherine Baldwin's Windy Hill Farm?"

Finally, I have his attention. "That's right. She's my father's sister. I lived with her when I was a teenager. That's where I learned to ride." And do everything else that matters when it comes to horses. Aunt Kate never left a thing out. Her precision was legendary in old Virginia equestrian circles, and that's really saying something.

"Well no kidding." Jim eyes me with new appreciation, as if I'm one of his fancy jumper friends in the Grand Prix arena. "Katherine Baldwin's niece. I'd lead with that around here, if I were you."

"Excuse me?" I blink at him, confused. "You want me to go around introducing myself as someone's niece?"

"Well, not just someone. Katherine Baldwin...she was a very big deal back in the eighties and nineties, wasn't she? All those championships, the Washington International, the National Horse Show. And she's been incredibly influential as a breeder. Do you have any Windy Hill horses in the barn?"

"No," I say flatly, drawing back and resting my hand on the table to keep it from curling into a fist. I don't need my aunt's name as a calling card; I can ride and I should be able to do all this quite well on my own. "And I've be*en* here quite a while, Jim. I don't think I need to walk around introducing myself to everyone for a second time, dropping my aunt's name."

"I'm just saying, if you want a password into some of the bigger trainers' barns around Legends, mentioning your aunt is not a bad place to start."

I look at him for a moment, trying to make up my mind about a few things—whether I actually like him, if I feel like dating is necessary to become a well-rounded adult human, if I'm hungry enough to demand he take me to the dinner I was promised or if I should just leave and stop for a burger on the way back to the farm. Jim is turning out to be a real disappointment.

But, I remind myself, we are people lacking in social skills, people who have instincts around horses, but not necessarily around others of our own species.

I decide to give him one more chance.

The thing is, I'm very hungry, even after the eclair.

"Maybe we shouldn't talk about horses," I suggest. "Or watch them. Maybe we should just go eat some dinner, like some real food, and get to know each other."

Jim pauses a beat too long before he agrees.

"Let's head into the hotel," he says at last, standing and pocketing that damn phone of his. "We can grab dinner at the Bit and Bridle."

"That would be nice," I say, moderately impressed at the upgrade from the original offer of pizza. "I haven't eaten there before." The hotel restaurant is a little outside my price range, like most things that aren't taco trucks or gas station delis.

There's a crowd at the bar inside Bit and Bridle, most of them shouting about a football game. I have to swallow my annoyance at that; why can't we just have one place that's all horses, all the time, without having to deal with all those silly human-only sports? And then I remember that I've suggested to Jim we don't talk about horses, and I realize that I'm the unreasonable one here. What the hell else are we going to talk about?

"So, um, you seem to know everyone in the Grand Prix," I say, once I have a napkin in my lap and a wine list in my hand. "That's fun. I've only seen you at the weekday shows, so I didn't realize you were so busy here. Do you have a GP horse yourself, or do you mostly do sales, or teach…"

I trail off as he grins at me. "Thought we weren't talking about horses," he says.

"I realized that was a no-go," I admit. "I don't have anything else going on in my life, do you?"

"Not really." He glances at the football game. "Unless you like the Patriots?"

"Not at all."

"Horses it is. I mostly teach, to answer your question," he says. "And of course sales. That's an important part of any teaching outfit, right? But I keep my eyes open for the right horse. Lauren's looking for me. She knows some folks down in south Florida who might be ready to invest. I did my early years on the circuit with Manning Stables and—"

And he's off again, name-dropping like *that's* his specialty. I only know about a third of the people he's trying to impress me with, mostly from doing deals with Malcolm's sales horses. While he yammers on about all the fancy riders he knows, I peruse the wine list, pretending to have a real opinion about what kind of vintage is going in my mouth (anything over fifteen dollars is exotic to me). Then he says something that surprises me into attention.

"Now, Cary Davies, that's an interesting proposition you've got going on there."

What? My gaze flicks up to his. "Proposition?" I repeat. And then, "You know who he is?"

"I got word he was in town," Jim says, like he's on the coconut telegraph of former child-star movement. "Decided to play it cool, though. My idea is, he might be ready to buy into a horse or two. For himself, for a rider, either one. Unless you think you got him on the hook for an eventer already?"

I shake my head, breathing out a little laugh. I'm oddly relieved that's what he thinks I'm doing with Cary...and amused, too. "You've got it all wrong with Cary," I tell him. "He's not here to invest in a show horse."

"But he's connected in Hollywood, right?"

I nod reluctantly. "I guess?"

Jim leans forward, looking like he's got something he wants to school me on. "Listen, if a man with money, or a man who knows people with money, walks into my barn, he's walking out buying into a horse or I've done something wrong. You telling me you aren't trying to get him to buy into something of yours? Surely you've got some syndicate that needs fresh investment."

"Absolutely not," I retort, not sure if I should feel like a spring chicken for looking at Cary solely as a student on a timeline, or like a businesswoman of remarkable ethics for not chasing him for every penny in his bank account. I don't even know if he really *has* any money. He's had a moderately successful YouTube series—how much could that really pay a man, anyway? Could he have riches in a trust fund leftover from his child-star days?

I think about the way Jim was letting Cary egg him on, explaining the ins and outs of every horse and rider on the course with remarkable patience, and realize with disgust that it was a game the entire time. That whole schtick wasn't about showing off how many pretty girls in breeches he knows. Evie and I had it completely wrong.

Jim was trying to hook Cary into wanting to invest in a horse, using his Big-Time Connected Trainer act.

And what's more, he did that all the while believing that's what I wanted from Cary, too. He was perfectly content to try to steal my mark while I stood there and watched. Unbelievable!

I chew on my tongue as Jim prattles on about the proper way to hook a millionaire, and when the waiter finally appears, I order a twenty-five dollar glass of wine, just to see Mr. Moneybags squirm.

Chapter Seventeen

"AND THEN WHAT happened?" Evie asks, holding out her hand.

I put a jumping whip into her gloved fingers and she tucks it into her grasp alongside her reins. Bucky, her tall and talented bay eventer, leans against the bit and makes a choking sound, sticking his tongue out of the side of his mouth.

"Ugh, Bucky! Please stop doing that," Evie begs him.

"Where did he pick *that* up?" I fiddle with Bucky's bit, but there's nothing wrong with the fit or the way the simple snaffle sits across the horse's tongue. "You're fine."

Bucky pokes his tongue out and makes the choking noise again. He's nodding his head, too, eyes bright with mischief. It's all a game to him.

"Auditioning for stupid horse tricks?" I ask him.

"Yep." Evie sighs and nudges him into a walk, circling him around me. We're standing in the sunny jumping arena behind Malcolm's barn. I stopped by with a tray of coffees for everyone in the barn and the intense need to talk out my disastrous date with Jim. Evie managed two sips of her coffee before Malcolm asked her if she was going to fall behind schedule for the day. At the moment, I felt bad about it, because keeping Malcolm on a tight schedule had been one of *my* contributions to Fine Day Farm, and I'd taught Evie how to write and manage the schedule herself—effectively creating the situation she found herself in right now.

But he wouldn't be so successful today if I hadn't done it, and if he wasn't a successful trainer, then Evie's path never would have led to him. So on second thought, I don't feel that guilty, after all.

"I don't know where he learned that sound," Evie sighs again, looking down at her gleaming horse with the same kind of resignation a mother reserves for a toddler trying to eat a telephone. "He just started doing it one day. Probably from some delinquent horse he got stabled across from at an event, I guess."

"Well, at least he's only doing it for fun and he's not complaining about the bit," I say, because grasping at straws is what the optimist equestrian does to stay sane.

"Yeah, there's *that*. Now tell me what happened after you ordered the pricey wine! Malcolm would have made the most ferocious face at me."

"But he's in love with you," I remind her. "And you're an established couple. That kind of stability makes a man cheaper. He doesn't have to impress you."

"So you're saying that because he's trying to get into your riding pants, Jimmy-boy went with it."

"He went with it, didn't even make a peep. And then he ordered the filet. I think he was trying to prove he wasn't afraid of a big bill."

"Hot."

"Truly." We roll our eyes at each other, on the same page about the wonderful Jim. "I got chicken. Cheaped *myself* out."

"Maybe he can take that big-money energy and put it into taking you on a shopping spree at a tack shop."

"If only. When we met I told him I was on my way to buy tack, so if I suggest it now, he'll definitely think I have a problem."

"So, did you take him home?"

I burst into laughter. "To my attic above the tack room? No, Evie, I did not. I would have felt like Little Orphan Annie if I showed him my tiny apartment, after all that big-name trainer talk he threw at me." My tiny apartment and my shabby, third-hand furniture. My stacks of clothes, because I don't have a closet. And my banged-up kitchen cabinets, and the hollow door to the bathroom with a hole kicked through one side of it. My apartment has been through the wringer. I've never wanted to ask Nathan about the previous tenants, but they seemed to have some anger issues.

"I don't think Little Orphan Annie entertained male companions," Evie says thoughtfully. She picks up the reins and moves Bucky into a twenty-meter circle, walking around me so we can still shout to each other. "I also think she was rich. So what, you went to his place?"

"Ugh, no. First date, Evie? I wasn't out there looking to score. I just hoped he'd be a nice guy who liked the same things I did. And he's really not. Besides horses, I mean."

"So, when are you seeing him again?"

I sigh. She's got my number. "Next Saturday."

Evie shakes her head and urges Bucky to lengthen his walk. "Come on, lazy daisy," she chides. "It's a jumping day, stretch out a little." To me, she calls, "What are you getting out of this, Alison?"

It's a fair question. Nothing I've told her should endear her to Jim. He was pompous, he was a show-off (is that the same thing as being pompous?) and he was definitely more interested in my aunt—and even Cary—than in me. Not exactly the recipe for everlasting love, or even a satisfying few weeks of knocking boots. So why am I seeing him again?

"He asked me to come back out with him," I admit lamely, shrugging. "I don't get a lot of invitations, I guess."

"Oh, Alison," Evie says, voice full of sympathy.

I watch her nudge Bucky into a trot and the pair of them move around me in a big, bouncy gait. And I realize suddenly that everything is backwards in my life, at least, backwards from where it was just six months ago. When Evie showed up at Fine Day Farm, she was very much in crisis, and Malcolm and I took her in. Now look at her!

Evie on top of that big, flashy horse while I stand here on the ground; Evie running Fine Day Farm with precision while I struggle at my dilapidated rental. Evie in control of her life and moving forward at the pace of Bucky's fine trot while I try to keep one jump ahead of my demons. Evie connecting with the horse who dropped into her life like a gift from the eventing gods while I'm struggling to recapture the magic of my first ride with Hansie, a horse I can barely afford. Evie living a life of rapturous love with my former boss, while I accept a second date with a guy I truly dislike.

When did my life stop behaving in such an orderly and satisfying fashion? I don't really have to ask myself that, because the answer is obvious. It was the day I decided to stop saving and investing, and put every single dime I'd amassed into starting my own farm. It was the day I chose to leave Malcolm's established business in order to try establishing my own.

I've been tumbling like a falling star ever since.

And so now, when a self-absorbed, emotionally unavailable guy like Jim who has his professional shit together and knows everyone on the prestigious jumper circuit seems interested in me, instead of telling him to hit the road as I should, I feel like, "Hey, at least someone wants to see more of me."

This isn't even rock bottom, I think morosely, kicking at the tidy white footing of the jumping arena. I have so much farther I can fall.

CARY'S AT THE barn when I get back, fiddling with the new flowerbed outside the barn doors. I smile to myself as soon as I see him bent over the flowers. He looks like an overgrown child, wearing baggy cargo shorts and a surf shop t-shirt, watering the flowers with a contented look on his expressive face.

He holds up a hand as I pull my truck next to his SUV, and accidentally sprays my windshield with water in the process.

"Whoops," he laughs as I hop down from the cab. "Forgot I had a hose in my hand."

"It's fine. A million degrees out and I don't think it's going to rain today, so a little extra water won't hurt anything."

"It really is hot," he agrees. "Did you want to skip my lesson today?"

"Your lesson?" I give him a surprised look. "Yesterday, you told me that I was a terrible riding instructor. You sure you want one?"

"That was mean of me, and I said I was sorry." Cary switches off the hose and gives me a contrite puppy-dog look. "I really am sorry. I was out of line. I got frustrated with all the walking around the arena, that's all. No excuse, I know."

"I'm not a yeehaw kick-'em-up kind of rider," I tell him, as if there was ever any room for confusion on that point. "If you ever got that impression, just know right now I'm always going to choose the opposite path."

"You never gave me that kind of impression," he assures me fervently. "I don't think you could ever give that impression, even by accident."

I glance down at my breeches and paddock boots, which I put on this morning like a uniform before I went over to Fine Day Farm.

"Yeah, casual isn't really my vibe," I agree, and crack a smile when Cary laughs. "Come on into the office when you're done with the plants and have some air conditioning," I say, heading into the barn. "I'll be in there, going over boring admin work until we get a friendly cloud to block some of that sun."

Or an unfriendly cloud. Either is acceptable on a steamy day like this, I think, as I swing open the office door and breathe in the slightly mildewed scent of the window air conditioner. Lily Marlene looks up from my chair, exactly where she was sleeping when I left this morning, then hops down and heads for the open door, pausing to stretch and brush against my paddock boots on the way out. "Bye, baby girl," I tell her. "Make good choices."

Her tail flicks to let me know that if she makes a choice, it's a good one, simply because she's the one who made it. Confidence, I think, watching her disappear around the corner. I should be so confident. I should call Jim and tell him what I really think of him, then get a whole bunch of clients and make a ton of cash just to annoy him.

There's something in the middle missing from that plan. If I knew what it was, I'd be profitable. Solvent, even.

I'm flicking through spreadsheets and wishing I still had some of the money I used to pay the deposits and buy equipment for this place when Cary pokes his head inside. "You're looking grumpy," he observes.

"I *am* grumpy. Enter at your own risk."

He pops inside immediately, a huge smile on his face. "Let me cheer you up."

I shake my head at him. "How? And before you answer that, can I ask you something? Last night, did you feel like Jim was trying to manipulate you into buying in on a horse?"

Cary's face cycles through several expressions before he settles on amused skepticism. "Is that what he's doing? Man, L.A. would eat that guy alive."

"So, you're not planning to invest in a Grand Prix horse for him."

"Absolutely not." Cary plunks himself down in the chair opposite mine. "In fact, I thought he was kind of a blow-hard. If I were going to buy a horse, it would not be from him."

"A blow-hard—well, then, why were you hanging out with him?"

"I was hanging out with *you*," Cary says, lifting his eyebrows in surprise. "You needed rescuing from that guy. I didn't want to leave you alone with him. I was surprised when you left, actually, but now that I know you were trying to protect me...that's really sweet, Alison."

"I was on a date!" I protest. "I wasn't trying to protect you!"

Wasn't it obvious I was on a date? Was it really so surprising that someone wanted to take me out, so shocking that Cary couldn't even see it?

Cary swings his chair back and forth, still looking somewhat incredulous. "You were on a *date* with that guy?"

"Yes," I snap, thoroughly annoyed. "He's a successful trainer, and he asked me on a date, and—"

"That was a *date*." Cary looks at the ceiling. "They do things different in Ocala, don't they, Lord?"

"Who do you think you're talking to?"

"Zeus," Cary answers promptly. "The God of Bad Dates. Have you read any mythology? That dude had problems with consent."

I shake my head at him. "You're unbelievable."

"*You're* unbelievable," Cary counters. "But in lots of ways, not just the extremely dramatic one that you seem to be attributing to me."

At this point, I am sure I've lost control of the conversation, or even the ability to follow it. So I just gesture at my laptop and say, "I have some financial stuff to finish."

"After that, can we ride?"

"Not while it's this hot."

"But there's a friendly cloud," Cary says. "Just like you wanted."

And right on cue, thunder rumbles.

It's almost like this guy can make it rain.

Chapter Eighteen

THE CLOUDS STICK around after a quick downburst of rain, and a breeze that can actually be considered cool flits through the barn, flicking at Nando's forelock as he stands in the cross-ties waiting to be groomed.

"It feels like fall," I remark, throwing myself into a director's chair Cary has left sitting by the office door. "This is the first time I've gotten to say that this year."

"This is fall?" Cary grins at me from over Nando's back. "Two days into September, you get one nice breeze and you're changing seasons?"

"In Florida, we take what we can get," I inform him. "We can't all be blessed and from California where the sun always shines and the temperature is always eighty."

"That's not even close to reality in Los Angeles. You're thinking of San Diego...sorta. Not quite. I think you're describing a place you imagined."

"Fine. Are you actually from L.A.? Or did you just move there to be an actor?"

"Oh, I'm from there. Born and bred in the city of angels."

I cock a skeptical eyebrow. "That's really what you locals call it, huh?"

"No." Cary tosses a rubber currycomb into the grooming box. "Nothing but net, oh *yeah!* No, I just thought I'd call it that so you'd feel sexy and cosmopolitan while we're talking about the Sunset Strip and Rodeo Drive and, uh, Knott's Berry Farm."

"Sexy and cosmopolitan!" I snort inelegantly, then wish I hadn't. "That's not likely. I have no interest in all that."

"Ever been?"

"You just told me I made up my idea of L.A., remember?"

"A person can have a faulty memory."

"I've never been," I admit, giving in. "Never even to California."

"It's very sexy," he says.

"Oh, stop. It's a *place.*"

"Well, what do *you* find sexy, then?" he asks, busying himself with a body brush. He flicks it along Nando's chestnut coat with sure, even strokes. The guy's a quick learner.

Probably you have to be, to work in film. And then to build a career out of learning other people's jobs as quickly as possible.

"What do I find sexy? A sub-twenty-five score on my dressage test," I say, leaning forward and resting my chin on my hands. "A perfectly braided mane that I didn't have to braid myself. White breeches without any last-minute slobber stains on them before I go into the ring."

Cary grins, still leaning into Nando with his brush. "I didn't ask what you *liked*. I asked what you find *sexy.*"

"All of those things turn me on," I tell him.

Cary turns slowly and gives me a very eloquent look.

I match it, turning up my lips slightly to give him a saucy little smile.

"I'll remember that," Cary promises—or warns.

An excited little flutter tickles my nerve endings, like a feather brushed along my fingers, up my arms, across my chest.

Oh, he's such a flirt!

"Sure you will." I lean back in my chair and cross my legs at the knee, toes pointed. The feather slips its way up the nape of my neck, leaving goosebumps behind. "And when you show up at four a.m. to get my horses braided before an event, just remember that I can tell if you rush at the end and make the last few braids bigger than the rest. And I *will* rip them out and re-do them myself."

"Does perfection ever exhaust you?" Cary asks, peering at me curiously.

"All the time."

"You should ride with me," he remarks.

"What?" Sometimes this guy's quick changes of direction in conversation are enough to make me dizzy. "What does that have to do with anything?"

"I want a riding buddy. We're doing the same thing today that we did yesterday, right? I'm feeling Nando's motion and learning to move with it?"

I nod.

"So, come do it with me. It would be more fun with a friend."

"I can't do that."

"Why, because you don't have horses to ride?" He looks up and down the barn aisle with elaborate slowness. "It could save you some time."

Actually, he's kind of on to something. I could hack a horse out and it would be good for their fitness—and it's not like I have this guy going around on a lunge line like I do with the little kids. Maybe it's not such a bad idea to hop on a horse and walk alongside him for half an hour.

"Okay," I say.

"Okay?" He looks surprised. "Seriously? I never thought you'd give in so easily."

"Yeah, well, I need to take Hansie for an easy walk today. I'll do it with you."

"Oh, I get you with *Hansie*, too?" Cary claps his hands. "I feel so honored! And I can get some video work done from the saddle, too. I'll bet Nando won't mind if I use one hand to hold up my phone."

I've taken entire video call conversations from Nando's saddle, so I know the horse won't mind.

But I'm not sure I'm still keen on this idea of filming Hansie's early days with me. The project seemed fun and innocent at first, but since things have been going poorly with him, I really don't know that we want a record of it floating around. Some things are best forgotten. Like Marlee's mom filming her daughter bopping around in Nando's saddle—in a few years, Marlee isn't going to want that video getting out, but it'll already be on Facebook, to haunt her for as long as that website lasts.

And what if Cary doesn't know to be discreet with footage of a tense, unhappy horse, and shows it to people because he thinks Hansie was just being high-spirited? If I reach any level of success with the horse, I won't want old video making the rounds. Not when so many difficult moments could be taken out of context.

"Maybe we better not do the movie," I say.

Cary tilts his head. "But what if he's better today? You don't want to miss the ride that turns it around for him. And maybe what Hansie *really* needs is a walk around the pasture with his old pal Nando. Maybe today's the day he cheers up."

I start to remind him Hansie really doesn't know Nando; they don't even get turned out together. But Cary looks so pleased with his idea, so hopeful, that I don't have the heart to bring him down.

"We'll see," I say instead, and head into the tack room to get another grooming kit.

IT'S AMAZING, THE way Cary always gets his way. I'm too in awe of it to really be annoyed, fascinated by how his easygoing smile opens whatever locked door he happens upon. The guy wants to ride out of the arena, and despite all my protests, that's exactly what ends up happening. How does he do it? What's it like to live such a charmed life?

Side by side, our horses stroll through the knee-deep grass of the back pasture, a sprawling few acres which I always hoped would be scattered with jumps and a few cross-country obstacles. The time for that, obviously, has not yet materialized. Instead, it's just a mess of somewhat weedy grazing and a scattering of scrubby trees which have needed pruning for at least a decade and throw dead branches across the field every time a windy storm blows through. Despite its messiness, the field is a pleasant one; if I look past the obvious tidy-up projects awaiting me, I can even relax out here.

The farthest fence line is lined with grand old live oaks, their long and undulating branches studded with resurrection ferns that wave in a verdant fan, deliriously happy with the rain that has just washed over them. They're gorgeous at any time. Right now, they're especially beautiful.

The rain-darkened bark of the trees is in deep contrast to the newly refreshed grass spreading around them; beneath the cloudy sky, the green pasture seems to glow. It might be the prettiest time of any day in Florida: after the storms, yet before the sunlight, with departing clouds in the distance so dark they are more blue than gray.

I take a happy breath, sucking in the clean and humid air. There's still a soft breeze; I know it will fade in a few minutes and we'll be left with a stuffy summer afternoon, but for now, for this fleeting moment, life is glorious.

Cary looks over at me and smiles.

I find myself smiling back.

He holds up his phone with his left hand to get some footage of Hansie moving contentedly. "You guys look so happy," he remarks. "You should ride out here more often."

I ride out here more than he thinks, but of course I can't tell him that, or he'll think we should do all his lessons out here. And knowing Cary, he'll get his way.

Normally I wouldn't allow a beginner to ride out of the arena, let alone take a horse into my largest pasture, but Nando is reliable and that western saddle gives Cary plenty to hold on to, should the horse spook or take a few quick steps. And he's very comfortable in the tack, something I've noticed more and more as his first few lessons have gone by. Cary might complain about learning to sway with the horse's motion, but he's doing a damn fine job of it, and it gives him a secure, natural look as Nando walks along beneath him, the horse's head held low and ears swinging in a relaxed position.

I'll make a cowboy of that man yet.

Hansie seems oddly relaxed, too, to the point where I find myself touching his neck a few times with the back of my hand, trying to feel if he has an elevated temperature. The constant tension in his back seems to have vanished, and his walk swings with such a long stride that I occasionally have to rein him back to let Nando catch up. His ears swivel between watching the path ahead, capturing the movements of squirrels bouncing along the tree trunks, and flicking back to listen to Cary and me as we chat idly. In fact, Hansie is acting for all the world like an old, contented trail horse, out for an afternoon stroll on the same paths that he treads every day of the year.

"Nothing wrong with a little field dressage," I concede finally. "If Hansie works better out here, we can do some schooling out of the arena."

"Maybe he doesn't want to school for a while," Cary suggests. He has his phone up to film, so he catches my annoyed glance on video. "Maybe he wants a break," he says.

"Well, he picked the wrong time of year to want a break," I say jokingly. "It's crunch time."

Cary lowers the phone, and I notice a crease in his smooth forehead. "Maybe this is what he needs, though," Cary says. "He needs to have some fun and get used to you. You could just ride him out there, like this, for a while. Or you could put him in the trailer and take him somewhere fun. What about the forest?"

I laugh shortly. "*Ocala* National Forest? You want to take him out there?"

"Well, what's wrong with that?"

"The forest is full of crazy people. Hunters, survivalists living in the scrub, Juggaloes..."

"Really?" He looks at me with interest. "Ocala has Juggaloes? I'm surprised you even know what they are."

"Please, everyone knows about the fandom of the rap group Insane Clown Posse," I joke. "Even Ocala horse girls."

"I guess so. I wonder if they're disappointed they're so mainstream," Cary says thoughtfully. "I mean, can't we assume that horse girls are as mainstream as it gets?"

"I feel like you're insulting me, somehow."

"Just finding common cultural touchstones," Cary says. "What do you know about musical theater?"

This conversation is derailing in the weirdest way.

"Nothing," I say. "Anyway, I don't go out there. It's not that nice, anyway. Deep sandy paths and a lot of pine trees, mostly."

"Oh. Well, that's disappointing. The survivalists sound a little scary, too."

"Yeah. I think we're better off staying in our pasture."

"Fair enough. Nice and safe here, I guess."

"As safe as anything can be." I don't mean to sound grim; that's just the reality of horses. And life, I guess. It's not safe. You do what you can despite that.

Nando takes a funny step and lurches a little. Cary grabs at the saddle horn, caught off-balance, then grins at me. "Whoa! That felt a little bit like a boat hitting a swell."

"A boat! Are you a yachtie, too?"

Hansie reaches for a juicy clump of grass and I let the reins slide through my fingers, not bothering to push him on when he comes to a complete halt and starts chowing down. Nando does the same thing, nearly yanking the reins through Cary's hands.

I don't bother hiding a satisfied grin as Cary yelps and grabs at them. "You almost had to dismount to get your reins, Mr. Trail Ride."

"That was close," he agrees. "Phew! Well, yes, I can get around a protected harbor on a clear day with no swells, but I generally prefer to be a guest on someone else's boat. Much safer and easier access to drinks. What about you? Ever get on the water?"

I've noticed how our conversations seem to veer in and out of personal space. Jokes, then a question about my past. And it's all orchestrated by Cary. When I ask a question, he'll give me a surface answer, but not really dig into the depths to give me a real story or anything, and then he'll turn it back around and ask me for my version of the answer, hoping that I'll give him a story.

It's like he doesn't want me to notice that he's not giving away much of anything about himself. All I really know is that he's from Los Angeles, he's been using self-produced work to survive outside of the movie business but he wants back in, and that he enjoys boating if someone else is doing the hard work of captaining the boat.

Not a ton to go on, really, and suddenly I'm consumed with curiosity. I want to know everything about him. That's what happens when you're withholding. The other person gets thirstier and thirstier while they're trying to live on little drips and dribbles, until they want a whole bucket, all at once.

"I don't boat," I answer at last, and Cary waits for more, but I don't have anything else to say about it. He's not going to get my whole life story out of me without giving me anything in return. Anyway, there's nothing interesting to say about it. I grew up in the foothills of the Blue Ridge. Not a lot of boating going on there.

A silence stretches between us. I watch him grow more uncomfortable as each second ticks by, his shoulders stiffening, his heels coming up. He stops looking as though he's comfortably settled around his horse, and starts to look like a beginner again, perched on top.

The horses grow bored with the grassy patch and walk on. Cary lurches a little in the saddle, as if he's having trouble finding Nando's rhythm.

"Where do you live now?" I ask him, breaking the silence.

It's the simplest of questions, but when Cary turns to look at me, I can see him preparing to deflect, to lob it right back at me.

But before he can say anything, Nando stumbles again, harder this time, and Cary rolls right over his shoulder and onto the ground.

Chapter Nineteen

"CARY!" I CAN'T help the unprofessional shriek that escapes my throat. I mean, the guy is wearing a helmet and everything, but he doesn't know how to fall properly and I'm afraid he fell wrong and hit some hidden chunk of limestone—this part of Florida is scattered with outcroppings of ghostly white rock. If he did, he might have broken his arm or his collarbone, or worse.

This is my fault. I shouldn't have tried to throw him off guard; the poor guy forgot how to ride because I wouldn't just give in and let him run the conversation. Comfort zones are so important—for other people, I mean; I don't allow myself that luxury.

Meanwhile, I can't hop off right away to check on him, because while Nando stops and stares down at his fallen rider in quiet astonishment, Hansie finds the whole situation very alarming and bounces backwards, spinning on his hind legs in a quick, agile bid to head back to the barn and leave this terrifying scene behind. Horses are very every-man-for-themselves; there is no question of him sticking around to reassure Nando that he didn't do anything wrong. There is only flight.

"Ho back, ho back, *ho back!*" I demand, reining back hard on Hansie, spinning him around again so that he can't take us back to the barn.

Nando stares at me from above his fallen rider, his ears pricked and his eyes wide, as if to say, "But I *did* ho back, and I'm standing right here!"

"Just *ho*," I snarl at Hansie, and as the horse finally comes to a staggering halt, I kick my feet free of the stirrups and hop down. By now, Cary is already pushing himself out of the patch of thick grass he ended up in. There's a smear of manure on his face that is *very* unfortunate. "Oh, shit," I say.

"Yeah, I smell it," Cary sighs, getting to his feet. He rubs a hand tentatively along his cheek and looks at the residue on his fingers with resignation. "All I can say is, the shit broke my fall. Like landing on a pillow."

"Oh god, that's so disgusting." Limestone would have been damaging, but a manure pile is just gross.

I drag Hansie forward and snatch Nando's reins. The school horse gazes at me in quiet astonishment, then leans past me and gives Hansie a sharp nip on the cheek. Hansie jumps backwards and snorts, giving Nando a look of pure hurt in response. "Kids," I say. "Be nice to each other. Nando, I know Hansie abandoned you in your hour of need, but some friends are just not helpful in a crisis, okay?"

"I'm not going to test your friendship by asking you to help me mount again," Cary offers, flicking at the manure on his face. "I'll walk this guy back to the barn."

"No, you should mount." I eye him, looking for a clean spot where I can put my hands and give him a leg-up. There isn't much of one. His entire left side is spattered with some fairly moist manure. "I'm sure there's a tree limb or a stump you could stand on."

Cary's grin flashes at that. "Precisely the kind of help I would expect," he says. "This is not a hands-on experience. Well, it is for me.

Have I passed some kind of rite of initiation, by falling in a manure pile?"

I don't have the heart to tell him that neither I nor anyone I know has ever fallen directly into a manure pile. This is a true first for me. "Sure," I lie. "You're a real rider now."

Cary looks grimly satisfied. He swivels his head, looking for a likely mounting block, and at the same time, we both spot a long, low limb reaching down from a live oak a few dozen feet away.

"I'll try getting a boost from that nice tree over there," he says.

It's an effort to convince Nando that he should line up alongside the hanging branch, which dives all the way to the ground, balancing the massive tree's weight before climbing back up towards the sky. I finally get Hansie involved, and he seems to enjoy shoving his barrel up against Nando's nose to make the horse hold still as Cary tries to find a spot along the tree limb where he's hoisted high enough to get a foot in the stirrup. The branch shakes and rustles and creaks dramatically, giving both horses a case of the spooky eyes, but I manage to keep them immobile so that poor Cary isn't forced to attempt hopping onto a moving target.

"Here we go!" he says finally, and mounts the horse with surprising capability.

"You're really a rider now," I blurt, impressed, and I mean it this time.

Cary grins, and a few flakes of manure fall from his cheek to his collar. "Yeah, I know."

UNDER RIPPLING GRAY skies, we ride the horses back to the barn, get them showered, and put them away with fresh hay. I can hardly bear to look at Cary, he's so filthy and streaked with manure, but at the same time, I want to look at him constantly, to assure myself he's okay. An odd nervousness has come over me, like a delayed reaction to seeing him fall, and there's a tremor in my hands as I hose off Hansie and give the horse a carrot for his trouble.

With Nando put away, Cary takes one look at himself in the bathroom mirror and comes out grimacing. "I'd better get out of here and clean up," he says, tugging at his ruined shirt. "Unless you want to just hose me off in the wash-stall?"

"If you have a change of clothes in your car, you can just use my shower," I suggest, surprising myself. I never invite people up there for a reason; I don't want anyone to see my tiny living quarters. Cary wouldn't make fun of my apartment, though. And anyway, he's already leaned in the door and gotten a look, assuming his eyes weren't totally consumed with my moon-white thighs sticking out of my riding breeches or my hands covering my sports bra.

God, I can't believe that's the way we met.

"Thanks," Cary says, "but I don't have anything else to wear." He looks up and down the barn. "I really meant to help you do barn chores. Tell you what, what if I come back around seven and take you to dinner to make up for leaving so early?"

"Dinner, huh?" I think of my prior dinner plans. I had a hot date with a pot of pasta all planned out. It wouldn't exactly be missed. "Yeah, dinner would be nice, actually. You have a place in mind?"

"I was hoping you'd make a suggestion," Cary says. "Since you know the town and all. Anything but that giant equestrian center," he adds, shaking his head. "You can't just hang out at work like that all the time, Alison."

"Try and stop me," I say with a grin, but I agree to figure out a place for dinner that *isn't* Legends Equestrian Center, and Cary heads out into the cloudy afternoon, leaving a faint smell of manure in his wake.

I turn to Hansie, who is working his way through a pile of hay in his stall, and tip my forehead against the stall bars to watch him for a few moments. The horse looks content, his eyes quiet and his energy focused on his food—just as a healthy, happy horse should be.

"You really liked that ride out in the field today, didn't you?" I ask him. "Why is that? Why do you hate my ring, when you were clearly fine with Malcolm's arenas?"

Although, he hadn't been perfect in the covered arena, either. He'd spooked hard in that corner when Malcolm was warming him up, and he hadn't liked going near the corner again. The video that had sold me on the horse in the first place had all been taken out on the cross-country course. He'd been okay in the outdoor jumping arena, but Malcolm's outdoor ring is enormous.

What if Hansie's claustrophobic?

The idea makes me sigh. There will be a host of issues if Hansie has trouble with small riding arenas—not least that at the Novice level, eventing dressage tests take place in a small, forty by twenty-meter riding arena. If I'm constantly fighting a horse who hates feeling caged in, our judged tests are going to turn out yucky.

But at least I'd have a good reason for his tense body and behavior, and with a reason, I can find a solution.

"I'm going to figure you out, Hansie," I tell the horse.

He keeps chewing, nosing through his hay for the morsels of alfalfa leaves that fall to the floor.

And as for dinner with Cary tonight, I think...well, I'm going to try again to get some real answers out of him. I can't have all the new men in my life acting all mysterious and confusing. It's too stressful. I want to know where he lives for real, not just the vague answer of Los Angeles. I want to know what drew him into acting. I want to know more about him, in general. Cary's a charmer with the witticisms and the innocent smiles, but I'm curious about who the *real* Cary is, the one who isn't all about Hollywood facades and capturing his best side on camera.

Because I'm pretty sure I saw his best side earlier today, and it was streaked with manure, smiling through the embarrassment. There's nothing quite like a guy who can laugh at himself.

"Imagine if Jim fell in a manure pile," I say to Lily Marlene, who has come over to rub against my legs, purring until I scoop her up for an ear-scratch. "He'd probably kill himself if anyone saw him as filthy as Cary was today."

Lily Marlene hums a rusty tune, pressing her head against my throat.

"You're right," I say, "Jim is probably a jerk. You're a very wise and all-knowing cat. So who should I date instead? Because if you haven't noticed, I'm pretty much on my own here, and I like the idea of having someone to eat dinner with every now and then."

Lily Marlene gives me a sharp glance with those olive-green eyes of hers.

"Yeah," I say, shaking my head. "I'm *aware* I'm having dinner with Cary tonight. But he doesn't count. He's not going to be around that long."

The cat struggles in my grip and jumps down, and I try not to read too much into it. She never wants to be held for very long.

Lily Marlene is content to be the lone queen bee of her kingdom. I should really take more life lessons from my barn cat.

Chapter Twenty

"YOU HAVE TO be kidding," Cary says, staring through his windshield.

"What? You're going to love this place."

He points at the restaurant in front of us. "This is a Mexican grocery store," he says.

"And restaurant," I remind him. "See, it says right there. Above the sign that says 'tacos'. Are you telling me you don't like tacos?"

"I'm from southern California," Cary says. "I like *real* tacos."

"Are you saying you didn't like the ones we had last week?"

"They were fine, but they weren't like SoCal tacos. This is Florida, Alison. Admit your tacos will be inferior here."

"Oh, buddy. Those are fighting words." I unbuckle my seat-belt. "You're going to take that back, I guarantee you."

I freely admit that when Cary asked me for a good restaurant recommendation, I struggled a little. There are probably some decent places in downtown Ocala, but I never go down there and so everything would be a mystery to me. Ocala also features an outpost of every chain restaurant known to mankind, but I get the feeling he isn't looking for a deep-fried onion or a half-pound burger. He doesn't have the physique of a guy who indulges in a lot of fatty food, and I respect that lifestyle choice. As for my personal favorites, I lean towards quick and close to home, which means learning which gas stations and taco trucks in the area are best and cleanest.

But for a restaurant where we actually sit down indoors, not at a picnic table alongside a highway or a greasy bag we take back into the truck to eat in the air-conditioning? Well, maybe it's lacking in charm, but for delicious food, I'm not afraid to take friends to the nearby Mexican grocery-slash-restaurant.

"This place is perfect," I say, as Cary dogs my footsteps through the front doors. "You're just going to have to trust me, okay? Horse girls know how to find good food on the cheap."

"I was willing to pay more than twenty bucks for dinner," Cary says. "If that wasn't clear before."

"Great! That means we can get dessert."

We push past a rack of Bimbo snack cakes and I lead him around a case stuffed full of baked goods—conchas and guava pastries and fat loaves of fresh bread. A doorway beyond opens into a little restaurant. It's half-empty, but the cluttered table-tops reveal that a lively early dinner hour has already passed.

I lead Cary to one of the few clean tables and a girl with a long ponytail gives it a spray of bleach water anyway, nodding and smiling as she wipes it down. She sets down menus, loud with color and illustrations. It's entirely in Spanish.

"Do you speak Spanish?" Cary asks, impressed.

"I do not," I say, "but I can get through an order without regrets."

"What do you recommend?" He looks resigned to his fate.

"The barbacoa, the carnitas, the chorizo, the pastor." I say, ticking off my favorite taco fillings on my fingers. "Red and green salsa, when she asks. I don't know which ones go with which tacos and I don't care. They're both perfect."

"Fine," he says. "But you're going to hear about how good California tacos are."

"I think you're wrong," I tell him, "and I cannot wait for your apology."

With chips and salsa on the table and two bottles of Modelo between us, we set into relentless idle chit-chat. Cary asks about the winter eventing schedule and I list all the events I want to do, and then list all the reasons I might not get through such an ambitious roster.

He assures me I can do it.

I remind him that he doesn't know anything about eventing or horses and has no idea the part that chance can play in it.

"We blame everything that goes wrong on the eventing gods," I add, watching him choke on a sip of beer as my words sink in.

"The eventing gods?" He lifts an eyebrow in an admirably practiced pose.

"Yes, someone started using that phrase years ago. I don't know who, but it stuck. You'll hear it all the time if you hang out with eventing people. Like, 'I just have to trust my horse and hope the eventing gods are kind,' before a tough cross-country course, that kind of thing."

"Are they often kind?"

"Almost never." I heap a scoop of salsa on a chip and pop it into my mouth. I glance over towards the kitchen to see if our tacos are on the way, and as always, the painting over the bar catches my eye.

In spirit, it's a combination of velvet Elvis kitsch and an earnest preschooler hitting the coloring pages with a new package of Crayolas. Flowers in lurid shades of red, purple, and yellow surround a green pasture; a mare and foal gaze out at diners with limpid brown eyes. To top it all off, a gleaming rainbow arches over the horses. It's simply the most magnificently unhinged painting I've ever seen.

Cary's gaze follows mine, and he chokes on a chip. "My god, that's a masterpiece," he gasps, once the chip has gone down.

I glance at him, skeptical. "It's a lot of things, but I don't know that it's a masterpiece."

"How can you say that? Look at the colors! The thick brush-strokes! The sense of chaos that somehow ekes through all the peace and plenty!" Cary is just getting warmed up. "I wish I had that painting on my living room wall. Nay, my bedroom. So that I can feel it watching me in my sleep, like a guardian angel."

I can't help the giggles bubbling out of me. "You're insane, you know that?" I chortle. "That painting is wild. I always think how crazy it would make my aunt Kate."

Cary looks at me curiously. "Does Aunt Kate hate joy?"

"She hates disorder," I say.

"Ah. Sounds like someone else I know."

"Hey, I'm not ashamed to be like my Aunt Kate. She's a legend in the horse world."

"The horse world," Cary echoes. "You know how funny it is when you guys say that? A whole world, where only your kind live."

"Like you don't live in a world of your own making, Hollywood," I snort.

"Fair, fair." Cary looks back at the painting. "What kind of art does Aunt Kate approve of?"

"Oh, hunting scenes, obviously. Landscapes. The English romantics, that kind of thing." I can feel the taut, reserved atmosphere of Aunt Kate's nineteenth-century farmhouse. Footsteps creaking on wooden floors, cream-colored drapes and burgundy walls in the living room, a writing desk beneath a wood-framed picture of a horse leaping a ditch alongside foxhounds on the scent, their mouths open and baying. "Very traditional," I say, and it almost feels like an understatement.

"Sounds homey," Cary says, and I hear the skepticism in his tone.

"It was home," I say. "But it was mostly work."

He gives me a concerned glance, opening his mouth to ask another question.

Luckily, the tacos arrive at that moment.

"Smell that," I command, as the server slips a foil-lined basket in front of me. The tacos are open corn tortillas, the filling smothered in chopped onions and cilantro. "Oh my god, so good."

Cary surveys his tacos with surprise. "These look...pretty good."

"Dude. I told you. I would never lie about tacos."

"Would you lie about other things?"

I'm already stuffing a taco in my mouth, so I just nod in reply.

Cary grins and shakes his head, like that's exactly what he expected me to say.

WE CLEAN OUR plates in about five minutes, which is normal for me whenever I come here. These tacos are too good to be eaten slowly, and anyway the soft corn tortillas just split and go all over if you do something crazy like set them down for a minute to take a drink. I'm scooping up the last of my pastor filling, chasing little bits of pineapple and pork with a tortilla chip, when a shadow falls over the table. I look up with a smile, ready to greet a fellow equestrian, and am slightly dismayed to find it's Jim.

"Goodness," I say, choking a little. "I didn't expect to see you here."

"Late sales showing, and this is the closest food to my place," Jim says. "Lucky me, right?" And he glances between Cary and me pointedly, clearly asking me what I'm up to with this guy.

"Pretty lucky," Cary says blandly. "We had to drive all the way across town to get here."

Is it me, or did he emphasize the word *we?*

"Cary helped me out at the farm today," I say. "He's learning how to manage a barn."

"Really?" Jim asks him. "Why is that? Surely you're not getting seduced into the lifestyle by this one."

"What's that supposed to mean?" I demand, but Jim just shrugs.

"Oh, I like to learn new things," Cary drawls. "Never stop learning, they say."

"Mm-hmm. She get you in the saddle yet?"

"I'm learning to ride, yes," Cary says, suddenly defensive. He glances at me quickly, as if he's worried I'll mention his fall.

To Jim? He should give me more credit than that. Evie will hear about it for sure, but she's as far as the story will go.

"Well, that's good," Jim says. "Always nice to have a husband who can ride. In the *future,*" he chuckles, as Cary sits up straighter, clearly confused about where this conversation is going. "You know, it boosts your value. Especially if you stick around Ocala. You sticking around, Cary? I don't remember if we talked about that the other night."

I chew on my tongue, wishing Jim would lay off Cary. I know he's doing this to punish me for having dinner with him right after I said I'd go on another date with him, but is it any of his business?

I'm not sure, actually. What are the rules of dating, anyway? *Are* there rules, or is that just a sitcom thing?

God, I am prepared for just about every kind of horse situation, but I have no idea what to do about men.

Cary squares his jaw, then replies, "I'm going back to L.A. in a little over a month, to start shooting a new movie."

My heart sinks.

And then I have to ask myself why.

I *know* he's going to L.A. This was always the schedule.

And also he lives there, I remind myself, and he is literally only in Ocala to get good enough in the saddle to play a cowboy in a movie for a couple of horseback scenes. Not to learn to run a barn with you, not to hang out with you, not to be your best friend.

Not that I think of him in any of those ways. Cary's a student.

A nice student who took me to dinner. I need more like him.

"Well, too bad about that," Jim says. "I do fly out to do some business on the west coast from time to time. The Coachella circuit." And he pauses, leaving room for Cary to make a fool of himself.

"I'm a little old for Coachella," Cary says, walking right into the trap.

There it is. Jim's smile twinkles maliciously. "I'm taking about the *horse shows,*" he says. "In Coachella Valley. The Desert Circuit."

"Okay," I say, flattening my hands on the table. Time to end this nonsense; it isn't going to get any better. Cary didn't fall for Jim's investment trick, so now the guy is going to give him hell for hanging out with me? Maybe agreeing to see Jim again was the wrong move. Then again, free dinners don't grow in hay-fields, and I don't really want to start an argument with him in front of Cary.

Both men are looking at me expectantly.

"Nice to see you, Jim. I think we're still on for the weekend, right?" I give him a tight smile to let him know our next date is contingent on him not being an asshole.

"Can't," Jim says, confounding me. "Meant to tell you. Taking a horse in the evening class on Saturday. What about Friday night instead? We can come right back here and have tacos. I mean, I already know you like the place."

There's no way he's getting off with buying me a plate of three-buck tacos. This is payback for the twenty-five-dollar glass of wine.

Cary kicks me under the table, and I realize I'm hesitating. I glare at him while saying to Jim, "I'll text you about it, okay?"

"Sounds good. Bye, now." He waggles his fingers at Cary and gives me a wink before he heads off to pick up a takeout order from the counter. I watch him walk away, reflecting that Jim does not have a great personality, but he does have a fantastic ass.

Cary looks at me as I drag my gaze back to him. "You're not going to come back here and have tacos with him, are you?"

"How could I?" I say, trying to make a joke. "This is our place, Cary."

"Let's keep it that way," Cary says sternly, as if he's taking me fully seriously.

I like that about him. He takes me really, really seriously.

"I'm going to cancel our date," I tell him.

"Good," he says. "You deserve better."

"I know."

We look at each other for a moment. Cary opens his mouth as if to say something, then closes it again. Like he's second-guessing himself. I wonder what he's hiding from me. Probably nothing. He probably was going to ask where the restrooms were and then decided he can wait until we get back to the farm.

It's better not to read extra emotions where there aren't any.

"This was fun," I say, tapping him on the hand with one finger. "Even with *that interruption*. I really liked showing you that Ocala has the best tacos in the country."

"Shh," Cary says. "Bite your tongue. While I admit these were good enough to make me cry a little on the inside, you still can't beat

Cali for tacos. We have tacos back home that would take these tacos out back and whoop their asses."

I realize that my intent to ask him more about California and his home went completely by the wayside. Somehow, he made the entire conversation about me and the horses. Again.

This guy is *good* at deflecting. Or maybe he's just really nice about listening? Possibly too nice?

"I forgive you for your foolishness," I tell him. "But you're still wrong."

"Maybe someday I'll take you to my favorite taco stand and prove it to you," Cary says, and then his gaze flicks to the cashier. "Now, finish your beer so we can pay up and leave. I want to look at all those crazy pastries in the grocery store."

"Okay," I say meekly, tossing back the beer. I watch him for a moment, letting him get up and walk to the cashier without me. Did he just say he'd take me back to California and get me a taco from his favorite place?

I'm sure he's just messing around, but...hey. I'd go.

Anywhere for a good taco, right?

Chapter Twenty-One

A FEW DAYS pass with nothing much to say for them. Hansie is a pain in the arena, and a doll in the pasture—which is where I end up riding him each day when, in desperation, I give up trying to find feel and comfort from him in my riding ring. If he was just going to be a field hunter, I suppose we'd be in business. The horse loves galloping in the open. But there are *three* phases in eventing, and two of them take place in arenas. If I don't get this horse to settle in the next couple of weeks, I won't be able to compete with him in October as planned...and the closing date for the first event of the month is rushing up at me.

Meanwhile, Cary is busying himself around my farm, gardening like a busy bee when he isn't messing around with the horses or cleaning out stalls. I can't really say no to the barn help, even if he is a tad bit wasteful with shavings and tosses out more good hay than he should. His help actually opens up a few hours in my day, which gives me time to work on the admin side of business—specifically, getting some boarders in to help pay my bills. I take pictures of the barn with flowers bursting into color on either side of the door and send the pictures to Evie.

In return, Evie comes through for me, calling me up to say she has two clients she's going to send my way, both of them with two horses. "Four stalls will help you out, right?"

"A *ton*," I say, feeling dizzy with relief. "When are they coming?"

"Next week. They're in a rush *and* they don't want to be more than fifteen minutes from Malcolm," Evie says. "Good job with the flowers! Now you can skip staining the stall fronts for another season."

This isn't as comforting as Evie probably thinks, because now all I can see is the glaring raw wood lining the barn aisle. I should have stained them...

Suddenly, the barn looks so dirty I can hardly stand it. When did I last sweep? Where did those shavings come from? Who scattered loose hay on the floor?

"They're emailing you all their health info and they're bringing their own feed to start," Evie is saying, brisk and efficient in the way that I taught her. "So, you should be all set."

"Okay," I say blankly.

"Okay? Are you alright?"

"I'm fine. I'm great! Thank you!"

"You're welcome, Alison." Evie pauses, then says, "Take it easy, okay? I know it's going to be busy this winter, so we all just have to remember to breathe, you know?"

"Sure," I reply. "I'm breathing."

Sort of.

"Right," Evie says, and ends the call.

The prospect of four paying horses in my barn makes me lean back against the barn wall. This is going to be a huge help. But, I think, I need to *clean*—I grasp for the broom hanging next to me without looking.

In the process, I knock down a pitchfork—one of those heavy steel ones used for cleaning out straw bedding. It clatters against the concrete floor and sends Lily Marlene running for cover, while the horses who are inside the barn push their heads over their doors and stare at me in astonishment. Hansie blows hard through his nose, his eyes so wide they have a white ring around them. The noise and their reaction bring me back to reality.

"Sorry, sorry!" I bluster, holding up my hands. "God help us if I make a noise in your serenity garden, you big babies."

Cary comes out of the feed room, where he has been doing heaven knows what, and picks up the pitchfork. "Were you planning on murdering someone with this thing?" he asks, eyeballing the sharp tines. "I thought it was just hanging on the wall for decoration." He stands it up on its handle and poses like the old man in *American Gothic.* "How do I look?"

"You need a hay straw sticking out of your mouth," I tell him. "And maybe a corncob pipe?"

"Hay *and* a corncob pipe? In this economy?" Cary hangs the pitchfork back on its nails, where it settles into place with a screeching sound of metal on metal. "Ugh. Terrible noise. So listen, I was reorganizing your feed room—I did an episode of my show on organizing closets and I had a few ideas for all those vitamins and stuff—and I just wanted to ask, did you actually adopt and name any of the spiders in there? Because they're all so large, I can only assume you've been caring for them like they're your own children."

"If you're asking for permission to kill the spiders, be my guest." I shake my head. "I never had spiders in Malcolm's barn. Why is this place so *dirty?*"

Cary looks around as if he's trying to figure out what I'm talking about. "It's an outside barn," he says eventually. "I think a few cobwebs in the rafters are to be expected."

"No, there's no reason for any of that." I sigh and run a finger along the wall, then hold it up. "Look how dusty this place is," I say, showing Cary the black dust on my finger.

He eyes me like I'm going crazy right in front of him. "Do you have any meds you should be taking for this?"

"Excuse me? For what, the crime of wanting a clean barn?"

"This barn *is* clean. I'm working in a feed room so spotless that NASA could use it as a clean room to build satellites. Even the spiders were confused and looking for an exit. I promise you, there's nothing wrong with this barn, Alison."

He looks genuinely concerned, which is kind of him, but also annoying. I know where his brain is heading with this.

"I don't have an obsessive-compulsive condition, if that's what you're thinking," I say.

Cary does not look convinced.

"There are *spiders*, Cary. What does that tell you? Clearly, the feed room needs a good cleaning!"

"It's Florida," Cary says. "I was given to understand this state is forty-seven percent spider. It's in the orientation video they show everyone at the state line."

He might be right about that percentage, actually. But *still*.

"Thanks for working on the feed room," I say, picking up a dust mop I use for clearing the stall fronts of cobwebs. "I'll start dusting the stalls out here. We have clients coming in a few days, and I need this place to look as immaculate as Fine Day Farm."

"Don't go too crazy," he pleads as I jab the dust mop at the closest stall door. "I'm sure everyone who sees this place will be impressed with the hyper-cleanliness."

"I should have stained the stall fronts," I mutter, annoyed with myself.

"We can still do that, if you want," Cary offers.

I glance at him. "You want to help me stain the stalls?"

"I mean, if that's what will make you happy."

"It will," I say eagerly. "That's what would make me happy."

"Okay," Cary sighs. "I will go to Lowe's and buy the stuff. You stay here and dust off the walls. Then we'll slap a coat of stain on them. Sound good?"

"Yes." I dig the dust mop into the track of the sliding stall door. "Sounds perfect."

Cary hesitates for a moment, watching me as if he's worried about what I might do next, then finally leaves.

"I THINK THE farm is looking good," Cary says, running his hand along Nando's neck as we ride side-by-side towards the back pasture.

"You know...you're right." A bubble of tension that has been present in my chest for the past few days suddenly seems to release, and I find I can breathe a little easier. "The stalls look amazing now." True to his word, Cary brought back some pails of wood-stain and we slapped it on all the stall fronts, giving the old, raw wood a bit of polish. "And the whole place looks greener, doesn't it?"

"Thank goodness for rain." Cary smiles at me, and I remember thinking just a few days ago that he seemed to make it rain.

Truly, ever since Cary got here, the weather has gotten wetter. Yes, too wet, at times, but that's just the way Florida operates. We've had almost a week of intermittent storms, with muggy mornings that heat up quickly, before noon brings rumbles of thunder and layers of clouds. Sometimes the rain pours down, sometimes the sky just drops extravagant numbers of lightning bolts. Either way, with all the clouds, the afternoon temperatures have slowly been tumbling from the middle nineties down to the eighties, and everyone is grateful for the change.

Since I've changed Hansie from my first ride of the day to an afternoon ride with Cary and Nando, it's meant gray, damp rides for my big horse...and he seems to enjoy them. The pasture rides have become the highlight of our days. Even Nando enjoys pretending to be a western pleasure horse, shuffling his hooves as if he's been moving at one mile per hour for his entire life, instead of wheeling around a show jumping arena leaping fences against the clock.

"It really needs mown," I say as we walk the horses through the pasture gate, because I can't see anything without the critical eye my aunt ground into me. "I don't think I can ignore it any more."

"Now, now," Cary warns. He has been after me to stop worrying about the way the place looks. He says that I have four horses coming in with signed boarding contracts and I should stop fussing.

He doesn't know that fussing is in my blood, that the need for perfection has been trained into me as surely as inside leg to outside rein.

"Well, the grass *is* getting long," I insist, but he shakes his head.

"Then let the horses eat it. Problem solved."

"I don't think they can keep up with it!"

"If we had grass like this in California, no one would live in Florida," Cary informs me. "Ocala would be in Los Angeles. Instead, it's a desert and people like me live there. So count your blessings that you get tropical rain and accept that means rapid plant growth, okay?"

"Well, at least look out for any broken or loose-looking boards on the fences and tell me if you see anything," I insist. "Safety is still a priority."

He's fiddling with his phone, holding the reins one-handed. "Mm-hmm," he says without looking up.

"Hey, now, buster! You should be paying attention to the road, not texting and riding."

"Not texting," Cary says, holding up the phone and pointing it at me. "Documenting!"

I shake my head at him. "This again? I told you I'm over the whole 'let's-make-a-movie' deal. You're going to have to tell your ego to sit and wait for your big cowboy romance to start filming."

"I want to capture everything about your farm," Cary pleads. "Trust me on this."

"Absolutely not. I have boarders coming; what if you catch some of them in the background?"

The very idea of Cary filming the incoming boarders puts me on high alert. They're not going to like having him wandering around making home movies while they're trying to school their horses. Equestrians are private about these things.

"Sorry, but that's just the way it is going to be," I add, as he gives me a hangdog expression.

"I clean your barn," Cary begins mournfully. "I plant your gardens. Weed your flowers. Muck your stalls. Buy you dinner. And for this...I get...what?"

"The privilege of remaining a client," I snort.

He laughs. "You're a tough cookie, Alison. You'd scare some people in Hollywood, you really would. And I mean that as a compliment."

"Well..." I consider him a moment, decide he is being sincere. "I appreciate that," I say finally. "I mean, my aunt raised me to be tough. So did my parents, actually, by letting me live with my aunt. They knew it would be good for me in the long run."

"Not a lot of parents would do that," Cary remarks. "Most prefer to raise their children at home."

And now we're talking about me again. He's a wonder.

"Well, I knew what I wanted and I couldn't get it in D.C.," I say, shrugging. It's not something I discuss often, because no one ever understands that my parents simply allowed me to move to Aunt Kate's. No one seems to see what a gift it was. I wasn't sent away. I asked for a change of address, and they gave it to me. "My parents were so busy with work, always running around the congressional offices and staying at meetings until late, and don't even ask about the nights before a big vote! They were always working. So for me to go stay with my aunt and have someone around all the time made a lot of sense. The horses just made it a no-brainer. I wanted to ride. That was all I wanted."

Cary says, "From what you've said about your aunt, she sounds a little...strict."

"Hey! She was the best. Worked me like a dog, obviously, but—"

"Obviously?" Cary interrupts, giving me an incredulous stare. "*That* made her the *best*? Were you accidentally sent to a Victorian orphanage? Alison, my god, what if that wasn't your aunt at all?"

"Oh, stop," I say, laughing. "You're *so* dramatic. Of course, she was my aunt. And she taught me the proper way to take care of a stable. No shortcuts. The *proper* way to do things, that's how we did it and that's how I still do it."

Aunt Kate always said it like that. The *proper* way.

"And now you're afraid of dust in a barn," Cary muses. "It's all coming together."

"There's nothing wrong with the way I was raised," I inform him tartly. "I do things the right way. That's a *good* thing. It's just..."

He glances at me as I trail off.

No doubt expecting some dramatic realization to come bubbling out.

"It's just harder to do things correctly in Florida than it is in Virginia," I finish, giving him a massive eye-roll. *That's for thinking I'm having some kind of family trauma breakthrough, Cary.*

He scoffs. "Everything is harder in Florida. It's the spider content. Unnaturally high, like I said before."

"And there's the humidity, and the lightning, and the palmetto bugs, and the mold..."

"Paradise on earth. What's keeping you here?"

"The eventing community. I came down here, got a job with Malcolm, a few years go by and now this is home."

"You couldn't feel at home somewhere more hospitable to human life?"

"Like Los Angeles, you mean?" I ask lightly.

He shrugs. "Not necessarily, but...yeah. L.A. is great. There are even horses there."

"Will you have a horse when you go back?"

The question was meant to be casual, but saying it aloud seems to tighten some muscle in my chest, one that doesn't usually get much operation in my day-to-day life. I realize that in the nearly two weeks Cary has been here, I've gotten used to his company. It will be hard to go back to an empty barn when he leaves.

Then again, I reflect, I'll have my boarders this winter. They'll keep me company.

Maybe.

"I've been thinking about it," Cary says. He runs a hand along Nando's neck.

"You can't have Nando," I tell him.

"Damn."

"But I could help you find another horse. When you're ready."

He glances over at me. "Yeah?"

"Of course. That's what trainers do for their students."

"I thought I might ask *Jim*—"

I snort. "You better not! He only wants to sell you a six-figure jumper that he can show with your money."

"You don't want me to do that for you?"

"Naturally, I do," I say smugly, "but a wise trainer knows to wait until the right moment."

"Well, you better hurry," Cary replies amiably, "or I'll be gone."

The word hits me like a fist to the stomach. My mouth runs dry, my lungs are empty, my vision narrows until I'm peering at the watery sunlight through a dark, black tunnel.

Gone.

We ride in silence for a while after that, the horses sauntering side by side, tails swishing. Thunder grumbles in the distance, then subsides again, unsure if it wants to come back or keep rolling towards the ocean.

Back at the gate, Cary takes out his phone, and I realize for the first time he put it away the way I'd asked him to. "Selfie," he says, holding it up. "If you won't let me document our rides in movies, at least let me take some pics."

I nod and position Hansie near Nando's hindquarters so that we can be seen in the selfie, and fix a smile on my face. It's so fake it makes my skin ache.

As we ride back to the barn, I swallow the lump in my throat and ask if he's excited to get back to work in another month.

A few weeks, and he'll be gone.

"I guess I am," Cary says blithely, watching Nando's ears bob from side to side. "I mean, we have to get to Colorado to do the winter scenes, all the snow and stuff, and then the studio work, and then a long break until we do the summer scenes. It's a complicated production, but Kat says it's going to be worth it."

It's hard to believe this guy riding alongside me is going to be in the movies. I mean, has been in the movies. When I think back to the day Evie had me Googling his name to see what he looked like as a teen heartthrob, it's hard to connect the dots with the goofy, thoughtful man who has been in my hair every day for almost two weeks, making himself such a part of my life that I hardly remember what the farm was like without him.

Empty, I think. Lonely.

"Will you miss me when I'm gone, Alison?" Cary asks. His tone is light. He's joking around, thinking happily of his resurrected movie career, his Colorado adventure to come.

I focus on a line of trees far in the distance, then on Hansie's pricked ears. They blur. "Of course I will," I say.

That strange muscle in my chest tightens again until I feel like I can hardly breathe.

Chapter Twenty-Two

OLIVIA JACKSON IS tall, thin, and blonde. When she unravels herself from her rental sedan, I'm reminded of a giraffe. A really elegant giraffe with a nice smile and friendly brown eyes, I mean. Well, and a short neck, for a giraffe.

What I mean is, Olivia Jackson is all legs, with a swan-like neck brushed by a platinum-blonde ponytail. I can immediately tell she is a young woman who loves matchy-matchy saddle pad sets and riding her jumping phases with that sleek, straight ponytail falling directly down the center of her back, in defiance of two hundred years' worth of hallowed hair-net tradition.

Aunt Kate would die. I have a box of hair-nets in my tack trunk and I'm not afraid to double them up in order to keep every flyaway hair hidden beneath my helmet.

Despite the fact that she has arrived before the van shipping her horses down from northern climes, and that she clearly won't be riding the poor, travel-worn beasts today, Olivia is wearing gleaming field boots with an extra-slim calf, slate-gray breeches, and a sun-shirt in pale blue with floral accents. She looks like she is ready to ride in a clinic, or maybe shake back her hair in a catalog photo-shoot. I can't help but feel a touch inferior, even though I'm dressed in my usual uniform of fawn and dark green and know that I look like the successful professional I am not.

Dress for the job you want, I've always heard.

Cary slouches out of the barn and stands next to me. He's wearing light khaki shorts and a pair of hiking boots he has decided are perfect for barn work, and in his sweat-stained blue t-shirt, with a hat pulled over his forehead, there's really no identifying him as a movie star. In fact, I think, giving him a slightly despairing once-over, he looks more like a random guy I once hired off the side of a highway interchange to strip twenty stalls so Malcolm's regular stall-cleaners wouldn't have to do such hard work.

Olivia fixes us both with a toothpaste-commercial smile. "You must be Alison's barn manager?" she calls. "I'm excited to meet her."

"Oh," I say, as Cary puts one hand to his face, no doubt to cover a mischievous grin. "I'm actually Alison."

"Whoops, how embarrassing!" Olivia has a touch of a southern accent—the Atlanta private school kind, not the twangy mountainous kind—and she titters with complete control. "Well, shoot. I'm Olivia Jackson, and I would just love if we could start over. You must be *Alison!* How was that?"

Well, she has a sense of humor, anyway. "That's me," I say, grinning back. "You nailed it. Welcome to the farm."

For once, I feel utterly confident about my farm. The gardens are blooming, the grass is green, the stall fronts are gleaming. And I know the barn interior is perfectly clean, because yesterday I had Cary help me drag everything out of the aisle before I pressure-washed the place until the aisle was so clean a person could eat damp spaghetti noodles off it.

And if you've ever dropped a damp noodle on the floor, then picked it up and looked at it, you'll know just how clean that is.

"Thank you," Olivia says, looking around with an approving expression. "Such a pretty place! I was a little disappointed not to get into Fine Day, not gonna lie to you...my friends go there every winter and I've heard how gorgeous it is. Perfectly clean, they all say, you can eat off the ground..."

"That's because of me," I can't help boasting. "I was the barn manager there. I just started this place at the beginning of summer. My old working student, Evie, is the barn manager now." This is a slight misstatement; Evie was Malcolm's working student, not mine. But I was the one who told her what to do and taught her how to keep a barn the Windy Hill way.

Cary shifts next to me, then holds out a hand. "Hi, I'm Cary," he says.

Olivia glances at him curiously before taking his hand—slightly gingerly, as if she didn't expect to touch the farm-hand standing next to me. I know Cary well enough to notice the way his shoulders come forward; he's trying not to laugh. He loves this.

"Let me show you where your horses' stalls are, and the tack room and everything," I say quickly, drawing her away before he can keep messing with her. I cast a scolding look over my shoulder as I usher Olivia into the barn. Cary grins and gives me a thumbs-up, then pulls his hat brim down even farther. All he needs is a hay-straw in his mouth to complete the local yokel look. I hope he doesn't get any ideas about standing around posing with that pitchfork again. He's liable to hurt somebody while he's playing comedian.

"Your barn is lovely," Olivia says.

I still think I hear the disappointment in her voice. Being clean isn't good enough; this woman wants fancy, too, and she'd have gotten it at Fine Day Farm.

I sigh; my place is workmanlike, and safe, but it's still not fancy, despite all my efforts. "Thanks," I say, trying to recover my bright tone. "Here's the restroom, and the tack room."

She looks around the tack room, the empty wall I've cleared for boarders' trunks, the wooden saddle racks and bridle hooks. "No lockers?"

I *sent* pictures of the tack room. It should have been pretty clear there were no lockers. I swallow my annoyance and say, "I made room for your tack trunk, and you have these saddle racks. Is that enough room? I can always shove some of my storage bins into an empty stall."

That won't kill me or anything.

"No, it's fine," Olivia says, and she gives me a determined smile. "We'll make this work!"

Well, she's being nice about the place, even though it's not what she wanted from her season in Florida, and that endears me to her like nothing else could. I can't blame Olivia for wanting more; I want more, too. But we'll both make the best of this.

"We're going to have a great winter," I tell her, smiling.

"Really fun," Cary says from the doorway. And as we turn, he sweeps off his hat and turns on his movie-star smile.

Olivia makes a little *peep* of excitement.

Great, I think. Now she recognizes him.

AFTER OLIVIA HAS finished fawning over Cary and explaining what a fan she is—including his guest appearance on *Mermaid H2O* ("You were so handsome I cried.")—I send Cary out to bring her saddle and bits of gear in from her rental car while I drag Olivia into the office to sign a release form and go over the barn rules. Lily Marlene crouches on the desk and watches the proceedings with half-closed eyes, clearly ready to pounce if Olivia seems like she might object to any of the clauses.

"I'm glad I didn't bring my dog," Olivia says, giving Lily a scratch behind the ears that makes the cat's eyes flutter closed in contentment. "He's a cat-chaser, so he stays home with my mom when I go to the barn. Usually that's just for the afternoon, though." She laughs ruefully. "It's hard to leave him for so long!"

"Is this your first time wintering in Florida?" I ask. "You get used to it. Or you just move here year-round."

"Yeah, so I'm told! This is the first year I've been able to work fully remotely, so I decided to go for it. Who knows if I'll ever have another chance, you know? Skip it this year and the next year you're pregnant, and then you don't have time to ride at all..."

"Oh, you're planning on getting pregnant next year?" I ask, surprised. She doesn't have a ring on her finger, but I suppose I shouldn't be so quick to assume everyone follows the same old social status quo.

"No, no kids on the horizon," Olivia laughs. "Not even a boyfriend. But you know how it is. Life surprises you. I've seen marriages happen, babies, when the person least expected it. And hey..." She lowers her voice. "If I should happen to meet a cute horseman while I'm in Ocala this winter, I won't complain. I figure my chances are better here than back in Illinois."

"True," I agree, because numbers are on her side.

"You know of any?"

I laugh and think of Jim. "Cute, yes. Nice, on the other hand..."

"I guess having a movie star for a groom doesn't count," Olivia says with a little pout. "How long is he going to be here for?"

"Just until the end of October," I say.

The tightness comes back to my chest as I imagine the barn without him, and I take the waiver and pen back from Olivia with a swiftness that startles her. "Sorry," I mutter. "Thought I was going to drop everything."

Cary swings into the office, one hand on the doorframe. "Saddle in the tack room, ladies," he says cheerfully. "Bag is waiting for your trunk to come with your horse. Anything else?"

"Thanks for helping," I say. "I think that's all we need, right, Olivia?"

Olivia watches Cary with a hunger anyone could see.

"Yup," she says, her gaze locked on his face. "That's all I need."

Cary grins.

Chapter Twenty-Three

I DON'T HAVE time to be annoyed about Olivia's clear interest in Cary; her horses arrive shortly after and while we're settling the two nervous, tired geldings into their stalls, Cary says something about a plant sale at some botanical garden I've never heard of and pleads the rest of the afternoon off.

Less than a half-hour later, Olivia makes a few sounds about dealing with her apartment rental and she heads off as well. I find I have to brush away some stray imaginings about her following Cary to the botanic garden. She wouldn't be that creepy, would she?

On the other hand, could anyone blame her for chasing after a Hollywood leading man she's been into since she was still carrying a learner's permit?

"Me," I tell Hansie, leading him from his stall for a solo ride. "I could."

He snorts and rubs against me, hard. I pause mid-step and run my hand up his dark face, beneath his forelock. "Sweet boy," I murmur, utterly in love with him. He laps up the attention. In the barn, he is always my lovely Hansie. It is outside, despite all our attempts to find a reason for his tension, that he's a strange, difficult version of the horse I have risked everything to own.

When he's tacked up, I ride out to the back pasture just as if we were working with Cary. What's the point of taking him into the arena when he just fights me there? I'll do field dressage until he's going so well he can't even remember why he hated the arena, and then I'll sneak him in there one day with Nando at his side, so he won't realize what's going on. It may not be the most sensible training plan I've ever come up with, but when I'm out in the field, Hansie feels more like the horse I fell in love with, and the desire to find that horse again easily crowds all the other thoughts out of my head.

And anyway, I think this plan will work. I'm good at working out training and conditioning programs for quirky horses; it's one of my talents, an instinct Aunt Kate loved in me, and one of the reasons Malcolm's riding career became so competitive while I was running his barn—although I suspect he doesn't know that.

So while the pasture riding might not be the most scientific approach to Hansie's arena aversion, I know I have a chance. And that's enough. Nothing is sure in this business. That's why we blame everything on the eventing gods. Often, we can't find any other reason for the way our plans go awry; it *must* be capricious and uncaring gods.

Thinking of them, I sigh.

Hansie sighs, too. Then he swings his head from side to side, looking for Nando.

"I know, buddy," I say. "I miss our guys."

More than I should. But, probably, not more than I will in another month.

My chest tightens again.

Get over it, Alison.

I'm here to train horses. That's my purpose. It's what I've been training for all my life.

Everything else is just noise, and I better remember that.

The sky begins to cloud over as we trot in big, round figure-eights across the flattest part of the field. I'm loving his trot, the way he blows out gently through his nostrils every time we change direction and he has to think about shifting the curve of his spine, the way his dark mane flutters along his arching neck like a black flame. A black flame! I laugh to myself. I'm really deeply in love with this horse; there's no other excuse for the way my brain goes haywire when I think about him or look at him or simply remember he exists and he's in my barn.

This is the perfect ride, I think, elated.

A cool breeze caresses my cheeks as the clouds thicken. I hear a rumble in the distance, the first hint of the storm to come. But that's fine; we've got time. It might not even rain here at all. I guide Hansie in a large circle, gently push his shoulders towards the center. He dips his head into the bit, and I feel his living mouth quiver against my fingers.

"Good boy," I croon, barely saying the words aloud, so afraid of ruining this precious, perfect moment of oneness with my horse. "Good boy—"

And then a sharply cracking peal of thunder races overhead, like the sound of sheet metal being ripped in two. I glance around, startled, as it echoes through the pasture; I didn't even see a flash of lightning. "Where did that—"

Hansie's rippling breath turns into a sharp, hard snort and he shies sideways as if he's seen something frightening.

Boom!

A metallic scent that fills my nose as the world turns white, blinding me.

I HEAR MY name from underwater, someone on the side of the pool calling me. I try to swim to the surface, but my arms and legs don't want to move. Panicked, I open my eyes, but instead of water flowing in to sting at my corneas, I see a blurry face very close to mine.

Something hits my cheek once, twice. The person above me is slapping me. How freaking rude! I'm trying to come out of the pool, I'm going as fast as I can—

Suddenly my vision focuses.

Cary.

He's close to me. Why is he so close to me? Oh, of course. He's going to kiss me! I flutter my eyelids closed. I knew this day would come. I knew—

"Alison. *Alison?*" Cary's voice is high, panicked. He doesn't sound like he's going to kiss me after all.

I open my eyes.

Cary's staring at me with huge eyes. He sucks in a breath and says, in a strange, strangled kind of voice, "Are you dead?"

"Dead?" I ask, or I try to, but my mouth twists and my word falls out garbled, not the way I meant it to sound at all. I purse my lips with an effort and manage to say, after a lot of concentration, "No?"

He rears back, hands in his hair. "*Jesus H. Christ*, Alison, I thought you were *dead!* Why were you out here in a thunderstorm? Why were you riding alone? I was coming back. Didn't I say I was coming back? I just wanted to grab a couple plants for the garden—" Cary stops and looks around. "Ambulance. We need an ambulance."

"No," I say, my brain slowly coming online. Riding in a thunderstorm? What's he talking about?

"Yes," Cary insists. "You need checked out. You could drop dead on me."

I scramble to a sitting position and reach out, grabbing his arm as he tries to dial his phone. "My copay on an ambulance would be insane."

He shakes his head at me. "Are you seriously talking about your health insurance right now? You fell off your horse! God knows how long ago! You could have a concussion! You could be—I don't know—bleeding internally."

"I'm not." I tap my helmet, still secure on my head. "My head doesn't even hurt. *Nothing* hurts, actually. But my teeth taste funny."

"Huh?" Cary peers at me. "Your teeth taste funny?"

"Yeah, kind of—" I suck at them thoughtfully. "Metallic? Like dimes?"

And then I remember the metallic smell in my nose, and the flash of light.

"Holy shit," I breathe out. "I think I almost got struck by lightning."

Cary looks at the sky with round eyes, like the lightning might come back, but the storm has moved on and there are just a few patches of gray left overhead. "Almost struck might be as bad as getting struck," he says. "I don't know. We should still call an ambulance."

"ER," I suggest, okay with that compromise. I have a decent emergency room copay on my insurance plan, whereas the ambulance costs would max out an empty credit card, and I don't think I have any of those left. "Can you take me to the ER?"

"Yes, emergency room, right away." Cary pushes back onto his heels, then reaches out with both arms, and before I know it, he has scooped me up.

"Cary!" I screech. I'm pressed against his chest like a damsel in distress, my face dangerously close to his chin. I can hear his heart thumping against my cheek; honestly, this guy could probably use an EKG for himself. His heart rate is out of control. "Put me down, silly. I can walk."

"Nope," Cary says, starting back for the barn with my body still tightly clenched against his. "I'm carrying you, I'm putting you in my car—"

Something occurs to me.

"Hansie," I say. "Where's my horse?"

"Right there." He turns a little and I see my horse watching us from a few dozen feet away, a dazed expression on his face. As we pass him, Hansie starts after us, determined not to be left alone. The reins dangle loosely over his neck.

"You have to untack him and put him away first," I tell Cary. "Or I won't go."

"I'll take care of your horse, Alison," Cary says patiently. "Close your eyes and relax. It is a lot easier to carry a limp rag-doll than a tense crazy woman."

"Sounds like a problem you inflicted on yourself," I murmur, but I try to relax anyway, listening to Hansie's tack jingle as he walks a few feet behind us.

It's funny. Pressed against Cary's chest, I almost feel...

I don't know, content?

Is that a real feeling?

* * *

"THEY'RE MAKING ME stay for observation," I tell Evie miserably. "Right when I have a boarder for the first time, and the second one arrives tomorrow."

The white lights of the hospital room are harsh; the scent of disinfectant burns my nose. Why is a place for convalescing so unpleasant? I'd be better off in my own bed, Lily Marlene draped over my feet, while I watch TV on my laptop. But no; even though it's pretty clear I wasn't *actually* struck by lightning, what with not being dead and all, the retinue of doctors who have gone over my vitals again and again insist that they want me flopped in this miserable bed for at least a night, probably two.

"It's going to be okay," Evie says, but she's already looking at her phone and I know she's checking the barn schedule, feeling jittery about offering to help, and guilty about her hesitation. She has a full house at Fine Day; she can hardly be expected to go and manage my farm, too. "We'll figure it out. Maybe Sydney can help—"

"I can manage things," Cary says, barging into the room so quickly I suspect he was hanging outside the door, waiting for the right moment to sweep in and be the white knight. Heaven knows the man is theatrical. I'm surprised he doesn't go down on one knee and present me with a rose as he declares, "You don't have to worry about a thing. I will run the barn to perfection."

"Cary, no," I begin, but he talks me down. And I realize he's probably fully capable of taking care of the barn, assuming nothing goes wrong. He's been working with me nearly every day for almost three weeks, and it's really not that complicated when you come down to it. Horses go in, they go out. They eat, they drink. They need their stalls cleaned and their hooves picked. There's not much else to it.

Once you take out everything I consider essential to running a showplace-style stable, anyway.

"I guess you can manage," I say begrudgingly.

"Now that's a ringing endorsement!" he jokes.

"I'm sorry, I'm just getting used to the idea of being stuck in this bed for goodness knows how long."

He pats my hand. "There, there. Our little lightning rod needs some quiet time."

"That's not my new nickname," I warn him, but Cary grins and winks at Evie.

She gives me a sheepish smile, and I know Cary's larger-than-life personality is beginning to wear on her right now. She's tired, and we're only adding to her stress. Cary the ham and me, the little lightning rod. "Go," I tell her. "I know you're falling behind. I'll be fine."

"I'll go to the farm and check everything once a day," Evie promises, clearly relieved to hand the reins to Cary. "And who knows? You might leave tomorrow."

Chapter Twenty-Four

IT TAKES FOUR days to get released from the hospital.

There was nothing wrong—not a thing wrong with me—besides the icky taste in my mouth, but the doctors wanted to run every test in the book on me, anyway. Apparently, despite Florida being the lightning capital of the world since forever, they don't get a lot of near-miss lightning strike victims. I guess the average lightning strike just ends in a fatality, and so that doesn't give researchers a lot of information to work with.

While I was being poked and jabbed and prodded by an army of white-coated men and women, I worried incessantly about the farm. Cary texted me constantly, usually sharing pictures of him standing with a horse or a clean stall or even Lily Marlene, giving me a thumbs-up and his huge child-actor smile. When he just sent a picture of horses grazing contentedly, I felt oddly disappointed. I wanted to see *him*.

Too. I wanted to see him, *too*.

When they finally let me go, he's the person I call to come and get me. He's the only logical choice, I reason. Evie's busy. Everyone in Ocala is busy. They have horses to train and events to school for and students to teach. Cary is the only one who is free to chauffeur me home. That is what I tell myself, anyway, as I call him and ask for a ride.

He sounds elated when I give him the news, and he's in front of the hospital doors twenty minutes later, which is alarming because my farm is half an hour away. Seeing him pull up gives me a rush of happiness, and I'm glad the heart monitor isn't beeping next to me right now, or the doctors would really have something to talk about.

"You came to rescue me," I say as he walks up, his smile ear to ear.

"Your knight in shining armor," he replies, but I notice that his eyes are flicking up and down, taking all of me in, as if he thinks I am still fragile, as if he's afraid I might be broken.

"I'm fine," I tell him.

"I know," he says, and attempts a laugh, but it's shaky. "I'm just realizing that I didn't sweep the feed room this morning, and I'm afraid you're going to fire me," he jokes, taking my arm.

His fingers are more firm than they used to be, I think, enjoying the friction of his touch on my skin. He's toughening up, my Hollywood man.

My student, I mean. My Hollywood student.

My hand closes over his and I give it a little squeeze, grateful for the warmth of him.

I've been alone a little too long.

Cary helps me into his black SUV, closing the door so carefully that it doesn't latch and he has to open it and try again. When he's finally in the driver's seat, he lets out a long breath and says, "Alison, I am so glad you're okay."

"I was okay four days ago," I tell him. "And I've been okay every day while we've been texting back and forth. There was never anything to worry about."

"Sure you were. Just fine and dandy. And, just curious, does your mouth still taste like you're sucking on a dime?"

I smack my lips. "No, but now I miss it. You have any spare change?"

He laughs. "You're crazy, you know that?"

We drive back to the farm, filling the half hour with all his stories about running the barn that he didn't send me in text message form. Carrots were distributed, mice were captured, hoses in pasture water troughs were forgotten and mud ponds were created. The usual daily reel of adventure and misadventure. I smile through all of it, relieved to be going home at last, happy to be in Cary's company.

"I'm so lucky you came out here," I say as he turns down the limestone driveway.

Cary reaches over and squeezes my knee. "I know you are," he says earnestly.

I TRULY, REALLY, seriously feel absolutely *fine*, but I let Cary fuss around me, even going so far as to let him walk behind me up the staircase to my apartment, because, he says, I might fall backwards if I should suddenly lose my balance. I feel like reminding him, as I kept reminding the doctors, that I was *not* struck by lightning. I was very close to lightning. This seems, to me, like a significant difference that no one else is giving enough weight to. I was death-adjacent. Not dead and resurrected.

Cary settles my overnight bag—which he packed after I was admitted to the hospital, incidentally, and I don't even want to think about him rummaging through my underwear drawer or I'll blush so red my face will burn up—on my rumpled little bed and looks around the tiny apartment with a proprietary air. "Should I make us some lunch?" he asks, rubbing his hands together.

I snort. Does he think I'm still going to play convalescent? I have work to do. "Absolutely not! I'm going to go downstairs and start riding. We can have dinner up here later, if you want," I add, softening my tone as he gives me a dismayed look. "I'm sure I have something in the cabinets we can turn into a meal."

"Oh, yeah, you're a real Suzy Homemaker," he says admiringly. "Listen, before you go down and ride, there's something I have to tell you."

I don't like the way he says this. As if he's been keeping a secret from me.

"What?" I eye him warily. "What did you do?"

"I took care of the barn, like you said." Cary holds up his hands— *I'm innocent!*

"Uh-huh." I fold my arms across my chest. *Spill it.*

"I only rode Nando at a walk," he continues.

"You rode Nando? Alone?"

"I did, but—"

"That was really unsafe of you!"

"But I have a program I still have to finish," Cary argues, albeit gently, "and Kat has been telling me every single night to make sure I am riding every day, so I couldn't exactly stop while you were in the hospital."

"For crying out loud—"

"Kat can be really formidable!"

"I know she can," I say, "but Cary, if you don't get to the point…"

"I hacked out Hansie."

"You *what?*" I sit back on the bed so quickly I nearly rap my head against the wall behind it. I feel blood rushing to my head and a roaring sound in my ears. This is easily the worst I've felt since I woke up feeling like I was underwater and sucking on loose change. "Cary, please tell me you're joking," I say thickly.

Cary looks at the floor. At least he's ashamed of himself.

"But, *why?*"

"He needed it," Cary says. "You said yourself you need him ridden every single day, no excuses. I asked Evie to do it, and she said she'd try, but every day she was too busy. So after feeding, I got on and rode him around the field, two times in both directions. I didn't hurt him! I left the reins loose, I swung with his back like you taught me —"

"I can't believe this," I interrupt. "My good horse, my *top* horse—"

"So I could have ridden Plato or Sebastian and you'd have been fine with it, but not Hansie?" Cary goes on the defense more quickly than I would have expected. "It's just *Hansie* you have irrational rules for, do I have that right?"

"I'm not being irrational!"

"All I did was walk him!"

"And *did* you ride the other two?"

Cary shakes his head. "No, I didn't see the need. You don't talk about their future the way you do with Hansie's. I mean, if they had a vacation, it seemed like that wouldn't be the end of the world. I was only trying to help," he adds sulkily. "I figured you'd be a little mad, but if you think about it, you'll realize it was a good thing. He really enjoyed himself. He was relaxed and happy the whole time."

"Cary, you could have—" I stop, because the list of things I *think* he could have done to Hansie is too long to know where to begin, and the truth is that half or better of those things are all injuries Hansie could do to himself while just turned out on his own.

But I can't wrap my head around Cary riding him without my permission. It's just too big. Too crazy. I can't think of a groom in

Ocala who would think of getting on the trainer's big horse without permission.

This is what happens when a civilian gets too much freedom in a stable. They don't know the rules. The etiquette. The unspoken, iron-clad rules about who gets on a horse and who stays on the ground.

He meant well, a tentative voice says in the back of my head. *And he said Hansie enjoyed it.*

He broke the rules, and my trust, I tell the little voice.

Maybe, says another voice, that sounds suspiciously like Cary's, *you should write your damn rules down so we know what they are.*

I have to stop this mental conversation before it turns into a mental argument. I have just gotten out of the hospital. I cannot be sent back.

"I need a few minutes alone," I tell Cary—the real one, not the one in my head. "Please, can I have that? Five minutes, and I'll come down and we'll start over."

Cary looks like he's about to protest again, but then he nods and heads out of the apartment.

He has never gone against my requests. If I had said not to ride any of the horses, he wouldn't have.

Instead, I just assumed he wouldn't. I forgot Cary isn't a groom. Forgot this isn't his world.

Forgot he's just visiting, learning about this life as a tourist, because that's his *brand.*

Alone, I coil myself up on my bed and try to fight the panic surging through me. I can't quite explain why I'm so freaked out about this, about the idea of someone else on Hansie without my supervision. But it has given me such a quaking, horrible sensation in my stomach that I feel tears spring to my eyes, and I feel like I might throw up.

I pull a pillow over my head and wait for the feelings to go away.

It takes a lot longer than five minutes. So long, in fact, that I'm worried Hansie isn't the only reason I'm upset.

Chapter Twenty-Five

I FULLY EXPECT Cary to show up the next morning in time to help with feeding. I mean, he's been doing it without me, and I'd assume he'd be eager to show me what a great job he can do with chores. So it's surprising when he doesn't show up until nearly ten o'clock. He pulls into the parking lot while I'm riding Plato in the arena, just cantering along enjoying the taste of fall in the air—it's not even ninety degrees yet this morning, so things are definitely cooling off in Florida.

I feel a weight lift from my shoulders when he gets out of the car. Until this moment, I hadn't realized how worried I'd been that I'd really hurt his feelings yesterday. He'd been quiet last night, and left soon after feeding, which had me thinking he was still sulking about the way I'd spoken to him. And I did feel bad about it, then and now. No, of course he shouldn't have been riding Hansie...but should I have freaked out like that?

I'm honestly not sure.

And it's unusual for me to not be certain of the way I feel. I don't like the edginess, the way my brain can't seem to commit to right and wrong, black and white, correct and incorrect, anymore. Maybe it was the lightning strike?

It wasn't the lightning strike.

That's just a convenient scapegoat, and I know it.

"Hey," I call, letting Plato drop to a walk and taking him over to the arena gate. "Where were you this morning? I missed you."

It just comes out, without my even meaning to say it. *I missed you.* I wonder how he'll take it.

He doesn't acknowledge that I'm floundering, that I don't know my own mind anymore. Maybe he doesn't even see it. "I went to the botanical garden," he says, leaning against the fence.

"You went *back* to the botanical garden?" I eye him suspiciously. "Do you have something going on there? Are you apprenticing with someone else?"

Maybe he's already tired of his little foray into the equestrian world. The part of him that thinks it's a good idea to dabble in different lives has probably hit its limit. Next, he's going to be tending giant water lilies or something.

Cary shakes his head and squints up at me . "No, I just wanted to pick up some cuttings they said they'd have for me today. But that's not why I'm so late. I was there at seven o'clock this morning, I swear. *This* is why I'm late."

Cary opens the back door of his car with a theatrical swish of the wrist. A small white dog pops out and takes off running, streaking across the parking area and under the arena fence.

"Oh, shoot!" Cary cries, smacking his forehead with the heel of his hand. "Tony, come back!"

"Tony?" I echo, watching incredulously as a tiny ball of muscle and wiry hair goes streaking across my arena, barking rapturously. Even at its tremendous rate of speed, little legs blurring, I can tell it's a Jack Russell Terrier—the kind of short, devious ratter that used to be the most common canine attendee at horse shows. Fashions change and you see fewer of the little dogs nowadays, but they're still completely equestrian, and I've always liked them.

From a distance, that is. They're famously bratty and I wouldn't actually choose to have one in my home or stable.

If Cary thinks I'm going to keep this dog...

The terrier reaches the far side of the arena and runs along the paddock fences, still barking. My horses glance at him without much interest before going back to their grass. It would take a more formidable presence than this one to tear them away from late-summer grazing.

"Cary," I say, "where did you get that creature?"

"Found him," Cary says, shielding his eyes with one hand to watch the dog gallop happily along the fences.

"Found him *where?*"

"Side of the road somewhere in the middle of Marion County," he says. "There were no houses around and he was just sitting there on the shoulder, looking confused. So I scooped him up and took a few pictures to put on all the pet-finding sites, and then I came here so I wouldn't be too late for a morning lesson. I have to be somewhere this afternoon."

"So that's someone's dog," I say, ignoring his mention of an appointment. We'll get to how he's not helping me with chores at all today. First, the creature he has sprung on me. "It's a lost dog."

"I guess so. Unless no one wants him, and then he's *my* dog." Cary's voice tilts up at the end there, a tone of hopeful anticipation.

I look from the dog back to Cary. He is a big, overgrown child, playing at being an adult. No wonder he loves acting. He's acting every minute of his life. "No one's just giving up a JRT," I warn him. "They're expensive dogs. One puppy can set you back a grand or two, easy."

"Well, I guess we'll see," Cary says, lifting his chin defiantly.

The dog does a huge loop of the parking lot and heads for us, still barking rhythmically. Plato lifts his head and watches the creature with interest, but he's not bothered; after a minute, he drops his head towards the fence and shifts his weight, resting one hind leg. In the paddocks, the other horses are grazing as if nothing strange is happening. I guess the dog is safe, or they'd all be watching him warily.

"He seems horse-proof," I observe as the dog sniffs around Cary's boots, utterly unimpressed by Plato standing two feet away. "As long as no one gets chased, he can hang out for the morning."

"Great," Cary says, beaming. "And then—"

"And then you can take him to a vet and get him scanned for a microchip," I say.

Cary shrugs. "Of course I will," he says. "Just as soon as we're done with my lesson."

"That's someone's dog," I repeat. I don't want to see him hurt. "Don't get attached, okay?"

He squints up at me. "Who, me?" he asks, his expression impenetrable.

And then he walks into the barn to get Nando tacked up, the dog leaping at his heels.

OLIVIA ARRIVES WHILE Cary is riding, and by the time we head back into the barn, sweaty and satisfied with Cary's improvement at the trot, she has her leggy gray gelding named Early standing in the cross-ties and her tack situated on the rack next to the tack room door. She stops curry-combing her horse long enough to put a hand on one jutting hip and regard Cary with admiration.

"Look at you, putting in the time in the saddle," she exclaims, as if Cary is the first person who has ever taken riding lessons. "I saw you trotting out there like a pro!"

"Well, thank you," Cary says, delighted. "I really appreciate the compliment!"

I know the guy loves an audience, but the sparkling smile on his face is almost *too* much. "Put Nando in the wash-stall," I bluster. "You got him all hot and sweaty."

"Yes, ma'am," Cary says obediently, and with a wink for Olivia, he leads Nando into the wash-stall. Since it's right across from the cross-ties, this doesn't really separate them by much. Dammit, Nathan, why did you have to be proactive and build the wash-stall indoors, instead of sticking it outside the barn like half the farms around here have?

I decide to chaperone the two of them, hanging out and messing with bits of tack while Cary hoses off Nando and Olivia makes eyes at him over the back of her horse. The dog drinks all of Lily Marlene's water while she watches from the stairs with quiet astonishment, then belly-flops onto the aisle and sticks his tongue out, panting happily.

What a happy little kingdom, I think morosely, and then I have to ask myself what about Olivia's attention to Cary makes me so upset.

But why ask questions I won't like the answers to?

Leaving them to their chit-chat, I go into the office and, after a moment's hesitation, close the door.

Wouldn't want the cold air to get out.

CARY SCOOPS UP the dog and takes off before noon, while Olivia is still riding. She waves to him from the saddle. He toots the horn in reply.

"Oh, give it a rest," I mutter, and stomp back into the barn aisle. Lily Marlene hops down from the first step of the staircase and gives me a single, prudish *mew*.

"You're not wrong," I agree. "Come upstairs and pout with me in the air conditioning, okay?"

She looks back and forth, checking for anything more interesting, then gives a feline shrug (more a vibe than a physical move) and leads me up the staircase.

Cary comes back around four o'clock, looking sheepish. I come downstairs again, rubbing my eyes as if I'd taken a nap instead of letting on the truth, that I sat and watched reruns of Parks and Rec on my laptop. What can I say? Leslie Knope's relentless pursuit of organization soothes me.

I immediately see that Tony is nestled in the crook of his arm and swallow a little sigh. Of what...relief? Did I *want* him to keep the stupid dog? Honestly, my emotions are simply off the wall this week. I might need to go on some herbs or something.

"Well? No chip?" I ask, walking over to the pair of them. I rumple the dog's ears while I look at Cary. His dark eyes are alight with triumph.

"No chip," he announces.

"So, he's yours?"

"Unless someone gets in touch. I put ads all over social media. If no one claims him, he's mine."

"Congrats." The dog licks my finger. "He's cute, I'll give you that."

"Thank you! I've wanted a dog for a while." He scratches Tony behind the ears and the dog licks at his face, trying to get his chin. "You don't mind having him around the farm?"

"Not as long as you're watching him," I say. "And no horses get chased. The truth is, he probably has some very troublesome flaw, and that's how he ended up on the side of the road. No one lets go of a JRT without a good reason. So you'll just have to keep a close eye on him until you figure out what that reason was. And you'll probably want to crate him back at Mrs. C's house. Don't let him just run around the place unsupervised, or he'll get into trouble."

"Well, actually..." Cary shifts his weight, getting ready to ask me for something.

"What?" I ask, full of foreboding.

"I have a favor to ask," he says.

I know what's coming. "Of course you do," I say tartly.

Cary gives me his most winning smile. "I need for Tony to stay here."

I sigh. How did I guess?

"Please?" He all but bats his eyelashes at me.

The truly worrisome part of this situation is how much I *want* to give in to him. How much I want to make him happy. Before you know it, I'll be doing his laundry. And then he'll have horsehair all over his clean clothes, just like I do. I square my shoulders and try to ignore his pleading expression.

"I don't have room for a dog, Cary. You've been in my apartment. You see how much space I have. Also, I really don't want a dog. No offense, Tony." I give the dog another ear-rub. He smiles up at me, pink tongue curling. "I know, you're very nice."

"But he's only a very small dog," Cary points out, injured tones indicating he is the very epitome of reason, "and anyway, he *loves* you. Look at him! He's not even offended that you don't want him. He just wants to hang out with you for the next month. Only a month! Four tiny weeks. It's nothing."

I swallow, feeling that tightness return to my chest. I'm starting to wonder if I have a heart condition. But no—I just had every diagnostic test available to mankind, and no one said anything about my heart.

It's fine. Four weeks and then Cary leaves forever, but it's fine. There's no reason for it to make my internal organs seize up. I can get past it.

"He *doesn't* love me," I retort, latching onto the only reasonable argument I've got, but even so, I can't resist taking a peek at the dog's soft brown eyes. Sure enough, they're fastened on me with something that looks suspiciously like doggy worship. I'm reminded of the way Hansie watches me. Look at me, the animal magnet. I shake my head and look back up at Cary. "Anyway, why can't he stay with you?"

"Kat doesn't want a dog in the guest-house, apparently. Says they tear up nice floors and dig up the gardens, and she won't lose another gardener just so I can keep a stray." Cary looks sadly at Tony. "As if this little guy could be called a *stray*."

"No, he belonged to someone who doesn't want him back, which is probably a red flag," I remind him. "Mrs. C is no dummy."

But if there's one thing we horse-people can never do, it's turn down a dog in need.

And Cary seems to know it. His own puppy-dog eyes put Tony's to shame.

"*Fine,*" I agree at last, knowing this was never a fair fight. "But you're going to Ocala to buy him a crate. And it's going in the tack room. I'm not going to have him rip up my apartment while I'm trying to sleep."

Chapter Twenty-Six

"THIS ELECTRICAL OUTLET doesn't work."

I look across the aisle, tearing my attention away from the horse I'm tacking up. Edward is looking at me without pleasure. It's the expression he's used on me since the day he arrived with his two warmbloods, three tack trunks, and five—*five!*—saddles.

Not my favorite boarder, Edward. Even with Olivia. blatantly flirting with Cary, I prefer having her around to this guy.

Edward is currently holding a laptop in one hand, a charger in the other, and a scowl on his face. "The outlet in the office works," I say. "You can use my desk. It's fine."

It's not fine, but if Edward insists on doing his Very Important Remote Work at the barn, I can hardly tell him he has to stay in the tack room, where the electrical outlets do not, in fact, work.

I've asked Nathan to fix them, but they aren't worth shouting the barn down over, since there are outlets in the aisle to handle my clippers and things. I try to save my outrage for things that *really* upset me, like the way heavy rainstorms flood the aisle. Not that Nathan cares if I'm mad or not.

Edward makes a face like I've insisted he plug in his laptop to the transformer at the top of the light-pole out in the parking lot. "I have a good set-up ready to go in the tack room," he informs me. "I would prefer to work in there, rather than starting all over again."

Why is everyone such a baby? I want to scream. Is this why Malcolm turned into a colossal, world-class hard-ass that everyone in the eventing community is half-afraid of? Everyone who doesn't truly know him, like yours truly, or Evie, or even Sydney, his working student, thinks he is the scariest man in the sport. And that's because if Edward whined to *him* about a laptop needing charging, Malcolm would simply growl that he didn't build a beautiful equestrian center so people could sit around and do pretend work on computers.

And he'd be right, too.

But this is having boarders, I remind myself. Customers aren't always right, but it's good for them to think they're getting their way. Or they leave and you end up broke.

"I'm sorry," I say as sweetly as I can. "I'll let my property manager know there's an issue."

It won't matter, but Edward takes the promise and heads into my office.

I sigh and go back to saddling Gidget.

"Argh!"

Gidget jumps backwards, her hooves skidding on the wash-stall floor. "Easy, mama, easy, easy," I say urgently, taking hold of the cross-tie. "Edward, what on earth happened?"

He's outside my office again, his eyebrows drawn together. His expression right now makes me want to laugh, or it would if I weren't annoyed with him for spooking my horse.

"There's a *dog* in there," he says accusingly.

"Oh, yeah." I keep forgetting Tony is hanging out here. Which is fully to Tony's credit. The Jack Russell is clearly crate-trained; the moment Cary put his newly bought crate in my office, the dog trotted inside, curled up, and went to sleep. Except for some post-breakfast zoomies, he's been in there all morning, snoring contentedly. "That's Tony, and—"

"I'm *allergic* to dogs."

I blink at him. While animal allergies must exist in the equestrian community, few of us would bother paying them any mind. I've heard a few people complain about cat hairs on their saddle pads, but those same people usually just happily down a few pills and go on with their life. Animal dander is just part of the lifestyle.

He throws out his hands, still holding his laptop and charger. I'm reminded that people who can hold an open laptop with just one hand are people who don't feel anxious about money. Honestly, it's a dead giveaway. "What am I supposed to do now?" he demands.

"Work at home?" The words come out before I know what I'm saying, and I wish I could claw them back into my throat. "I mean, uh, the dog is only here temporarily, so it won't be a problem for more than a few...weeks."

I swallow; every time I think about Cary's departure, about the way the days keep speeding up and passing us by, I feel a thickness in my throat that threatens to choke me.

Edward gives me a narrow-eyed glare before he stalks back to his car. A few moments later, I hear the motor start.

I look at Gidget. "Well, I didn't do that relationship any favors, did I?"

She nudges me gently, looking for cookies.

Maybe, all I should do is set out cookies for my boarders. A daily peace offering. It would be easier than trying to guess their every want and desire, which is how I've approached the past week—my first week with strangers in the barn.

I thought it would be like it had been at Malcolm's—as Malcolm's barn manager, it was indisputable that I was in charge, my word was law, and Malcolm was the god who was only approached during riding lessons. But instead, I find myself with a crew of three who see me as their housekeeper—someone to cater to their whims and clean up their messes. Malcolm is still the god, but he's off property, and without the threat of his glowering presence stalking about the barn, I have no one to grant me authority.

It's disappointing to realize all my power derived from him. What an illusion I'd been living under!

I'm in the arena when Olivia arrives, looking like a beautiful flamingo in pale pink breeches. She leans on the fence, which I assume is my signal to stop working my horse and ride over to see what she needs.

"Is Cary here?" she asks without preamble.

I glance at the parking lot, where Cary's black SUV is conspicuously missing. "No," I say after a pause just long enough to be rude.

I've really had enough today.

Olivia pouts and shakes back her curls, which today somehow exist in tangle-free cascades that defy Floridian humidity. It's unfair, really. Everything about her is unfair. I didn't use to feel jealous of other people for anything; I had it all. But this week, this month, this season, this year...it's all starting to wear on me a bit.

"Do you know when he's coming back?"

"Not until late. He has a wardrobe meeting with Mrs. C," I say. "She's coming by later to watch him ride after her kid's lesson," I add. "So he won't be up for social hour. He'll be busy with the boss."

Olivia chews at her lip for a moment. "Fine, I guess. Do you think you could drive my horses over to Fine Day? Evie said Malcolm has a cancelation this afternoon and we can fit in an extra lesson."

Is she *serious?* "I don't know," I say evenly, somehow biting back a furious retort about having my own schedule to keep. "When are your truck and trailer getting here? I thought you said you were buying one while you were here. To get you to lessons and events."

"Oh, I haven't had time to do all that shopping yet," Olivia laughs. "I figure I can pay you to do some hauling for me. It's not far."

"I'm riding," I say, gesturing to the horse between my legs in case it wasn't obvious enough. "I can't just get off and haul your horse for you. Not even if you're paying me."

"I mean when you're *done*, silly," Olivia laughs. "But, you know, soon. I need to be there in an hour."

EVIE WALKS OUT to say hello as Olivia and Sydney walk the two horses into the barn. "Thanks," she says, wincing apologetically; she's aware this is all her fault. "I know that was late notice."

"She said she was going to buy a rig here. When I asked her how she was getting to lessons, she said she would take care of it."

"Yeah, that was what she told us, too," Evie says vaguely. "Thanks again for getting her here, though."

"I can't be her taxi."

"Charge her fifty bucks a trip and it's good money," Evie suggests.

"I don't have the *time*." And more than that, I don't have the desire to be her cabdriver, whatever the money is worth. Evie can stand here and make suggestions for how I can serve these people, but it's easy for her, because she's standing in the position I once held.

Ugh, I just want my authority back. I want my pedestal back.

I want what I freely gave Evie. I traded my identity for the hope of something bigger, but damn, it has not paid off, has it?

I sigh and turn away, leaning against my truck for a moment. The metal is hot, scorched by a season of blazing sunlight. I feel a surge of exasperation; endless summer isn't as nice as people imagine. When will the first frost come? Sometimes it's as early as mid-October.

That's only weeks away, now.

Looming on the horizon.

"I'm sorry," Evie says again. "But, if you don't mind my saying..." She trails off.

"Yes?" I demand, when her silence drags on.

"This is the hard part," Evie says, shrugging. "I know all about the hard part. But you're bigger than it is."

I wish I knew what the hell she was talking about—so *many* things are the hard part right now, I don't even know where to begin defining them, let alone thinking about how I can overcome them— but Evie just gives me a squeeze on the shoulder, turns, and walks back into the beautiful barn I taught her to run.

And, resenting the fact that I have to be back in two hours to return Olivia's horses to my barn, I get back into my truck and drive home again. I have Hansie to ride, Cary to teach, and, of course, Mrs. C's terrible daughter.

Olivia will just have to fit in where I have time for her.

"LET ME SEE this new horse of yours," Mrs. C announces the moment she gets out of her car.

I look behind her for Sarah, but the girl doesn't appear. "Where's Sarah?"

"Oh." Mrs. C shakes her head. "You know, she didn't want to come, and I didn't have the heart to force her. Her therapist says—"

Mrs. C dives into a lot of clinical talk about feeding the inner child, which seems redundant to me, since Sarah *is* a child, while she strolls into the barn ahead of us.

I glance over at Cary, who is climbing out of the passenger seat. He gives me a sheepish shrug and says, "Who knows? But she's excited to meet Hansie, so that probably outshone Sarah's disappointing her."

"Have you been talking up my horse?" I ask, falling into step beside him. Tony leaps beside us, rapturously happy at having Cary back. Even though the dog is living with me, he clearly regards Cary as his true partner in this life. It's only slightly insulting. After all, it's a good sign when a dog chooses a person, and Cary's clearly a good guy.

"Oh, you know," Cary replies vaguely, running a hand through his hair. "I like to give her all the barn buzz." His hand falls by his side, and our fingers brush.

I feel a little thrill race through me, as if his touch is electric. Then again, I don't taste loose change, so how electric could it be? I smile grimly to myself. I still can't believe that this will forever be remembered as the year I was almost struck by lightning. Not exactly what I wanted it to be famous for.

Maybe it will also be remembered as that crazy year I had a movie star working on the farm. I glance at Cary, letting my gaze linger on the stark lines of his cheekbones, his slightly Roman nose. His slanting forehead, running up to that dark thatch of hair falling over his eyes. Our fingers brush again, and this time I know I'm not imagining the heat rising on my skin.

Then Tony hops up between us, licking at our fingers. I snatch my hand back.

"Dirty mouth!" I tell him. "I know where you've been!"

"In the pasture, eating poop?" Cary asks, gazing fondly at the dog.

"His one true love," I say.

"This relationship was meant to be. Look at this happy little farm dog!"

I wonder which relationship he means. The one between the dog and me? But it's not my dog! Or does mean—

"Mrs. C loves to get the gossip," he says, interrupting my confused thoughts. "That's how she knows about Hansie."

"I hope you don't tell her everything," I say coyly, then wonder what game I'm playing. It's like my mouth is running without any input from my brain.

"What does that mean?" He turns his gaze on me, a smile playing on his lips.

I honestly have no idea. So I shrug in reply, then stumble on the lip of asphalt at the barn entrance. Cary grabs me by the arm before I can go down and skin my knees like an eight-year-old.

"Careful there, sweetheart," he murmurs. "Don't want to go back to the hospital."

I swivel my head to look at him. Sweetheart, again? But there's nothing smoldering in those dark eyes of his, no secret passion I hitherto have not noticed. Just 'sweetheart', just a friendly endearment for a pal who tripped.

I'd better be careful or I'm going to be reading all kinds of crazy hidden messages where there are none. And of course, it doesn't mean anything that I'm mistaking Cary's friendship for a deep affection. It's just the frustration of the tough year, and the difficulty getting used to working alone, and the lonely hours he has filled by being here, by being my friend.

There's nothing else to tell, nothing else to look for.

Ahead of us, Mrs. C has already reached Hansie's stall and is gushing over him.

"Oh, he's beautiful," she trills, poking a finger through the stall bars.

Hansie pricks his ears and gives her an interested nibble, flicking his lips along her manicured nails.

"Thanks," I say, sidling up alongside to attract his attention away from Mrs. C's fingers. I can't imagine what an acrylic nail would do to his digestive tract, but I'm sure it wouldn't be good.

Mrs. C asks for a rundown on Hansie's life history and I give her everything I've got, finishing with my intent to start him at an event in a few weeks.

It's all so close now.

"Well, that's exciting," she enthuses. "I wonder if we can make it to watch. Cary? What are you doing the weekend of Alison's horse show?"

Cary shrugs, scooping up Tony and pressing the wiggling dog against his chest. "I dunno. I'd have to check, but I think I might have to fly back to L.A. that weekend."

Something leaden settles over my chest.

"Oh, of course you do," Mrs. C sighs. "Well, dear, I'm going with him, so I think we'll have to miss your big debut. Maybe next time, though!"

"Sure," I agree, not that I ever expected Mrs. C to come out to one of my events. But I suppose someone like Jim would be laughing at me right now, for not immediately pushing to get her out to another event, or even because I didn't start working on her the minute she became a client. *She's got big bucks,* he'd say, smirking, *and you need to put them to work buying you horses!*

Suddenly, though, I can see the potential of a woman like Mrs. C as a syndicate investor or even a full owner of an event horse, and I want to kick myself for not working on the idea sooner. I have just been so tired this summer. It's no wonder I didn't have the mental bandwidth to think outside of my current income stream. What gave me the room to see it now, though?

He did, obviously. He came and gave me a hand with my work, and offered me friendship and support that I so badly needed. That handsome, silly, dark-eyed man standing just to the other side of my horse's stall door, hands on hips while he jokes with Mrs. C about going back to California—and when he does, he'll be leaving me right back where I started.

Chapter Twenty-Seven

ONE OF OCALA'S charming horse-capital quirks is that there are too many "recognized" horse shows and events on the weekend for trainers to get out young horses to school in cheaper shows that aren't organized under national governing bodies. So a Wednesday morning jumper show is a perfectly normal thing, attracting professionals and well-heeled adult amateurs like my boarders who can leave their laptop for a few hours to get in a few schooling rounds, prepping for the next event in a show atmosphere without giving up a recognized event on the weekend.

With our first October event just ten days away, I hitch up the trailer and load Sebastian, Plato, and Hansie, alongside Olivia's horses Early and Archie, and we head off to a nearby jumper show to give our horses a look at the colorful jumps.

Cary insists on coming, of course. "Mrs. C got me thinking about how I'd miss your big event," he told me, "and I want to see you in action, Alison! Plus, of course, I'll be able to help out."

"You want to groom for me?" I'd asked him, feeling a bit suspicious. He hadn't been making any more of his videos, at least, not to my knowledge, since the boarders arrived. But 'Show Groom' did feel like a good candidate for one of those brief, quirky jobs he'd built his online career with. Maybe he was shoring up potential episodes in case the movie didn't work out as he hoped. "This is a gag, right?"

Cary twisted his face into a pout of unimaginable hurt. If I hadn't known what a remarkable actor he was, I'd have felt guilty. "Alison, how could you? I love working for you. I want to help."

Well, I couldn't deny I wanted him there. I suggested he try to keep a low profile, since horse shows were very public places where emotions ran high. "You might see some crazy stuff," I told him, "and that makes it the kind of place where it's best to keep your eyes on your own work."

Olivia goes a little over the top when she discovers Cary is joining us for a little light show-grooming. The good show-coat comes out, despite the relaxed atmosphere promised by the show organizers, and her black field boots get buffed to a military gleam. Olivia is going all out in the wardrobe department, as if we're showing in the Grand Prix arena at Legends instead of at a local farm.

I know it's all for Cary.

Even though she already sees him around the barn every day, Olivia seems to think that being the star of the show-ring will make her look extremely impressive to him and he will absolutely have to ask her out to dinner. Olivia's so obsessed with Cary that I don't risk telling her he actually eats dinner with *me* more often than not—though it's not dating, just two friends chatting and looking at our phones over salads and pasta. I don't want her to wind up resenting me and ultimately looking for somewhere else to keep Early and Archie.

And the thing is, even if I didn't need her money to pay the bills, I actually like Olivia. Yes, she's a bit spoiled and entitled—but a *lot* of the people in this sport are, so that's a meal I have learned to take with a generous helping of salt. She's nice to ride with, friendly to hang out with, and adds needed conversation and laughter to a barn that has been just me and the horses for too long. While the other boarder, Edward, is basically a ghost who whooshes past me, rides his horses, complains about my wi-fi, and leaves for the day without saying goodbye, Olivia is a pleasure to have around.

When Cary's gone, I'll still have Olivia, and that's not the coldest comfort in the world.

WITH THE TRAILER parked in a shady corner of the farm's front field, and Cary back at the trailer to mind the horses while hopefully fending off Olivia's fashion-show advances, I walk over to the show office in the main barn. I feel pleasantly official, like a real riding coach, as I check-in both my horses and Olivia's. She's not my student, obviously, but the vibe is nice. I imagine having students like Olivia, or even some really talented, ambitious teenagers. That could be good. Once Hansie is rolling and bringing me some attention, maybe I can lure some to the farm.

I linger outside the office for a moment, taking pictures of the course diagrams, when Jim strolls up. He looks athletic and handsome in breeches and a technical fabric shirt, his farm logo embroidered on the chest. His tan is deeper than the last time I saw him. He should be more careful about the sun, I think.

"You didn't text me to set up another date after you canceled on me last time," he says, hands going to his hips as if he's going to lecture me. "I waited."

But I was never going to text him, and surely he knows that.

I can't remember who I was a few weeks ago when I said I'd go on another date with him. I can't remember what I meant. Things have been so...different.

I've been so caught up with Hansie, and the boarders, and Cary.

"Oh, sorry. I was busy and forgot. You know how this time of year gets. How are things at your barn?" I add, just to be polite.

"Great," he says heartily. "Everything is going great. Just sold a nice Dutch mare, got fifty-k for her, and she was barely in the barn for two weeks. That's my kind of turnaround."

I swallow reflexively. There was absolutely no *polite* reason for him to drop how much he sold his horse for; that was just to show me what I'm missing. A big, strong, experienced horseman who can sell fifty-thousand dollar horses for fun. "Congrats," I say at last. "I hope she has a good career."

"If she doesn't, she can make babies." Jim shrugs, following me as I step aside to let some other competitors look at the course maps. "That's the great selling point about a mare, in my book. Yes, they're harder to deal with, but hormones can be zapped with some Regumate and then you've got the back-up plan of getting a foal off her if she doesn't hold up or gets hurt. You have any mares? You really should."

"Just geldings right now," I say. "Just the way it worked out, not on purpose. I better get back, my client—"

"Brought some clients?"

"Yes," I say, fudging the quantity; what's one letter, what's one imaginary person to make the plural true? And technically, Cary is my client, even though he's somehow turned into my employee as well. "And I'd better take back these numbers so we can get tacked up and over to the ring."

"Have a nice ride," he says casually, using the eventing phrase for a luck on a cross-country round, and I have to wonder if it's on purpose, because he knows I event...or if he's already forgotten what I do for a living. "See you out there."

"Yeah," I say. "See ya."

But I don't think I'll see Jim outside of chance meetings at horse shows. If his attitude just now is anything to go on, he's happy to wash his hands of me.

Well, that's fine. What were the chances I was going to meet my dream guy while accidentally getting my truck stuck in the mud because I drove off the road?

Because I was looking at a text about Cary, I remember, smiling to myself. I was looking at a text about Cary, and it's like I was somehow subconsciously aware that my lonely summer was about to turn around and become something so much more satisfying.

Suddenly, I feel like I'm in a very big hurry to get back to the trailer and see him. It's as if this last conversation with Jim has opened up new knowledge in my brain. Two key points are flashing in bright neon, self-discoveries I should've made weeks ago.

One: that I was never looking for love or a relationship, even casually, amongst the ranks of Ocala horsemen.

Two: that I'm already dealing with a major crush, one I didn't even realize I had until right at this moment. A *big-time* crush with my groom and riding student.

And now I just can't wait to see him again.

What's this feeling, this flutter in my chest, these butterflies in my stomach? It's nothing like show-ring nerves at a big event. Those are deeper, grabbier, claws ending with hooks that threaten to scrape my insides raw right before I turn down center-line and everything leaves my brain but mastering this dressage test with my horse, or bursting out of the starting box to make mincemeat out of a cross-country course before it can best me.

No, this feeling is something straight out of high school, when I ducked through the corridors of the county public school a few miles from Windy Hill, my mind on the horses I'd ridden already that day, then rounded a corner and saw *him*—*him* being an assortment of boys, their names and faces changing with every school-year, who never saw me back—and my entire brain went animal.

This is like when I first started working for Malcolm and for a few silly weeks, I fell for his gleaming smile, brooding gaze, and devilish good looks. I remember barely sleeping, barely eating, just thinking about that gorgeous man I had to call my boss. Then I figured him out, and the crush turned into friendship and that was that.

This is like that, but the opposite, because Cary has been my friend all along and now, *now,* my brain and my body are craving so much more of him.

I speed-walk down the rows of trailers, as horses are backed or led out of compartments and grooms buckle on jumping boots and check saddles with quiet competence. The air is filled with whinnies and the deep thud of hooves on trailer ramps. I hear Hansie's high-pitched neigh and smile to myself because I can pick his voice out of a crowd. I walk around the side of the trailer, expecting to see a line of horses tied and eating their hay, and instead encounter Olivia with her hands on either side of Cary's face.

He's looking down at her, back against the horse trailer. Her face is turned up to his. She smiles. And he smiles back. That slow, delicious smile of his...the one I somehow thought, in my ignorance, was something he saved just for me.

He's going to...to kiss her?

No.

No.

What are they doing?

"Hello?" I bleat, interrupting those smug smiles before they can take things any further.

When they're done explaining themselves, I'll pick my guts up off the floor and wander off somewhere private to put myself back together. But for now, I hold what is left of me upright by stiffening every muscle I've got.

It's the very least I can do for myself.

Olivia whirls to face me, her gorgeous eyes widening. I see her look me up and down, taking in my state. Deciding if I'm truly a threat to what she wants.

She smiles and shrugs. I guess I'm not.

"Sorry I'm so taken with your stable-hand," she says, laughing. "I hope you won't judge me too much. It's just a silly crush, right, Cary?"

I look past her to Cary.

He stares back at me, then flicks his gaze at the ground.

Ashamed.

As well he should be.

We're at a *horse show.*

Surrounded by people who should be my peers. People who will be watching me at my first few outings without Malcolm, without the power of Fine Day Farm backing me, and wondering if I can hold a business together on my own. I'm here under the microscope and *this* is what goes on back at my trailer?

"That's not very professional," I snap, stuffing every emotion I've ever had to the back of my brain, where they belong. This is a *job.* We are here to *work.* I'm angry with Cary for being a spectacle in public; this has *nothing* to do with me. "Can we keep it together at horse shows, Cary?" I demand, pointedly laying the blame at his feet, not hers.

He had a choice. He didn't have to smile down at her as if he wanted to kiss her.

He could have saved that smile for me.

Cary swallows, his throat bobbing, and says nothing. His eyes bore into mine until I want to turn and run away. *What does he want from me?*

But I can't read his emotions. Not this time.

As the silence stretches between us, Olivia takes a step away from both of us, holding up her hands as if I've got her at gun-point. "Look, Alison, I'm sorry. I didn't realize you were strict about this kind of thing. We were just fooling around, honestly. I won't, uh—"

"Thanks," I say, looking away from her. "Here's your number."

She takes the paper sheet with her number and watches me for a moment, then walks to the truck and opens the door, pulling out her show bag so she can slide the number into her pinney.

Cary is watching me. I ignore him, walking past him to the rear tack compartment. The horses are groomed already; all I have to do is take out the saddle and pad, the boots and the bridle, and pop on my own pinney and riding helmet. I can be mounted and away from him in five minutes.

Away from both of them.

And so of course he follows me, even though I'm not sure my body language could be any more clear—I want to be *alone,* and every rigid muscle in my body is proclaiming it. But he sticks close. He takes down Hansie's bridle and slides it over his shoulder the way I've taught him, then slides out the saddle and drapes the pad and girth over it, holding it all against his chest with one arm.

He looks at me beseechingly, draped in my tack, but doesn't say a word.

"Please don't," I tell him, annoyed by the slight quiver in my voice.

"I wasn't going to do anything with her," he whispers, glancing towards the truck cab. Olivia is still there, rifling through her show bag as if the answer to how to deal with me is hidden somewhere inside. "She kind of pinned me there, and I thought she was just flirting, and then she moved in like she wanted a kiss."

"Would you have let her kiss you?" I demand.

He tilts his head, his gaze suddenly curious. "Would you care? Outside of it being unprofessional, I mean?"

I shake my head, unwilling to let myself be sucked in again. I say, as firmly as I can, "Being professional is the only thing I care about. I thought I'd made that clear to you, over and over again. And yet here you are, smashing up against a client when, for all anyone knows, you're just the groom!"

Cary's eyebrows go up at that. "Just the groom?"

"You know what I mean." I've said the wrong thing, but there's no time to back-pedal. They're already calling the first riders in Hansie's division. I move to walk around Cary, and he steps into my path, blocking me.

"Move it," I hiss, careful to keep my voice low. "I need to get my horse tacked up now."

"I don't think I like the way you just put me into a lower class than you or Olivia," Cary tells me. "Look, we've been having a good time, but you have to treat me with a little respect, Alison."

"Respect? What do you know about it?" My voice goes up sharply; I see Hansie shift his weight to look in my direction. "You have been walking all over me since the day you got to Ocala. Giving yourself a job at my barn. Demanding we ride the way you want and going against my lesson plans. Riding my *horse* without permission. Stowing a dog in my apartment. When have you wasted even one moment of your precious movie-star time on *respecting* me? You've done what you wanted and used me to have fun, that's all."

Heads are turning, equine and human. At the truck, Olivia has given up pretending to look through her show bag and is staring at us with undisguised astonishment.

I realize, with a rush of furious embarrassment, what everyone will think. That *I* have been having it off with the groom. It doesn't matter that the groom is a famous movie star, or a once-famous movie star, or whatever he is. It doesn't matter that nothing has happened between us, or that he has been underfoot for the past month while I have tried and tried to keep things professional.

No, in this moment, everyone at this horse show will earnestly believe they've just witnessed a lover's spat between a young event trainer and her groom, and they will happily take that gossip to all four sides of Marion County, back down to Wellington, and anywhere else they happen to be riding in the next few weeks.

"Dammit, Cary," I mutter, tears of embarrassment spilling over my cheeks, and I shove past him, listening as my saddle slides from his arm and hits the ground, letting him swear and pick it up, because by *god* he's still choosing to be my groom today and he better just scurry after me and get that saddle on my horse.

Chapter Twenty-Eight

HEARD THERE WAS a little bit of a show at the jumper thing today. You okay?

The message is from Evie, popping into my texts to let me know in the nicest way possible that the news about our horse show altercation is already flying through Ocala's equestrian telegraph. If anyone would know, it's her—Evie was once the gossip queen of Marion County. She gave up her crown when she found out what it was like to hear *her* name on everyone's lips, but she still hears plenty. She just doesn't usually share it with anyone else.

I shove out my legs full-length on my bed and type back that I'm just fine. I mean, I am. I have my whole bed back, for one thing, since he took his stupid dog back. So that's nice.

Except I kind of miss the dog now. I didn't expect to let him sleep in my bed, but he looked so sweet and sad when I tried to leave him in the crate overnight...and now here I am, hurt again.

Hansie was pretty good, I add, hoping she can read my sarcasm. *He didn't totally blow up in the jumping ring.*

Actually, he jumped clear in both his rounds and brought home our first ribbons as a team. A second and a third. I'm pretty damned proud of my horse for pulling it together, even though he wasn't happy with being penned up in an arena again.

That's great, Evie responds. *I promise I'm glad. But what happened with Cary?*

What happened? That's a great question.

"I don't know," I say aloud, wishing Evie would just come over, preferably with booze, so I can talk all this out instead of having to find the words to type. I don't feel like I know the English language well enough to write out what happened, what's happening, what I'm afraid will happen. I just have these memories, which sit frozen and incomprehensible in my brain, like chips of ice fragmented in the folds...

Cary silently working at the trailer to make sure my horses were groomed and tacked up and cooled out properly.

Cary riding in the backseat of the truck in stony silence while Olivia tried to make conversation all the way home.

Cary scooping up Tony and saying he had appointments in the afternoon, and leaving before I could corner him alone, to apologize properly for talking down to him at the show.

Those are the facts of what happened, but I don't know what words I've got that can possibly explain the reality of what happened.

What it *felt* like.

What it *feels* like.

This icy chill that hasn't left my skin since he first turned back to me with my saddle, the one I'd let fall to the ground and ignored, forcing him to choose between picking it up and storming away. The piercing stab of his stare when he'd looked at me, my saddle over his arm, and I sensed an anger in his hooded eyes that went far beyond all his acting skills. *You're just a groom,* I told him.

Unforgivable. Who *says* things like that? I don't say things like that! And yet it happened. I can't even say where the words came from.

I must be losing my mind. The burnout of the long summer, the exhaustion of the endless preparation for show season—it all finally got to me, right when I need to pull myself together and be an impressive, tough, Ocala horsewoman who can run with the big boys all season. The person I have been practicing to be all this time, finally called out on stage...and I forgot all my lines, missed all my cues, and just about fell off the stage.

I'd insulted him, I'd hurt his feelings, I'd behaved badly, and it will take a mother of all apologies to make it up to him...but I suppose he isn't ready to hear it, or he wouldn't have taken Tony and swept away.

Are you okay?

Evie, trying so hard to help me. Evie would never say something so stupid to a friend. She is warm where I am cold, she is sweet where I am sour. She is a warm morning sleeping late, and I am the cruel stepmother banging on the door, barking there are chores awaiting.

Wonder where I learned to be like this.

I'm fine, I type back, but I don't hit send.

I'm not fine.

I'm cold.

I swear I still have goosebumps.

And who wouldn't have a chill on an afternoon like this? Alone, with the miserable realization that I've well and truly messed things up between Cary and me, the truth sinking into my bones like freezing rain on a wintry Virginia afternoon. I can almost hear Aunt Kate's feet on the stairs, coming up to rouse me from my lunch-break and send me back out to work.

Then I realize I really do hear footsteps outside my door, and I leap up to fling it open, my heart pounding.

Cary is standing there, his hands shoved in his pockets, his expression oddly bland.

"Hey," I breathe.

"Hey," he says. "Listen, I just came by—"

"I'm sorry," I blurt.

A dimple shows in one cheek, like he's biting back a smile. "That's not why I'm here, Alison."

"But—" I need him to know. I need him to understand I was under a lot of pressure, and I cracked a little—just a little—but it's fine now. Everything will be fine. Especially if he could stop messing around with Olivia. That would really help things along.

The words are all there, crowded and crammed into my throat, as he says, "I have to get back to L.A. tonight. I'm really sorry to leave so suddenly, but duty calls."

I have no words now. Not in my throat, not in my brain, not anywhere. I just stare at him.

He drops his gaze. "I appreciate everything. I had a good time."

"I'll bet."

I don't know where that came from. It was so unnecessary. But at least it gets his eyes fastened back on mine.

"I'll *bet?*"

I refuse to blink.

"Is this still about Olivia?" he asks, voice incredulous. Again, at least it's not stiff and empty anymore. At least we've got some emotion going.

Not sure what I plan to do with it, though.

"Alison." Cary pauses, sighs. "Can you just admit one thing to me?"

"What?" I ask suspiciously.

"Can you admit you were jealous?"

I swallow.

He shakes his head as if I've disappointed him. "Take it easy, Alison," he says, turning to leave.

"I was jealous," I blurt, desperate to keep him another minute, another second.

Cary turns back to me and I feel his dark eyes searching mine like a physical touch. For a moment, there's a tug between us that makes me think a kiss is inevitable.

Then he reaches out his hand and touches my cheek, tracking a line from my brow to my chin. I feel a roughness to his skin that wasn't there a month ago. Hard work and horsemanship, leaving their mark. It makes him incredibly attractive, a million times more than any Hollywood glitz could ever do.

"I'll be thinking about you, Alison," he promises, and then his hand falls away.

THE SUN IS sinking below the horizon and I'm cleaning stalls under the barn lights when Evie finally comes over, pizza box in one hand and bottle of white in the other. She stands outside the stall door, looking like a lost waitress in breeches and paddock boots.

I keep tossing soiled bedding into the wheelbarrow. "Hey, Evie," I say dully.

"It's seven o'clock at night," Evie says. "You're still mucking out?"

"I started evening chores late."

"That's not like you."

"I fell asleep." Kind of. I turned the air conditioner onto the High setting, then pulled my duvet over my head and just stayed in my own personal cave until the horses were kicking the walls in frustration. Then I finally gathered the energy to go downstairs and feed them their dinner, sleep-walking through feeding and turnout, my brain drumming with the memory of Cary's fingers on my skin, the gravel in his throat when he said, *I'll be thinking about you, Alison.*

What did that even mean?

Evie sighs. "I'm taking this pizza to the office and you're going to come with me and help me eat it."

"What about Malcolm?"

"He knows how to cook, remember?"

I do remember. I've sat down for dinner with Malcolm a few times. Back when I let him handle the bills, and I just made sure the business ran like clockwork. Was that really me back then? I was so certain of myself! I miss her.

Following Evie to the office, I say, "I made a mistake giving up my job like that."

"No, you didn't." She sets the pizza box on the desk and flips it open. The room is filled with the scent of garlic, and my sleeping stomach comes to life with an enormous growl. "You did the right thing. Remember when I left my galloping gig to work for Malcolm? Remember how much I regretted that, for the longest time?"

I really don't remember, because at the time, Evie was just a working student and her worries didn't matter to me. The only thing I cared about was getting through each day on schedule. But at some point, Evie turned into a human, and a friend, so I just mutter, "Sure, I do."

"I was *comfortable* riding at the thoroughbred farm," Evie continues. She slides pizza on paper plates and puts them on either side of the desk, then unscrews the bottle of wine. So smart, buying a screw-top! Finding a bottle opener in my office would mean a lengthy delay before wine gets consumed. "I was comfortable, with my own little place. I was comfortable, and I wasn't getting anywhere."

I know where she's going with this. "Let me stop you," I say, holding up a hand. "You had to get out of your comfort zone and now you're a better person."

She puts a plastic cup of wine into my hand and my fingers close around it of their own volition.

So wise, my good friend Evie.

"I know," she says, nodding at me to take a sip, get it started. "I know what it feels like right now. But I also know what it's going to feel like when you push through the hard part and come out on the other side. And you don't want to miss that feeling, not for anything, Alison."

She's only talking about my business. And she might be right. But she doesn't know about Cary.

I'll be thinking about you, Alison.

Ugh. Absolute murder, those words. I don't know what to do with them.

The wine is cold and slightly tart. Nothing spectacular for *Wine Spectator* to write about, but it does the job. I feel a little prickle beneath my skin, as if the frozen flesh is coming back to life, thawing out at last.

"Here's the thing," I say.

She looks at me.

"I messed up today," I say, sinking into the chair near the door. The chair reserved for guests, and occasionally for Lily Marlene's afternoon naps. I cede my own chair to Evie; she can be in charge for a while. I've had my fill of power for today. "I messed up everything."

"With Cary?"

"He came back," I say. "And he asked me to admit I was jealous, and I wouldn't. Not at first, anyway."

"Why not?"

"I was embarrassed."

Evie sips her wine thoughtfully. She nods to herself, and says, "Being embarrassed in front of someone seems like a big part of love."

"Who said anything about love?" I demand.

"Easy there, killer."

"I'm not in love with anyone."

"I know, I know," Evie says. "Alison is in love with Alison. Everyone knows that."

I stare at her.

She shrugs. "Sorry."

"Is that what people think?"

"That's the vibe you give out, sweetie."

"Oh, god." I shake my head. "This is all too much effort."

"Emotions?"

"Absolutely yes, emotions. Kill them with fire. I don't have time for this."

"But, Alison," Evie says, tilting her head and blinking at me in the most innocent forest-animal way imaginable, "if you let people in, then you're not on your own anymore. And I kind of got the impression you wanted to have someone else on your team. That's what Cary has been for you, right? Someone else on Team Alison? But you need to let those emotions in or he can't be there for you."

I snort. "Okay, okay, the doctor is *not* in. We aren't doing novice therapy."

"It's not therapy," Evie retorts, annoyed. She picks up her pizza and takes a bite. Still chewing, she mutters, "You're difficult."

I just shake my head and pick up a slice of pizza for myself. Sure, I'm difficult. But don't I have the right to be?

Don't we all?

My Aunt Kate likes to say that horses are difficult, but they are a piece of cake compared to humans. "At least horses are generally interested in what we have to say," she'd tell me, often after some student had the gall to complain about her critique of their riding—she did not sugarcoat her assessments. My aunt doesn't know the meaning of sweetening her statements when she can just pour salt directly into a wound. She figures she'll get faster results if it stings like hell. And she's right—if you can survive a Windy Hill riding lesson, you *will* be a better rider. That's just a hard fact.

When I went off on my own, it seemed easier to work with clients by being cool and professional, rather than harsh and demanding. Hey, we all have our own way of dealing with others. But I learned my lessons at Aunt Kate's knee. Honesty is a virtue. And dogged determination, to the death if necessary, is the only way to improve.

Cary once asked me if I'd been sent to a Victorian orphanage instead of a relative's farm, and he was joking, but he also wasn't too far off. My teenage years were hard. There were tears. Sleepless nights with my entire body aching, wishing I could just quit and go back home.

But I broke through.

I figured out my aunt, I got strong enough for the work, and I put everything I had into my horsemanship and my riding.

I became *me,* and would I trade this version of myself for some softer, gentler, less-driven version of me? Even if that person wasn't deathly afraid of letting someone else in?

A person who was capable of admitting she was jealous and giving a nice guy something to hang on to?

I wouldn't. I don't think I would, anyway. I can't be softer. Don't want to be softer. The outside world is hard.

I look up at Evie, my eyes widening with a revelation.

She looks back at me, swallows a bite of pizza, then nervously asks, "Is there a spider on my head or something?"

"No, of course not," I snort. "This is *my* barn, remember? And anyway, we'd both be screaming. No, listen. You're right."

"Well, I know I'm right," she says reasonably. "The question is, about what?"

"I mean—yeah, you're right. Things are going to get better. Because *I'm* going to get tougher." It all makes so much sense! I wave my hands around in the air. "I shouldn't have let Cary get to me like this. I let my guard down. I let things get emotional. That is *not* the way forward. I've got this now, though!"

"Um." Evie shifts in her chair. *My* chair, actually. The boss's chair. That's okay. She can have it for another few minutes. But then I need it back. She says, choosing her words cautiously, "I didn't quite mean you had to get tougher. You're already made of steel, and it's scary sometimes. I meant that *things* will get easier. Nothing ever stays awful forever. You have a breakthrough and things get easier, and—"

"Nope," I say. "Things don't get easier. It's *us,* Evie. *We* get tougher. Trust me on this."

"Okay, let's say you're right. That's good, then!" She smiles, a satisfied *I helped!* expression that makes me love her all the more. "And in the meantime, pizza and wine help, right?"

"There's no in the meantime," I say, standing up. "There's only right now, and how I'm going to handle it."

Chapter Twenty-Nine

HANSIE, I THINK, throwing back my sheet in the morning.

I am not going to think about what's missing from my life this morning. Only what I've got.

Cary is not coming, Tony isn't wiggling up from the corner of my bed, his tail going a mile a minute. Two gaps in my day that I'm not going to think about.

Only Hansie. I am going to fill my head and my heart with my horse, who gave me a brilliant performance yesterday and is only going to give me more brilliant performances.

Hansie is the only thing I've got going for me, so I better make every minute with him count. Why wallow in bed wishing for a guy when I've got a literal dream-horse in my paddock? I'm not going to be that girl. I don't even think she was ever an option.

"Up we go," I say to myself, swinging my feet to the floor. "Let's get this show on the road."

Lily Marlene is waiting by the feed room door, her olive-green eyes bright. She rubs carefully against my ankle as I unbolt the door, pressing only the parts of her nose and cheek that she wants to touch me against the leather of my paddock boots. She is so precise, so demanding; I've always liked that about her. About cats in general, really.

Cats remind me of my Aunt Kate.

"You're my little boss, aren't you?" I ask Lily Marlene, who darts behind the line of shining trash cans storing horse feed, anxious to surprise any mice who might have lingered past the witching hour. "Keeping me honest and on-time."

What people don't understand is that I hold no resentment against Aunt Kate for making me the person I am. I hold no grudges against her for treating me like, to borrow Cary's words, a Victorian orphan. Clearly I inherited her nature, her obsession with perfection and organization, or I wouldn't have taken to her training program like a duck to water—after the first few painful months of breaking-in.

The strict program at Windy Hill was a *gift*, and that's what they don't realize. I was always going to be like this.

Aunt Kate was the only one who saw my potential to rise instead of my eventual downfall.

And if that means that I can't have a normal relationship with other people, and if that means I'm a lonely woman working with horses just like my Aunt Kate surely always has been—why else did she take on a teenage niece, why else has she lived alone her entire life, if not because she is a lonesome loner who simply can't function with a second person who isn't as neurotic as she is?—well then that is what it *means*. I don't have a good answer to that. I can't change how I am. I don't want to.

But of course, Cary already made his choice. He let me chase him away. Because he would have said he'd come back, wouldn't he? If he could have handled my particular brand of crazy? He would have said "I'll be back soon, Alison," instead of simply, "I'll be thinking about you, Alison."

That was a break-up line if I ever heard one. And we were never even together.

The horses hear me tossing grain and the whinnies begin, echoing across the foggy paddocks outside. *"They* want me," I tell Lily Marlene as I return the buckets to their shelf above the feed bins. She stares patiently at a single point behind the corner feed bin and does not flick so much as an ear in my direction.

So, I leave her to her work. I understand all about slavish devotion to the work.

It's all we've got, people like me, and Aunt Kate, and Lily Marlene. The work is all we've got.

I bring the horses in to eat their breakfast, then set up Hansie's tack by the cross-ties, ready to go exactly twenty minutes after he cleans up his grain. With everything set and ready, I stand and drink coffee, watching him lick his manger, watching him dig into his hay. Mentally, I plan out on our ride, envisioning the way I would like for things to go. First a long, ambling hack out in the field, then some trotting and cantering on a loose rein, then back to the arena to do a little work up in the bridle, thinking about our dressage without getting too tense. It's going to be a good ride. I'm ready for it.

Today, we're going to do the work.

The work is all I've got.

BUT THE WORK isn't always enough to fill the day...or my racing thoughts.

Especially when my Thursday evening lessons cancel.

And then my Friday evening lessons cancel, too.

The ground feels a little less stable beneath my feet, even after an excellent ride on Hansie is followed by several nice hacks and workouts on my other horses.

They're all innocent enough cancelations. The texts drop into my phone one by one, each detailing completely relatable situations. A nasty cold crops up out of nowhere. A birthday party is suddenly revealed by a younger sibling, commencing at the exact same time as the older sibling's riding lesson. A car is in the shop and Lyfts are expensive. A forgotten visit to Grandma and Grandpa's house in Siesta Key, planned months ago, can't be delayed.

All very reasonable, and over the course of four or five weeks, this many cancelations might have been manageable.

All of them occurring in one weekend is financially daunting. But I take a breath each time and carry on. I have managed this place for six months on a shoestring budget. A weekend without riding lessons sucks, but we can carry on. After all, I have the boarders now, padding my account at the beginning of the month. And I have Mrs. C's riding lesson payment, which is covering Hansie's payment and then some. It's going to be fine.

And then, on Sunday, something truly terrible happens.

Mrs. C's weekly payment does not appear in my Venmo account.

Okay, yes. Obviously, I should have known she wasn't going to pay me for the two weeks Cary skipped by leaving Ocala early.

Obviously.

Maybe I should have had a contract to make her pay for the entire program ahead of time, but I trusted her and I never thought it would end early. So that's on me. I can take responsibility for this. Should've known.

Even so, it's still completely horrifying to look at the app and *not* see that hefty sum, with a lovely plus sign next to it, indicating that for once, the big money is going *into* my account, not out of it.

The loss of it all, Cary leaving *and* the brief period of financial stability he brought me, hit like a punch in the gut.

"But it's okay," I tell myself. "It's fine. You'll get paid board money in another..."

I look at the calendar on my phone.

"Two and a half weeks."

Something wobbles dangerously in my gut. October, which rushed at me like a rampaging lion during the hot days of September, is going to last forever now that I'm flat broke, waiting on November first's board payment.

THE ONLY PLACE I feel better is in the saddle—and even then, it's only marginally. Sebastian and Plato are schooling nicely, but neither of them are going to win at the event coming up this weekend. Their dressage tests are going to be passable, at best. Both of them have weaknesses we're still working through, and basic things like staying connected through the bridle in downward transitions are challenging enough that the most generous of judges will note we still have miles to go.

And in Ocala, a passable dressage test is not going to get you a top spot going into cross-country.

Sometimes, I regret setting up my business in the most competitive region in the sport. But only sometimes.

Like right now, when I could use a win and a quick sale on a horse to keep everyone fed.

"They're sure to be gone by New Year," I tell myself, tacking up Hansie on a cloudy morning mid-week. There are just a few days left before our event. Our *debut* event. I dropped our entry down to Beginner Novice, a slight downgrade from the Novice courses he's been competing over, to give us an easier dressage test, less to think about on the jumping phases. Hansie has settled into work with me at last, but I can't shake the memory that he wouldn't be going so nicely if it weren't for Cary.

Cary, insisting that we ride out in the pasture, insisting that Hansie and Nando needed each other's companionship.

How did he know?

He had instincts, that man.

Not enough instincts to stay in touch with *me*, but maybe that's his superior intellect at work, too. Telling him that I was getting too dependent on him—for companionship, not just for help around the barn—and that he'd better keep his distance from the crazy horse girl in Florida, before she did something nuts. Like get attached.

"I don't miss him," I tell Hansie, fastening his noseband in place.

Hansie turns dark eyes on me.

Skeptical eyes. A horse shouldn't be able to give me a skeptical look when I'm talking about emotions, but of course, Hansie is special that way. A horse who gets it. I give him a rub between his eyes, knocking his long, black forelock askew, then gently pulling it back into place.

"You were half his horse, you know that? You loved me the moment you saw me, and I appreciate that. But you fell for him, too. Come on, now Hansie. You should know that a little loyalty goes a long way with me."

He blinks, his expression a very clear: *And what about it?*

"Nothing," I tell him. "It would just be nice if we weren't both thinking about him."

"YOU'RE DEPRESSED."

Evie is in my barn aisle again, this time without the wine and pizza. I wonder if she's got at least got a bag of doughnuts behind her back. It seems pretty rude to show up at someone's barn unannounced, tell them they're depressed, and not bring snacks.

Anyway, I don't have time to stop and talk to her. The stall fronts need dusted. I keep running the dust mop up the stall bars while I say, "Don't be crazy, Evie."

"I'm not crazy." She puts her hands on her hips. No doughnuts, then. "I'm worried about you."

"I'm just tired." Up and down, the dust mop slides. Dust and cobwebs flutter around me. How does a barn get so dirty in just a week or two? "I lost my only help. I should probably get a working student, but I can't afford one right now. That's funny, right? I can't afford free help?"

"Working students aren't free," Evie says, dangerously reasonable. "You have to either pay them or feed and house them. Usually a horse, too. I can see why you wouldn't have the extra cash right now."

"Extra cash!" I laugh. *"Extra!"*

"It's going to be okay," Evie says. Bless her, she has no idea.

"Based on what?" I move to the next stall. Up and down. Cobwebs down. Shine the bars. "My students are all canceling on me. They were all I had week to week. I'm running on fumes until the end of the month. I have an *event* this weekend and I can't afford to go to the grocery store."

Evie nods.

Suddenly, I appreciate Evie's forbearance. She doesn't ask where the hell my savings went (hay, mostly) or how I let things get this bad (poor business skills, I presume) or what the hell I'm going to do to survive until the end of October (eat shoe leather, most likely). She doesn't ask those things because she knows I don't have the answers, and Evie is always thoughtful like that. She doesn't put a person on the spot.

A large spiderweb, still housing a large spider, falls at my feet and I jump backward with a yelp. Evie gives a little yell and scampers away as well. We back up against the opposite stall and watch the critter high-tail it back towards the wall it came from. I have seen a lot of spiders in my time, but this one has a presence which can only be described as monstrous, and a wash of nausea churns in my gut. That thing lives in my barn. Up high, next to my apartment. And it's probably spawning more.

Spiders that are going to take over my barn, their webs defying my constant attempts to bring them down, and the boarders and students I manage to bring here will run away screaming, telling all of Ocala about the horrific spider-barn...

I swallow something acidic.

"That was quite a large spider," Evie says, downplaying the situation with admirable aplomb.

I shake my head. I can't speak. Literally, I can't think of any words or even how to open my mouth. My knees are trembling, my thighs are pins and needles, and suddenly I'm sliding down the stall wall, hitting the ground, and just sitting there, staring into space.

Evie's next to me immediately; she's got her hands on my shoulders, she's looking into my eyes. I shake my head at her—at least, I try to. But none of my muscles seem to be working properly. And also—am I not breathing?

"Alison," Evie says urgently, "if this is a panic attack, this is the weirdest way anyone has ever had one."

I'M UPSTAIRS AND on the couch, glass of water in my hand and Lily Marlene at my side, before I start to feel normal again. And even then, I don't like it. I don't want to feel normal right now...my base level is not a comfortable place.

Evie is pacing back and forth, clearly on her way to a panic attack of her own. "You're not helping at the moment," I tell her, not wanting to sound ungrateful for her help, but also unable to regulate my words the way I usually would. The carefully rehearsed and always appropriate Alison seems to be missing right now. I hope someone finds her and brings her back soon. "Can you just sit down and relax?"

She throws herself on my bed and stares at me. "What am I going to do with you?"

"Trust I can manage myself?"

"Now is not the time to be snarky. You just lost your shit over a spider."

"The single spider was not the issue," I say. "The thousands of spiders that it represented..." I give a little shudder, abandoning that line of thought before it can overtake my brain again. "Listen, I just haven't been keeping the place up. I have to work harder. I'll be fine."

"You can't work harder." Evie shakes her head. "I'd send over Sydney, but we're so swamped now..."

"It's winter. This is the game. This is what we signed up for."

"How can you be so cool about this?" Evie asks.

I shrug. "I don't have any choice?"

I think that's what people don't always understand. They freak out and cry and carry on about things, but sometimes there's just nothing to do but grin and carry on. Aunt Kate taught me that. Life is hard. Hard is life. Blah, blah, blah. I'll get over it.

Even if right now, I don't know how.

"I had a crush on Cary," I say, because nothing is sacred and I feel like letting all my insides out.

Evie leans back on her hands. "I know."

"It was obvious?"

"Maybe to me, because I know you."

"It was just a crush. I'll get over it."

"Is he not coming back?"

I swallow against the lump that rises in my throat; apparently the emotions here are just as raw as ever, and it's harder to shove through them than all my other fears. Or maybe it's just that I haven't learned to handle these emotions yet. I'll tame them in time. I've got my chair and my whip, and I'll teach this lion who the boss is. "He said he isn't coming back."

"Oh, wow. But...but he really liked you."

I'll be thinking about you, Alison.

Not the kind of promise a girl needs, is it? Thoughts and prayers?

I glance at her and shake my head before I explain, "Liking me doesn't matter, though. Or he didn't like me enough. He isn't coming back! He could have at least said he'd visit. I don't need someone hovering over me all the time, but knowing someone is out there? Someone's coming back to see me? That would be pretty good."

There's no one here but Jim. And yes, I'd rather die alone than see Jim again, with his stupid name-dropping and hungry horse trading.

"I could do long-distance," I say. "But this was one-sided."

"I'm not mistaken," Evie insists. "He really does like you. A lot. It was pretty obvious."

"He's an actor," I remind her. "It's easy to believe everything they do is real and has meaning."

"But..." Evie sighs. "Cary isn't a particularly *good* actor."

"Evie! The man is a movie star!"

She shakes her head again. "He had some roles when he was a teenager and didn't get another job for over a decade. I think we can both admit Cary was never a great actor. He was just a really cute guy, and now he's a really handsome thirty-year-old going into a knock-off Hallmark movie. That's not exactly Oscar-worthy."

"That's so mean of you," I say, but I'm wondering if she's right.

Wondering if Cary might be scared of his future, too.

That makes things so much worse. He should have stayed! He should have said he'd be back! We could have kept helping each other! *Why* isn't he here?

I put my face in my hands and make a noise that's halfway between a wail and a moan. And when I'm finished, I feel much better. Almost like I can take on the world again.

Evie and Lily Marlene are both staring at me in horror. "What?" I ask innocently. "You never had to make a good moan before?"

"Alison," Evie says, "sometimes I really wonder about how you were brought up."

"Oh, please." I wave my hand at her. "Everyone's always saying that. It's not a big deal." I get up and head for the door, where my muddy boots are sitting on a mat.

"Where are you going?" Evie asks, alarmed.

"To finish sweeping the aisle for the night," I say matter-of-factly. "And then I'm going to drive to Publix and get some fried chicken. You want to have dinner with me?"

Evie gets up slowly and joins me at the door, her gaze wary. It's like she never saw someone suddenly resolve to conquer all their problems and make their life better through sheer willpower before. "Are you sure you're alright to...drive?" Her tone makes me think she really wanted to finish with, "stand upright" or "walk down stairs unassisted."

"I'm going to be fine," I assure her, tugging on my boots. "I've got a plan."

I don't actually have one yet, but I'm going to.

I've decided that much. The rest, the *actual* plan of action, I'll figure out on the way. I'm going to treat life like a difficult horse. As long as I keep it moving its feet, I've got a shot at controlling where it goes.

Chapter Thirty

AND SO FOR the next two days, I keep my farm clean, I work my horses, I prep for the event, and I am fine. *Fine.* Because I choose to be. Take that, depression. Take that, Cary. I am on the move at all times, never sitting down unless I absolutely have to (certain things require taking a seat). My feet keep moving, and I can only assume they are heading in the direction I need to go. Because even if Cary's unexpected departure has thrown me through a mental loop, I can't let up right before the event.

I can't give up on my horses. In fact, as a plan slowly unfurls in my mind, I come to believe it's more important than ever that we have a good outing this weekend. I need my horses to look fantastic.

By Friday at noon, I am forced to call a halt to my relentless feet... because, incredibly, I have run out of work to do. The trailer is packed. The horses are clean—enough, anyway. I'll still want to bathe them early tomorrow morning before we head over to the show-grounds. My show clothes and my back-up show clothes are set out and ready to go. My keys are even in the truck, sitting on the console so that I cannot misplace them somewhere in my apartment or office.

Feeling aimless for the first time in days, I simply sit in the center of my spotless barn aisle, legs crossed in front of me, and stare out at the parking lot.

Except for my truck and trailer, and Olivia's parked rental, the lot is empty right now; Edward took both his and Olivia's horses to Malcolm's farm this morning so that they can ride with the master before showing. October hasn't yet brought a slowdown of the afternoon rains, so there are some round puddles in the packed white sand, masking deep potholes I'll have to cajole Nathan into filling in once the dry season rolls around. The flowers that Cary planted along either side of the barn doors are flourishing with the rain and the more forgiving sun angle of autumn, growing around the corners and peeking into the aisle with nodding fuchsia and lemon-colored blossoms.

They're beautiful. Possibly the only truly beautiful thing about this farm.

But they came from Cary, and I think...no, I *know*...I need to forget that guy.

That's what the past few days of nonstop work have given me. Not a plan to get Cary back out here, which I admit is what I was hoping for. But instead, I've got the idea that maybe I can do a better job of picking up my life and putting it back together without him around.

After all, what did Cary really do for me? Besides amuse me and keep me company and help me with Hansie—and, let's be real, he didn't actually know Hansie would go better in the field; he was just trying to get out of working in the arena, too. Besides those things, which I am going to downplay for my own mental health, didn't Cary kind of get in my way? Didn't he make for a strained relationship with Olivia, someone I actually kind of liked, until I caught her trying to kiss Cary? Things would be better now, I think, if Cary had never been here to get between Olivia and me. I could have used having her as a friend, instead of a client who tiptoes around me, not sure how to behave since I became an irrational jealousy monster at a horse show, in front of everyone.

And dammit, Cary shouldn't have left in the first place!

He should have chosen me. After all the days we spent together, all the rides and the meals and the work and the laughter, he should have chosen *me*.

I pull my knees to my chest and wrap my arms around them, squeezing myself together.

I should have known sooner that my friendship was turning into a crush. I'm partially to blame here. I should have given him some signal that I was open to a kiss, like Olivia did. She just beat me to the punch. Is that really his fault?

This line of thought is making me angry.

Those flowers are making me angry.

Everything he touched here is just another reason to be filled with a righteous rage.

I glance at my tools hanging along the wall, the sharp edge of the shovel calling out to me. *Rip them out,* the shovel whispers.

Yes, I think. Yes.

What better way to get rid of my memories of Cary than to rip out those flowers, destroy all that work he put into making sure I'd never forget him?

After all, what gives him the right to leave a permanent calling card right under my nose? He left. His flowers can go with him. Maybe I'll even put a handful of dead blossoms in an envelope and mail them to him.

Okay, maybe that would be excessive and weird and slightly serial-killer. I won't do that.

But the flowers are still going down.

I take down the shovel, ignoring the spider that scurries away from beneath it—I'll deal with *him* later, I think grimly—and head to the barn door. The flowers wave on either side of me, blossoms gleaming in the midday light. A lizard wiggles his way along the woody branches of a hibiscus bush, his smooth scales green as a sun-ripened lime.

Sorry, buddy. Find a new house.

I raise the shovel to make the first stab. I'm going to whack these flowers into oblivion, and it's going to feel so good. I think I even let out a cackle.

And then, before I can drop the shovel on those unsuspecting blooms, a truck pulls into the parking lot.

A UPS truck, to be precise.

Hmm. Probably won't score any points with my UPS driver if I'm stabbing a garden to death when he shows up. And when you live out in the countryside, you definitely want to be pals with your delivery guys.

I slide the shovel back into the barn aisle. Hopefully, it just looked like I was doing a little light weeding...not embarking upon a full-scale garden massacre.

The UPS driver hops down from the cab and walks over, neatly sidestepping a puddle. He's in his late twenties, with muscles that fill out his brown uniform nicely, and a jutting chin that could stop traffic. I try very hard to be attracted to him, because he's good-looking in a way that is nothing like Cary's chiseled cheekbones and soulful dark eyes. This isn't a man that will make you breakfast in the morning. But he might be convinced to let you cook for him—as long as you promise to leave immediately after doing the dishes.

"Alison?" he asks, glancing from his tracking device to me.

"That's me," I say. "Whatcha got? I can't remember ordering anything. You know how that goes."

"It's a real big bag," he says, without cracking a smile. "Got a wheelbarrow?"

Confused, I go and fetch one of my wheelbarrows while he opens the back door of the truck. I'm astonished when he pulls out a fat brown bag roughly the size of two feed bags. "What on earth?"

If I was drunk-shopping after one of my wine-nights with Evie, I was definitely erring on the practical side of self-indulgence.

"Feels like seeds," he says, dropping the bag into the wheelbarrow. It shudders gently with the weight. "You planting crops out here?"

"Crops?" I repeat blankly, staring at the bag. The return address is printed on the shipping label. *Florida Wildflower Association.* "No," I say, pressing a hand against my chest. Hopefully, I can keep all the feelings in that way. "Not crops. Flowers."

"Pretty," he says, and hops back into the truck, leaving me with a wheelbarrow full of what can only be Cary's handiwork.

THE WILDFLOWER SEEDS get parked in the hay-stall alongside the week's stack of bales, with a tarp thrown over them so I don't have to look at them. But I want to; I want to stand and stare at the forty-pound bag of future flowers that surely came from Cary. What was he thinking? Why would he do this to me? I stare at my phone, wondering if I should text him.

In the barn aisle, the shovel leans against the wall, laughing at me. I pick it up and put it away. So much for my righteous rage against the flower-beds. They gleam and nod happily, a collection of flowers that seem to know they've escaped certain death.

"For today, anyway," I tell them, and get out a broom to hunt after that spider I saw earlier.

A half-hour later, a FedEx truck pulls into the lot.

"What could *this* be?" I mutter, putting down the broom.

Maybe a boarder ordered something from a tack shop that they need by tomorrow for the event.

That's probably it.

I walk out to meet the driver...and she hands me a flat envelope. I flick my gaze to the return address.

Los Angeles, California.

I sigh so hard the woman, who is already getting back into the truck, looks at me. Her expression is clearly sympathetic.

I wonder how many envelopes filled with bad news pass through her hands.

But this isn't bad news, I tell myself as I stand in the parking lot and rip the envelope open. Just...unexpected.

I nearly drop the sheet of paper folded inside. It's a letter. A *handwritten* letter. Who does that?

I mean, obviously it's from Cary, but why is he like this?

Hey Alison,

I ordered these wildflower seeds from the botanical garden last month. A couple of days ago, I got the shipping notification and realized you wouldn't know what to do with them, but I didn't know if I should call. Or text. And I wanted to send you an email, but I was afraid maybe I'd use the wrong email and you wouldn't get it. It's a lot of seeds, and they have a purpose, seriously!

So anyway, I decided to write you a quick note and FedEx it to you so it arrives on time. I hope that's okay.

I just know that you don't have time to mow like you want to, and it always bothers you when the grass around the barn gets scruffy. So, here are the magic seeds that will save you—for six months or so, anyway.

Spread these seeds all around the barn and along the driveway to the road. All those sandy areas? Seeds. Rake them in so the birds don't eat them. I know you don't have time, but this will help you out later!

Do it now, or in November at the latest. Be generous, that's why I ordered the big bag. And when it warms up in March, you'll see... wildflowers everywhere! No need to mow. And the place will be so beautiful. It'll be famous. Just like you always wanted.

Enjoy them.

Cary

I stare at the letter, reading it over and over again. His handwriting is loopy and round—the writing of a person with a sense of humor, I think. The writing of a person with a big heart.

Enjoy them.

Couldn't he have signed off with something a little more personal?

I sigh, crumpling the paper a little, then catching myself and straightening it out again—because I can't let anything happen to this note. Handwritten, the last piece of Cary I've got. I know what I'm going to do with it. Stick it in my desk drawer, where it's safe, and where I can look at it ten times a day, running my fingers over his name like a lovesick teenager.

I never was a lovesick teenager, I reflect, trying to swallow the lump in my throat. Maybe that's why I'm having such a rough time now. Another life lesson I didn't learn at my aunt's knee, because I was too busy becoming the world's most obsessive horsewoman.

Well, this is the lesson, Alison. Sometimes you get a crush on your friend and then they break your heart by just...staying your friend.

Your thoughtful friend, who sends you wildflower seeds in the mail and makes no promises that you'll ever see them again.

"This is why I should stick with horses," I tell Lily Marlene. She pauses in her wanderings and blinks slowly at me. "They stay where you put them. Most of the time, anyway."

With a mew, she disappears around the corner of the barn door and disappears into the flowers.

"HE BOUGHT YOU wildflower seeds?" Evie asks, face incredulous.

I nod grimly, tipping the bottle of wine over her tumbler. "So that I won't have to worry about mowing next year. He knows I get upset that the place always looks scraggly, so he told me to seed the sandy areas around the barn with these seeds so it won't need mown."

"That's...pretty thoughtful." Evie sips her wine and considers the bag of seeds. We're standing in my hay stall, because I felt like I had to show her, in person, the sheer gargantuan five-hundred pound gorilla of it all. "I'm trying and failing to imagine Malcolm making a gesture like this."

"Oh, please," I say. "Malcolm has other pluses. Being thoughtful about gardening is a pretty specific trait; I don't think you can expect all men to demonstrate it."

Evie laughs. "You're being pretty cold about this."

"That's because I'm all shriveled up inside," I say thoughtfully. "I'm like one of those little capsules you drop into water and they turn into, I don't know, an elephant. Except, there's really no room for an elephant when you didn't have one before, you know? Where do you even put it?"

She gazes at me thoughtfully and says, "You truly come up with the weirdest metaphors."

"I guess that's one of my skills."

"So what do you do with the elephant you don't have room for?"

I sigh. "Get rid of it, I guess."

"And how do you propose to do that?"

"Business as usual, until the elephant knows it isn't wanted and lumbers away."

"Or shrinks back down to the size of a dry sponge?"

"Yeah," I say. "That would be fine, too."

"It won't go back in the capsule, you know."

"Close enough." I shrug again. "What other choice do I have?"

Evie sits down on a hay bale and crosses her legs. She gazes out at the empty barn aisle as lightning flickers through the doorway and the windows, accompanied by a low roll of distant thunder. She flinches a little, but I don't, even though I remember the taste of loose change in my mouth every time a storm blows through. It's just one of those things. The lightning came for me, but it didn't kill me. It just made me stronger...maybe.

Strong enough?

Maybe not.

I lean back against the wooden slats of the stall wall, ignoring the possibility of spiders. The hay stall is glaringly tidy; I have been scrubbing all the walls in this barn, every day, all week. If there's a spider here now, he must hate his sparkling-clean new life. But I need it this way. I need the perfection.

Just rubbing my hands over the smooth wood makes me feel more confident. The slats are slick with soaked-in soap. I have taken control, I think, sliding my reddened fingertips against the burnished surface. I have everything under control.

"Malcolm's going to wonder when I'm coming back," Evie says finally. "We have to leave for the event early in the morning."

That's my cue to let her go. "Thanks for coming over. I really appreciate it."

"So formal." She smiles up at me. "Alison, you're going to be fine. I really believe that."

"Fine, with wildflowers," I suggest as lightly as I can manage. "Even better, right?" *Look at me, I've got jokes!*

"You should eat something and go to bed," she says, standing up and dusting off her breeches with both hands. "You have an early morning, too. You're competing three horses of your own tomorrow! That's a big deal! I'm really proud of you."

"Thank you," I reply, touched but not willing to let it show—if I let out any emotion, who knows what crazy will escape? What if I'm afraid, what if I'm secretly scared to death that this weekend I'll fail and I'll *really* have nothing to show for a summer of hard work, for all my life savings, for the guy who bought me wildflowers and yet still, somehow, got away? "That's kind of you to say," I add, aware it sounds strangely formal but not sure how to say it any other way.

Evie gives me an odd look, like she knows something is up with me, something that wasn't there an hour ago when I texted her and asked if she could come over after work. I know she wants to stay. I know she thinks there is more to say. She might even be right. Maybe if she stayed, and we finished this bottle of wine, it would all come out. Everything I am determined to jam back into that stupid capsule.

But Evie is a horsewoman with a huge event tomorrow, too, so she puts down the tumbler, gives me a soft hug, and heads out into the approaching storm.

"See you tomorrow," she calls over her shoulder, and I raise my hand, waving goodnight.

Chapter Thirty-One

HANSIE LOOKS AROUND the sunrise glow creeping over the show-grounds with his head high and his ears pricked, and I swear I can see satisfaction in his gaze.

I know how to do this, he is telling me.

"I know you do, buddy," I say, patting the firm muscle of his neck. We're almost out of time. Naturally, I scheduled a hand-walk around the show-grounds into my day, even though the day is going to flash by with all the horses I have to get through three phases today. I'm glad I made the time for this walk. Everything about his relaxed, but interested, demeanor tells me that my new horse feels just fine.

What a relief!

If everything in my life has been angst-ridden and difficult as hell in the past week, at least Hansie seems sorted out. And that's what counts. Every day since the jumper show, he has been a little more level-headed, until I have been able to start a ride in the field and finish it, neatly and without panic, in the arena. He still has a ways to go, but Hansie is figuring out his phobias and dropping the tense act.

I'd like to think I would have figured out Hansie eventually, but I can't deny it was Cary who put us on the right track. It was Cary who insisted on all that field riding, who *said* Hansie would feel better out of the arena. Yesterday, when I was busy trying to hate

Cary, I pinned his pleading to take Hansie for a trail ride on his desire to avoid hard work in the ring. But today, as the sun rises over a hundred or more horses, riders, and their teams, with a forty-pound bag of wildflower seeds and a handwritten letter back at the barn, I can admit that Cary did the right thing for all of us when he said the horses wanted to get out of the arena.

I can admit that Cary got us here today, prepared for a solid show day instead of a three-phase panic attack.

And of course, the event is custom-made for a horse who wants to be out in wide open spaces.

First, the dressage test, to be ridden in a grass ring with a low, fetlock-high fence that is hardly a barrier at all. Cross-country, a collection of obstacles flung across thirty acres of open fields. Only the stadium jumping round will be in an arena, and the show-grounds' jumping arena is huge, bigger even than the expansive ring at Fine Day Farm. Hansie can't get claustrophobic today, even if he tried for it.

This horse lives to work outside, and today he's going to get his wish.

Now, for the tight-rope act of competing three horses at the same level!

Hansie, Sebastian, and Plato are all in the same division, Beginner Novice. This level has friendly heights and simple combinations in both dressage and jumping, so it is packed with riders starting out their horses for the season. The sheer size of this division works in my favor; I was able to get the scheduler to put twenty minutes between each of my rides. That means Hansie is the first horse out; Plato is nearly last. But even with the gap, I need help to get the horses tacke up, over to the arenas, and cooled out after their rounds.

I'll have just enough time to hop off a horse, hop on the next one, and warm-up the next one...for three separate phases.

Although event grooming is complicated and it helps to have someone experienced to change out saddles, bridles, and boots, I know it would have been a big plus to have Cary around today. When it was clear he wasn't going to be here after all, I ended up begging Malcolm and Evie to lend me their working student, Sydney, for the division.

They agreed readily, although Malcolm is acting as if it's a huge inconvenience. That's normal behavior for Malcolm, though, so I ignored him, thanked Evie, and welcomed Sydney to my team for the day.

She's already at the trailer grooming Sebastian for his dressage test, so I walk back Hansie and tie him by his hay-net to get him tacked up as well. We have a half-hour to his dressage time. That's just enough time to saddle, do a light warm-up, and spring into the arena on time and with plenty of gas in the tank. The one thing I don't want for our dressage today is a horse behind the leg, worrying about the corners of the arena. We're going for *big* today. If he loses some finesse in his gaits and movement because he's a little too boisterous, that's okay. I'd rather have more horse than less.

Sydney smiles at me as she sprays detangler in Sebastian's tail, then adds some to Hansie's as well. At age seventeen, she's whippet-slim and effortlessly beautiful in her expensive riding clothes. Frankly, I never thought we'd whip this one into shape; she was one of Malcolm's most spoiled winter riders for several years. And then she rebelled against her own privilege, ended up as our working student, and made it possible for me to hand the reins to Evie so that I could start my own farm.

I'm not sure if I should love her or hate her for that.

Maybe things will make more sense after my last ride today.

One way or another.

"Sebastian's such a love," she says, placing his saddle gently atop the white quilted dressage pad. "I'm going to buy him for myself."

"Oh, please do," I suggest, grinning. "I need the cash to pay for Hansie."

Sydney glances over Hansie. "You're lucky they didn't offer him to me first. I'd be all over that beauty."

"You'd have gotten Mommy to buy him?" I tease.

Sydney shrugs, unashamed. "I mean, use what you've got, right? If she's willing to pay, who am I to tell her no?"

"That's very wise of you. Some people would let pesky things like pride get in the way."

"Would *you?*" Sydney counters. It's like she knows I agreed to teach a has-been actor to be a cowboy in exchange for enough money to make a down payment on this horse. I guess Evie might have told her; it's probably not a secret. Sydney fastens the girth with a gentle tug and says, "I mean, I don't think pride has any place in this sport. It costs too much, and it pays nothing. If I'm learning anything from working for Malcolm, it's that there is never, ever enough money."

"You're not kidding," I snort. Hansie leans into my curry comb, his lips fluttering with contentment. I have to hurry up this procedure, but it's hard to tell him no when he's so happy. "I'm in a pretty cash-free zone at the moment, actually. I don't think I have any pride left to burn me, either."

"Well, if you need money, I know where to find it," Sydney says, so casual it's hard to believe she's for real. But I know she is. "I can talk Mom into a syndicate buy-in if you want. She's already in on one of Malcolm's. What's another share of a horse, if it makes you feel included in your daughter's life?" And Sydney smirks at me before walking back to the tack compartment to get Sebastian's bridle.

"Damn," I tell Hansie, giving his coat broad, firm strokes with the body brush. "She's tougher than me, I think."

In my head, I hear Cary's voice chuckling as he says, *Not possible, Alison. She wasn't raised in rags and wooden shoes like you.*

It's a different kind of tough, I suppose. Being handed everything on a silver platter because your mother would rather buy your love than spend time with you, earning it, fosters a certain kind of calculating personality. On the other hand, my parents were willing to send me to chase my dreams with the understanding that my taskmaster aunt was not going to give me the gentlest upbringing in the world. They showed their love by setting me free. What kind of person has that made me?

A confused one, I think reluctantly. A person who can't quite figure out what love is. Not between humans, anyway.

"Well, at least there's no confusion when it comes to loving you," I tell Hansie, flicking the brush down his face. He closes his eyes and steps a little closer to me, and I feel like I could groom him all day, except that Sydney comes over yelling "Chop chop, boss-lady, get on that horse!" and I realize I'd better hustle or I won't even have the twenty-minute warm-up I promised myself.

HANSIE'S WARM-UP goes beautifully. The morning grows warm quickly, and there's a sheen of sweat on his neck and beneath the straps of his bridle as we trot into the dressage ring, but his head is in the game, his ears flicking towards the judge and scribe at their table beneath a tent at the arena end, then back to me as I sit deep and think *whoa* just before the center of the ring.

He halts square and only wobbles a little behind as I salute the judge. *Forward,* I think, leg on, and he bounces eagerly down the center-line, his gaze fixed on the humans watching him and making their cryptic notes.

I can imagine what they'll say as we reach the end of the arena at C and make our turn. *Over-bent to left, good impulsion.* Not the worst for a Beginner Novice test. And then I realize that if I keep thinking about what the judge is saying to the scribe, I will go off-course. *Be present.* It's one of my strengths; I suppose it says a lot about Hansie that I am capable of wandering in my thoughts during a dressage test.

He grounds me in a way unlike any other horse.

Hansie prances through his dressage test as the minutes tick by and the sun beats down, so that I forget everything but the way he feels, the way he moves, the opposite twins of impulsion and submission marking every move I make in my seat bones, my legs, my abdomen, my shoulders, my fingers. Maybe even my nose—when I turn my head to look where we're going next, every bit of me is communicating through saddle and bridle to the dancing horse beneath me.

And then it's over, my final salute a nod, a bursting smile, a feeling that my heart is on my sleeve to show the world how much I care about this horse as I lean down and pat his slick neck.

"You're the best boy," I tell him, as he shakes his head and snorts.

The judge and scribe nod and smile and look down at their work, finalizing the test score-sheet, prepping the next one. They will watch dozens and dozens of pairs go through this ring today. It's almost impossible to truly stand out, especially at this level where the movements and requirements are relatively simple, but maybe for at least four or five minutes, they were impressed with what they saw.

"Gorgeous," a few other riders say as we head out of the arena and back towards the warm-up. "Really nice test."

I hold my head up high as I wave my thanks with one gloved hand, feeling dangerously near tears.

Happy tears, lost tears, triumphant tears, they're all mingling in my eyes right now.

I can't help but wish Cary had seen this. The test he helped make possible. I don't know if I'd have gotten it without his help.

I really don't know that I would have.

Imagine if he'd been here with his iPhone, filming us out there in our first test.

It would have been prefect for that movie he said he'd make, the documentary of Hansie's first season with me. The one I told him to forget about, because I didn't want to record our failures. Now I know that was foolish; I would have been recording our triumphant rise. Why'd I have to be so short-sighted?

Sydney has Sebastian tacked and waiting at the edge of the warm-up area. He watches us approach with his head held high, looking astonished that Hansie is out here, too. Sydney just looks down at her phone, ignoring the show completely. I hop down alongside her and she glances up.

"Hey, how'd it go?" she asks, pocketing her phone.

"It went awesome," I gush, and she raises her eyebrows, not used to seeing me so unguarded.

"It *must* have. You look almost crazy, Alison!"

"I *feel* almost crazy," I laugh, patting Hansie and unbuckling his nose-band.

"Here, let me do that," she says, taking his reins in her free hand. "You need to get on this horse and go."

"You're right, thanks," I say. A quick check of the girth and I swing into Sebastian's tack, breaking my usual rule of only mounting from a block. There isn't time to go back to the trailer. I'm settling myself onto Sebastian's narrow frame, looking around idly while he waits for me with his usual patience, when I spot a slim, long-legged man power-walking away from the dressage arenas. I feel a startled flip in my abdomen as my stomach takes one for the team. Who is that? It's not—

He's moving through a crowd hanging out near the stadium jumping, where the Intermediate division is hopping the biggest fences of the day, and then he's behind the show office and out of sight.

It's no one, I tell myself. This is Ocala; we have an abundance of long-legged men here. Almost too many, if we're honest with ourselves. They have such cursed natural balance on horseback.

It's just my brain playing tricks on me, thinking so much about Cary that I think I'm seeing him back in Florida, when I know he's in California. Where he lives. Where he'll stay.

"Come on, Sebastian," I say. "Let's go dressaging."

BY THE TIME Plato finishes a finicky, head-tossing dressage test— there was a bee by his ears the entire time, I swear—Sydney has Hansie in his jumping tack and is starting on Sebastian. I have just enough time to drink some water and hit the port-a-potty before they're calling my name at the jumping ring, so Sydney has a quick word with the in-gate steward while I jog Hansie to the jumping warm-up to hop him over a few sticks. Sydney waves to show me she's bought me some time and then heads back to the trailer to finish up prepping Sebastian, and I'm profoundly grateful for her entitled upbringing in that moment. The steward is looking my way and shaking her head like I broke the entire day's schedule, but I can't help it that my dressage ring was running late by the end of the division.

Hansie snorts and blows at the warm-up fences, but clears them all with feet to spare, nearly jumping me out of the tack. I find myself clinging to his neck a few times while he puts enough oomph into a jump to clear the standards.

"Well, *someone's* excited," a fellow rider calls, and I laugh.

"He's been jumping in the field for the past month," I explain. "These colored sticks must look highly suspicious!"

"Take him around once more and see if you can contain all that energy," a cool voice commands, and I look around to see Malcolm standing by the jumps, his arms folded.

"Malcolm!"

"I have five minutes," he says, unsmiling. "Let's get it right, please."

The woman at the in-gate shouts my number.

"Five minutes," Malcolm shouts back. The in-gate steward shakes her head and points to another rider hanging out nearby, who gladly picks up her reins and trots into the arena. Malcolm says to me, "Do it right, please."

I'm so grateful for his help with warm-up, I decide to just take the attitude without complaint. Five minutes later, Hansie's jumping much more reasonably and he sends me to the show-ring.

The steward looks at me for a moment, her chin jutting. "*Now,* are you ready?" she demands at last.

"I'm ready," I say meekly.

"Fine," she says. "As soon as that horse in the ring goes through the timers, get in there."

Yes, *ma'am.*

The dressage scores aren't up yet, so I have no idea where we stand going into the stadium jumping. It makes our round go by with a lack of urgency I find refreshing. There's no mental energy wasted calculating how many poles Hansie can drop and stay in his place, or a sense of futility from knowing that even a clear round won't give me a good finish overall.

Instead, we just canter around the course with the easiest, most careful approaches and biggest, roundest turns we can manage. I know a lot of kids like to ride stadium like they're peeling out in the Grand Prix arena at Legends, but at Beginner Novice level, that's just not necessary. All you need is to be careful.

And Hansie is so careful after our mini-lesson with Malcolm, picking up his hooves and putting them down again with such precision, he might as well be counting his strides for himself. There is a smattering of applause from the moms and coaches and kids watching the round as we canter through the timers, aware that we put in a picture-perfect equitation round even if our style was not being judged.

I have about two seconds to tell Hansie what a good boy he is before Sydney is thrusting Sebastian at me. "I'll walk him while you jump these two and then you can trot off and do your cross-country," she says.

I can't help but be impressed with her efficiency. "Can you water him, too?" I ask.

She gives me a glare which says there was no chance she was going to skimp on the water break.

Damn, Sydney, I think. *Okay.*

BY THE TIME Hansie is stepping out of the start-box, his ears already locked on the first log a dozen strides away, I am entertaining the idea of stealing Sydney away from Malcolm and Evie. Of course, I don't have enough horses to interest her now...or anywhere for her to live, or the money to pay for her horse's care and upkeep, or a small salary—all things she's getting from Fine Day Farm. Also, I lack the prestige and intensive training she's getting from Malcolm.

Dammit, what is it going to take to get me on Malcolm's level? How will I ever—

Unfocused on my ride as I fixate on my future, I forget to sit back and take Hansie in hand quick enough, and he throws himself at the log fence with so much gusto he picks a long spot out of the blue, nearly unseating me. I blink in confusion as we gallop away from the fence, the reins slipping through my hands. Did I just nearly come off at the first jump on a Beginner Novice cross-country course?

Get it together, Alison.

The voice is in my head, but it's my aunt's voice, stern and soul-crushing. Silly mistakes like that wouldn't have flown at Windy Hill.

It's effective, though. I sit up, take Hansie in hand, and balance him up for the second fence on course.

We take the little wooden barn jump in stride and canter up a slope towards a pleasant scattering of easy log fences set amongst tall pine trees. Hansie pulls on me, saying it would be easier to just drag along on his forehand, and in reply I lift my hands, telling him to sit back on his hind end and use it to propel him uphill. Up and over the first jump, a swing around a clump of palmettos, and over the second at a slight angle—tricky, for most young horses, but Hansie has no problems. His ears are pricked, his canter is rhythmic, his breath flutters from his nostrils with each stride in a loose, happy snort.

For a few minutes, I am able to let go of the empire-building and the perfectionism and the emptiness that comes with thinking about both, and simply enjoy the ride.

Chapter Thirty-Two

THE RIBBONS GO up in the tack room, on a rail under the window: a second place streamer for Hansie, a fourth for Sebastian, a hard-fought eighth for Plato. I can't stop admiring them. Since I started on my own, I've gotten some smaller ribbons for the schooling shows we've done over the summer, but these are the first long, impressive ribbons for an official horse trials that I've won under Highbury Sport Horses. The gleaming satin fills my heart with pride.

"Look at this!" Olivia gushes, coming into the tack room with her own ribbons. "Can we put ours up in here, too? Like we're one big, happy stable family!"

"I don't know about *stable,*" I laugh, "but yes, that would be great!" I'm happy Olivia and I have been able to put the jumper show altercation in the past. I really do like her.

She puts up her blue and pink ribbons—having won a first and a fifth in her horses' divisions—alongside mine, with just a little space dividing them. Then she rushes out and pulls Edward into the tack room as well.

"Hang up your ribbons," she urges him. "Go on, be a part of the team."

I watch her hand on his arm, the way her fingers press with easy familiarity on his skin. Edward doesn't seem to mind. Which is interesting, because up until this point I hadn't thought anyone could touch grouchy Edward without being turned to stone or something. The guy has been a pill since day one. Now, though, he just pats Olivia's hand gently, and she lets it slide off his bicep. He asks, "What are we doing now?"

"We're hanging up our ribbons like we're twelve!" Olivia laughs. "Look how cute!"

"Not hanging them on the stalls?" He raises an eyebrow.

"Bugs will get on them," Olivia says. "I was just going to take mine home, but hanging them up here is so much better. We can do it all winter long and fill this wall with ribbons!"

Edward shrugs and opens his tack trunk, taking out another red ribbon and a green one. "Molly's first time at this level," he says gruffly, nodding at the green sixth-place ribbon. "I'm proud of her."

"She's a nice mare," I say, watching Olivia pull Edward close and give him a little hug. So, just how close are these two? It seems like she didn't waste any time making a new friend once Cary was out of the picture.

Wish I could move that quickly. But it's silly to think there's any guy in the cards for me. If the best I could do around here was Jim...I shake my head to myself.

Edward shakes his head at Olivia's insistent cuddling, making me think they're not fully an item just yet. But I suspect Olivia is the type who will simply act like they're a couple until she gets her way. And Edward, as gruff and unpleasant as he has been with me, could do a lot worse than having a big-hearted and beautiful girl like Olivia fall for him. Whether it's just a winter show season fling or something that lasts, I think it would be good for him.

And here I was mad at her for chasing Cary. The moment he left, she was probably following Edward around, calculating her new plan for an Ocala romance. Like Sydney, Olivia possesses the ability to see what she wants and make it happen.

I used to think I had that ability, too, but now I can see it was just wishful thinking and the pride of prominence as Malcolm's right-hand woman.

"We're going to get some dinner," Olivia says. "Do you want to join us? I'm thinking Italian..."

"I'm thinking *pizza*," Edward corrects her. "You do what you want, but after an event, I deserve a pizza with all the meat."

"Oh, Eddie," Olivia laughs, slapping his arm with the lightest of touches.

Eddie, I think, hiding a smile. No way I'm going to be a third wheel with these two.

"You kids go get dinner," I say. "I'm ready to be in for the night."

UPSTAIRS, THE AIR conditioning is humming gently on low—even though the October nights are cooling off, I like the company the sound gives me. I put pasta on to boil and sit on the sofa to cuddle with Lily Marlene while I look at my laptop. There are pictures from the day to admire, there are praising comments on my social media to answer, lots of love and likes for the pictures I posted of each of my horses wearing their ribbons. I pause for a moment when I see a comment from Cary, my heart surging up into my throat.

It's from his secret account, the one with the simple profile name *C Davis*. He added me as a friend just a few days into our riding lessons, saying that it was a huge honor to be allowed to know a Hollywood star's secret social media profiles. I'd laughed and pretended to delete his friend request, but I accepted it later that night, after he'd gone home. He'd responded by sending me a message with a picture of two glittery kittens.

His profile picture is new—Tony, smiling for the camera with his tongue hanging out. I look at my bed, remembering when Tony would be passed out asleep on my pillow before I could get to bed in the evening. I don't necessarily miss him getting sand and hair all through my sheets, but I do miss that little dog's sunny disposition.

And I miss his dad.

C Davis has hearted my picture of my three horses wearing their bright ribbons and beneath it he has commented, "Proud to say I knew them when."

I nod at it for a moment. *Knew them when.*

You should know them now, Cary. Come back.

I feel grateful for this one glimpse of him, even though in the long run, it probably means it will be harder to get over him.

But I will push through it. That is what I do, right? I just keep going.

"The problem with pushing through things," I tell Lily Marlene, "is that I never know when I should have stopped and tried something else."

She blinks at me lazily, debating the merits of listening to me whine or simply going to sleep.

"What if this isn't working because it isn't the right path?" I ask her. "I mean, yes, I brought home three ribbons today, but that doesn't mean my problems are going anywhere at all. Almost winning the Beginner Novice division is a long way from bringing in paying clients or selling horses for six figures."

Lily Marlene hops down from my lap and pads over to the door. She sits down and looks over her shoulder at me. Evidently, her choice is neither. She is picking the thrill of the hunt over relaxing with me tonight.

"Fine," I sigh, setting the laptop aside. I let her outside and watch her move sinuously down the stairs, off to terrorize mice in the hay stall. While I'm standing on the landing, I notice a cobweb and reach inside for the broom.

Five minutes later, I've swept the stairs and banisters from top to bottom and the pasta water has boiled over on the stove.

"Damn, damn, damn," I mutter as I clean up the mess with a tea towel. I burn my finger on the steaming water and pop it into my mouth, feeling the day's good vibes burning off like fog under the sun. Jeez, this isn't the first time cleaning has made a bigger mess for me. Why can't I just leave it alone?

Because that's not how I'm wired. That's not how my brain works. That's not how I was raised.

And *that's* the problem I never want to face, really.

"Cary was right," I tell my pasta, which is boiling in a more controlled fashion now that I am paying attention. "I *was* raised in a Victorian orphanage."

Finally settling down with a bowl of buttered noodles, I open my laptop again, just as my messenger app chimes. I nearly drop the bowl when I see it's from Cary.

And it's a video.

Cautiously, as if it might jump out of the screen and bite me, I press *play* and make the video window full-screen. To my astonishment, I see that it was taken today—Hansie's lovely face looks towards the camera, and I'm on his back, in my good white shirt and gray show jacket.

As my pasta grows cold, I breathlessly watch a highlight reel of my day, from Hansie's first bouncy trot down centerline to Plato's redeeming clean round cross-country, splashing through the water obstacle like he'd never given puddles a second thought before. All three of my horses look like a million bucks, and it's not just because Sydney has them groomed to perfection or because I've trained and conditioned them for this day. There is a professionalism in this video—it has been carefully shot and edited with sunlight, angles, and backdrops thought out.

It can only mean one thing.

Cary was here today, and he made me this video.

The realization is almost as awful as it is amazing. That was him I saw, wasn't it? Why? Why did he come all this way, back across the country, and spend a day filming me—without my knowledge?

Is this a thank you, or a goodbye?

Or is it both?

I put my head in my hands after the third viewing, unable to process what he could possibly mean by it all, and too unsure of myself to simply open the messenger window again and *ask* him.

Sydney would ask him.

Olivia would ask him.

Hell, Mrs. C would ask him.

I get up, close my laptop, and start washing dishes, forgetting that my dinner is getting cold on the sofa behind me. I've completely scrubbed the kitchen and the microwave clock tells me it's half past nine before I remember that I didn't eat yet.

Once again, I've vanished into my work. I'm starting to see it now.

Have I always been like this?

YOU'VE ALWAYS BEEN like this, Evie replies the next morning, around seven thirty—just about when she'd be heading into the barn to start for the day. *I didn't realize you didn't know.*

It's nice of her to not say anything snarky about my ten p.m. text; I'm sure she was asleep when I sent it. Evie goes to bed crazy early, even for the average equestrian. She started doing it when she worked in racehorses and had to be at the barn by five thirty every morning, which sounds like a nightmare to me, but she always says she liked only working four hours a day and that made up for the early wake-up. There just wasn't any room to move up. It was kind of a dead-end job.

"Plus, there was no Malcolm," I like to remind her when the topic comes up, to which she always giggles and kind of tosses her head, acknowledging that having him around is a big perk of her work-day.

I mean, I get it. I was in more of a hurry to get downstairs and get to work when I knew Cary was going to be here. I'm in no rush at all this morning. It's the day after an event. I only have a few horses to ride today, and no motivation whatsoever. I flick through my phone after reading Evie's text, not bothering to get out of bed. Work will wait. It's always there, anyway. Waiting.

Although, I do feel weird right now, wanting to stay in bed. I thought I eliminated that urge from my system as a teenager—through simple self-preservation. Aunt Kate wasn't big on hitting the snooze button. We were on a schedule, a strict one, every day.

Come to think of it, I've been on a strict schedule for half my life. What would it be like to live without every hour, every minute, planned out and regimented?

I can almost imagine it. With the first event of the season is over, the goal I've been pursuing single-mindedly since Cary left has been achieved. The ribbons are hung, the horses are turned out, and the tack is put away. I admit, the laundry needs to be run, and the trailer needs cleaned out, but what if those are the only things I do today?

Just bring in the horses to feed, turn them back out, throw the saddle pads in the wash and muck out the trailer, and then...what?

I shake my head. Sure, I could try not having anything on the schedule today, but all that will do is give me time to miss Cary. I'm going to have to stick to my regular routine, I realize, and make sure there's no room for mourning that relationship. Swinging my feet out of bed, I push myself into my usual mindset. Get. Things. Done.

Dressed, my face washed, and my hair tucked into its taut bun, I pick up my phone on the way out of the apartment and see Evie has texted again. *Hey, Malcolm said to remind you Hansie's next payment was due yesterday.*

I stop with my hand on the door-knob and stare at my phone for a moment, feeling a cold tide washing over my skin. Then I look at my calendar app. I flick through the dates marked with red, wishing they'd change somehow. But no. Hansie's payment was absolutely due yesterday.

I'd forgotten because of the event, which is understandable, I think.

But the problem is that I can't pay it today.

Or tomorrow.

The money just isn't there.

Look, I had a plan. It just wasn't a good enough plan. I was counting on a certain amount coming in for the next few weeks. And then Cary left. And my students cancelled last week.

If that twin blow hadn't landed, the boarders' first-of-month payments would have stretched to cover Hansie's payment. But as is, I have just enough in my account to cover this week's feed delivery... and nothing else. I'll have to charge anything else that comes up.

It has finally happened. I'm tapped out. My heart beats an uneasy little tattoo against my ribs.

"Shit," I mutter, pacing my little apartment, from kitchen to bed and back again. "Shit, shit, shit."

It doesn't give me any great ideas. What good are swear words, anyway, if they don't immediately fix everything? We need to stop giving them special status; it just gives desperate people like me inflated expectations of their magical properties.

My phone chimes again. Is it Evie? It must be. I can't look. I shove the phone deep into my pocket, fling open my door and head out into the barn. The horses in their paddocks rumble deep in their chests as they hear my footsteps on the staircase. That's right, guys, it's time to feed breakfast.

The normalcy, the inevitability, of farm chores reaches out to embrace me like a warm hug. I'm safe in the work. I know what's expected of me, and I know how to do it well. There are no real surprises waiting out there. Everything can be done blindfolded, one-handed, empty-minded.

And I set my phone upside-down on my desk before I get started, closing the office door. I'll just leave it in there, where it can't hurt me.

Chapter Thirty-Three

LOCKING UP MY phone does not make the problem go away. Surprise, surprise, I know. But hey, I am running low on options. It was worth a shot, right?

By nightfall, six fresh voicemails are waiting on my phone. But at least my farm is sparkling. The cleanest it has *ever* been, and that's saying something. I'm worn out from the feverish cleaning; my fingers are red and wrinkled with bleach, detergent, and water. The horse trailer has been pressure-washed and sanitized inside and out, there are horse blankets drying on the arena fence after a pre-season scrubbing and waterproofing application, and every single white saddle pad has been bleached, dried, and folded carefully on a freshly lined shelf.

I even took out the rickety old seed broadcaster left behind by another renter, cleaned it out, and filled it with bucket after bucket of wildflower seed. Then I went out and walked the sandy, scruffy ground around the barn, along the driveway, right up to my mailbox, spreading those seeds everywhere I wanted to ignore come spring. Now, the big brown bag sags half-empty in the hay stall, and I don't know how I'll feel in spring if those wildflowers really do blossom all around the barn. But I'm hopeful that by then, I'll be over this crush on Cary.

I turn the horses back out for the night one by one, with a glowing moon showing us the way. I take care to do everything correctly: right hand below the halter, left hand carrying the rest of the lead-rope bundled up in a neat butterfly loop. The horses walk politely at my side, keeping their shoulder alongside my shoulder. When a horse surges ahead, I make them practice halting with me, then walking precisely at my shoulder once again. I insist Plato walk between the paddock and the barn three times before I'm satisfied with his behavior on the lead. Each time we turn away from the gate, he gives me a confused look, his face betraying his emotions: *Mom, what on earth is going on?*

We're doing everything *right*. That is what is going on. It's as if Aunt Kate is watching me, her arms crossed over her chest, her mouth a thin line that doesn't give away a thing, so that I can't glance at her to see if I'm hitting all her marks or not.

"This is what I've got," I tell Plato as he tugs impatiently at the lead-rope. "I can take care of horses like nobody else. Let me enjoy it."

It's past seven o'clock when everyone is finally turned out, their halters hung with precision on the covered hooks I installed myself next to each gate, the lead-rope looped over top so it can't fall into the sand and get dirty. The horses exchange looks as they walk away from the gates and head back towards the far end of their paddocks, united in their belief that Mom has gone crazy.

"Get used to it," I call, watching the moonlight dapple through the oaks and onto their smoothly swaying hindquarters, as they put as much space as possible between them and me. It really looks like they're trying not to be too obvious about it. I can basically hear them whispering about what a whackadoo I'm being.

"We've been slacking off! Not anymore!" I remind them.

A snort echoes and multiplies, shared between them like nervous laughter.

I shake my head—*kids*—and check each water trough in turn, running a hand through the cool water, topping them off as needed. The moon's reflection ripples in each trough, silvery and smiling. So many nights like this, in hot weather and in flying snow and occasionally on those elusive evenings of perfect temperature ambiance, when the air seemed to be like smooth water on my skin, I strode along paddock fences beneath the watchful moon and checked the water troughs *one more time,* conscious that Aunt Kate would ask me before I had taken off my boots at the door, certain she'd find out if I fudged the answer even once.

Night-check was always my responsibility, looking over both the inside horses and the outside ones for the entirety of my teenage years. There was a reason I'd given that task to Evie the moment she'd moved into the barn apartment at Fine Day Farm. For the first time in fifteen years, I could go to bed at night with the knowledge someone else was making sure all our horses would survive the night. I remember going to bed early just because I could, turning out the light around nine, sleeping all night and waking up fresh as a daisy.

I turn off the last water faucet and silence descends on my ears, a pressure that's quickly relieved by the intermittent sounds of a countryside that never fully sleeps.

A truck drives past on the main road, the whir of its tires cutting through the night. A dog barks, and then another, and a distant horse whinnies. An owl in the oaks at the back of the property hoots, and closer, something rustles in a palmetto clump, the fronds rattling together like castanets. Enough noise to be a panther hunting in the shadows, or at least a bobcat, but probably just Lily Marlene, chasing the last cicadas of the year through the underbrush. I spot her, the silken white patches of her coat glowing in the moonlight, and cluck encouragingly. She looks back at me and opens her mouth to offer a single mew of acknowledgment, then carries on with her work, disappearing into the dark shadows of the palmetto fronds.

I'm a little disappointed. Everyone has work to do, I get it, but it would have been nice if she came home with me.

Alone, I walk the sandy path back to the barn, the arena a dull blue-white oval at my side. Accompanied only by my work, I think, how apt. It's all I've ever had.

Upstairs, my phone is pulsing through another cycle of vibrations. *Evie,* the screen tells me. My only friend, and I can't answer her calls. I must have made a mistake somewhere between Windy Hill and here, to have come to this, but I'll be damned if I know what it was.

No, that's not true. I turn on the faucet in the tiny shower stall of my tiny bathroom. I know what it was. What it is. What it will likely always be.

I just don't want to face it.

The water is steaming; thank goodness Nathan didn't shirk on a hot water heater the way he did on everything else. I got lucky in that department. It beats down on me while I concentrate on everything except my fatal flaw; on my toenails (short, battered against the toes of riding boots all day long) and on my thighs (thick, muscled, from pushing against saddles all day long) and on my chest (pale, ghostly, from being hidden under ultraviolet-ray blocking shirts all day long). Soap in a bottle, a stream of vanilla-scent from a dollar-store brand, cheap fragrance filling my nostrils as the steam rises up and fills my eyes. I'm not crying, the water is crying. You're crying.

No one is crying.

Aunt Kate: *I don't take on crybabies, so if you're going to be emotional, this isn't going to work.*

I swallowed my tears after that; it was just the first night after all. I was tired and cold and I missed my parents, my bedroom with the window overlooking our postage-stamp backyard in the D.C. suburbs, the things I hadn't realized I was trading away for horses. And I was terrified this arrangement wouldn't work out, more frightened I'd have to go home than I was of sleeping in the creaking, likely haunted bedroom at the back of Windy Hill's venerable old farmhouse, or the prospect of starting at a strange new school the very next morning.

I laugh to myself now, because little had first-night Alison known that I'd never be troubled by ghosts because I was always too exhausted to do more than fall face-first into my pillow at night, little had first-night Alison known that I'd never have to worry about what the other kids thought of me because I'd be too busy training horses and working in the barn after school to ever bother with a social life.

If you're going to be emotional, this isn't going to work.

And I never was again.

EVIE'S OUTSIDE MY door when I get out of the shower. I hear her knocking, picture her standing on the landing. Has she come as a bill collector, or as my friend? Maybe she's tired of being the latter. Maybe all my drama has chased her away. This isn't what she signed up for when we first met. Although I'd like to think I've been keeping my melancholy under wraps lately. Really, it was just the wildflower seeds that made me feel moody again.

"Let me get dressed," I call, sitting on my bed with the towel wrapped around me.

"Hurry up," Evie grumbles through the door. "Now that I know you're alive, I'm going to kill you and it's getting late."

"That's not encouraging," I say, not bothering to raise my voice. She can hear me through the cheap laminate.

"I'm not here to be encouraging," Evie snaps. "I'm here because you won't answer your phone, and we have a problem."

"Coming here will not solve it."

"I don't think we can solve it," she says ominously. "I'm just here to tell you what's happening."

WHEN SHE'S GONE, I turn myself face-down on my pillow and try to give myself permission to cry. But it has been too many years since I had that privilege taken away from me, and not even now, with the end of my dreams in plain sight, I can't get myself worked into a state. As much as I'd love to have a breakdown, my body refuses to cooperate.

Such a frustrating turn of events.

Evie sat on my bed (once I finally pulled on a shirt and shorts, and let her inside) and told me everything that was going down. The way she and Malcolm had gone to bat for me to get Hansie's owner to take payments. The fact that he wasn't going to budge on the three-day grace period for late payments. The timing of the trailer which would come to pick up Hansie and take him back to Fine Day Farm if I didn't have the late payment turned in by Tuesday at five p.m.

"You might as well send the trailer now," I'd told her, a grotesque grin pulling at the edges of my lips. "The money's not there."

Evie stared at me, aghast. "You have two more days to figure out where to get the money," she'd reminded me.

"Which gets me out of trouble for thirty days," I said, suddenly feeling very certain that I was doing the only thing I could, "and does nothing for all my other shortfalls. It's over, Evie. I am officially in the red. If something doesn't give in the next few weeks, I'm going to be giving away horses I can't afford to feed."

She'd shaken her head, so very slowly, as if I'd dropped her into a tank of water and she needed all her energy to stay afloat. "You never told me it was this bad. How—when did you know?"

"That it was all going to fail?" I'd laughed, a flinty sound that made her flinch. "Probably the day I signed the lease and saw how little I was getting with that big, impressive pile of dough I'd worked for. I think on some level I realized I was living in a fool's paradise, thinking I could turn this into a profitable venture."

She sighed, impatient, and I knew this wasn't the time to be flippant. Evie still believed in me. Bless her.

"No," I'd said. "Of course not. It was just in the past few weeks. When I had those cancelations, and Cary left at the same time...I was hanging on week to week, Evie. Paycheck to paycheck. And now my paychecks seem to be coming monthly. With school going now, my students are all over the place. They keep canceling. And so now there's a lot of space between those pay-days with nothing filling the in-between spaces. Nothing that's a sure thing, anyway. And I can't keep horses that way. You know that."

Can't feed them, can't house them, can't show them, can't train them...

Can't even *sell* them, if none of the above are going right.

"There's nothing left?" Evie asks.

"I have one savings account left," I admit. "But if I use that for the horses, or to try to keep things going, then when things go south again, I'll have nothing left at all. I'll have to live in the woods." Or go back to Windy Hill, but the idea of returning to my aunt after all these years is completely unthinkable.

"You'd get a job," Evie says. "You wouldn't have to live in the woods."

"Metaphorically," I say. "I'm not willing to find out."

"There *has* to be something we can do," Evie said desperately. "Some way we can help."

"If you had any open stalls, you could have my sales horses for a song," I told her. "But I know you don't."

"We'd figure something out. We'll get you set up with some space for them. It doesn't have to come to giving them away! I'm sure we can work something out. *Not* that we'll have to, though, because everything's going to be fine!"

Such optimism! I didn't have the heart for it. I sent her on her way.

"Things were looking up," I say to myself. "They really were. And then they all just crashed."

And though I won't say it out loud, I know when it went wrong. The day I lost Cary, that's the day my house of cards came tumbling down. The man that could make it rain, the man who could make me laugh, the man who knew a hot horse needed time out in the pasture and a cool customer in the saddle didn't need extra arena time, either...Cary had something special to him, some quality like a drifting good luck charm in the kind of Westerns they don't make anymore.

That's what he is, I think. He's the kind of person they don't make anymore.

And I wish I could have him back, but he's probably drifting through someone else's life now, making his little movies about the jobs he doesn't understand, and acting like a heartthrob cowboy for an actress who doesn't know what kind of guy she's got.

Chapter Thirty-Four

THE GUT-PUNCH comes the next day, as if the universe was saving the real kicker for me when I least expected it. Another FedEx truck, another driver hopping down, another envelope with my name on it. Inside, a note and a DVD.

I worked on this for you. - C.

Just C.

I touch the letter, tracing it with my finger. Why didn't he write the entire thing out?

What does it matter? He's sent me something—I suspect it must be the early sessions with Hansie, when I was begging him not to record us and he did it anyway, swearing I would want a record of this someday. I do, but not for the reasons he said back then.

One day Cary had teased me about the age of my laptop, remarking that he hadn't seen one with a DVD player in years. I feel the ghost of that day in this plastic disc. He might have messaged me a file, or a link, but he went out of his way to remind me of an afternoon when we were together. That's just like him, a guy who cherishes private jokes and intimate moments between friends.

I walk into my office to fetch my laptop and find Edward at my desk, typing away.

He gives me a narrow-eyed look as if I've wandered into his private C-suite on the fiftieth floor of Rockefeller Center. I wish Olivia was around; she's the only one who can coax a smile out of this guy.

"I'm just getting my laptop," I say, letting him have my office, because my horses' next meal depends on his good graces. But he's still a jerk.

Back upstairs, the staircase creaking beneath my feet, skipping the step Nathan has chosen not to replace but just mark with duct tape as a potential hazard. My air conditioner is humming to itself as I push the door open, and Lily Marlene shoves past me impatiently. For a little while, during the brief week or two Tony was here and then for a few days after he was gone, she would pause in the doorway to make sure That Dog wasn't going to pounce on her with his cheerful greeting. But she's decided he's gone for good now and so she slides inside with her pert tail twitching at the top, heading for the dish where I heap her meals of Purina Cat Chow even though everyone knows you should underfeed a mouser.

While Lily Marlene hunches over her breakfast remnants, I sit down on my sofa and convince my laptop to play the DVD. For a few moments, I don't think the computer will comply, but at last it whirs to life and starts sorting through the media files. A blank screen pops up, a play button prominently in the center. My finger hovers over the trackpad, momentarily stilled by the tingling of my nerves.

Don't be silly, I tell myself, stern as ever. *It's just a video of Hansie from over a month ago. Nothing to get worked up about.*

I tap the pad and the video begins to play.

My eyes fill with tears almost instantly.

This isn't just a collection of clips taken of us riding. This is an elaborately prepared (to me, anyway) production, with close-ups of my face as I work with Hansie, of Hansie's big, dark eyes as he watches me move around the barn, and of everything else that goes into my days here. *Our* days here, because Cary turns the camera on himself from time to time, and when he opens his mouth to narrate what it was like working here, I feel like my heart is going to burst from my chest.

"Working with horses feels so natural and right to me," Cary says —said—as he runs a hand along Nando's neck. He's on horseback in the back pasture, and I can see myself in the background, trotting a twenty-meter circle on a newly compliant Hansie. "I always had a thing for them, but thanks to you, Alison, I feel like I've unlocked a piece of my heart that was closed off before. I simply didn't know this would become a love-of-my-life type situation!"

A love-of-my-life type situation.

God, what a thing to say.

A half-hour passes by in a blur, my thoughts a hazy confusion of happiness and longing as Cary shows me what a month in my tutelage meant to him. And when it's over, I watch it again.

And again.

By the fourth viewing, I'm able to look past Cary and the way my heart seizes up every time I feel like I'm gazing into his dark eyes again. Now I can see what he meant to be the star of the show—me —and honestly, I'm not thrilled by what he has captured.

I look so tired. So hunted. So...in some angles, anyway... *gaunt.* Were there always shadows like that under my eyes? Hollows in my cheeks? I look like I haven't been eating.

I glance guiltily at my kitchenette, knowing there's not much behind those cabinet doors besides pasta and boxes of rice and beans

—the kind you're supposed to mix with a protein or eat as a side, while I've been having them for dinner. And suddenly I wonder if I'm not feeding myself properly.

I think of the big lunches we used to have at Fine Day Farm, financed by Malcolm and insisted upon by me, because I knew what it was to work through the day without time to eat and I didn't want to do that again—or push it on my employees. When had I fallen back into that habit of skipping meals in favor of working all day? Just in the past few weeks, surely, right? That's not too bad. I'm not falling apart yet.

There is still time to fix things.

But I can't help but think it was easier when I wasn't alone. I think I need someone else nearby, someone to keep me normal, to stop me from sliding into bad old habits I learned at Windy Hill. Someone to remind me that there is more to life than horses, even if it's just managing basic life skills to stay alive and healthy enough to keep working with said horses.

Am I not really capable of doing this on my own?

I look at Cary's face, freeze-framed as he gazes away from the lens, looking at a figure in the distance. I know he's watching me.

I CAN'T REALLY figure out how to thank him for the DVD—should I text, should I email? I finally settle on email, because texting is so immediate, and since we both have iPhones, I'd have to see the *read/delivered* option beneath the message, and I don't want to deal with the agony of watching for a reply from a read message, or to flick back and back and back again to see a delivered message, wondering why it hasn't been opened.

It's a short email: *love what you've done so much, how can I ever thank you,* blah-blah-blah. As I write pointless words which skirt around how I really feel, how much I want him here, I think of the last lines in his wildflower letter: *It'll be famous. Just like you always wanted.*

And I add to my email:

You probably know a thing or two about how fleeting fame is, and the cost of keeping up appearances. I'm learning that lesson now. I wish I'd known it sooner.

I think for a moment, my fingers pressing lightly against the keys. A sentence that means something, because why not go for broke?

I type:

Sometimes I think I was better when you were here.

A pause. Lily Marlene finishes with her bowl and turns around, mewing gently. A horse whinnies from the barn below. I look at the words, deliberating.

I delete the word "sometimes", then hit send before I can change my mind.

Chapter Thirty-Five

ON TUESDAY EVENING at five-thirty, Malcolm and Evie arrive together to repossess Hansie.

I lead him up the ramp myself, my fingers numb as the lead-rope slides beneath my callouses. I pat him on the neck and clip the trailer tie to his halter. He nuzzles my shoulder and the permanent lump in my throat rearranges for just a moment while I gulp back a sob, and then settles back into place.

Malcolm looks even more upset than Evie, and Evie is downright distraught. "We'll keep him from selling the horse again," he promises. "I'm putting him straight into my program. At a discount to the seller, just to keep him sweet. We won't let this end here."

I run my hand over my hair, feeling how the frizz of summer has finally subsided. It is late October and the warm, dry days of autumn are settling over Ocala. A layer of white dust coats my flower-beds, which desperately need watered. I think guiltily of Cary putting all that work in, and wonder if I'm going to let them die waiting for another rain shower.

"You're too good to me," I tell Malcolm. "I messed up. You don't have to fix it."

"Let us fix it," Evie says. There's a tremor in her voice. "You always fixed everything for us, all the time. Can't you let us help you?"

"You help me plenty, so there's no reason to pretend I'm over here refusing all assistance like some kind of proud crazy person," I say, grimacing in an attempt to smile.

"Clearly, we didn't help enough," Evie mutters. "I can't believe this is happening."

I can't either, and at the same time, I'm able to step back, outside of my body, and see that it was going to happen all the time, that it *was* happening, a slow-motion fall of dominoes, and we were foolish not to have noticed them toppling one by one.

"We'll help with the sales horses," Malcolm promises as they start for the truck. "You let us know what you need, and we're here for you. No one is being given away or sold for a few hundred dollars, Alison. Promise me we can help you."

"I promise," I say, because hey, I might have recently realized I'm crazy, but I'm still not stupid.

Olivia looks up from her grooming as I walk back into the barn, orange light filtering around her horse's legs. "Where is Hansie going?" she asks innocently.

"To Malcolm's, for training," I say, leaning against the wall. I run my fingers along it, checking for dust, the very motion of my hands a tic I can't control. My fingertips are still red from bleach; I curve them under my palms so I don't have to see the damage.

"Oh." Olivia looks at me for a minute, her gaze searching. I gaze back as blandly as I can, hoping I'm not giving a thing away. Finally, she goes back to grooming. As she rubs Early's chest with a curry-comb, she says, "Have you heard from Cary recently?"

"I got an email from him a few days ago," I say, looking at the aisle so she can't see my face twist. In response to my moment of soul-bearing, Cary had replied, *I'm glad you like the video.*

That was it. The entire email. Like a meeting that could have been an email, I had an email that could have been a text, in place of a friendship that could have been so much more, if I'd just been paying attention to anything but my work and my stupid, stupid need to keep up appearances.

Or if he'd wanted to come back, I remind myself. If he'd so much as offered to make this work long-distance, but of course, he didn't. He said he'd be thinking about me, not that he was in love with me.

I keep forgetting that part, shouldering all the blame because that's what I do, but he's part of this situation, too. He just doesn't know it, because he doesn't know there's a situation at all. He's moved on, making his life in Hollywood like he always wanted.

"How is he?" Olivia asks, trying very hard not to fish for information.

"He's fine," I say. "Busy."

I hope he is, anyway. Being very busy is a better excuse for that email than that he simply was finished with me, that the DVD was his final gesture and now our lives could continue on two different paths, our crossroads disappearing into the past like that perfect little town you stop at on a road-trip, where you love the pie and swear you'll come back again someday, but of course, you'll never pass that way again.

"I might have a work trip to California in a few weeks," Olivia says. She runs a hand down Early's foreleg, squeezes above his fetlock. The horse obediently lifts his hoof for her to pick out. "I was thinking I might see if he's free for lunch."

"I'm sure he'd like that," I say, and I'm about to head upstairs and hide when I hear a truck pulling into the parking lot. Who could this be so late in the evening? With daylight nearly gone, I'm ready to call it a day. Sighing, I walk down to the barn doors and gaze out.

"Mrs. C?" I ask, astonished, as she climbs down from a shining black Suburban. "Nice truck," I add.

"Thank you, dear. It's for the new place," she says, shutting the door with a careful shove. "I bought a farm out on the west side. You'll have to come out and see it! I could use you for some training, to be honest. I don't know what I'm doing." She trills a happy laugh.

"You bought a farm?" I repeat, gobsmacked. She'd never indicated she had any interest in horse ownership before, content with her big house on a sprawling lot in a gated subdivision.

"Oh, well, I guess spending so much time here, I caught the bug. And Cary kind of goaded me into it. I was just out on the west coast with him, you know. He's buying something for himself. All those dusty hills and brown mountains, they shouldn't be pretty, but they are. I'd rather have green though, don't you think?"

I stare at her, feeling dazed. "Green, yeah," I manage, although I hardly know what I'm agreeing to. "Um...what brings you here tonight, Mrs. C?"

"Well, it's that horse you have, that big dark one," Mrs. C says. "I've been doing some thinking, and I believe I want to buy into him. That was an option, right? You still have shares, don't you?"

I know I'm still standing upright, because my head doesn't hit the ground, but it feels like I'm falling backwards. I can literally feel the pull of gravity tugging at my stomach as I tumble like an abandoned satellite falling from my orbit. And yet I remain on my feet, Mrs. C standing in front of me, all smiles and bright interest. A marvel of physics, I think, grateful I never had to take it in high school.

"Can we go and look at him?" Mrs. C asks. "Is he out in the pasture?" And she squints through the dying light towards the paddocks, where my horses are out, swishing their tails and grazing on what's left of the summer grass.

"He's—uh—actually at my friend's barn right now," I say, trying hard not to stammer and almost managing it. "For some training stuff."

Mrs. C looks disappointed. "Oh! Well, hopefully nothing serious."

"No...nothing...serious."

"And he is going to keep competing this winter, right? Like you said?"

"Yes, of course." I straighten my shoulders and try to suck down some extra oxygen. Maybe this is the chance I needed. Maybe Mrs. C can make it all work out. "Do you want to sit down and talk about it?"

"Absolutely! Yes. I have some time. Your...ah...office?" And she swats her hand around her face as if a cloud of gnats has descended over her head.

Wondering just how Mrs. C will adapt to farm life, I lead her into my office. It's not empty; for some reason Edward has felt the need to work here every day this week.

He looks up and slams his laptop shut as if I've ruined his night, possibly his life. "I'll move," he says curtly, removing himself from the office. Mrs. C looks after him with interest.

"He's got a real high opinion of himself, doesn't he?" she asks loudly.

I have to put my hand over my mouth to stifle my bark of laughter, and she looks at me fondly.

Suddenly, I like Mrs. C quite a lot.

"So," she says, throwing herself into the guest chair. "The dark horse. Let's talk."

"Yes," I say, pulling my laptop out of my desk drawer. Somewhere on the cobwebby depths of my hard drive, there's a file with plans for this very conversation, built for Malcolm and repurposed for my own small farm. I hadn't really planned on trying to syndicate Hansie, but if selling pieces of my heart horse is the only way to get him back, then I'll bite the bullet and set up the chopping block.

Or something. My head is mixed up, metaphors charging around like a herd of loose horses spooked by storms.

"Here's what it could look like," I begin.

WHEN MRS. C finally leaves that night, promising to go over everything I've presented to her and get back to me as soon as she can, I slide to the ground and slump against the barn wall. I don't have the strength to get up. Everything I had left went into presenting myself as a normal, well-adjusted businesswoman to my potential investor...when the reality, of course, is far from that buttoned-up truth. I'm just a mess of mashed potatoes in human form at this point.

Crickets sing a shrill song across the fields, and a frog peeps from the flowers next to me. His throaty little call reminds me that I never watered the gardens. I look out at the night, the eastern sky just beginning to lighten with the coming moon, and wonder if I've got the energy to turn on the hose and sprinkle these flowerbeds with water, or if I'm just going to sit here on the dusty asphalt of my barn aisle and wait until I keel over from exhaustion.

Lily Marlene wanders up, opening her mouth in a pink-tongued mew. She looks towards the staircase, then back at me. Wanting to go in, wanting her dinner. "I know, baby," I tell her, summoning the strength to run a finger over her tipped-back ears. "But Mama's so tired. Let's just sit a few minutes."

And Lily does, settling down on her haunches beside me and staring out into the night.

Peep, the frog says on my other side.

In the distance, a horse snorts.

Tonight I watched my plans fall apart, only to be given some weird new hope from Mrs. C. But the truth is, I don't know if her buy-in is enough. In fact, I *know* it isn't. She could be paying half of Hansie's bills, which would be great, but I still won't have the money to pay for Hansie's purchase. I'm that far behind.

It's time to face the facts. I channel the cool, calm Alison that I have always been, the Alison that Aunt Kate raised. No more ugly emotions, no more panicked breathing, no more comparing myself to a pile of mashed potatoes held together by a burlap sack in the shape of a human. Just...reality. The only thing there is.

You are Alison.

And here's what happened to you.

I started a business, I had a solid business plan, I did everything right.

And the business has failed.

That's okay. That's normal. That's what businesses do, half the time, if not *most* of the time.

"It's okay," I say aloud.

Lily looks at me questioningly.

"I just need a new plan."

And then I grin to myself, because yeah...that's the hard part, said like it's the easy part. A new plan, she says, as if I can run to Publix and grab one from the produce section. A new plan, to replace the one I'd been working on for five years, from the day I came to Florida to take the job at Fine Day Farm.

It didn't work out, but at least I worked at Fine Day Farm. At least I distilled all that knowledge and discipline I gained at Windy Hill, refining myself into a woman who can run a training center with military precision. I can go back to that, I figure.

"Ugh, though." I run a hand along Lily's soft back. She arches her spine against my touch. "I don't want to do that again."

The realization is surprising, but I'm certain. Suddenly, I *know* what I want, with a terrible clarity.

I want a break from this life.

I want to take it easy for just a little while. I want to stop being this version of Alison, fire-hardened and ice-cold. I want to have a little time to breathe, let my shoulders slump, and gather my thoughts. If I can't have some help, then stopping is the next best option.

"I'm burned out," I realize aloud. "That's what this is. This is burnout."

"Mew," Lily Marlene says, giving me a little head-butt of encouragement. She glances back at the stairs again.

"In a minute," I promise. "Let me just...let's watch the moon rise, okay? I don't remember the last time I watched the moon rise."

Alone with my cat, I wait for a sign to tell me what I should do next. And as the golden disc of the moon slides menacingly up from the eastern horizon, my thoughts begin to slip inexorably west.

Chapter Thirty-Six

I WANT A break, but you can't just drop everything when you have horses. It takes me a few days to formulate a plan and start informing the other players of their role. Some are astonished—Evie actually gets teary-eyed and has to blow her nose as I explain what I need her to do, and even Malcolm looks a little heartbroken, like it's all his fault.

"It's not you," I assure him, when he ventures to say he hopes he didn't burn me out on his horses by working me to hard when I was his barn manager. "This was a long time coming."

This might have started when I was fifteen years old, now that I think about it.

"And it's not forever," I add. "It's just a little break. I'm coming back."

"Don't take too long," Malcolm warns jokingly. "I've had my eye on Nando for a while. I might not give him back."

"You treat my Nando like the rock star he is," I say. "And always say please and be respectful to him. Or he'll bite you."

Malcolm laughs, like I planned. I'm not looking for pity or sympathy or even disappointment. I just want to hit pause on my life, sort some stuff out, and then come back refreshed. Usually, you can't do that kind of thing when horses are involved. Lucky for me, I have good friends.

Malcolm and Evie don't balk when I ask them to take on showing and possibly selling my project horses while I'm away. Their schedule is full, but I know they'll figure out a way to add a few more horses to their program. If Evie needs any help with drawing up the new plan, she can always come to me, and I'll sort it out. I'm still the queen of organization and scheduling around these parts.

Olivia is the wild card in my plotting, but she falls into line with surprisingly little prodding, agreeing to supervise the care of her horses and Edward's while I'm away. "I'm going to turn the apartment into a little office," she decides happily, "and just work from here. I might sleep here some. Does it come furnished? Yes? Oh, this is so fun. I mean—" she puts her hand on my arm. "I'm sorry you're leaving, Alison. I really am—"

"It's okay," I assure her. "I need the break. And I'll be back. So don't change too much, okay? By the time you head back up north, I'll be back. Probably a lot sooner than that."

I don't know for sure if that's true, but I think it is. And I feel safer having an exit strategy from my exit. A place to return to, when the creases have been ironed out and I feel like myself again.

I'm stripping down to the bone, but even restless bones need a place to feel comfortable and at home when the wandering is over.

"And Lily?" Olivia asks, as the cat jumps onto the desk and waves her tail, looking between us as if she knows this is a division of assets. "Where does Lily fall in all this?"

"She lives here," I say, swallowing yet another lump in my throat. "I'd take her with me if I was moving full-time, obviously, but I'll be back, so...you'll give her whatever she wants, right?"

"I'll give her everything," Olivia promises. "Darling girl." And she rubs Lily Marlene behind the ears with her third knuckle, exactly the way my barn cat likes it.

With the farm in good hands, Lily Marlene wrapping Olivia around her soft white paws, and the horses in a program which will have no problem selling them to good competition homes, there is only one piece left in this puzzle of a plot.

Well, make that three pieces, but they're all inter-connected.

I start with Mrs. C.

"BUYING...HIM?" I echo, confused.

Mrs. C—Kat, she wants me to call her now, and I keep forgetting —raises her eyebrows and pours me a glass of wine. It's eleven o'clock in the morning, but I take it from her, anyway. Medicinal.

Should I have done this part first? I didn't expect the pieces to start moving without me. I guess I should have considered that they're all living people, with minds of their own.

"Well, don't look so shocked, dear," Kat says, not unkindly. "But when I made a few inquiries and found out you didn't actually own him, I was a little surprised at you! And his owner was very motivated to sell. Annoyed with that whole crew over at Fine Day Farm for protecting the horse like that. He told me to make him an offer. And I did."

She sips her wine and looks at me expectantly. It's my turn to say something. To apologize for pretending I owned Hansie and could sell her a share in him, I guess.

But I can't speak.

This isn't how the conversation was supposed to go. I had a whole thing planned out, and she has thrown me through a loop.

Hollywood types! They are always doing back-room deals. Can't be trusted. I should have known.

"Are you alright?"

"I thought—I thought—" I sputter. "I mean—"

"Drink that down," Kat says briskly, pulling out a stool and gesturing for me to sit at the marble bar. "It'll loosen you up so we can have a chat. I bought a horse you like riding, so what? Stop looking like it's the end of the world. We'll work something out."

We sit side by side and gaze out the floor-to-ceiling windows lining the back wall of Kat's gleaming white kitchen. She hasn't moved out to her new property yet, saying there are a million things to do before she can consider giving up this house. The backyard is a green, tree-filled space with a little cottage near the back fence. I know it's the guest house where Cary stayed and the idea of him living here is enough to put a tight knot back in my stomach. I sip the wine, then gulp it, hoping she's right and the alcohol will loosen up all these clenching muscles.

She owns Hansie, I think, over and over again. This isn't how this meeting was supposed to go.

But maybe I can still salvage the plan.

When the glass is half-empty, I set it on the marble—a little too hard. It clinks alarmingly—and look at Kat. I can feel a flush on my cheeks from the wine, from my nerves.

She smiles at me. "Now," she says. "What is it you want to talk about?"

"I still want to train Hansie," I say. "And I'm sorry about the whole ownership thing. I thought that was a minor snafu."

"Well, dear, you didn't *own* him," Kat says reasonably. "Snafu is an interesting way to put it."

"I did for a while—never mind. That isn't important now." I square my shoulders. "I want to train him," I say again. "Can we do that together?"

"Well, I certainly wasn't going to ride him." Kat's smile broadens into a grin. "What did you think was going to happen?"

"I thought you'd leave him with Malcolm," I guess. "And actually, I need him to stay with Malcolm for a little while, because there's something else I need to do."

"Oh?" I get the feeling she knows what is coming.

"I need to go to California."

Kat nods triumphantly. "Of course you do."

HANSIE AND MRS. C—Kat, I mean—are in their places at last. Not the way I expected, and I have some soul-searching to do about Kat's name on Hansie's papers, but I force myself to exhale through my mouth as I drive back to the farm, expelling the fear from my lungs and, hopefully, from my heart. One thing at a time, I tell myself, as the fences and fields of horse country slide past. I stop for gas near the spot where I ran off the road while trying to imagine Cary's face, and remember meeting Jim here all those weeks ago. I was a different person then, and if *he* had been a different person, things might be so different right now.

I'm really grateful Jim's a jerk.

Because if he'd been the nice, confident horse trainer I'd been hoping for, I would have kept going, pushing forward while I ran out of gas, slowly disappearing beneath the sea like a sailor clinging to the crows-nest of a sinking ship, denying the whole thing was even happening.

But instead of dating Jim, I spent my working hours and my spare time with Cary, and he helped me see something about myself that

I'd never dared to look at before...the side of me that was, indeed, raised in a Victorian orphanage, starved for affection and willing to work my fingers to the bone for a scrap of praise.

I don't feel bad for teenage Alison. I got what I wanted. I like who I am. But my fingers are red with bleach and I realize that things have gotten out of hand, and now I need to step back and reassess my life, before I let it break me in two.

And yeah, I'd like some affection without having to muck out a thirty-stall barn, ride six sales horses, and feed fifteen broodmares in a downpour in exchange for it.

Which is why the last piece of the puzzle is Cary.

But I'm not the one calling him to say that I'm coming to California to fight for him.

That job falls to Kat.

Chapter Thirty-Seven

A LIGHT RAIN begins to fall as I pull into the farm parking lot, low gray clouds hanging above the trees with a wintry look to their folds. Outside the truck, the air temperature is foreign to my skin; I glance at the thermometer hanging just inside the barn aisle and am astonished to see the long hand has fallen below seventy degrees. It's the first cool weather of the season, and it blustered in while I was driving back from Kat's house just across town. Florida can be wild sometimes.

Most of the time, even. I give an involuntary shiver as a distant rumble of thunder crackles over the paddocks, and dart into the barn where it's safe. Is it weird to admit I am not afraid of lightning I can see, but the invisible stuff now gives me the willies? I run my tongue around my molars. The taste of metal is gone now, but somehow the memory of it is always there.

Someday, maybe, a reporter will ask me what the most important moment in my riding career has been. And I'll caress the gold medal hanging from my neck (What? This is a fantasy) and say, "Well, the day I was almost struck by lightning was the day I realized I shouldn't be doing this all by myself anymore. And it took some time to fix that, but at least now I've got someone looking out for me if there's a thunderstorm moving in."

That's a good fantasy. I think I'll hang onto it, shape it every night before I fall asleep, make it come true through sheer force of will.

I bring the horses in quickly, still glancing around the low-hanging clouds in case more lightning approaches, but the sky stays quiet as I get them inside and settled with hay. The chilly rain falls in a quiet curtain, a different kind of animal altogether from the huge, tumultuous droplets of summer. I walk up the aisle with my arms folded across my chest, feeling cold outside for the first time in months, and look at each horse in turn. Sebastian, Plato, Gidget...

I've made memories with these horses, and I feel bad leaving them. But for once, I remind myself, I have to put myself first. And they're going to be in impossibly good hands. I am not letting these horses down, and that's what matters. I need a break. I need to fix things. And then I can come back to them—if they're still with Malcolm and Evie—and do better by each of them. A whole person is a better trainer than a half one, and I haven't felt like a whole person in a long time.

I look around and try to imagine coming back to this barn, finding it empty, in a month or two. Will I be back before winter?

Will I be back before spring?

I don't know. My schedule is wide open. I feel uncomfortable just thinking about it, but I also suspect this is the only way forward. The only way to stop scrubbing, stop obsessing, stop grinding myself down to the very bone, and start living.

A car crunches on the gravel outside and I walk to the door, wondering if it's Edward or Olivia. Surely they won't want to ride in this weather. I stop in the doorway, confused.

It's a black SUV.

It's Kat's new Suburban. What is she doing here?

And then I see the figure in the driver's seat.

My heart stops beating. It just stays still, for a long, agonizing moment.

And then it's thudding wildly all at once, blood rushing in my ears.

Cary gets out of the SUV, his dark eyes fastened on mine, our gazes locked in a way that feels eternal. I'll never stop drowning in his eyes, and he'll never stop reeling me in. The whole world becomes Cary's eyes, and then they widen, expand, taking in everything around me, until I realize, with a squeak of surprise, that I'm falling.

I WAKE UP in his lap, my legs nestled against the side of the barn aisle. Cary's sitting with his back up against the wall, my head in the curve of his arms, gazing down at me with a frightened expression.

"Oops," I whisper. "Did I faint?"

"Have you been eating?" Cary demands, as if he's the sheriff of healthy eating and I broke the law right in front of him.

"Of course I have," I say, indignant. "Why wouldn't I be eating?"

"You *look* like you haven't been eating. And you feel—" he pauses. "Light."

"I always feel light."

He smirks. "Answer the question, Alison."

I haven't been eating *much,* sure, but that's neither here nor there. I worked out a fix for that. My feed bills are someone else's now, so I can worry about feeding myself. It's not anything he needs to worry about. "You're here," I say, instead of answering with all those details he doesn't need.

"Yes." His smirk untwists itself into a gentle smile. "I missed you."

"You missed me." *I'll be thinking about you, Alison.* "For a long time, right?"

He nods, smiling. "A very long time. Did you miss me?"

Miss him? He doesn't know the half of it. Doesn't know the lengths I've just gone to in order to see him again. All the plans I just put into place, using Olivia and Malcolm and Evie and Kat so that I could get to California, because I missed him so much. And yet, here he is. Maybe all I had to do was ask him to come back.

Wouldn't that be something?

I mean, I'd still be the proud owner of a failed business and still responsible for a half-dozen equine mouths I couldn't feed, so it wouldn't entirely solve everything.

Cary is looking at me nervously again. "Are you okay?"

I say, "I was going to come find you. Didn't Kat call you? Didn't she tell you our plans to come out to California—"

"I was already on my way back," Cary says. "She told me, but, sweetheart, do you really want to leave Ocala?"

Sweetheart. I push my lips together before I cry out something incoherent. He makes me lose control of myself. No one else, no one on this planet, can do that. Just him.

"Here," he says, when I don't answer. "Why don't you sit yourself against this sparkling clean barn wall and tell me what's going on? Because, and I hate to admit this, my left leg is falling asleep. Even with your marshmallow weight on it."

I slide off him begrudgingly and lean against the wall, as instructed. Cary snuggles up against me, tucking me close to his side. "Now, spill it, Alison."

The rain patters gently on the roof.

It's a comforting sound. I used to dread it at Windy Hill; in Virginia, even a gentle rain could be an all-day soaker. Rain on the rooftop was the sound of getting soaked doing morning chores, of sloshing down to the school bus in muddy boots, of feeling damp all day with bedraggled hair falling into my eyes. I was never more of a poor little match girl than on wet winter days in northern Virginia.

In Florida, a steady rain can be the calling card of a gentler season arriving. It means summer has passed and the cool days are coming. These are small raindrops, without any agenda but wetting the flowers, unlike the massive cannonballs of summer.

I tuck my head against Cary's shoulder and he wraps an arm around me. "My business is failing," I say.

"That's alright," Cary says. "We can fix it."

"And I've been lonely."

"I'm sorry for that." His arm squeezes me a little closer.

"It wasn't your fault."

"Still sorry," he says.

"I have unresolved trauma from my childhood."

"Of course you do. We all do. But yours was pretty tough."

"I didn't realize it was," I admit. "That's part of why it's unresolved."

"So, what do you want to do about it now?"

I think for a moment. "Move on," I say. "Not wallow around in it. I'm pretty sure I can't, anyway. It's not in my nature."

"Those eggs are cracked," Cary agrees.

I turn my neck and look up at him. The firm line of his chin slides upward as he smiles at me. "I think you broke me," I tell him. "I was fine before."

"Were you?" That smile. So irresistible, even when he's being a skeptic.

"No," I sigh. "But when you left, I started to realize my life was kind of a wreck, and then I realized I was broke on top of that, and *that* was when it became really clear I'd failed at...everything."

"Everything?" Cary sounds skeptical. "You have a lovely farm. You have horses that love you. You have friends." He runs a hand over my head, stroking my hair with a calming touch. "So you need to change a few things. You need some help. That's all fixable."

He has no idea. Or does he? Is that why he's here?

"I *do* need help," I whisper. "But—"

"But, nothing," Cary says. "I'm here to help."

And he leans down, fingers curled beneath my neck, and places the softest kiss imaginable on my lips.

It's good, so good. But it's not good enough. With a growl in my throat that surprises even me, I lunge upwards and catch his mouth with mine, curling my hands into his hair and tugging him close. And this kiss...it's not soft at all. Not sweet. Not thoughtful or gentle or caring.

And that's just fine by me.

Chapter Thirty-Eight

"YOU'RE BACK!" I wave to Cary from horseback as he hops out of his shiny red SUV. He grins and pulls a bag from the backseat. Since he decided to spend half his time in Florida, he's bought his own car and stopped relying on Kat's production company to pay for a rental —a decision Kat says she would have made for him if he hadn't reached the conclusion on his own.

I always miss Cary when he's in California for work, but he was only gone for a week this time, shooting some promotions for the cowboy movie, and I've kept myself busy with Hansie, schooling him over at Fine Day Farm where there are more jumps, more arenas, and more people to keep me from feeling so alone.

Keeping Hansie over at Malcolm's farm was the best decision Kat ever made for me.

Well, maybe the second-best.

And it wasn't one I ever would have made for myself, which makes me appreciate having her as an owner even more. Kat has a way of looking people over and figuring out what they need before they know it themselves. She says that's how she knew Cary would make a great cowboy, even though he didn't know how to ride when she cast him for the role. "I just knew he had a horseman's heart," she declared after his first week of on-set riding out at the Colorado ranch they'd hired for the shoot. "And," she added, "I knew he'd be the perfect foil for you."

"Foil?" I'd asked, looking back at her over the zipped-up neck of my fleece jacket. Colorado was freezing cold and a total shock to my system; even though it was only early November, the peaks of the mountains were swathed in snow and there was a sharpness to the wind that the ranchers working as extras swore meant snowfall before the next morning. I'd been secretly excited to see snow, even though I was pretty sure I'd hate being that cold. It had been years since I'd spent winter in Virginia, and it didn't snow there more than a few times a season, anyway.

Colorado snow was on a different level.

Anyway, Kat had grinned and said yes, a foil was a character's challenging opposite. "A person who brings out all the best parts of you, even the ones you've been hiding," she'd said.

"I would never hide my best parts," I told her, and she laughed.

"You're hiding them all under that huge coat right now, Florida," she'd said, and I'd snorted.

Then Cary rode over on the chunky quarter horse gelding they'd cast as his cow horse, asking what all the giggling was about, and I'd told him we were making fun of the way he held his reins. He'd looked so aggrieved, though, that I sighed and told him the truth.

He liked the idea of bringing out my best parts about as much as I'd figured he would.

"Show me your best parts!" he calls now, leaning over the arena fence with his bag slung across his back. "Wave them in the air for me!"

"Sir, some decorum, please," I scold in my best dowager duchess voice. "Some of us are trying to ride horses."

"Sebastian looks ready for a break." Cary pulls out a tube of peppermints wrapped in foil and waves them in the air.

Sebastian makes a beeline for him. My reins might as well be cut off at the bit for all the good they do when Cary's waving mints at him. When Cary decided to invest some of his Hollywood big bucks (a joke, he isn't rich by any means, but things are going better in his career now that the Arrowhead movie is getting good buzz) in buying Sebastian, I tried to stop him, reminding him that horses are only a good way to lose money. But he said Kat was having too much fun telling him about all the clever things Hansie and I did, and he wasn't going to let her be the only investor in Team Alison.

"Aren't you glad I'm your daddy?" he croons to Sebastian, giving the horse three mints at once.

"One at a time, please," I warn. "He's got a bit in his mouth!"

"Sorry, Sebastian," Cary says, his face very close to Sebastian's muzzle. The horse snuffles at his chin, still chewing. "Mmm, you smell so minty fresh!"

This is what it's like every time Cary comes home. Whatever I'm doing has to take a backseat to his antics until I finally give up riding and go inside with him.

We've been doing this routine all winter, and I'm not sick of it yet.

"NEXT EVENT?" CARY asks as I throw a cooler over Sebastian. The March afternoon is chilly, and steam is rising from the horse's back after his bath. I put him in his stall with some fresh hay and a reminder not to roll in his blankie. Sebastian snorts into his hay, letting me know he'll do what he needs to do.

"This weekend," I reply, hanging up the halter carefully on its hook, positioning the lead-rope just so. Yes, I have a few obsessive tics, but I'm okay living with them when they're managed. And I manage them by not allowing myself to become isolated and overwhelmed. Impressive, right? A few sessions with Kat's therapist over the winter and I'm practically a mental health goddess. Included as a perk of training her horse, since she says Hansie is too nice to be slowed down by his rider's personal neuroses. (She said it with a smile, anyway.) "Novice for Hansie, Plato, and Sebastian. And it's the Training Level debut for Pigeon," I tell Cary.

"Oh! I'm excited for Sebastian," Cary says, "but maybe more excited for Pigeon. Is Olivia coming?"

"Yes, she's riding her two and cheering on Pigeon." Olivia breathed a sigh of relief when she found out I wasn't slinking off to California for the winter after all. It turned out she'd gotten a promotion at her remote job, which meant more work along with more money. She hadn't been sure how to tell me she was going to struggle with keeping the barn while I was away, and had actually been thinking of hiring someone to do the work for her.

When I told her I was staying in Ocala after all, with just a few trips to join Kat and Cary on filming locations as a paid consultant, she'd been delighted. "So we're *both* making more money now," she exclaimed. "What a win!"

And then, because she had all that extra money she'd planned on using to hire a barn manager, she bought an off-track Thoroughbred named Pigeon Pie who was already running at Novice. He was firecracker-hot and needed a lot of steadying to quiet his brain on course, which didn't really end up working for Olivia. But she said she liked him and preferred watching me ride him to trying to manage him herself, so she put the horse into training with me.

It's funny the way things turn out. Six months ago, I was ready to wash my hands of this place and give up on the winter season.

Now it's mid-March and I'm moving a client's horse up a level, looking to qualify for the national championships on Hansie, and perfecting Sebastian's dressage at last. I think he might even score in the top five this weekend.

And of course, I have Cary around better than half the time, helping in the barn during the day and keeping me excellent company by night.

Who could have known he'd fall for horses and shop for farms in California, only to decide he'd rather be in Florida with me?

Me, probably, if I'd just asked him before he'd left in the first place. But there's no point dwelling on the past. Everything good is right now.

I watch him now with hungry eyes, eating up his movie-star good looks, his mellow smile as he flicks his eager gaze around the barn. He's making sure I haven't gone on a cleaning bender, of course, but he's also just taking in the sights of a place he now calls home.

"The flowers are looking beautiful," Cary says, peering through the far end of the barn aisle. Outside, the wildflower seeds I scattered back in October have turned into dancing fields of pink blossoms. It's phlox season, apparently. I'd had to ask an old-timer at the feed store what those beautiful flowers were when they'd started appearing everywhere.

"I'm so glad I don't have to think about mowing," I say, watching the flowers nod in the cool breeze. "That was an inspired move, sending me wildflower seeds."

"I'm just happy it turned out the way I expected." Cary laughs. "I mean, I'm not exactly an expert on Florida landscaping. I just talked to the folks at the botanical garden until we came to a solution."

The office door opens behind us and Olivia comes out, a wiggling ball of fur in her hands. "Someone heard Daddy!" she sings, putting Tony on the ground.

The Jack Russell races for Cary, his claws digging into the grooves in the asphalt. Cary stoops and scoops up his dog. "Hello, son!"

Olivia smiles engagingly at me and I smile back, walking over to join her. "Thanks for keeping him in there while I was riding. He's been underfoot a lot lately."

"That's just Jack Russells for you," Olivia laughs. "And Lily sat on the desk giving him the evil eye the whole time. If he hadn't been so intimidated by her, I think he would have realized Cary was back a lot sooner."

We watch the dog and his human cuddling for a few moments. Then Olivia says, "Kat called on the barn line, so I answered it. She said the papers are finalized."

"Oh, wow." I take a deep breath. This is turning into quite a day.

"Dare I ask?"

"Yeah, it's...this arrangement we came to. She's selling me back Hansie."

"You're kidding! That's amazing news." Olivia rubs my shoulder conspiratorially. "I figured it was killing you that she owned him."

I grimace and shrug. All winter, it had been there in the back of my head, that now Kat owned Hansie and not me. I've never loved a horse the way I love Hansie, so much it's unreasonable, really. And while I'd been grateful to Kat for buying him before someone else could, then giving me total control of his training, it really had bugged me that someone else's name was on his paperwork. "It's really just a swap of names on paper," I say, trying to take a pragmatic view of things. "There's a second contract, naming her a shareholder in his syndicate."

"But you're the primary now, right?"

"Yes."

"So, it's all the same thing." Olivia smiles. "And since she's an investor, she's still paying his bills, right? That's what counts."

I have to laugh. "Yeah, I guess it is."

It's a joke on the surface, but Olivia's right. The business is working again, better than before, and that is what counts on a lot of levels. I have help with the competition horses, whether it's Kat owning shares in Hansie or Olivia paying for me to train and compete Pigeon. Cary owns Sebastian, making that horse one less I have to feed. My students eventually figured out their school-year lives and came back to their lessons, and two of them have actually mastered posting and are beginning to jump. I have friends to ride with at Fine Day Farm every day, so that I'm not totally alone during the weeks when Cary is away working.

And I have Cary here the rest of the time, taking the burden of perfection off my shoulders so that I can focus on riding and selling horses for everything they're worth.

What a difference a winter can make.

I look across the aisle at my Hollywood leading man, playing with his little scrap of terrier like he's never been so happy in his life, and my whole body seems to fill with light and joy. Having him here is the greatest gift of all. "Thanks, eventing gods," I murmur.

Olivia glances at me, but doesn't say anything. She gets it.

Cary looks up and our eyes meet. An electric charge crackles between us, and it's not just leftover static from when I was almost struck by lightning. He puts the dog down and walks over to me as Tony scampers out of the barn.

"You have time to go upstairs?" he asks, as Olivia shakes her head and heads out after the dog. "Need to check your schedule?"

He knows I still live by my schedule, that the order keeps my head straight.

"I have exactly twenty minutes before I need to get to Fine Day and ride Hansie," I say.

"Good," Cary says, taking my hand. "But I can't promise you'll be on time today."

"I'll try to manage," I laugh. "But I'm only going off my schedule for you."

Acknowledgments

THE HOLLYWOOD HORSE was a sticky one! Thanks to Hurricane Idalia, which knocked me out of work for over a week due to hurricane prep, evacuation, and clean-up, this book ended up well over a month late. To make matters worse, my idea of the ending grew a lot less clear while I was away from the draft. It took some marathon days of writing, deleting, and rewriting to reach a satisfying conclusion.

Thanks so much to Rachel Kuntz Killian for getting me to some shows and riding lessons while this book was being written; all of it helped inform the riding and training scenes in this book. In some ways, you made the book take longer, but in lots of ways, you've made it better!

As always, a special thanks to the Patreon and Ream members who read my first drafts, often one or two chapters a day for several weeks on end. This one took forever, right, guys? Thanks for sticking it out. And letting me know when Chapter 28 just wasn't good enough. I fixed it! I think.

You can join us at patreon.com/nataliekreinert or at Ream Stories, a new subscription site just for storytellers, at reamstories.com/ nataliekreinert. Join for free and follow my weekly updates, or join at a tier level for special access to exclusive stories and early chapters!

My Patrons and Ream subscribers include: Renee Knowles, Silvana Ricapito, Annika, Alyssa, Susan Lambiris, Heather Voltz, Shauna, Lisa Leonard Heck, Dianna, SailorEpona, Megan Devine, Michelle Beck, Lynne Gevirtz, Sweetwildrain, Mary V, Agavehurricane, Cat, Stacy Verrell, AshleyO, Miranda Mues, Ashley Swink, Eris, Erika Thomas, Shelby Graft, Nicole Russo, Karen Wolfsheimer, Pamela Allen-LeBlanc, Raina Kujawa, Kellie Halteman, Jennifer Williams, Megan McDonald, Adrienne Brant, Sally Testa, Becca B., April Lutz, Heidi Schmid, Mel Sperti, Cathy Luo, Elana Rabinow, Laura, Dörte Voigt, Empathy, Tayla Travella, Gretchen Fieser, JoAnn Flejszar, Nancy Neid, Libby Henderson, Maureen VanDerStad, Jean Miller, Leslie Yazurlo, Nicola Beisel, Mel Policicchio, Harry Burgh, Nicole, Kathlynn Angie-Buss, Peggy Dvorsky, Christine Komis, Thoma Jolette Parker, Karen Carrubba, Emma Gooden, Katie Lewis, Silvana Ricapito, Sarina Laurin, Di Hannel, Jennifer, Heather Walker, Cyndy Searfoss, Kaylee Amons, Kathi Lacasse, Rachael Rosenthal, Hannah, Diana Aitch. Liz Greene, Zoe Bills, Cheryl Bavister, Sarah Seavey, Tricia Jordan, Brinn Dimler, Rhonda Lane, and C Sperry.

What an incredible list! It just keeps growing, and I'm so grateful for your support. Thank you all so very much.

Do you want to see more of the Ocala Horse Girls? I hope you'll join me on my Facebook Reader Group (facebook.com/groups/ nataliesreaders) or at my Patreon or Ream, so we can discuss which characters you'd like to see next, and what kind of story you'd enjoy!

About the Author

A FULL-TIME writer, I work from my farm in North Florida, where I live with my family and two horses. In the past, I've worked professionally in many aspects of the equestrian world, including grooming for top event riders, training off-track Thoroughbreds, galloping racehorses, patrolling Central Park on horseback, working on breeding farms, and more! I use all of this experience to inform the equestrian scenes in my novels. They say that truth is stranger than fiction, and those of us in the horse business will certainly agree!

Visit my website at nataliekreinert.com to keep up with the latest news and read occasional blog posts and book reviews. For previews, installments of upcoming fiction, and exclusive stories, visit my Patreon page at patreon.com/nataliekreinert or Ream Stories at reamstories.com/nataliekreinert and learn how you can become one of my team members. Visit my store at nataliekreinert.shop for the best value on print and ebook editions.

For more, find me on social media:

Facebook: facebook.com/nataliekellerreinert

Group: facebook.com/groups/nataliesreaders

Bookbub: bookbub.com/profile/natalie-keller-reinert

Instagram: instagram.com/nataliekreinert

Join my email list and receive an ebook at https://subscribepage.io/getbold

Email: natalie@nataliekreinert.com

Podcast: adultingwithhorsespodcast.com

Made in United States
Troutdale, OR
12/12/2023

15738948R00213